HERMES

CONSPIRACY

Martin Grant

Published by The Margrant Press

ISBN - 978-1-7396631-0-0

Cover design by Bob Russell

Printed in England.

Dedications

To my family.

To Trafford Libraries for applying for an Arts Council grant to support a creative writing course for the celebrations for VE 75 (the seventy fifth anniversary of Victory in Europe) and then publishing the stories that were written in the course as an Anthology of Stories

To Charles Lea our tutor on the course for his advice and support.

To Reggie my History teacher of many years ago and his fascination in what was called the "Eastern Question" and the Ottoman Empire which gave me the idea for this book.

1

Although it was a bright, clear, September morning in North London, beyond the scattering of light cloud there lurked a darker sky that threatened rain later. That was why the maroon and black liveried 1908 Renault had left town early. The car was almost new and the kind of reliable motor your doctor might drive; exactly why the driver had stolen it for today's job. His knowing face disfigured by a long scar, he was dressed for once in a shirt and tie underneath the somewhat garish yellow check suit that made him look like a bookmaker straight off the racecourse. He was usually hired for a robbery or to 'put the frighteners' on a slow payer, but this job was different and special. Unusually it was, as the boss put it, 'rubbing out' some woman living way out in the northern suburbs near Golders Green.

"We on time?" his short stature, fox faced passenger queried again. Impatient as always.

"Of course!" The driver's testy tone signified his growing displeasure with the man. "Damn it! Sit still can't you."

"Shut it! I need to reach my goddam raincoat."

"What the hell for?"

"To get my gun."

"You stupid goop! You don't need that now."

An instruction that the passenger chose to ignore. He knew that he was the key man on this job. "Hah! I know what I need. You mind yer words."

"I told yer. Stop fidgeting!" the driver shouted, referring to the man repeatedly fingering the concealed Webley revolver. "Damn you! You make me effing nervous. Stuff it."

"Keep your bleeding hair on. They shouldn't 'av gave me this damned thing. I wanted a Luger. I always use a Luger."

"Leave off the grousing! You're getting plenty of dosh for an easy job ain't yer. A real soft, easy job."

"Shut it!" the passenger responded sharply. "I know 'ow to do my job. Just make sure you do yours."

Having climbed up to Hampstead village, the car was reduced to a crawl up the final steep ascent to the Whitestone Pond, forced into low gear with its engine labouring. The enforced snail's pace was the kind of painful, stop-start, climb, that the Renault hated. But eventually, with the engine pounding loudly in protest, they reached the top and the driver gratefully pulled in to the kerb, near where a horse drawn cart had driven down a ramp right into the Pond to allow the horses to drink. The Renault, too, stopped to allow its overheating engine to cool down. But it set off again ten minutes later, passed Jack Straw's Castle and motored down the other side of Hampstead Heath, a steady drop down the hill for more than a mile to Golders Green.

"I'll stop for fags at the shops. We 'av to wait for the signal," the driver observed, pulling the car abruptly into the kerb near a tobacconist's shop, just outside the offices of 'David Strange. Solicitor.' It was in an arcade of shops facing the newish Golders Green Underground station and it was just before ten in the morning.

At that moment Robert, David Strange's son, now six months newly qualified as a solicitor, stepped briskly out of his father's office. He intended to cross the road but had to stop dead in his tracks because a maroon and black Renault suddenly pulled into the kerb almost on his toes.

"What the hell!" he exclaimed, annoyed at the driver's dangerous behaviour. "Mind where you're damned well going can't you!" An objection that was casually dismissed with a mere shrug from the driver.

A well-built young man in his early twenties, of more than average height, Robert had an open, warm, countenance and a wide nose over full lips. His healthy, dark, bronzed complexion often made people who didn't know the family history think he had just returned from somewhere hot: a good Mediterranean holiday perhaps. His smart, black jacket, rather than the traditional long morning coat that many lawyers still wore, his striped trousers and bowler hat, rather than an old-fashioned silk topper, marked him out as a thoroughly modern man of business. He avoided the Renault, with a scowl at the driver, who ignored him, and crossed the road. As he did so he quickly checked the bulky contract in his black leather briefcase.

He strode on and was nearing the Underground station when he spotted a figure approaching from the other direction. It was someone he immediately and instinctively recognised. Vivid, overpowering images from the past immediately flashed through his mind.

My God! I'll be damned if it's not Anna! I'm sure of it! It's Anna Gibson to be sure.

The sudden realisation was so completely gripping he stopped dead on the pavement. Indeed, a man walking too close behind him had to dodge to one side to avoid him.

"Sorry! I didn't realise ..."

Yet he had known her at once. How could he not, she had once been so special, for many years a childhood playmate until they were both fourteen and their paths had diverged. He had heard she was now a university graduate and realised that a great deal had happened to them both in the last six or more years.

Maybe it's too long ago. So much has happened she won't remember me.

Indeed, the reality was that there was good reason she wouldn't want to. For since they last met, they had entered very different worlds. He to work long hours as a lowly legal clerk in an office in the City, living in cheap digs in the East End, while she stayed on at school, made it to the Sixth Form and then to the elevated heights of a degree course in English at University College London, in Gower Street.

Anyway, why should she want to remember me? He felt shamed now by remorse at recalling the shallowness of their parting.

For, although they had in the past been close chums, their once regular encounters had rather run down as the time approached for him to leave school. And when it came to him finally leaving both home and school to start his legal clerkship, he had just simply left, preoccupied and excited at his prospective new life in the City. All too ready and eager to abandon his schoolboy memoirs to gather dust on the shelves. He could not even remember if he had properly said goodbye to her. He realised he probably hadn't, had just drifted away, just parted without a word.

Even if she does remember me, she might not want to know me now. Too much has happened.

That was the worst thought. She was always a live wire; she must have met many interesting people at university. As she was also a pretty girl she had surely met many eligible young men in her three years at college. Anyway, as she was nothing less than a university graduate, one of only a handful of women, he had another unpleasant thought.

Maybe she'll think I'm beneath her. She'll think I'm just another boring tradesman. An uneducated jobber. She'll think I know nothing that matters.

Such uncertainties raced through his mind and troubled him. Years of daily grind, working in the heart of the City of London and living in digs in the East End had taught him growing self-reliance. Yet here he was in a hopeless dither, shilly-shallying just because he was surprised to see a pretty girl from the distant past. Perhaps it was because whatever the past, she was a beauty in the present and he was an instinctive opportunist. With a conscious effort to seize the opportunity he pulled himself together to greet her.

"Anna! What a delight!"

He was indeed pleased to see her; she had become an eye-catchingly attractive young woman. Moreover, merely the sight of her flashed a mass of happy memories through his mind; the childish games and pranks that years ago they had enjoyed together. He remembered again her gorgeous auburn hair, her alert, wonderful, blue-green, doe-like eyes and her small pert nose. His hesitations vanished like a shot and propelled by a sudden overwhelming impulse he embraced her with a 'bise' on the check in the now fashionable French manner, one that he had picked up on one of his excursions to Paris. Although she was clearly startled at the unexpected nature and boldness of his move, he was aware that she did not repel it. Maybe she was even rather flattered by the evident public attention of a good-looking young man.

"Robert! How nice to see you!" So after all she had remembered him: his brightly shining, dark eyes, short, frizzy, black hair, and thick eyebrows. And did seem at least pleased at the unforeseen encounter, if not, though, exactly overjoyed.

"Robert! I thought you were working in the City."

"I was. But now I'm working in my father's new office across the road. I'm on my way into town on business. Are you by chance going into town as well?"

"Yes, I'm going to Tottenham Court Road on the Underground and then I'm going shopping."

"Wonderful! What jolly good luck. I'm headed to Town myself. I can take a cab from Tottenham Court Road to Grosvenor Square, and I can easily drop you off wherever you like. I have a building contract for one of our clients to agree." He indicated his full briefcase.

"Looks important."

"It's for a new construction company we're forming. Our client in Mayfair will back it financially. There's a lot of building around here now in the Garden Suburb. Look, let's go through and I'll get the tickets."

She made a gesture of refusal that he brushed aside. The idea of a girl travelling with him and buying her own ticket was simply not in his philosophy. He was no longer a penniless, gawky, articled clerk but a thoroughly professional salaried man. But he was aware from her attitude that she had really meant to buy her own ticket and might embarrass him by offering him money. She did exactly that.

I remember, she was always damned independent. She's determined to make a point. Maybe she's picked up some modern ways at college.

Indeed, if he had not been blinded by just seeing her face, her fantastic eyes, and auburn hair, he would have spotted the small broach on her blouse and known she had indeed changed. An outer circle of green garnets, reflecting the greenish blue of her eyes, entwined in a double band of white enamel with a fine violet amethyst in the centre. Green, violet and white: these days the colours of the Woman's Social and

Political Union, adopted only at the beginning of the year. Wearing the badge marked her as a supporter of the WSPU, the campaign for Women's Rights and especially for the Vote, the growing campaign that was causing so much political upset.

They went up to the platform and boarded the waiting train for Town. "Anna, it's been ages! I've only ever seen you once or twice in passing, and it's years since we talked. It's so good to meet again."

"Yes, it has been a long time." It was said with no sense of her interest in the unexpected reunion, just a bald statement of fact. It had indeed been many years and he had gone off to the City with barely a word. Moreover, staying on at school and then going to university had not been easy for her, or for her parents, because of the money. Her achievement was of course that much greater.

Her tepid response did not undermine his enthusiasm. "Anna, we were both school kids then. And now look at us. My mother told me you've finished your degree. A graduate. Terrific Anna! And I've not yet congratulated you. I must do! Well done, Anna! It's so brilliant! You must feel so pleased. One of the very few women graduates. You are changing the world. I envy you. So much is open to you."

That clearly pleased her, and she smiled nicely in acknowledgement, though doubtless she had enjoyed thousands of compliments, and his was after all rather late in the day.

As they drew into Tottenham Court Road Station the time seemed to have flown. It had been interesting, and he had liked hearing her story, but it left him feeling that his first instincts were right: they had been close friends in childhood, but that was a world they had both long left behind. He noticed also, with some hurt, that she had not asked him anything about his own experiences, or future plans.

But face it, that's that! It's exactly what I thought, why should she be bothered about me. I'm sure there must be someone else in her life now.

But then, thinking of his own likely engagement to Sybil, a nice girl with whom he had over the past six months become increasingly intimate, that certainly had to be for the best. And anyway, why on earth should Anna be interested in him, they had both become different people, and for her as a graduate in these modern, progressive times the world was surely her oyster.

Nevertheless, as they left Tottenham Court Road station, he spotted a flower seller's barrow beside the pavement and could not resist stopping to buy her a red rose, which she accepted with a flush of embarrassment that he failed to notice. He then took a cab down Oxford Street and dropped her off on Wigmore Street near Debenham and Freebody, a palatial Department Store recently built in an ornate Edwardian baroque style.

Anna thanked him politely for the lift.

"Perhaps we may see each other again!" Robert remarked, handing her down to the pavement. He thought of making an actual suggestion but hesitated; she had said nothing to encourage it and it could be tricky with Sybil.

"Indeed," she answered in a flat voice. Her indifference confirmed his impression. But what of it? This was no more than another casual passing encounter. He noticed that she had left the rose in the cab. He thought of picking handing it to her, but on second thoughts didn't bother. He would keep it and give it to his client's wife in Grosvenor Square.

She walked off purposefully, content with both herself and the world. The year had been good: studies completed, the prospect of good, secure, teaching employment ahead. It had also been a nice surprise to meet Robert Strange after so many years. He was no longer the lanky, unkempt, young rascal of yesteryear, and seemed to have turned into a pleasant, uncomplicated, straightforward young man. Handsome too. She wondered vaguely what his interests were these days, now he had a job to do.

She relished the feel of striding towards the Department Store through the covering of newly fallen leaves that the Plane trees were shedding as autumn approached. As her feet scattered the leaves it reminded her that, from the amount of walking she was doing to support the 'Women's Cause', she would soon need a new pair of shoes. But it was worth it, for thanks to the efforts of women like her the newspapers were now taking the campaign seriously. It was only a few months ago that 30,000 women had marched in Hyde Park in support of 'Votes for Women', observed by a great crowd of half a million people, the great 'Women's Sunday' event. The prospects of success had never looked brighter, even if everyone knew the battle was far from over.

She made her way to 'Ladies' Fashions' and was approached by a young assistant. "I'd like to see what you have in the way of smart wool skirts. I will need two. Something dark but I don't want black. It needs to be formal but it's not for a funeral."

"Of course, Madam. You mentioned 'smart'; something for a special occasion?"

"Yes. I need it for a job interview. At a School. I was thinking of something dark grey perhaps?"

The assistant looked interested, there were not many middle-class jobs at a school. And her customer was quite young. If it was a school job it must be a bursar or a teacher.

"If I may check your size madam, we have a very good selection and I'm sure that we will find the perfect thing for you!"

They did and Anna was pleased with her purchases. The girl had been helpful and polite. Anna had noticed that she had spotted the new brooch that Anna had pinned to her blouse. The girl had not said anything of course; it would not have been wise to do so because the Suffragette movement was politically controversial. But her whole manner left Anna in no doubt that she was a supporter. Given the poor working conditions and pay of a young shop assistant, Anna thought that the sooner there were votes for women the sooner would there be change for the better for people like her. Encounters like this always encouraged her convictions.

Leaving the store she passed through the elaborate entrance, with its ornate and carved Royal Coat of Arms, to meet Gerald Morris, who had invited her to lunch. She knew him from the Tennis Club and the Catholic Church in Hampstead village that both their families attended. Last Sunday, after Mass, she had happened to mention her proposed shopping trip, and he had immediately offered, indeed insisted on, lunch. In fact, he was already waiting for her in the entrance, looking incredibly smart in formal morning dress, a pink carnation in his buttonhole, wearing a silk hat and carrying a Malacca cane. He had indeed just stepped out of a taxi from his father's Bank in the City, for his family was wealthy and well connected, unlike Anna's, whose father was an insurance clerk. He had already annoyed her by indicating his approval of a potential marriage that would take

Anna dramatically upwards in the social scene. However, although Anna found Gerald amusing company, she had no intention of committing herself to any young man at any time soon.

"Anna, you look marvellous! And such a nice, jolly hat! It really suits you!" Gerald was always careful to compliment a girl, and anyway especially liked to please Anna. But it was true, she looked wonderful.

She really appreciated the compliment: she had gone to some trouble to choose the hat. It also occurred to her that Robert Strange had not said a word about the hat, or offered any kind of compliment about her appearance, just rushed in with that provocative and rather aggressive Parisian kiss. Perhaps he hadn't noticed the hat. But in fact, he must have seen it, and probably he was just a bit unsophisticated, lacking experience in polished social manners. Not his fault of course, but it must surely be rather a handicap if he wanted to get on in the world. But what she hadn't observed was that, unlike Robert Strange, Gerald had noticed her new brooch. Indeed, the quick tightening of his lips, when he spotted it, revealed his displeasure at the unwelcome antics of the women's campaign, although naturally he would never dream of talking serious politics with Anna. He just assumed it was a frivolous residue of her student days, something out of which she would soon grow.

The lunch with Gerald, in his father's club in Pall Mall, was of course splendid. Gerald was attentive, an easy conversationalist and excellent company. Afterwards she made her way back to Golders Green, arrived there before three in the afternoon and called at the butcher in Golders Green Road. Leaving the shop, she idly noticed a maroon and black liveried Renault parked outside. She bought some lamb chops for a family supper and headed for the tram stop in

Finchley Road for the short journey to Temple Fortune and home. It had been a good day.

2

The Renault had indeed moved since Robert encountered it outside the office earlier that morning. A boy on a bicycle approached the car about half an hour after Robert walked past it and gave the driver a note.

"Good! That's our signal to move!" the driver told the passenger. Then he got out of the car, cranked up the engine and drove off. "It's only about a mile further."

At Temple Fortune he turned right into the outer parts of the Hampstead Garden Suburb and stopped.

"We're 'ere! The job's round the corner."

"Right!"

"I'll go slow at the end of the road. You take a butcher's up the street and tell me wha'ya see!"

The passenger did so. "There's an 'andcart about 'alfway up with a geyser and a lad."

"Anything about the 'andcart?"

"Writing on its side about knife grinding. The grinder was at work on something, the lad was turning an 'andle on the grinding wheel."

"Very good! Now tell me about the grinder."

"He had a scarlet kerchief! Why all the charades?"

"Not charades! It's the signal the house is all clear!"

"Right!"

"Ready?" The driver looked meaningfully at the passenger.

"I know my job!" the passenger said, pulled out his revolver and put it in an outside pocket.

"Right then!" the driver said. "You got ten minutes at the outside."

"I told ya, I know my job!"

"You'd bloody better! As soon as we're done, we'll lose the motor and scarper."

"Thank God I won't have to put up with you anymore!" The passenger snarled, descending from the Renault, straightened his coat and sauntered up the road towards No 14, the house where Maria Gibson lived. The driver watched him walk off and grunted. The handcart of 'John Plume, Knife Grinder' passed the Renault and disappeared out of sight. The driver kept the engine ticking over and waited impatiently for only about five minutes. The passenger returned on the trot, jumped into the car and the driver quickly engaged his gears and pulled away.

"Do it?" the driver asked.

"Wha'ya think!" the passenger sneered.

"Let's hope you're right!" the driver retorted. "Now we'll dump the motor and scarper"

"Except of course!"

"Yes, we collect the rest of the the brass. We meet the bloke from the Narodony Bank at three under the clock at Victoria. Be on time!"

So, the maroon and black Renault drove off, not too fast to avoid drawing attention, headed for the Finchley Road, and turned south back towards Golders Green where it was abandoned outside a butchers shop in the main street. The driver and passenger made their separate ways to the Underground station and disappeared without trace.

*

Later that day, sometime well after five, Anna Gibson managed somehow to drag herself into the Golders Green offices of David Strange, Solicitor. Flushed, beside herself with grief and gasping for breath, she staggered across the room and crumpled onto the chair that the receptionist hastily proffered. She looked dreadful, wild, frantic, in a state of hysterical distress, her face ashen and awash with tears. Her attire was completely deranged, her hair dishevelled and her hat almost off. She could speak only falteringly, and then only with effort.

"Please help me! I need … help! … It's my mother! … She's dead! … You see … they've … killed my mother! … She's been … murdered! … I must see David …"

She blurted it out with tears running down her face, her long auburn hair all over the place and her hat now falling onto the floor.

David Strange was upstairs and hearing the commotion rushed down to the pitiful sight.

"Uncle David! … It's so awful! … I went in…! And I found her there … She was … I can't …" she spluttered, the words sticking in her throat. She was unable to finish the sentence and broke down in tears.

"Anna!"

"Help me! Please help me!" she begged. "I don't know what to do!"

"Anna dearest! Whatever has happened. You can't surely mean it …" he said softly, and picked her up in big powerful arms, holding her tight but tenderly, as he would a daughter. Her parents were old and close friends.

"Uncle David! I can't tell you how bad it was!" she cried, trying in faltering, sobbing words, on the verge of losing control, to try to convey the horrific scene she had witnessed on returning home. Her mother still slumped forwards on the table, where she had been writing a letter when she was shot, the revolver thrown down on the carpet. Anna was too overcome to go on.

"Anna," he said, trying his best to comfort her and gently stroking her hair. "It's terrible but you must try not to distress yourself further."

She told him in a halting voice that a neighbour had called the police, who were now at the house, and her father, who knew nothing about it, was expected home from his job at the Prudential Assurance in Holborn. She wanted someone to be there when he returned - the sight would be a terrible blow for him. Anyone could see she was in a seriously bad state of shock, tearful, white faced and trembling.

"Anna! I'll go to your house right away and deal with the Police. And Robert's just back from town, he's upstairs and will look after you. You must rest. I think Robert should take you to our house so that Grace can be with you. You need someone with you, and somewhere calm. And you should lie down."

Robert Strange had indeed only returned a few minutes before Anna arrived. He was working at his desk when Anna arrived, heard the kerfuffle, and rushed downstairs. His father asked him to comfort Anna and then grabbed his overcoat from a coat stand and rushed out to take a Taxi from the rank outside the station.

"Anna! Whatever's happened!" Robert could see at once she was terribly disturbed and realised without having to ask that something awful had taken place. Although she had rallied a bit, she was slumped forward on her chair with her head in her hands and was gently sobbing. One of the clerks told him quietly what had happened. When a moment later Anna saw him, she looked up with her big round blue-green eyes reddened from crying. He was overcome with sorrow for her, hardly able to understand the enormity of the crime. Her mother had been such a warm, caring, lovable person, had treated him with the same affection as if he was her son. He knelt in front of Anna and, held her head between his hands and softly kissed her forehead.

"Anna! I can't believe it! Maria murdered! Your mother of all people. It makes no sense! She was such a kind wonderful person. It's wicked! I don't know what to say it's so unbelievably despicable. How could something like this happen to such a person! I'm so, so sorry! I can only guess what you must feel."

He had not been in such close physical contact with her for years, but the old protective affection was instantly recalled. She was again as dear to him as the sister he had never had. It was a moment that made him suddenly and profoundly aware that no-one outside his own family had ever been as close to him as Anna.

She managed somehow, struggling with the words and sobbing, to tell him what she found on returning home.

He could imagine the sheer horror of the terrible scene that met her. "Anna it's so appalling! So dreadful! To come to the house in broad daylight and murder Maria! Who would even want to do such a terrible thing. Your mother was such a sweet, good person!"

"Robbie! It's so good to see you!" she sobbed, unable to say more, the words were trapped in her throat. He stroked her hair tenderly and kissed her forehead again.

"Don't try and talk Anna. You are safe here with us. We'll look after you. There's no need for you to do anything. Father will deal with the Police and the house. You've had an awfully bad shock, a terrible shock, and you must rest. You must rest!" He held her hand in his and gently stroked it. "As father said, the best thing is I take you home to our house and you should lie down."

She did not reply at once, but her blue-green weepy eyes met his bright shining dark brown eyes and she tried to smile. "I don't know what to do! I feel so helpless!" her face crumpled.

"Anna! Do nothing! We will look after you! Just rest! It's been such a terrible shock!"

He carried her to a taxi and his mother, Grace, was waiting for them at the front door, tears in her eyes, for she and Maria Gibson had been good friends for many years. Robert lifted Anna from the taxi and carried her into the house. His mother insisted she must lie on the sofa in the Sitting Room. She sent Robert upstairs for a rug.

"Now Anna," Grace Strange said, "you will all stay here tonight!" She waved aside Anna's protests. "No, it's all arranged. David will collect your father and your brother. I will not hear of anything else."

She swept Robert, who had wanted to remain with Anna, out of the room and went to the kitchen. Then she sent Robert, who was reluctant to leave Anna, back to the office to return later when he could.

"She needs peace and quiet and must rest. She's had a terrible shock. I am here to be with her and look after her."

But Grace Strange had noticed Robert's reluctance to leave Anna. Indeed, she had to practically push him out of the house. More than that she had seen the expression on his face when he looked at Anna and she was concerned. After some six years in training as an articled clerk in a Solicitor's office in the City, living frugally in digs with no spare cash, he had for the past months been enjoying the relative luxury of paid employment. With money enough in his pocket he could enjoy some of the pleasures of life. Indeed, to the extent that his mother became sure that she needed to get him 'settled down', as she put it. It was clear to her that he needed a suitable wife. There should not be any problem in him finding a girl who would be an asset to him in his career. Not just that he was good looking and good company but that one day he would take over his father's successful legal practice. He would offer any girl the prospect of a secure and more than reasonably good income. And she knew that there was such a girl on the scene, Sybil, a nice, attractive girl who would be just right for her son.

The future looked bright for him. But, observing how he re-acted to Anna, she was seriously worried. His interest in her was all too obvious, and of course there was a history between them, even if it was now years and years ago that they had been pals. She couldn't help asking herself if Anna could possibly be the right girl for him. But much as she really liked Anna, and much as she liked her family to whom they were so close, she seriously doubted it. Anna had become a thoroughly modern woman, a graduate, a girl who wanted her own career, was moreover mixed up in controversial, militant politics and of course had always been very independent. Without any doubt, therefore, she was not a suitable girl for her son. Grace Strange feared the consequences of this terrible murder.

*

Meanwhile back at the Gibson's house David Strange was discovering from Inspector Thorpe from the Hendon Police Station that Maria Gibson's murder made little sense, although the bare facts themselves were crystal clear. Just before midday Maria Gibson was seated at a table in her sitting room at the back of the house writing a letter. She was shot dead from behind at close range. A single fatal shot to the head from a revolver that was then abandoned. The murderer had evidently stealthily entered through an unlocked French window behind her. After firing the deadly shot, he had immediately left the house by the same route as he had entered.

"The shot," the Inspector told David Strange, "was heard by the neighbour who was just in time to see a man in a dark coat running away from the Gibson's house towards a motor car down the street."

"You're saying he had a car waiting for him?"

"Yes. The car had its engine running and immediately started off. We have a witness who saw it parked by the kerb for a few minutes. We conclude that the murderer was driven to the street, walked up the street to the Gibson's house, fired the shot and ran back to the vehicle. It must have been all over in five minutes."

"Good God! It's like a carefully planned assassination. Any clues?"

"Nothing was stolen as far as we can see. All we have are a footprint or two around the French window. But no fingerprints anywhere."

"She knew nothing about the shot that killed her?"

"No! It killed her immediately! And there is no sign at all of a struggle."

"She was sitting, writing a letter when he fired?"

"Yes. He must have shot her while she was concentrating on the letter. I can't be sure, but I think that the killer came into the room with the revolver already cocked. Otherwise, she might have heard the revolver click when he cocked it, been disturbed and seen him."

"You mean he came into the room ready to fire?"

"Yes! It looks like that! But the question is why? Why would he have been ready to fire? Why if he was a burglar would he come into the room with a gun ready to shoot?"

"And indeed, immediately fire!" David asked.

"Exactly! A problem!"

"Anything else about the shot?"

"Yes. It was very accurate. One shot and death was instantaneous. It was either fired by a marksman or a lucky shot by an amateur!"

"And you yourself think ..."

"I think all the signs are that he was a marksman. My whole feel is that this was a professional who knew his business. He went there intending to kill her."

"Good God! But what on earth could have been the motive?"

"I'm afraid there is no obvious motive. Nothing was stolen, not even the little jewellery Mrs Gibson was wearing when she was shot. At the moment we are without any lead. There is simply no indication of who the killer might be, why he was taken there by car or the reason for doing it."

Clearly baffled by the circumstances of the crime, the Police announced that it must have begun as a speculative burglary, that for some unknown reason had gone wrong. Perhaps the burglar had gone to the house and panicked. The trouble was that it didn't look anything like an attempted burglary. The crime suggested a considerable degree both of resources and of planning. How many burglars even had access to a motor car? How many had chauffeurs? Moreover, the police were sure that the man had clearly planned to go specifically to the Gibson house. The question was why, and they had no answer.

"It doesn't make sense," David later told his son. "They say he was a professional. But what professional fires without a reason? What burglar goes in broad daylight armed with a revolver? There was no reason to fire, there was no sign of a struggle, and he shot Maria from behind."

"And why fire the gun and then run off with no attempt to take the gold necklace she was wearing?"

"The Inspector agrees," David continued, "there is too much planning for it to be speculative. Why carry a gun at all? Why no warning shot? Or a shot to disable rather than kill? So many questions and so few answers."

3

Five days later the Gibson's felt it was time to return home. James, Anna's younger brother, went off to school, John Gibson called a cab to take their luggage home, David Strange departed for his office and Grace Strange had gone to the shops. Robert, who had remained in the house to walk Anna home when she was ready, was reading the morning paper in the sitting room. The front doorbell rang and Mary, the family's cook-general, showed a well-dressed, blonde-haired young man of about Robert's age and build into the sitting room. He was announced as Mr Gerald Morris, calling to see Miss Anna Gibson. Robert had not expected the visit. He knew vaguely that Gerald was an acquaintance of Anna's from the local Tennis club. Yet as he was here to visit her, he must know her better than Robert imagined. Robert thought that he worked in the City and had an idea that his father was a banker, well connected with the City Corporation. A man therefore of some significant stature and influence. Certainly, the family had money to spare and lived in a grand old house with land not far away in the Finchley direction.

Robert was also surprised at Gerald's visit because he would have said, if asked, that Gerald was not Anna's sort. Not by any means a fool, but not much concerned with the world of books and ideas Robert knew to be the centre of Anna's interests. Apart from tennis, for which Gerald had the wrong build to be a good player, Gerald's other and preferred game, one that suited his temperament and frame, was rugby.

He seemed conventionally polite and introduced himself in an affable if distant manner. However, he used the kind of deliberately over-firm and unsubtle handshake that

Robert understood was intended to convey a message of superiority. Robert recognised the type, saw it coming and equalled it with his own powerful hand grip, useful for the self-defence classes at the Dockland club near where he had lived in the East End. He instinctively disliked Gerald as someone altogether too keen to impress others with his innate personal authority. An attitude reflected in his haughty manner, and the condescending way he eyed up the room.

"I hear your parents have given the Gibson's a bed. Good of them! It's been such a bad thing for them. How has Anna taken it? It must be hard for her."

A direct approach. Although, if he cared so much about Anna why had he taken several days after the murder to inquire?

"Yes, it's very hard for her. Anna was naturally badly shaken. But she's strong and I'm sure she will recover." Robert said it with some doubt in his mind. Anna was very clearly badly shaken by the events.

"Of course! Anyway, I've come to take her home," Gerald continued abruptly, in a way intended to cut any conversation short. "I've got my father's car outside. I'd be obliged if you could call her." But it wasn't a question; more like an instruction from someone who expected quick compliance. "I don't want to waste time."

Robert thought it a confounded cheek and was thoroughly irritated. But, he reasoned, it would be silly to make an issue of it. The man was a rich dandy, certainly not his type, and he was surprised he was Anna's. Maybe, it struck him, that just shows how much she had changed in the last few years.

"It's kind of you to drive her home. In fact she's still getting ready upstairs. But she is expecting to go home and will be down any moment. Do take a seat."

Gerald looked annoyed that Robert had not immediately acted on his wish and ignored the invitation to sit down. He looked tempted to renew his instruction, but apparently decided against it. "We'll give her a minute or two I suppose," he said with evident irritation. "And then someone could tell her that I'm here to collect her!"

He meant of course that Robert should do it. He began to pace around the room, rather ostentatiously and rudely sizing up the furniture and fittings, as if he was in an auction saleroom on viewing day.

"Quite a cosy little place! They say that since the Underground came here there's a building boom. All the fields round here will soon be covered in little places like this!"

"That is indeed the plan for the Hampstead Garden Suburb. We act for one of the co-operatives and some of the main builders, and of course purchasers."

"Shame to cover good farming land with rabbit hutches!"

What damned cheek! Robert thought. He was about to observe that he disagreed, and that the Hampstead Garden Suburb project was in his opinion a splendid idea, a model for the future. But his thoughts were short-circuited because Gerald had stopped in front of the mantelpiece. He was examining the array of framed family photos; he was up close, scrutinising them.

"My God what's all this tosh! Just look at him! That one there! What a clown! For gawd's sake it's panto time! What a farce!" He was examining a photo of Robert's grandfather as a young man in Nigeria, standing in front of a large, intricately carved, black, tribal throne and wearing the elaborate ceremonial state robes that fitted his rank as the son of a Paramount Chief.

"That photo? That's my mother's father. My grandfather, at home in Nigeria. Just before he came to England to study medicine."

Gerald laughed loudly. More a guffaw, a long-drawn-out throaty roar of derision. "Gawd save us! Your grandfather you say! For pity's sake a proper savage in a suit! A Ju Wallah you say, a medicine man. That looks right!" He then turned to the adjacent photos, Robert's grandfather receiving his degree in Medicine at Edinburgh University and later as a newly appointed consultant at Guys Hospital in London.

"There's another one all dressed up! And just look at him in that Witch Doctor outfit! Looks almost civilised, but you can always tell!"

He turned to stare rudely at Robert. "My God! I knew there was something damned odd about you. Now that I look it's obvious! I see now I should have brought you a bunch of bananas! You must miss not having them outside on the trees!" It was not spoken casually or carelessly; it was meant to insult. His derogatory manner expressed complete indifferent to any hurt his words might have caused.

At an early age Robert's father had taught him never to tolerate such behaviour. But while he was fuming at Gerald's blatant insolence, he was determined to keep control. He had been in such situations many times before. It was best to keep calm and anyway the fellow was a guest in his house. But then he looked again at Gerald's sneering face; the man had gone too far.

"You were looking at photos of my grandfather at his degree convocation and then when he was appointed as a consultant physician. How dare you come into my house, Mr Morris, insult me, and insult my family!"

"Dare? Dare? My dear chap I'm just saying it as it is!"

"Well Mr Morris, then I too will say it as it is! You are no longer welcome in this house. You will kindly leave. And you will do so now."

"I don't take orders from monkeys. I'm going to wait for Anna."

"No. You are not. I told you to leave!" Robert's blood boiled and he had to consciously restrain himself.

"When I'm ready! Then I'll leave. Not before." Gerald stood there defiant. His stance brazen, declaring that he, Gerald Morris, would not give ground to someone he saw as someone clearly not 'one of us'. He, Gerald Morris, would not be moved. Robert stepped closer towards him, but Gerald showed his contempt by standing with his body leaning slightly forwards and his chin stuck out. His manner showed he completely discounted any likelihood that Robert would even think of forcing him out of the house. He wouldn't dare, he would know his inferior place. And if, stupidly, Robert did try something, Gerald's attitude showed he was completely sure he would regret it.

"No! You will leave right now," Robert said, the quiet steel in his voice a warning that he would tolerate no more.

"I will not! Hah!" Gerald sniggered rudely.

That was it: the last straw. Robert stared at him for a long five seconds, his face expressionless and cold, and then moved fast. Two small, quick steps forward, right up to Gerald. Then a sudden, raised, left knee propelled powerfully upwards at close quarters, hard into Gerald's groin. Not of course anything like the pretty, polite, socially acceptable, way that gentlemen fight. The Queensbury Rules and so on. Rather a simple, effective, disabling, streetfighter's move. Something picked up in the East End. For in Robert's eyes Gerald's calculated offence did not merit a gentleman's consideration. Robert had learnt in the Docklands how to dispense with niceties in dealing with scum. His blow dropped Gerald to the floor, sobbing and doubled up in pain. Incoherent words came out of his mouth. Robert gave him no quarter, seized his right arm, pulled him roughly to his feet and twisted his arm round behind his back in a half-nelson wrestling hold. Gerald had been completely taken by surprise and yelled in pain.

"What … the hell …"

He tried to say more but the pain stopped him.

"No-one speaks to me or my family like that!" Robert spat the words and tightened the pressure. Gerald squealed.

"You are leaving! And you will never return. Do you understand?"

There was no response. Robert renewed the pressure until Gerald conceded by a desperate nod of his head.

"So! Out you go!" He bundled Gerald into the Hall, called for the maid to open the front door and frog-marched Gerald down the path to the road where his car was parked. Without ado he propelled Gerald towards the car's bonnet and used his foot to hasten his passage.

"Don't come back! Ever!" he shouted.

Gerald collided with the car's bonnet and slid down to the pavement from where he tried to slowly pick himself up. "My God you will pay for this!" he cried, groping for the door. Robert walked away.

Anna came downstairs ten minutes later, apparently oblivious of the incident, and he told her that Gerald had called but had not waited. She was surprised he had gone, and Robert said he would call a taxi for her.

As soon as she had been driven off home, he picked up his raincoat and walked to the office. It had been, he reflected, an informative morning. He had seen Anna through a new perspective. It wasn't only that she was clearly no longer the girl of his childhood memories, or a girl whose academic accomplishments he suspected had put her out of his league, but rather that if she really had friends like Gerald, although she might be clever and beautiful, she was not for him. Which, given his relationship with Sybil was fine.

He went into his father's office to recount the morning's affair.

"My God! You did right to throw him out," his father said. "There may be repercussions, but you did the right thing. What a ghastly piece of work this Gerald sounds. How on earth can a nice girl like Anna like him?"

"It shocked me!" Robert answered. "He's just not her type. Or her father's for that matter."

David Strange hesitated. "John Gibson? There may be connections."

Robert waited until his father provided the information that was implied.

"Well ... You see for one thing the families are both Catholic. That could be important to them both. And another thing is that John bought their house with a mortgage, and the mortgage was then sold onto Gerald's father. He's a banker you know."

"Yes, the Catholic Church could be a link. Maria being Italian I know Anna was brought up a Catholic. Was it a large mortgage?"

"Yes, it was. John had no money. And then John had to extend the mortgage when Anna went to University."

Robert looked at his father, a hard, searching, look; the families had been very close, surely if the Gibson's were hard up and needed help for Anna to go to University, his father would have been both able and pleased to help them out financially.

His father got the message. "Look Robbie, I offered him whatever money Anna needed to go to college. I begged him to take it for her sake, we were delighted she was able to go to University. But he wouldn't take it. Not a penny. Insisted on doing it all himself. What could I do?"

Robert was surprised, but her father's money dealings could surely not explain why Anna should be a close friend of Gerald. At least the Anna he had known so well in the past had never been the kind of girl who would let herself be bought for a handful of silver. Maybe, therefore, it must be the religious connection; he supposed that Catholics would tend to stick together, being a bit different. He could of course understand that there were problems in being different. He knew all about being different. It was not therefore surprising that birds of a feather flocked together. That he supposed must be the answer about Gerald.

David Strange went on to say that the police had carried out further detective work. The registration number of the vehicle had been traced to a doctor in Kent, from whom the car was stolen the day before the murder. One witness had seen the knife grinder and careful questioning disclosed that he had looked for work only in the Gibson's street. All the evidence now pointed decisively to the murder being the product of a well-organised criminal cell, one with significant resources and the ability to plan a relatively sophisticated operation. The murder was clearly not the work of an incompetent thief and was in no way speculative.

"It is an important step forward," David told his son. "But it doesn't take us closer to actually understanding the murder."

"No," Robert replied, "what on earth was the point of such an expensive, sophisticated, criminal operation? Why in

God's name would anyone go to such trouble to murder Maria Gibson of all people?"

"Indeed, it makes no sense. My intuition is that the shooting was linked somehow, I'm not sure how or why, to the fact that Maria Gibson was born in Italy. You know she was visiting Italian relatives in London when she met John Gibson at a party. I think Italy may be the clue."

"Father, there's nothing at all to support that idea! How on earth does the fact she was born in Italy even begin to explain why anyone would want to murder her?"

"I don't have an explanation at the moment. I just think that an Italian connection might unlock what is otherwise a complete mystery. You have heard of Italian Secret Societies who carry out hideous reprisals, including horrible killings, sometimes years and years after an event that was somehow against the Society's rules. They may even kill grandchildren for something they have decided was a sin of their grandfather. The thing is that at present I can't see any logic to the murder. I'm just casting around for something that makes sense of it."

"Father, isn't your theory about Italian Secret Societies rather a leap into the dark? How on earth could Maria Gibson of all people have been connected to anything like that!"

4

It was a Sunday about four months after the murder, a cold January morning and Robert was sleeping late. Still in bed although downstairs in the Hall the telephone was ringing repeatedly. He was oblivious to it because he needed the sleep after a very late Saturday night out in Town with Sybil. But eventually the telephone's insistence broke through his slumbers, and feeling guilty, he did his best to get up. But as his feet touched the bedroom carpet the phone ceased. Feeling annoyed he wondered who would telephone on a Sunday morning. Overcoming the temptation to simply return to bed, he pulled his dressing gown close around him; for there were never fires lit upstairs unless someone was ill.

"Who," he asked himself again, "would telephone on a Sunday morning?"

It was probably his mother in Norfolk. His father's health had unexpectedly changed suddenly just before Christmas, and he was put under doctor's orders to rest, exhausted by overwork and too much stress. He had been told to recuperate in the family's cottage in Norfolk. Bought many years ago for holidays, although a hundred miles or so away the cottage was a simple train journey from London and easily reached by pony and trap from the station at Hunstanton. Robert had himself enjoyed many escapes there, especially sailing in the creeks along the north Norfolk coast, where he kept an old dinghy he had refurbished.

He went downstairs and made his way across to the kitchen, the warmest part of the house because Mary, his mother's cook-general, had lit the coke boiler before going out for the day to visit her sister. It was good, also, to light the new gas cooker and put the kettle on to make a pot of tea. As he sat waiting for the kettle to boil, he was jolted out of his still sleepy reflections by the demanding clarion summons of the front doorbell. Its abrupt command startled him. Who on earth could possibly be at the front door on a Sunday morning? First the phone now the doorbell. Another long ring. Quite annoying but he had better find out.

Standing there in the porch was an attractive young woman. About twenty-two or three, with a beautiful oval face with long sleek auburn hair loosely gathered at the back by a turquoise ribbon. On her head she wore a round, low crown, russet coloured woven reed hat carrying a naturalistic design in blue with a wide flat brim with a pale blue underside. She had large bluish green eyes and a short pretty nose. She wore a long tweed coat pulled closely around her neck. Her appearance was so completely unforeseen that it took him a moment to pull himself together. It was of course Anna Gibson, who he had last seen at her mother's funeral Mass in the Catholic Church in Hampstead. He was completely flummoxed at the utter surprise of finding her standing on the doorstep. Why on earth should she be outside his front door on a Sunday morning? Why except for what he immediately feared; something bad to do with her mother's murder.

"Anna!" he blurted out, in a state of confusion. Shock as well because he saw at once the paleness of her complexion and her tearful eyes. Something bad had happened, her distressed appearance bore the unmistakable signs of ill tidings. But standing on the doorstep in his slippers, pyjamas and dressing gown at mid-morning to greet a pretty girl, he felt both ridiculously self-conscious and very stupid. What would she think of him? But shamed or not he was in fact pleased to see her.

"Anna! It's wonderful to see you. Is something wrong?"

"Robbie!" she greeted him, tearful, barely in control. Then took in his garb. "You can't surely still be in bed! At this time of day. I've been trying to phone you. For ages. I rang and rang. There was no answer. I couldn't understand it and I had to come. I must talk to you." On the verge of hysteria, she sobbed freely.

"I'm so sorry!" he exclaimed, embarrassed that he appeared so lazy. "I was asleep when the phone rang. I'm so sorry. You must come in. It's cold outside."

"Robbie, you're not even dressed. I can't come in."

"Anna don't be ridiculous! Of course, you can. You must come in. We've known each other for years. We're practically family. You must come in."

He hesitated no longer and stepped into the porch. He gently lifted her into the Hall; she did not resist, although she did give him a look which indicated that she was doing so despite her better judgement. He gave her a cautious peck on the cheek and felt the bitter cold on his lips. He took her hand which was just as cold and, feeling he had to do something to warm her, enfolded her in a good enfolding bear hug. He hadn't done that since he was about fourteen and it felt good. But as he held her close in his arms, he could feel the shivers in her body, only partly due to the cold, and he held her tighter. She rested her head on his shoulder and just let go. She cried and cried. He tried to comfort her, holding her, whispering soft words, his hand rubbing her back and stoking her long hair. She must have rushed out of the house without a scarf or gloves. It must be really serious bad news. After a while she controlled her sobbing. She looked up at his face, with tears flowing freely from her eyes.

"Robbie I'm so sorry to disturb you ..."

He interrupted her. "Don't talk nonsense Anna! You're disturbing nothing. Except my lazing in bed. Something's wrong and I'm glad you came. Let's go to the kitchen. It's warm there." Putting his arm around her he guided her across the Hall. "I've not long boiled the kettle. But you really must tell me what's wrong."

She seemed to relax as they entered the kitchen. "Robbie it's been an awful morning. My father's in such a terrible state." The persona of self-control dropped, and she was tearful again. He held her hand tight. She was still shivering. He had feared something like that would happen, John had not taken Maria's death well, as Robert's father had told him several times.

The words now came tumbling from her lips. "You see, last night my father got a package from Rosina, she's one of my mother's cousins. It was a bundle of letters sent to my mother from Sergio, he's a distant relative in North Africa. Sergio must have trapped my mother into taking part in some dreadful political conspiracy. It looks as if there's a Secret Society involved. Father thinks she was killed because of something in these letters. He's worried sick that since they killed her, they will come after us too. I am really frightened Robbie."

She was in tears again and shaking, so he tried to comfort her.

"Letters? Italian Secret Society? What on earth is all this Anna?" he asked, thinking it sounded like some farfetched magazine fiction. Yes, but her words had immediately reminded him of his father's assassination idea, months ago at the time of the murder, that Maria's death had some kind of secret Italian connection. Then, there was nothing to support such a theory, but Anna's news put a different complexion on it. Robert was intrigued as well as anxious. If some Italian

Secret Society had indeed killed Maria, Anna was right to be afraid; the Gibson family might not be safe. He realised that he cared.

"Robbie, the secret societies are capable of doing anything to get what they want. Murder. Blackmail. Anything. They are vicious and unforgiving. I'm worried!"

"My God this is serious stuff Anna!"

"My father is beside himself. Can you come home with me and talk to him?"

"My poor Anna! I'm sorry about the telephone. Of course, I'll speak to your father. Whatever it is I'm sure it's something that we can manage."

*

John Gibson opened the door, his long, lean face ashen with exhaustion. He had never carried any excess weight, but he was now decidedly wasted.

"Robert! It's good of you to come." John's greeting was delivered in a shaky voice. "You see, yesterday, I got this parcel from Rosina, a collection of letters from Italy written to Maria, care of Rosina's address. I was never shown them. I'm afraid they open a new ghastly problem. They all from her cousin Sergio, written in Italian of course but I am reasonably fluent."

"And Sergio is who?"

"That's why it is so strange. He is only a very, very distant cousin."

"I think," Anna explained, "that his grandmother and my mother's great grandmother were sisters. Sergio is the son of my mother's great grandmother's sister."

Robert was completely lost in the complicated family tree.

"It means that he is only a very distant relation," John said. "But, nevertheless to an Italian, part of the family."

"Yes. I do understand that. In my grandfather's culture in Nigeria, he would also be simply part of the family, and treated like a brother to Maria."

"Maria never met Sergio," John continued. "He has been working in an Italian Bank in Tripoli for a few years."

"Tripoli?" Robert was lost in the geography, where on earth was Tripoli?

"Yes, this is Tripoli the chief city of Libya, in North Africa, just across the sea from Sicily. Libya is a province of the Ottoman Empire based in Constantinople."

"Intriguing!" Robert was trying to imagine the map of the Mediterranean. Libya must be next to Egypt. The Orient.

"You could say that I suppose. Sergio worked for the Banco di Roma, an Italian Bank that opened a branch in Tripoli a few years ago. The bank services a growing Italian community settled in Tripoli. Italy is encouraging Italians to settle there. They want to colonise Libya, economically and gradually."

He handed Robert a collection of hand-written letters in their envelopes all addressed to 'Maria Gibson' at Rosina's address.

"They are in Italian," Robert observed, "I'm sorry but I know no Italian."

"No matter," John replied, "I and Anna have translated the ones that matter. You see I think there is a message in the letters. If I explain you will understand my concern, and why I asked you to call."

The first letter from Sergio was about two years ago and told Maria of the sudden illness of a person Sergio described as 'Uncle Cesare'. After this Sergio sent letter after letter, giving her instructions about how to handle a large sum of money he was sending to her. Then he wrote that Uncle Cesare had died and bequeathed Maria a property near Rome together with a 'substantial' sum of money. Then he told Maria about Cesare's instructions about the money he had left.

"Money?"

"The first payment to Maria would be £10,000.00."

"Wow! Ten thousand pounds, that's a huge fortune!" It was indeed a staggering amount of money, enough to buy all the shops in Golders Green, and much more. And that was just the first payment. Whatever could be involved that could justify such vast sums?

"But you see we know it wasn't paid into her own Bank account in Golders Green. So, if she got it, she must have a secret Bank account somewhere else."

"Was there more money?"

"Yes, the letters mention another ten thousand pounds. Who knows there could be more?"

"Incredible! Such a huge fortune. Uncle Cesare must have been enormously rich."

"No! The point is that Uncle Cesare never existed. He was make-believe, never existed, a fiction."

"What! But then how did he give Maria the money? And to leave property in Italy on his death would require a lot of legal correspondence."

But John said there was a complete lack of legal correspondence. "All Maria got were letters from Sergio. There were never any Court or legal papers. It didn't look right. But she did get instructions from Sergio: she was told that Uncle Cesare wanted her to buy a 'little old fishing boat' to transport 'supplies' to the 'Italian settlers' in Tripoli."

Sergio wrote that Cesare had explained to him:

"... it is my patriotic duty and in the true spirit of the Sons and Daughters of the Carbonari to support the Italian settlers in Tripoli"

"The Carbonari? Who are they?" Robert inquired.

"The Carbonari? They were an Italian secret society in the early last century. They fought against Napoleon and later in the 1830's one of their leaders was Giuseppe Mazzini."

"Yes, I've heard of Mazzini. One of the heroes of the struggle to reunify Italy. He lived for a while as a refugee in London near my old School in Gower Street."

"I think Sergio uses 'Carbonari' to mean that the wishes of this alleged Uncle Cesare are about the ideals of 'Young Italy', Italian nationalism. Everything in the letters is couched as an appeal to Maria's Italian patriotism."

Robert realised his ignorance of modern history, what on earth was 'Young Italy'? John showed Robert the next letter:

Dear Cousin Maria,

Our uncle Cesare wants to make an important contribution to the cause of our new united Italy, that she may prosper and establish her true destiny as the mistress of the Western Mediterranean ... Italy must therefore claim her historic rights in North Africa as the new Rome. Tunis should have been ours by right, but we were tricked out of it by the French. Italy cannot afford to be tricked out of Tripoli. The Ottoman Empire who occupy Tripoli is finished .... The English call it the 'Sick Man' and they are correct. Tripoli must be wrenched from them by Italy ...

Our uncle Cesare wishes therefore ... first to support the Italian settlers in Tripoli, second to create fighting in Tripoli, in the streets and in the deserts, so much that the Ottoman Turks must use their army to regain control. That must be the moment when our friends in Rome take the opportunity to compel Italy to intervene with all its naval and military strength and seize Tripoli and all Libya by force.

Later Sergio wrote that that the money sent to Maria was to be used to buy the 'little old fishing boat' and to pay for the guns and explosives needed for an armed uprising in Tripoli. The plan was that when the Italian settlers in Tripoli revolted against the Turks and seized the city, the Italian government in Rome would have to invade Libya. Rome could not ignore public opinion and would be compelled to take military action against the Turks in Tripoli, who would be distracted by an Arab revolt in the desert.

"And Uncle Cesare? You are sure he doesn't exist?"

"I am sure he does not exist. I looked at Maria's family tree in her family Bible. There is no one who fits. She never mentioned anyone like that."

"Interesting!" Robert exclaimed. "If this Uncle Cesare is a fiction, why did Sergio invent him?"

"I puzzled about that! I think it's part of the mystic associated with the Secret societies. They never did obvious things, they loved hidden codes and meanings. Here is a letter:

"I spoke just now to someone who is hidden from those who wish him harm. It is none other than our dear uncle Cesare Onio. He says pointedly and proudly that he is not as he seems. But the meaning behind his words is clear to me, and will I hope be also clear to you. For this grandson of a great patriot of the Carbonari will be soon no more: history and Italy must never forget their struggle. Nor ever forget the bonds in blood that tied them together!"

"Quite a poetic touch!" Robert responded.

"You think so. When I concluded that 'Uncle Cesare' was an invention, there had to be a reason why Sergio invented him."

"Sounds logical."

"Robert, it was part of how Maria was induced, persuaded, or coerced to do things for Sergio's nationalist cause."

"Sure?"

"Yes. Sergio deliberately binds her to do as he asked. By putting his instructions in the mouth of 'uncle' Cesare he implies they are the instructions of the Carbonari secret society. That means he is threatening her."

"Threatening?"

"Yes, the Carbonari was a Secret Society bound together by strict oaths of loyalty and by terrible bloody sanctions if the oath was broken. Oaths taken in the name of the Carbonari are never to be broken."

"I understand your concern! My God!" For was not that exactly what had happened? The letters had drawn Maria into a conspiracy from which she had not escaped alive.

"You say none of the money mentioned went through Maria's Golders Green account in the Midland Bank. Yet as Sergio refers to a deposit of £10,000.00, if it didn't go through her Midland account, how was the money actually received?"

"I don't know!"

"And by cash? Cheque?"

"According to one letter Sergio was going to send her a Banker's Draft. A Banker's Cheque he calls it. I believe that is a cheque drawn by a Bank on its own funds. It is as good as cash."

"Do the letters say how she was to get this Banker's Draft?"

"Yes, it was to be handed to her in London. A meeting to be arranged."

"Wow!" Robert was impressed. "That's like a classic spy thriller. But what's missing is the actual money. If it was not put in her account in Golders Green, she must have opened another account. Do you know of one?"

"Absolutely not! I knew nothing about the money from Sergio until I saw the letters. What can he have said, or done, to persuade Maria to join him in this secret exchange? Maria must have been manipulated or forced into it by this rogue Sergio."

"Was it blackmail? Did Sergio know something that made Maria vulnerable?"

"That is my thought too. But how would he be able to blackmail her? What did he know of such power that would force Maria to engage in a secret conspiracy about so much money?"

It occurred to Robert, although he did not pass these thoughts on to John, that if some vicious Secret Society was behind the conspiracy, they would have had no hesitation in threatening the lives of her husband and children if she did not do exactly what they wanted.

"I'll do whatever I can to help!" Robert said.

"Thank you. I'm at a loss to know what to do. I called you to ask your advice: what should I do with the letters? I'm lost! What do you suggest?"

"If my father was here, he would at once think that his suspicions about Maria's murder were borne out. He always thought that there was indeed more to it than burglary. I think the same and these letters confirm it!"

"Should we then go to the police?"

"I'm not sure," Robert replied. "If there is a connection to the murder I suppose so. But I wonder if the letters don't raise other considerations that we might like to think about first before involving the Police."

"What then should I do?"

The story in the letters was both fascinating and worrying, but Robert felt out of his depth with all this reference to major power politics and the possible intrigues of the great Powers. If he was to advise John, he needed time to think.

"I suggest you need more information before going to the Police. There's nothing in the letters that bears directly on the murder and the police have in fact closed the case."

"I understand, but do you have something else in mind?"

"Yes. If the letters are credible, and they seem so to me, if they are therefore to be taken at their face value, they seem to me to raise important political questions, I mean questions of British national interest. And if so, it may be that the Government rather than the police are the people who should see the letters first."

"Yes, I can agree with that."

In saying so Robert was, however, acutely conscious of the limits of his understanding of current international politics. The story had so many potential issues of which he was only half aware, so many potential subtle nuances. He knew he was at sea without a compass or chart. Yet John Gibson was asking for his help, and he had rashly promised to help without appreciating that it might be beyond him. He was floundering and tried desperately to think of a way out of the problem. He then remembered from his school days some fascinating history lessons on what the books called the 'Eastern Question', which was all about the Turkish Empire's provinces in eastern Europe. And as Tripoli in Libya was part of the Turkish or Ottoman Empire that could be a route to follow.

"Look," he answered, "I would like to understand more about the background, the politics behind what Sergio is planning. And so I suggest that I have a talk with Dr Rands my old history teacher at school. This, the Ottoman Turkish Empire, Italy, the Mediterranean, is right in his area of interest. I think he could help us understand the situation better."

"If you think so," John replied, "you should do it."

"I would need to show him the letters in confidence."

"Yes, of course."

"And then you should have a better idea of what to do with the letters."

They agreed that Robert would ask Reggie Rands for advice about what to do with the letters. When Anna came down from her bedroom, in a change of clothes and refreshed, Robert explained that he had been reading Sergio's letters and mentioned his idea of visiting his old history master.

"That sounds good," she said, her eyes lighting up with interest. "I should like to hear his advice if it helps us to understand what to do."

He had thought of having a talk with Reggie as something he would do by himself. It was therefore a surprise that she told him she wanted to join in. But if she wanted to come that was alright.

"Good! I'll arrange a meeting as soon as I can."

5

Reggie Rands was intrigued by Robert's letter and invited him and Anna to discuss it with him at the school in Hampstead. Anna was keen to accept the invitation and Robert arranged to meet her at the underground in Golders Green.

"It's good to see you!" he said, noticing the pretty, distinctive brooch that he knew showed she was a supporter of the Woman's Social and Political Union. It did strike him that if she was a committed supporter of the campaign for votes for women, she had probably worn the brooch the first time they met, and that he had totally missed it. Not like him; but he knew why, at that time he had been so overcome at the unexpected reunion.

"You can't know," she said, "how good it is to feel I'm doing something real about my mother's death."

"Good! I'm so pleased."

"It's so important to me Robert. Thank you for suggesting it." He noticed that she was no longer calling him 'Robbie'; the relationship was to be formal, and that suited him well.

It was a quick journey and leaving Hampstead Underground station, they walked past the Georgian houses in Heath Street, then past Hampstead Parish Church, down Frognal and reached the school soon after the school day had finished. Reggie Rands greeted them in the main school Hall.

"Reggie, it's good of you to meet us," Robert said. "May I introduce Miss Anna Gibson?"

"Well Miss Gibson, I'm so glad you've come. And Robert, I've been hearing a lot about your sterling work in the

School Settlement. The boys think the world of your football training."

Anna looked puzzled.

"You see Miss Gibson, the school supports a Settlement, a kind of Club, in the docklands in the East End. It organises physical training, gym, football and so on for the local boys. Robert's been a terrific helper there for the last six years." Robert had indeed helped there while he was at school and had continued to do so regularly while working his legal articles in the City. He had trained the boys to play football, take part in self-defence classes and generally enjoyed a lot of physical exercise as an antidote to his sedentary life in the office.

Anna was surprised. "Robert, I had no idea!" Probably, Robert thought because she had not shown the slightest interest in his activities.

Reggie took them through the fine, panelled Great Hall used for morning assembly. Some classrooms led off it and a wide, first floor balcony round all four sides gave access to a further ten classrooms. The spacious, modern, and well-equipped building was so different to the cramped and inadequate school next to Robert's dockland club. He remembered his anger there, face to face with the poor overcrowded conditions under which the teachers were struggling to do their job. Was it not blindingly obvious that our country's future depended on the proper education of its young people? Working in the City he had seen at first-hand the myriad commercial transactions across the world that showed we were an incredibly rich nation, the hub of a far-flung trading Empire and the centre of a vast, prosperous, world-wide commerce. Surely, we were able to give good teachers the proper tools to do the job. The failure made him angry as did the huge sums devoted to bolstering the armaments necessary to support the Imperial image, also indeed to continually enlarge the Empire – even at that moment British troops were still engaged in securing the northern territories of Nigeria.

After they were all seated in Reggie's classroom Robert explained the background to the letters Maria Gibson had received from Sergio, and Anna showed Reggie the translations of the key letters.

Reggie read them thoughtfully. "You asked for my opinion about the letters. But you gave me only half the story."

Robert looked blank.

"You mention, and only as a kind of marginal note, that Anna's mother was killed. But you give no details."

Robert looked at Anna, but she nodded her agreement to tell Reggie the whole story. He did.

"So, I was right!" Reggie said. "It gives a crucial colour to the whole thing doesn't it. Maria Gibson was obviously murdered by professional killers who, given what the letters say, might well be an Italian Secret Society like the Carbonari. The letters virtually foretell her murder. What did you think of the letters?"

"It looks as if Sergio plans a conspiracy for Italy to invade Libya. The trouble is that the conspiracy involves Britain, and he has drawn in Anna's mother to traffic the money through London. We're not sure what to do. We need to know whether the conspiracy is credible or is just a wild delusion. And if it is credible what we should do."

"Well," Reggie said, "he clearly plans to bring about an Italian invasion of Libya, a province of the Turkish Empire in North Africa, and to turn it into an Italian colony."

"Is it a credible plan?"

"Yes. The colonisation of north Africa is a well-known Italian nationalist aim. They wish to re-create the old Roman empire. Which once included the whole of north Africa. But the plan has problems."

"Oh?"

"Yes. Italy would need the agreement of its official allies, that means Germany and Austria. And Italy would need at least the tacit consent of Britain and France, the big naval powers in the Mediterranean. The small Italian navy is no match for them."

'Look." He turned to a big school map of the Mediterranean on the wall behind him. His thin bony fingers traced how close Tripoli, the capital of Libya, was to the British naval base in Malta.

"Malta, you see this tiny island here, is the base for the British Mediterranean fleet. The Italian fleet would not dare anything against the Turks in Tripoli unless they could be sure that the British Mediterranean fleet would stay out of it."

"Yes, Italy would have to be sure we would not interfere in their invasion."

"And the other problem is that apart from a small Italian community in Tripoli, the local population in Libya is Arab and Muslim. Sergio's plan is not to liberate the Arabs but make them colonial subjects of Italy."

"Ah!"

"The Ottoman Sultan in Constantinople is also the Caliph, chief Muslim religious leader, and would not welcome the subjugation of a Muslim population to Christian Italy."

"I suppose not."

"Moreover, Libya is the last piece of north Africa remaining in the Turkish Empire. Once most of north Africa was Turkish."

His hand returned to the map. "Egypt is today only nominally part of the Ottoman Empire because we have controlled the Egyptian government since 1880."

Reggie's hand moved west along the north African coast. "The French seized Algeria from the Turks as a colony in the 1830's and took Tunisia as a French protectorate only a few years ago. Libya is all that's left of a once huge Turkish north African Empire. Libya is the only easy pickings left for Italy. If they want a colony in north Africa, Libya is all that is left to them."

"But does Libya really matter to Turkey?" Robert asked, thinking of Turkey as a decadent, spent and declining power.

"It does today. In the past the big European Powers just took what they wanted because Turkey was weak. But now there is a new nationalist movement in Turkey and a reform government is in power in Constantinople. Now they do care. They are really trying to improve the administration of the provinces. They would resist an Italian attack on Libya. They would fight."

"And would Britain be affected?"

"Yes. Bound to be affected. It's all tied up with British policy to support Turkey, to use Turkey to block Russian expansion, especially to deny Russia control of the Straits at Constantinople."

"The what?" Anna asked. "What are the Straits?"

"The Straits? They are the narrow waters at Constantinople that separate Europe from Asia and divide the Mediterranean from the Black Sea. They describe the waters of the Bosporus and the Dardanelles."

"But is Russian expansion not over?" Robert asked.

"No. Russia still looks greedily at India. Russian expansion in Central Asia has come close to the gates of India. and now there is a new Russian threat to the Raj through the back door to India. I mean Persia."

"Ah."

"But, while that is true, the rest of the game has fundamentally changed."

"Really?"

"Yes. The Russian threat to India remains real. But we face a new, greater, and immediate threat from Germany. Therefore, we need Russia as an ally to keep the Kaiser tame. That concern trumps all our old worries about Constantinople and the Straits, even about India. Russia is our absolutely key ally to control Germany."

"That's helpful," Robert said. "Can we ask you more about what the letters say about Sergio's plan to invade Libya."

"Well, it's a curious situation. All the big European powers secretly support Italy's claim to Libya. But they do so for opposite reasons. Germany because she wants to keep Italy as an ally. Britain because we want to lure Italy away from her alliance with Germany."

"That's why it's sense for us to help Italy get Libya?" Robert suggested.

"Indeed, but on the other hand we need to remain friendly with Turkey because we control Egypt and therefore the Suez Canal only with their consent."

"Sounds tricky! And a bit dishonest. Like running with the hare and hunting with the hounds."

"Exactly! Our policy is therefore careful. That's why we only secretly support Italy's claim to Libya."

"But surely," Anna interjected, "this looks like the proverbial diplomatic applecart."

"Indeed, and it is one that can be easily upset."

"Such a complicated set up," Robert exclaimed.

"A house of cards indeed."

"Or one built on sand."

"So," Anna intervened, "if Sergio's plan succeeds it could trigger a major war."

"Indeed."

"And what about Turkey?" Anna asked.

"A good question, Sergio's plan makes it look as if Britain is part of an underhand conspiracy to snatch Libya. That would make Turkey furious with Britain. They would ask Germany for support."

"And if there was a war in Libya?" Anna asked.

"Turkey would make an alliance with Germany. German influence in Constantinople has grown in the last ten years. A new railway is being constructed to link Constantinople to Bagdad. When built, German troops could be quickly transported to Bagdad and Germany would get control of all the oil deposits around the Persian Gulf. Oil is important. It could be a catastrophe for us."

"Wow! It's like a game of skittles. What else if Italy attacks Libya?" Robert asked.

"Not good. In a big European war, as Germany's ally, Turkey would close the Straits at Constantinople, cut off all access to the Black Sea. A major blow to Russia because most of their foreign trade goes through Odessa and the Straits. Moreover, with railway developments, a German army could be at the banks of the Suez Canal in no time and sever our main link to India."

"My God! The stakes are high," Robert exclaimed.

"Indeed! But if our Government has any sense, and I'm frankly not sure it has, we should do everything possible to keep Turkey out of Germany's grip. In any big European war Britain needs Turkey to be at least neutral. Not only does that keep the Germans out, but also Russia. If Turkey is neutral Russia has no excuse to attack her, would not be able to capture Constantinople and the Straits, occupy the Caucuses and strike south to the Arabian Gulf."

"Makes sense!" Anna observed.

"But," Reggie continued, "to ensure Turkish neutrality, Italy must be persuaded not to invade Libya."

"And Sergio's conspiracy?" Robert asked.

"Sergio's conspiracy must be put down at all costs. It is financed through London, would probably therefore use British gold sovereigns to pay for the native revolt in Libya, would use a British registered vessel that sails from a British port with a British crew and probably arm the natives with British made rifles."

"And the effect?"

"It would look like an underhand British plot and wreck our carefully nurtured international reputation for honesty and the rule of law. It would make the British Empire look like a bunch of pirates."

There was a silence. Robert had not anticipated such a strong statement.

"Thank you," Anna said, "for making clear that there is more to this awful saga of my mother's murder than meets the eye." She profusely thanked Reggie for his time in seeing them.

Reggie acknowledged her thanks. "I'm glad you showed me the letters. You may be wondering what to do with them. I think that they show a serious plot by your cousin Sergio to damage British interests. Especially the reputation of the Empire. I think they raise important issues for the Government to address urgently. I think that what you should do is talk to people in the Foreign Office."

"Wow!" Robert answered, not expecting that. It was odd to think that an Imperial sceptic like him was now being cast as a saviour of the Imperial reputation. He was not sure he wanted the role, but he felt obliged having come this far to at least explore the suggestion.

"Do you have any proposal how we might do that?" Suddenly the meeting with Reggie that he had dreamt up, only to get him off the hook, had taken on an unexpected and major new importance. Anna was being offered a way forward, but was it a road that he wanted to tread? However, he had promised to help her and the memory of her anguished state when she came to him was all too fresh in his mind. He guessed he probably had no choice.

"I've been thinking," Reggie continued. "One of my former pupils, Hugo Cavendish, is now at the Foreign Office. I think he could help you. He is quite sharp if somewhat unorthodox. He must be about thirty-two now. He read History at Oxford, but his heart wasn't in it, and he didn't get a good degree. He had to give up the idea of going for the Indian Civils, a government career out in India. Instead, he did some travelling around the Med for a year or so and later joined the Foreign Office. I would if you wish arrange a meeting."

"Would he be able to take this Sergio matter forward?" Robert queried.

"He is junior, but what I've heard he seems to have the ear of seniors in the Department. I gather that after he returned from the Med, he went to Manchester for the Home Office to do some difficult intelligence. As a result, he is well thought of."

Robert did not much like the sound of this Hugo Cavendish. Not his type. He smacked of being a rich self-indulgent, well-connected lay-about. A failed administrator of the Raj. Surely not the man to persuade a traditionalist department like the Foreign Office to take up the Sergio case.

However, he knew that Anna desperately needed to feel that something was being done. If he had any doubt on that score he had only to glance at Anna. Her face had lit up with delight at the hope of progress that Reggie now offered.

"That's wonderful news!" she exclaimed, with a broad smile. "Of course, we will follow your advice! Suddenly the whole ghastly business of my mother's murder has started to become intelligible. How can I thank you!"

She had decided. That was it, and Robert did not argue; it was after all not really his business. So, Reggie went ahead with arranging a meeting with Hugo Cavendish at the Foreign Office. A new chapter in the Sergio affair was opening.

6

Hugo Cavendish wasted no time to invite Robert and Anna to the Foreign Office in Whitehall. Anna jumped at the news and arranged to meet Robert outside Golders Green station to take the underground into Town. Robert went along, though, expecting that the meeting would be the end of his renewed acquaintance with Anna. Passing the matter of the Sergio conspiracy on to Hugo Cavendish and the Foreign Office did seem to signal the limit of what Robert could usefully do to help the Gibson's in the affair.

"That must be for the best," he thought. He had enjoyed meeting Anna again; their reunion had been the trigger for recalling many happy days in the past. And he had found her good company, although he realised she had changed a lot and noticed that while she was friendly, underneath she seemed indifferent to him. Anyway, what was preying on his mind was an awareness that he must end his role in the affair of the Sergio letters because of his prospective engagement to Sybil. Continuing regular meetings with Anna would become hard to explain to Sybil.

Leaving Strand underground station, they strolled across Trafalgar Square and continued down Whitehall towards Parliament Square. They threaded their way through the usual confused tangle of vehicles of all kinds manoeuvring for advantage. As well as the still numerous horse-drawn buses, Hanson cabs, carts and occasional carriages, the sign of the fast-changing times was the number of motor vehicle, cars, buses, lorries and vans. They neared Parliament Square and turned right towards the massive set of government buildings built in a palatial Italianate style, now fifty years old. It was an immense edifice, embracing three large interior courtyards, built to demonstrate the vast and complex scale of modern British imperial government. For the huge sprawling structure housed the India Office and the Foreign Office at the side overlooking St James' Park, while the Colonial and Home Offices lay beside Whitehall. Nearing the moment when he would have to confront the forces of the British establishment, Robert for the first time felt anxious. True that Reggie Rands had encouraged and set-up this meeting: he must therefore have been confident that Robert would take it in his stride. But this vast government complex was the bastion of traditional, conservative, British attitudes and Robert was not sure how he would be treated. Rather, he was sure he did know how he would be treated and did not look forward to it. Polite, if cold, to his face of course, but behind his back it would be different.

They reached the Foreign Office, were efficiently ticked off on a visitor list and were ushered up a magnificently opulent, ornate, and expensively marbled grand staircase designed in an overpowering Italianate manner. Halfway up Anna paused beside a variegated marble inset panel.

"Just look at all this overblown display of sumptuous luxury!" she whispered, nudging Robert's arm. "All these grand, marble, Corinthian columns and gilded capitals. It's far too much. Even for an Italian like me who loves a bit of show. I feel overcome by the sheer vulgarity of it."

"Vulgar?" he answered. "Yes, I suppose it is vulgar. But what do you expect? Surely, it's only what you must do if you want to impress gullible foreigners. Awe them with British Imperial power and wealth. If you set yourself up as a mighty Empire you must be sure to look the part. It's just an Act on the World stage. That gold leaf you don't like is there for a purpose!"

"I'm shocked at you Robert. It's all too much, tasteless." She was right but had missed his point.

On the first floor they were shown into a waiting room. In the centre was a small mahogany table with four upright chairs in the Chippendale style. The walls were hung with red and gold patterned wallpaper, and one wall was occupied by a neat stone fireplace with an open grate in which a coal fire burnt, whose comforting warmth they were quick to enjoy. Above the fireplace was an oil painting of some long past naval victory over the French, the country that was today Britain's closest ally against Germany.

At long last there was the sound of orders being imperiously shouted in the corridor outside, rudely rupturing the museum-like silence of the place.

"Carruthers!" a voice boomed. "Take these papers to my desk. Now!"

Then the mahogany door was flung open, and Hugo Cavendish almost bounced into the room. His attire was an immediate shock: it was so out of place. He wore the kind of brown tweed suit and brown boots appropriate only for a country walk, quite ill-chosen for the corridors of a great department of State. Moreover, his equally inappropriate tweed overcoat signalled that he had just arrived in the building. But what would a junior Foreign Office clerk be doing out on the streets at this time of day? Nor did his appearance fit, of average height with a tightly trimmed brown moustache, his fair hair brushed sideways from a centre parting was much too long and he wore no kind of hat. But perhaps his most striking feature were his large hazel eyes, alert and searching, indeed discomforting in their intensity. And then as he stepped lightly across the room, he seemed to move on the balls of his feet in such an odd way that his heels did not appear to touch the floor. To Robert, his light, careful, softly placed tread reminded him of a recent, and decidedly doubtful, client in the Kilburn area of north London who had been an unsuccessful cat burglar.

"Terribly sorry to keep you waiting in this hole!" He greeted them in a casual manner, and as if to order he spread an expansive smile across his round face. "Ah! It must be Robert Strange!" He stepped across the room and gripped Robert's hand.

Robert took the vice-like handshake to be a deliberate ploy, intended to test him. He made a point of returning Hugo's grip with interest, compelling him to be the one that disengaged. Hugo subjected Robert to an intense, uncomfortable, scrutinising gaze that made Robert feel he was being soundlessly but thoroughly interrogated, and then labelled for future reference like some interesting botanical specimen.

"Yes, I was told that I would find you … interesting." He paused still looking. "Yes … interesting was the word used. And they were right …. I do." He said it in a way that was quite disconcertingly affected; a rising cadence for some words like 'interesting' coupled with an unexpected drop in volume to a whisper as he came to the closing words of the sentence.

Robert did not care to be told he was 'interesting', which could only mean one thing. His initial reservations about Hugo, particularly about his apparently posh and idle background, were compounded. Robert's docklands experience told him not to trust the man: appearances mattered. Hugo did not fit the look of a junior Foreign Office clerk by a mile. The clothes and hair were wrong; he had publicly berated the unfortunate Caruthers in a way that did not belong to a junior clerk; he had entered the room as if he owned the place. And then there was the odd way he walked, his ability to flick on a plainly artificial smile at will, the affectations in his speech, his unconcealed and offensive scrutiny of Robert's face and his transparent attempt to disadvantage Robert with a power handshake. Robert feared for the rest of the meeting, thinking it would go badly and he would have to cope with a distraught Anna on the way home.

Anna had been keen on the visit but could not miss the blatantly rude way Hugo had drawn attention to Robert's appearance. Then, although he was a complete stranger, Hugo greeted her without more ado with a kiss on her cheek in the most forward, advanced Bohemian manner. Did he just casually assume that as a mere girl she would be flattered by such attention? Or worse, did he just take it for granted that because she was there to beg his help with the Sergio letters, he could take whatever liberties he wished? Was he indeed the sort of man who would not hesitate for a moment to take advantage of a situation where a woman had strayed into his power? As it was, she knew she had no choice but to defer to him because he controlled the success of their visit.

The moment passed and Hugo, oblivious to the poor impression that his guests had formed of him, led them into a nearby grand committee room with a large mahogany table and asked them to be seated. By way of chatting, he told them he was "not so long out of Oxford," so was still "a relatively junior hand at the job here."

Hugo looked at them steadily. "Well, you've come for a reason so let's sit down and get on with what's brought you here!"

He looked to Robert to start, and Robert explained finding the Sergio letters many months after Maria's death, John's investigations and theory and their visit to Reggie that had led to the arrangement for this meeting. He asked Anna to hand over the collection of letters and translations. Hugo looked carefully through the translations, taking some twenty minutes, and then shoved them to one side. He then immediately fired a rapid burst of searching questions about Maria Gibson and her cousin Sergio. The way he did so made Robert realise that he was an accomplished interrogator, knowing how to cut through to the heart of a matter.

"This Sergio person," he demanded of Anna, "what relation was he to your mother? You say a cousin, but what kind of a cousin exactly? Have you met him yourself? Why is he in Tripoli? Who does he work for? How long? Do you know his politics? What connections has he with any Italian political groups?"

Anna kept calm through the barrage of questions, refusing to be flustered by Hugo's barnstorming inquisition, giving the answers as best she could to most but not all the questions. Hugo showed signs of impatience when she was unable to answer or didn't address exactly the point of a question. He was clearly a man who was used to obtaining information and expected to get it.

Hugo then moved onto the issue of the money. Robert said it seemed that according to Sergio's letters a large sum had been received by Maria.

"Seemed to have been received?" Hugo queried, tersely. "Seemed? Don't you know?"

Robert was taken aback by the forceful, belligerent tone, as if he was being addressed like a lower order clerk, an inferior servant of the man. But he felt obliged to humour the fellow and so explained quietly that all the indications were that Maria had indeed received the money, but they knew she had not used her normal Bank account. She had therefore probably opened a special account somewhere else. Another Bank.

"At which Bank?" Not a question but an accusation of incompetent staff work.

"I'm sorry, we don't have that information."

"Clearly! You see if your version of this Sergio affair is remotely correct," Hugo continued, "and if a vessel of any size was to be purchased, Mrs Gibson must have received a very great deal of money. But where is the proof of any of it?" Hugo made it as a statement of the obvious, as if Anna and Robert were too naïve or stupid to have appreciated it.

"The evidence is surely there in the letters," Robert muttered.

"The letters merely express a wish. They do not establish the fact of an actual transfer of hard cash. Where are the Bank statements that show there was a real deposit?"

"We don't have them," Robert had to confess.

"No, you don't. Moreover, from what you tell me about Sergio he did not conceivably himself have the kind of money his plot needed. From where, therefore, did the money come?"

"We have no idea!" Anna replied.

Hugo gave her a searching look, dramatizing the long silence that followed her admission.

"Perhaps from Germany," Robert said, a suggestion plucked out of thin air, immediately thinking it was a silly thing to say and Hugo would relish making him look ridiculous.

But in fact Hugo smiled. "Germany. An interesting idea. A German conspiracy. Well, it would not be the first German plot against us!"

"It would work," Robert continued. "Germany has an interest in causing trouble for Britain in the Mediterranean, and in convincing Turkey to throw in her hand with Berlin."

"Interesting! That would indeed be a devilish plot. A German plan to finesse an alliance with Turkey. Clever!" Hugo looked at them quizzically.

"Yes, but it seems a sensible guess."

"But, nevertheless, you are of course merely guessing." It was true, only a guess, Robert was beginning to feel there were crucial holes in their story. Maybe they would be dismissed and told not to be silly or waste the government's valuable time.

Hugo remained seated, then looked hard at the pile of letters on the table, shuffled them into a neater pile, picked it up, starred hard at Robert and Anna for ten discomforting seconds, slapped the table hard with his palm and stood up abruptly. It signalled a decision. Robert had taken against the man and felt that their interview had not gone well. Hugo's questions had shown large gaps in their knowledge of the key facts. His aggressive tone indicated that he was about to dismiss the whole thing; they would be sent packing.

Anna then remembered Reggie's comment about the importance of oil in Mesopotamia. "There is one other matter Dr Rands suggested we should mention to you."

"Yes?" Hugo showed little sign of interest.

"Yes. Oil."

"Oil?" Hugo stood stock still.

"Yes, he thought that oil in Mesopotamia was the key to understanding the modern middle east."

Hugo's eyes brightened. "He is right, oil is important. There is a lot of oil in the south of Persia." He pointed to one of the big maps on the table. "Here, near the Persian Gulf there is a great deal of oil, oil that the Anglo Persian Company is busy exploiting on a big scale."

"And this Persian oil is important?"

"It is! It gives us a secure British controlled oil supply. A supply essential to our Navy."

"Ah!"

"Some of our warships are already converted from coal-burning to oil-burning and Fisher, the First Sea Lord, wants the whole British fleet to convert to oil."

"I recall seeing that in the papers," Robert observed.

"Yes. Our Battle fleet can't afford the time taken to re-coal if there was a surprise German attack across the North Sea. Moreover, oil burning gives them an edge, a few critical extra knots. And oil gives our ships a greater steaming range because they can carry more oil than coal in the same bunker capacity."

"That makes sense."

"Britain must therefore obtain and protect our own secure oil supply for our oil-fired Battleships. We dare not continue to be dependent on American oil."

"But why should we be concerned about Mesopotamia?"

"Well, Persia is sensitive for us because of the oil, and Germany is prospecting for oil in Mesopotamia, the Ottoman province next to Persia. People say that there is as much oil in Mesopotamia as in Persia. Moreover, Germany is also building a railway from Constantinople to Bagdad, the capital of Mesopotamia. If Germany had an oil supply in Mesopotamia on the shores of the Persian Gulf, think of the extra range it would give to their High Seas Fleet. Moreover, they could easily attack our own oil supplies in Persia."

"That is so interesting," Anna observed. "I have never before heard anyone talking about the politics of oil."

"Make no mistake, the politics of oil is the future," Hugo replied. "And who controls the supply of oil will soon have great power. And great wealth. Look at how much money Americans like Rockefeller are making out of oil. The importance of oil means that we must be very concerned what happens in Persia and the Turkish province of Mesopotamia."

"How come you are so interested in oil?" Robert asked.

"Oh that's easy! I got a small legacy and one of my friends in the City advised me to invest in the Anglo Persian Oil Company. It had only recently been formed and had just found a major oil deposit in southern Persia."

"Are you saying," Anna asked, "that because there is oil in Mesopotamia, Turkey will become an important oil producer. And we therefore need to be friends so that we have access to their oil?"

"I think Turkey will indeed enjoy the new oil wealth. Who knows, it could be vast. At present we have good relations with Turkey, and we should make them better still. Turkey will build two new battleships, Dreadnoughts, in England, and we are helping Turkish naval training; we should do more to help them build up their navy. But we are also interested in stopping the Germans getting their hands on any oil in Mesopotamia. We want the whole area from Egypt to Persia to be a British zone of influence."

"Yes, but surely there is no oil in Libya," Anna said.

"No-one has found oil in Libya. You are right," Hugo replied. "But the point is that Sergio's plot may completely undermine our relations with Turkey and do so in a situation where what we want is good relations for the reasons I suggested."

It was a discourse about the real politick of the impact of oil that left Robert amazed, as he was at the direction of the conversation. Reggie had presented Turkey as a valuable British ally, because of the need to contain Russia. And now Hugo was reinforcing all that with his view about the importance of the potential oil wealth in the Middle East. Turkey could be rich and no longer to be ridiculed and despised as the 'Sick man of Europe' of his schooldays. It was a complete reversal of how he had imagined Turkey.

Hugo sat silent, pondering, staring straight ahead at thin air. Then a smile crossed his face. "Right!" He announced. My friends, I've taken this mater as far as I can. I must now involve my Senior. Kindly remain where you are. I will return forthwith." Saying which he swept peremptorily out of the room without further explanation, leaving Robert and Anna somewhat aghast at his apparently contemptuous manner.

7

They were left in limbo, sitting there not knowing what if anything was happening. They looked at each other wondering what to make of Hugo's behaviour. Perhaps, Hugo had simply forgotten they were in the building, his casual attitude seemed to make him capable of such indifference. Then the door was suddenly opened wide, and Hugo entered behind his 'Senior', a man who strode briskly into the room and wasted no time in introducing himself.

"Good morning. I'm Blake. It was good of you to take the trouble to advise us about your case. I have responsibility for the Italy desk here and the matter you have brought to our attention concerns Italy. Cavendish has briefed me about your story." His style was very much to the point, formal, brusque and business-like.

Blake, unlike Hugo, did look the part of a Foreign Office civil servant. He was above medium height with a lean, sparse build. He was perhaps approaching fifty with the outward bearing, outward haughty manner and evident self-perception of a man who regarded himself as a person of some importance. He was dressed accordingly in morning dress, cutting an imposing patrician figure. Behind steel rimmed spectacles his eyes were bluish-grey and much awake. His greying hair was cut on the short side and brushed back. This, and his lean muscular cheeks, tended to exaggerate his long nose and a tight mouth beneath a trimmed moustache. He wore a red carnation in his buttonhole and, unlike Hugo, made no attempt to be 'modern'. He impressed Robert, who was inclined to be suspicious of such men, as a person of some overblown sense of self-importance. Much like the well-established senior clerks he encountered in the City; formal in their behaviour, well set in their ways, blinkered against the change that the contemporary world threatened, unpleasant in their manner when dealing with those they considered their inferiors. Especially people like Robert. In Robert's experience such people had the habit of summing him up with a single, quick, and disparaging dismissive glance. Relegating him to beyond the Pale, not 'one of us'. Robert felt on his guard with Blake.

Blake asked Hugo to introduce Robert and Anna. He shook Robert's hand and greeted Anna. Without more ado, he then took the bundle of letters and translations that Hugo handed him. Robert observed the mannered way in which he methodically arranged and re-arranged the letters on the table. It was all a bit theatrical, and Robert concluded that Blake was a typical civil servant, a careful, cautious man who would counsel prudence, take time to make judicious, discerning decisions. By no means, therefore, a man to whom John Gibson's bold assassination theory would have any appeal.

When he finished, which he signalled by laying down the last letter with a flourish, he looked up. "And so to business," he said in his thoroughly matter of fact manner. He turned to Robert. "And now, young man, your theory if you please."

"Anna's father," Robert said, "has examined the letters. He is sure that the uncle, Cesare Onio, who Sergio mentions often in the letters is entirely fictitious. There is no such person."

Blake raised an eyebrow. "Go on, I am intrigued."

Robert obeyed. "Cesare is invented by Sergio only as a code to tell Maria to read between the lines of the letters." He then explained John's reasoning in detail. He explained John's ideas about the reference to the Carbonari Secret Society, the nature of the binding oath into which Maria had been inveigled by Sergio and the tradition of brutal punishment for anyone who betrayed the Society's code.

Blake sat silent, turning to the relevant letters as Robert mentioned them and otherwise keeping his blue-grey eyes fixed on Robert's face. Absorbing it all. Then he spoke. "A first-class report. And a fascinating story. Miss Gibson your father is an accomplished armchair detective. I agree his analysis that this supposed 'Uncle Onio' is a fiction."

He turned back to Robert. "What you suggest is ingenious, young man. A very interesting, clever theory. I like the inventiveness of it. You put it well. What good research you have done, I congratulate you."

Robert held his breath; it seemed as if they were about to win the prize. But Blake had merely paused.

"However," he continued, "much as I accept this analysis, there are problems. The Carbonari Secret Society was active at the start of the last century, but is there any reason to suppose that they are still active now, in the twentieth century?"

"I suggest," Robert answered, "that Sergio was using the Carbonari's historical importance in the struggle for Italian Unity, and their significance to modern Italians, as a means of impressing on Maria Gibson the absolutely binding nature of her commitment to his scheme. We think that mentioning the Carbonari was a threat. If she did not comply with his demands, she would be punished in the same deadly way the Carbonari punished those who broke its code."

"In other words, she would be murdered if she displeased them. As has in fact now occurred. Very clever." Blake replied, turning over the letters as he considered Robert's case. "But only supposition. There is indeed a powerful nationalist movement in Italy. It is very influential and uses its influence quite openly. It wants its voice to be heard and it is heard. But is there any evidence at all that it operates like an old-style secret society? With secret oaths enforced by torture or death? I think not. But if I'm wrong, do show me the evidence. Do you have any?"

It was a challenge he knew Robert could not answer. If he had such evidence, he would have produced it already. Robert had to admit that he didn't have more than the interpretation of the letters he had just presented. But he wasn't going to give up the ghost and argued that the letters themselves were enough to show a credible scheme to cause trouble in Tripoli and put the blame on Britain. This was a plan that fitted a nationalist agenda, so it was reasonable to connect it with Nationalist politics.

"Well yes, I agree you are entirely reasonable to make the link." Blake said. "If you read them as you suggest, there could be that story."

Robert's hopes soared.

"However, the fundamental question is whether this Sergio saga is more than a good story. It is indeed a thoroughly good story. A good story rather than a real, dangerous conspiracy? That is the question. Why not read these letters of Sergio as merely a fascinating but crazy fairy tale? A fantasy existing only in Sergio's mind. Nothing more."

He threw the gauntlet down and Robert was not sure how to react.

"The trouble with your idea, young man, is that it's fanciful. Fanciful. This supposed international conspiracy scheme of Miss Gibson's cousin, Sergio seems to me to be merely an illusion, a fake, an unreal construction that has no substance."

Robert again took too long to think and feared that things were not going well.

"This plan of Sergio," Blake continued, "is of course devilish interesting. But the devil is surely in the detail. Where is the money? The money without which this so-called conspiracy is merely an illusion. In a bank? Where? Whose account? One must always follow the money. It's like a murder mystery, follow the money. And where is the money in this story of Sergio's? It is nowhere to be found because it doesn't exist. And when he wants to ship arms to North Africa, from where are the weapons coming?"

"It's clear", Robert said, "that he intends to arm the Italian settlers, and to supply rifles to the native tribes to revolt against the Ottomans."

"I agree he plans all this. But have you missed anything?"

Robert felt like a candidate about to fail an oral exam. He had to respond. "When the tribes rebel that will create an incident, enough to give Italy the excuse she wants to start a war of conquest."

"Yes, I agree that is what he intends. But there is a step before we get to that. To implement the plan would require a huge amount of money, money that he says will pass through Mrs Gibson's bank in London. The money is everything. But there is no evidence that Mrs Gibson received any money, there is no evidence of her having a bank account that handled such money. Moreover, Sergio's plan could only work if his financial resources were far more than anything you know. Where is the evidence that he has the money to pay for his grandiose scheme? Or indeed that he had acquired a huge amount of money from somewhere or other? If it was raised in Italy, would it have escaped detection by the Italian government? Or our own government if the money was raised here? Or anywhere in any money market in the world? And why if he commanded such immense resources would he need to make use of Mrs Gibson? He would surely use a professional. I'm afraid, therefore, that your story begins not to hang together. More like a delirious nationalist pipe dream than a real plan."

Robert was taken aback. Blake was taking the line that Hugo had. And they were right, the Sergio conspiracy could only work if it was backed by a great deal of money and organisation, but there was no sign of Sergio having such resources. Or indeed of any sums, let alone huge sums, being received by Maria Gibson. Had he and Anna got only half the story? Less than half the story? Robert was annoyed he had missed the crucial need for compelling evidence. It was a criminal offence for him, as a lawyer to be caught napping like that, such an obvious blunder made him feel ashamed.

All he could manage to say in response was a rather weak, "Yes, I see what you mean."

"Sergio's little plot is not a convincing plan. It lacks credibility." Blake continued, sounding as if he was enjoying himself, trampling triumphally over their silly illusions. "It is not a viable plan."

It was the cruel, cold judgement of Zeus, the ultimate and authoritative pronouncement, the hatchet job with which Blake effectively destroyed the heart of the claimed Sergio conspiracy. The debate was surely over. Blake's pronouncement produced a shocked and embarrassed silence. For what more could indeed be said.

It was Anna who broke the silence, her face resolute and her voice steady and controlled, although Robert guessed that underneath she was buzzing with suppressed feeling; the prospect of action over her mother's death slipping away.

"Would Italy just sit on the side lines?" She asked. "Be a mere spectator if there was an armed Italian rising in Tripoli?

If the Italian settlers were fighting for their lives in the streets of Tripoli? Dying by the score under a hail of Turkish bullets for their dream of Italy. Their blood soaking the green, white, and red flag of Italy, that we Italians know as the Tricolore. The banner that represents all that our glorious Italy stands for! You really think so?"

It was a powerful, emotive speech that gripped the room. Anna delivered it well, in a firm voice that was quiet but nevertheless commanded her audience. It reminded Robert of their playacting years ago, and he suspected she had indulged in amateur dramatics at college.

My God she's good! She'll be wasted as a schoolteacher. If women are ever allowed to sit in Parliament, she'd be great there!

"Ah! If that were so, Rome might then intervene." Blake responded carefully, sitting back comfortably in his chair. "But believe me Italy has devoted years of successful diplomacy in persuading the Great Powers, including Britain, to support the principle of their claim to Libya. They have done well. They have secured the support of all the Powers. Work that has been so successful is not to be thrown away on a hare-brained scheme like this. What they have in the bag is that they know that, in the right circumstances and by international agreement, all the Powers would support Italy in her North African aims. But the circumstances must be right and international agreement in place. Rome knows very well that anything like Sergio's plan would be not only a dangerous game but a foolish one."

"But if Italy is not supporting Sergio's plan," Robert observed, "and was never likely to do so, what is the point of it?"

"Indeed, there you have it!" Blake replied decisively. "You have it in a nutshell! Well done. What is the point of it? There would surely be none. This Sergio may be merely a nationalist romantic. His plan no more than a dream without substance. Rome would oppose his plan. If Sergio started a rising the Turks would simply supress it."

There was again silence, lasting only a few moments, but it felt like an hour. Blake just sat there looking blank. Hugo betrayed no sign of emotion and kept a steady gaze on Anna, but not making a move to close the meeting, just sitting at the table as if he expected something. Robert sensed he was waiting for something, but what?

"Are you saying then..." Anna said in a voice that took some effort to keep steady, and Robert realised she was struggling to control her deep disappointment at the way the meeting had worked out. "Are you saying that we should ignore the whole thing about Sergio? Ignore everything we know, all these letters?"

Blake looked at her with kind eyes. "On what we know we can take no action. But no, we should not ignore the whole thing. The letters exist and they should not be ignored. We can do nothing only because we do not know enough to take Sergio's scheme seriously."

The atmosphere in the room was tense, waiting for something, but what? What could avoid the meeting simply dissolving, frustrating any further investigation of the Sergio letters.

Hugo then leant confidentially across the table towards Anna. "You see, although the story is fascinating, as it stands it is unconvincing. As you have been told, the government can do nothing because we do not know enough to take Sergio seriously. So, what the Foreign Office needs is some new event. Some new occurrence, some new information, new evidence, some new fact that lights up our understanding of the situation and makes Sergio's plan look real!"

He looked at Blake, who seemed surprised at Hugo's intervention but said nothing. Hugo forced him to speak.

"Do you not agree?"

Blake nodded. "I agree with what you say. If that was indeed the case …" The pause that followed was strained to bursting point with expectation.

Hugo filled the pause. "If that was the case …"

"If …" Robert jumped in, picking up Hugo's unfinished words. "If the case was that there was new convincing evidence, could it lead you to accept that the Sergio plot is real?"

Hugo beamed and slapped the table with his right hand. "If that was the case, I'm sure it could be decisive!"

He looked at Blake for support as he spoke. "Absolutely. The letters would then be of real interest to the Government."

Hugo looked at Blake again, forcing him to commit. "Do you agree?"

Blake nodded. "I do."

Robert realised that the game that had only a moment ago appeared lost had miraculously been restored to life by Hugo's tactical intervention. The man was a greater mystery than he had thought. He had no doubt now that Hugo himself accepted there was a real Sergio conspiracy, and that he had gone out of his way to finesse Blake's approval for further investigation, albeit by Robert and Anna rather than the government. Robert wondered how to play the situation, to push for something more explicit, some clarity about what exactly what might be done to gain the 'interest' of the Foreign Office. Hugo turned suddenly to Robert, who wondered what he was up to.

"Have you thought of joining our Royal Navy Reserve?" Hugo asked. An extraordinary question out of the blue. "I understand you are a sailor, and the Navy needs competent, intelligent officers if there is a war. We could do with people like you."

Where had that come from? Joining the Navy Reserve had been far from his mind, but it was diplomatic to show at least polite interest.

"The Navy Reserve? Sounds interesting. Perhaps I should find out more."

"Please do."

Anna had used the diversion to think and turned to Blake. "May I ask if clearly proving the money exists might be the key to accepting Sergio has a real plan?"

Blake smiled. "Yes, it could be. We don't know enough about the money. Was money sent, how much, when and by whom? When and how was it received? In what Bank? How and to whom did she dispose of it? Many crucial questions!"

"If..." Robert said slowly, regaining his confidence and determined to get something concrete out of the meeting, "If we were to find cogent answers to those questions. If we establish the material facts about the money, and for what it was used, for instance that it was actually used to buy a vessel?" He was half suspecting that Hugo had asked him about the Navy Reserve to give them time to save the situation and put a proposal to him.

"If there were to be such new information, such new facts?" Hugo answered. "Yes indeed! That would be a new situation." He looked at Blake for confirmation.

Blake nodded. "It would. However, you must understand that it would be politically unwise, indeed in practice impossible, for the government to become involved. We must stand well away from it in all respects."

"But," Robert continued, sensing that Blake was giving him the opportunity to make his case, "if the Gibson family wants to discover the truth about Mrs Gibson's murder. If they investigate privately and find the key facts ..."

Blake looked at him and shrugged. "Then the Foreign Office can resume this conversation. And the matter may well move forward. The door will remain open. Perhaps, that is where we should leave it for the moment."

Then, turning to Anna, Blake said "And now I regret that I have to leave you. A pleasure to meet you Miss Gibson, Mr Strange."

With that he left the room.

8

Outside the Foreign Office, in King Charles Street, Gerald was waiting impatiently to collect Anna for lunch. He lost no time in condemning their visit as a total waste of time.

"Anna, these civil servants are useless idiots! They do nothing. Just blather. No wonder the country is in such a mess."

And then he turned aggressively to Robert. "And I'm sure you did a lousy job! A hopeless failure. If you worked for me, I'd sack you on the spot. I'll tell you what Anna, to hell with this pathetic messing about. Since it seems to matter to you, I'll do whatever the Foreign Office wants myself, and do it properly."

Robert would have squared up to him if Anna had not quickly intervened, physically separating them.

Gerald turned his back on Robert. "Just leave it to me Anna. Forget your pitiful friend."

Robert ignored him and spoke quietly to Anna. "What Blake agreed at the end is crucial. With more hard information about the money, the FO will have to think again."

Gerald had heard and snarled at Robert. "Strange! This is Anna's business not yours. You're out of it, Strange. Finished."

Anna tried to calm things. "Let's not argue. Robert's right, the message is plain. Somehow I must find the key facts."

Anna departed in a taxi with Gerald, saying he had invited her for lunch at his father's club in Pall Mall. Robert was rudely and publicly not included in the invitation – but would not have accepted had it been offered as he found Gerald's manner insufferable. Anna's friendship with Gerald continued to puzzle him.

What can she see in him? But she does seem to rather like being taken to these swanky lunches. How on earth does that fit with all that radical Suffragette stuff?

And now of course there was the new point; Gerald had inserted himself into the inquiry. Gerald had promised to carry out the critical investigation the FO wanted. Could he be relied on to do it? Robert doubted it, the chap was a slacker with a rich father and a sinecure in his father's Bank. But maybe if Anna was so keen on accepting Gerald's help, it meant that she wanted him, Robert, out of the Sergio game, side lined, if not cast out for good. But if so, he felt he had in fact faithfully fulfilled his promise to Anna to help the Gibson family. He continued his journey home somewhat bruised, but sure that his part in the Sergio affair was to all intents and purposes over.

*

Therefore, Anna's telephone call some four days later, was unforeseen. "Robert, I've been thinking how to deal with Blake's comments. I suggest we visit Rosina, my mother's cousin. She was the go-between for the letters, Sergio sent the letters to Rosina, and she kept them for my mother to read. It was Rosina who sent the letters to my father."

"I see." He assumed that she was thinking of taking Gerald on the visit.

"I'd be so pleased if you could come. It could be important. I feel I must try everything." Her voice was pleading and he didn't like to refuse.

The visit was, indeed, informative. Rosina told them she had sent the Sergio letters to Anna's father only because she had been visited by what she described as a "strange foreign man, a bit of a brute". He had frightened her and tried to badger her to hand over the whole bundle of Sergio's letters. He had told her some unlikely story about getting a telegram from Sergio, which she had not believed, and had sent him packing with a flea in his ear. However, she had also told him that he was wasting his time because she did not intend to keep the letters. Robert feared that the man would work out that she would send the letters to the Gibson's house. He would probably plan to go to the Gibson's house and steal the letters there. Not wanting to alarm Anna, Robert decided to keep his fears to himself, but decided also to talk to Anna's father about the security at their house.

His concern was justified. When he telephoned John Gibson the following morning, John told him that during the previous evening there had been an attempt to break into his house. A neighbour reported a suspicious looking man in the Gibson's front garden, standing beside the new gate to the back garden, as if contemplating whether to climb it. The man was medium height, well built, wearing a dark overcoat, having dark hair and a thick black moustache. The description fitted that given by Rosina. The neighbour was naturally alarmed and called out loudly, demanding to know what the man was doing. The man had apparently been startled at this and had quickly scarpered.

Robert was concerned. The same man who went to Rosina had evidently lost no time in then going to the Gibson house. Robert asked John how the house was secured, but as it sounded good, he advised John to be very careful to keep all the doors and windows firmly closed and not to open the front door to anyone he did not recognize. Robert also promised that later he would walk round and have a look himself to see if he could suggest anything else.

So, after finishing work at the office he walked round to the Gibson's house, about twenty minutes at a reasonable pace. It was by then towards the end of daylight and he called in at his parent's house on the way to pick up a torch and his 'special' walking stick, just in case. The 'special' walking stick was in fact a piece of thick, polished, oriental hardwood rather more than four feet long. It was fitted with a clever, removable handle extension that made it into an apparently ordinary walking stick. It had been given to him by his old self-defence instructor in the dockland settlement, part of self-defence training in 'fighting with sticks', a style derived from the Philippines that the chap had picked up in seedy ports out East. It had on various occasions for Robert in the East End, proved to be a useful skill.

It was fortunate he had prepared himself, because when he reached the path up to the Gibson's front door, he saw a man in a dark overcoat peering in through the letter box. The man heard the approaching tread of Robert's feet on the path behind him and turned round. Robert switched on his torch and shone it directly into the man's face.

"What do you want here? Who are you?" Robert shouted. The man fitted the description given to John Gibson, medium height, short dark hair, a dark moustache, wearing a dark overcoat a size too big for him and brown boots. He was carrying a small leather bag.

"Nothing. Just looking," the man replied, blinking with the powerful torchlight shining straight into his face.

"Looking? What for? Who are you!" Robert demanded, slipping the removable handle off his stick, and getting a good grip on the business part. Then as an afterthought he added in his schoolboy French, "pourquoi cherchez-vous à cette fenêtre?"

No answer, and the man shielded his face from the torch. So, Robert tried his little German instead. "Wo sind sie? Was wöllen sie den hier? Wo bist du?" Robert was sure from the man's facial expression that he had understood.

"Sorry. Pardon. Nothing. I go. No worry!" the man said quietly in broken English, and something like an east London accent.

It was a tricky moment. Robert had to act fast if he was to act at all. Should he detain the man while he called for the Police? He could, but arrest him for what? The man hadn't in fact yet done anything criminal. But if he was indeed up to something, detaining him would enable the police to question him and they might discover something useful.

On the other hand, the man could be dangerous. His overcoat was spacious and could easily conceal a gun, quite likely if he was part of the gang that had murdered Maria. If so, he was likely to use it.

But Robert had his special stick and did a quick calculation. It would take the man a moment to remove a gun from inside his coat, which was well buttoned up. And Robert was close enough to clobber him with his stick before the man could reach a weapon. It was, Robert decided, worth the risk. He would detain the man and disable him with his stick if he reached for a weapon.

"Stay exactly where you are!" Robert ordered loudly. "Still zu stehen! Halt!" He shouted in German, and repeated "Halt!"

The man understood "Halt!" and obeyed. He remained rooted to the spot. Robert ordered him to kneel but became aware of movement behind him.

"Of course, an accomplice!" And one getting ready to pounce on him from behind.

Robert pirouetted to his right, which neatly turned him to face the fellow approaching from behind. He bent at the knees, getting ready. He moved his stick through the air rapidly in a continuous figure of eight, a movement that bewitched and confused the attacker. Then he suddenly stepped forwards, placing his right foot slightly sideways to the man. At the same time, he pulled the stick back over his right shoulder, his left hand and left palm facing forwards for defence.

He had already marked a good target area for the strike, the man's left collarbone. He smashed the stick down on it in a perfect slashing strike that took the man by surprise. He yelled and clutched his shoulder in agony before receiving a swift second hard whack on the side of his head. He sank to his knees with the shock and pain. It had been a textbook exercise: Robert had been taught well by a master.

For a moment the second assailant would be out of the picture and Robert quickly turned his attention to the first man, who had drawn a wicked looking knife.

Robert was glad it was a knife and not a gun. Stick fighting had its limitations against bullets. But, observing carefully how the fellow handled his weapon, Robert quickly concluded he was no expert with the knife. He kept the man's attention focused on him by wielding his stick rapidly through the air in a continuous X pattern. He then took an angled stance and waited for the man to close. When the man moved, the stick once again went back over Robert's right shoulder.

He intended to deceive. He appeared to be about to bring the stick down on the side of the man's head. But the real target was the man's right wrist, holding the dangerous knife.

Robert hit the man's wrist hard, enough to make him yelp in pain and drop the knife.

Things might have gone well after that; Robert could have detained at least one of the men for the Police to question. But, unfortunately, at that moment John Gibson, decided to open the front door. The men promptly took the chance to bolt for the road. Robert would have gone in pursuit, but John yelled out.

"Leave it Robert! Leave it! They may have a gun!"

He was right and Robert let them run for it. They had attacked twice in one day; they must be determined. Robert was sure that it was the same man as the neighbour had earlier surprised.

It was clear to Robert that the culprits were unlikely to abandon their search for the Sergio letters. Given the history they would be prepared to use extreme violence to get what they wanted. There was both Anna and James to consider, they were still out but would be home at any moment. Robert therefore proposed that the Gibson family should leave the house empty that night and let their opponents break in and do their worst. If they were desperate to search the house, they would be back that evening. They would of course discover that the letters were not there, but it would be dangerous for the family to be in the house and possibly tortured for information about the bundle of letters. Robert's parents were still away, and his house was large enough for all of them to stay, which they should do for at least a couple of nights. If that was not enough, they should think of Police protection – though what good that might be against armed attackers Robert was not sure.

John was reluctant to accept the invitation but saw the sense of it and was eventually persuaded to agree. Anna and her brother, who came home together shortly after, also accepted that the plan was sensible. They all packed overnight bags, locked the house up and Robert collected them in a taxi. Robert was sure he had done the right thing but did wonder what his mother might say later. Mary, his mother's cook-general, fixed up two bedrooms for John and Anna, and Robert gave up his room to James and would himself sleep on the sofa in the sitting room. After dinner they talked for a while and then as everyone was feeling exhausted, they decided to call it an early night. But just before going upstairs John remarked that he should tell Gerald about the house.

"The house?" Robert said, nonplussed. What had it to do with Gerald?

"It's about the mortgage. I should tell him if anything happens to the house."

Robert knew that Gerald's father was a banker, that he had provided the mortgage for John to buy the house and that the loan had been extended. But the total loan must be large for John to feel like that.

"You are insured? Well in that case there is nothing to tell him yet." He wondered if Gerald's family had a more serious financial hold over John Gibson than he had previously believed. Once again, he wondered if that could be the reason why Anna was nice to Gerald. It still seemed improbable.

Anna's friendship with Gerald had always struck him as unlikely. If Anna was critical of Robert's social attitudes, how could she possibly view Gerald with any favour? He must surely be a backward reactionary in her eyes. However, since the murder John had been unwell and on sick leave from the Bank. His income would have been affected, and perhaps therefore he did have serious money problems and was in deep hock to the Morris family Bank.

*

One night away from home for the Gibson family was indeed enough; the expected break-in at their house took place that night. John and Robert went to the house the next day. The gate to the garden had been forced and someone had broken the glass in the French window in the sitting room. Gazing at the damage inside John looked grim. But nothing seemed to have been stolen, although there was some silver, candlesticks and other portable objects on display. A burglar would surely have taken at least the silver. Robert thought that this confirmed that the main target had been the letters. Indeed, Maria's small bureau in the Hall, John's own desk in the spare bedroom and three bookcases downstairs had been thoroughly ransacked, thrown to the ground and their contents rubbished. They had explored diligently everywhere they might find the papers for which they searched. All the drawers in Maria's bureau had been pulled out and thrown around, papers from it strewn all about. In John's desk all the drawers were left in a tangled mess on the floor, every pigeon-hole emptied, papers and files vandalised. In the bookcases all the books had been systematically ripped from the shelves and left in messy piles on the floor.

Robert regarded the scattered wreckage. "Thank God you weren't here last night! Think what might have happened!"

He knew from the past that Anna was more than capable of putting up a fight and would probably have done so, with perhaps dreadful results.

"They must have been searching for the letters," John said.

Letters that Anna had in fact left with Blake at the Foreign Office. Moreover, only a few people knew the letters existed. Apart from them, Rosina, Reggie Rands, Hugo, and Blake the only other person who knew about the letters was Sergio himself. And therefore, his fellow conspirators. But why had anyone wanted to recover the letters? To get hold of them to destroy them as evidence of the plan? Surely a bit late if the letters had been read. Might it be the opposite? Not to destroy them but to publish them, evidence of British betrayal of Turkey?

John wanted to call the local police to investigate the break-in. Robert had doubts about that, thinking that the break-in must be tied up with the whole Sergio conspiracy. Robert thought it better that the Foreign Office should be consulted. But the matter was taken out of his hands because the local police suddenly arrived at the house: alerted by neighbours realising there had been a break-in. Inspector Thorpe, from the Hendon Police Station, who had investigated Maria Gibson's murder, examined the state of the house, and spoke to John Gibson. John told him that he thought the criminals were searching for a bundle of letters. Robert then outlined the gist of the Sergio affair.

The inspector lost no time in coming to a decision. "I'm going to involve the Special Branch of the Metropolitan Police. They're the people for a job like this. I always thought that there was something more about the murder of Maria Gibson."

A man came that afternoon and introduced himself to John Gibson as Inspector Brown of the Metropolitan Police Special Branch. He came with two other officers who examined the house carefully, taking fingerprints. They were at once clear that the break-in had been a professional job and done to search for particular things, probably documents. They were very pleased with the prints they took from the French window, which had been broken. They left saying that they would be in touch.

A few days later Inspector Brown contacted Robert to say that the Special Branch had a result. The prints they took matched their records of a petty criminal, known as 'Adolf', who was implicated in other break-ins that involved the loss of material of interest to Germany. Moreover, the Special Branch had traced Adolf to a restaurant in Charlotte Street, Soho. This was in fact 'Schwarz', a well-established and respectable German restaurant. The Branch had chosen to be discreet and had not followed up this lead because movements at the restaurant were under surveillance for other reasons. But the Branch would keep a watch on the location and on 'Adolf' in particular, the Branch being particularly concerned with the suspicious activities of foreign and especially German agents in London.

It was all news that clarified the break-in. More than that it seemed to confirm Robert's growing suspicion that Berlin was behind the Sergio conspiracy. But it still left a lot of unanswered questions about Maria's murder. He was also left wondering what the next move might be.

His concerns were met by an unexpected telephone call from Hugo Cavendish, a message for Robert to contact him on important but unstated business if he was to be in town. As Robert had to be in the City on the firm's business the next day, he arranged to meet Hugo in 'The Albert', a Pub near the Foreign Office on Victoria Street. Hugo came to the point immediately. The 'Branch' as he called it, had reported to him about the break-in at the Gibson house.

Moreover, Hugo had other important news. The Special Branch had been unexpectedly approached by some respectable members of the Italian community in London, people who were now prepared to talk about what they knew of the Sergio plan. The difficulty up to then had been that the community had closed its ranks and declined to talk to the Police. The Branch had learnt that some members of the community knew of Sergio's initial plan to buy a fishing boat to take supplies to settlers in Tripoli. But they later became concerned when it became known in the community that Sergio's plan had been taken over by new people who were not Italians. New people probably connected with a government hostile to Britain, who planned to use Sergio's arrangements for their own ends. The Italian community had no wish for Italians settled in England to be contaminated by association with what they openly called 'a German scheme' designed to cause damage to Britain. The community wished to distance itself from all this malicious 'tomfoolery', as Hugo described it, and would therefore assist the Branch. Moreover, they talked about Maria's killing, angry that she had been murdered in cold blood and were alarmed not only at the revival of the violent activities of the old secret society called the Carbonari, but that it had been manipulated by a foreign power for its own interests.

Shortly after this meeting John Gibson received another visit by the Branch. The Inspector said they had reconsidered Maria's murder and now believed that it had been committed by agents acting for, or at least in the name of, the Carbonari, the Italian Secret Society. The actual culprits were probably professionals hired for the job. Whoever had set up the job was apparently claiming that Maria had to be killed because she was a traitor to the Society. The real reason being that she probably had become reluctant to co-operate any further in Sergio's Scheme or at least had started to ask questions. As for the break-ins at the Gibson's house, the Inspector put these down to a search for documents and was sure it had been the work of German agents looking for documents, probably the letters from Sergio to Maria Gibson. He said that there was no doubt that her murder was a political assassination, and that there was a German hand in it.

9

Robert was pleased that so much light had now been shed on Maria's murder. It confirmed the view he had already formed that his part in helping Anna to deal with the Sergio affair was over. He was not therefore expecting the further telephone call from Anna.

"Robert, the thing is we need to find more information to ask for another meeting at the Foreign Office."

"Oh?" But after his ridiculous, rash promise that was surely entirely Gerald's business now.

"Yes, I have an idea, Robbie. I think I can work out when and where the money was taken out from my mother's account." He noticed she was using 'Robbie' again, like the old days.

"You can?"

"You said the money was probably taken out of the bank as a cheque, or bankers draft. What I'll do is work through my mother's diary, which is written in a kind of shorthand Italian, which I can normally just about decipher. I don't think the police looked at it closely enough. I know her writing, I may find some clue."

"Surely the police examined the diary?"

"They did, but I think they probably missed the point. My mother used her own Italian abbreviations."

"Well, that seems a good idea, Anna." It did not involve him doing anything and he was sure that if her investigation did lead to anything, she would want to get Gerald to help her.

She did indeed look at her mother's diary and after going laboriously through page after page found an obscure entry in a shorthand Italian. The Police had not picked up its significance. She immediately telephoned Robert.

"I've got news! I went through the diary and found things. There's an entry for September 10th 1908. My mother wrote: *'M bca: racc: cambiale.'* What I spotted was the word *'cambiale'*, which is Italian and means draft, Bill of exchange etc. That is the key! I think, therefore, that *'bca'* means *'banca'*, Bank. I think *'racc'* could be short for *'raccogliere'* which means collect. So, what she has written means 'Bank; collect the bill of exchange'. This could mean the banker's draft she was to collect from the Bank to hand over to someone to pay for the boat Sergio wanted to buy."

"Excellent detective work Anna! If you nail that, you can go further and show that a vessel was actually bought by the conspirators."

"You know about these things Robbie. What do you think could I do with the information I've got?"

"What you've found is that September 10th was the approximate date when the banker's draft was drawn."

"Yes?"

"Well, that gives a date from which to search for a transaction to purchase a vessel."

"Yes, I see that."

"But vessels come in all sorts of sizes and value and to tie down the search you need to know the amount of the banker's draft."

"Is that possible?"

"Yes, but you need to know which Bank your mother used. You said that the diary mentioned *'M bca'*, so 'M' could be the name of the bank."

"Yes?"

"There aren't many Banks beginning with the letter M. My guess would be Martins Bank. It used to be just a small private bank but grew at the end of the last century. Their base is in Lombard Street in the City. It's still quite discreet. Could be ideal for a conspiracy like Sergio's."

"And how do we find out?"

She had used 'we' again. "It's not straightforward if you want the Bank to give you information about a client's account. Normally you would need a Court order."

"That could take ages."

"Yes. And might be refused. The information is confidential to the client. The only other idea I have is to ask Hugo. He seems to have contacts in unlikely places." Robert meant criminal contacts, the underworld. He was resolved to refuse her next request, which might mean ending his relationship with the Sergio saga. But that was just fine for him now that Gerald was mixed up in it.

The expected request came. "In fact, could you do that Robbie, ask Hugo? He seems to like you."

Robert did not want to ask Hugo for a favour; he did not trust the man and suspected that Hugo would want something back in return. "I don't know why you think he likes me. In fact, it would come better from you, I'm sure he likes you."

She must have picked up the firmness of his tone because she accepted his refusal. She did, in fact, exactly as he suggested. Hugo was apparently surprised at the request but receptive and put the desired inquiry underway. He provided an impressive letter of authority, signed by a senior officer in the Metropolitan police, saying that Anna Gibson was investigating financial circumstances relevant to her mother's murder. A further letter asked the Bank to assist her in her inquiries. A telephone call obtained a formal appointment for her with the branch manager and when she attended, she was accompanied by not one but two officers from Special Branch.

For the rest it was up to her to use her charm. It worked; Martin's Bank in Lombard Street confirmed that a banker's draft for £22,000.00 had been drawn by Maria Gibson on 10th September 1908. The draft had been presented in Liverpool five days later on 15th September and taken in cash. What had happened to the cash was not known. The amount of the banker's draft was of course a staggeringly large amount of money. If true it suggested strongly that Sergio's plan was being financed by someone, or some country, for whom money was no obstacle. Moreover, Hugo's men in the Special Branch had accessed and examined Maria's account in the Bank, it showed there had been deposits amounting in total to some £24,000.00. A balance of £2,000.00 therefore remained in the account. Had, Robert wondered, Maria baulked at further co-operation in the Sergio Plan? Having been part of the Banker's draft transaction, then drawn the line at any further shenanigans? If she had refused to co-operate further, was that why and when they decided to kill her? However, the important thing was that now the information existed with which to track down the purchase of a ship.

Anna was delighted with her success and told Robert so on the phone. "It is marvellous Robbie! And it gives me another idea. My mother must have passed the banker's draft to someone, someone who then travelled to Liverpool and cashed it. We know the date she got the draft and if I look in her diary, I may be able to see where she went in the next two or three days."

"That sounds a good idea, Anna."

"I'll do it now; the diary is here." She searched, quickly found a note for 11th September 1908, '*Tea pom. Ho. Adel. 3.30.*' She phoned Robert to pass on the news.

"I think that this looks like an engagement to have Tea with someone. '*Pom*' may be pomeridiano meaning afternoon. So, a meeting over afternoon tea?"

"Brilliant detective work Anna!"

"But a meeting where? What is *Ho. Adel*?"

"That could be the name of a hotel!" Robert suggested. "That's the sort of place people meet for a transaction like this. *Adel* could be the first letters of the Hotel. Have you a telephone directory?"

Anna looked at the directory and worked out it was the Adelphi Hotel close to Charing Cross Station. It fitted.

"That's wonderful! I'll find out!" she told him.

He noticed he was not being asked to accompany her to the Adelphi Hotel and assumed she would ask Gerald. She did and the Hotel confirmed that her mother had made a tea reservation for 11th September. Intending to claim credit for the whole discovery, Gerald hired a private detective who found the waitress who had served Maria that day. She recalled it because the gentleman who had met Maria in the Hotel was 'very foreign', 'not the type she would have expected such a nice lady to know.' The waitress described the man as having a thoroughly sullen look, being rather course, not good looking and with a scar on his left cheek. Moreover, she thought there had been an argument and the man had stayed for tea only about ten minutes.

Anna telephoned Robert, pleased that the quest was moving forward. The banker's draft drawn by Maria Gibson on September 10th was handed over the very next day to this 'foreign' type. It was therefore a good guess, given the speed of that transaction, that if the money was used to buy a ship, the purchase would be soon after 11th September. Robert was glad for Anna's sake that the story was unfolding so nicely and assumed that she would now ask Gerald to complete the last pieces of the jigsaw. At the same time he realised the full horror behind the new information: the conspirators had murdered Maria only days after she handed over the Banker's draft.

*

Anna's note some days later, an urgent invitation to meet her in Fuller's Café in Golders Green Road to "discuss the FO question", was not expected. Robert had felt sure that by this time Gerald would have carried out his brash promise to lay bare the 'facts' that the Foreign Office needed to accept that the Sergio investigation merited their attention.

"Robbie, I'm sorry to drag you out of the office."

"I needed the break." Having concluded that his part in the Sergio affair was now closed, he was curious why she wanted this meeting.

"Blake told us that the Foreign Office wanted to find new facts."

"He did." And of course, they both knew that Gerald had promised to do all the finding of facts.

"Gerald says that knowing my mother handed over a bank draft is not enough. I must prove to the FO that it was used to buy a ship."

"Indeed." Gerald was merely stating the obvious. But why? What was he up to?

"He says I need to prove a ship was bought."

"Indeed." Where was this repetition leading? Why was Gerald just mucking about? He should be just getting on with it.

"Well, we know the bank draft was cashed in Liverpool on 15th September last year."

"Yes."

"So, Robbie, if it was used to buy a ship that could well have been done in Liverpool about that date."

"Yes. But they may have paid the cash into another Bank account and drawn on that later for the purchase. Or merely sat on the cash for a while. In other words, there could well be a time gap before a purchase."

"Alright. But given the amount sent to my mother, allowing for the purchase of guns and so on, the cost of the ship was probably between £20,000.00 to £22,000.00."

"Indeed." He waited to hear how Gerald had used all this information to identify the ship that had been purchased.

"Robbie, how do you suggest we might do this?"

Not the reply he expected. Where was Gerald's big promise to do exactly that? He saw it unmistakeably. Gerald was all words and no action; he had in fact done nothing and was now playing pass the parcel.

"What does Gerald suggest?" Two could play that game and so he threw the parcel back. Gerald worked in the City, so it was surely simple for him to come up with the answer.

"Gerald said that as you used to work in shipping, you would know at once what to do."

Gerald was of course right. Robert did know exactly what to do and how to do it. But why, having made that rash promise, why was Gerald not doing it himself?

"Did Gerald not offer to do this?" The bombastic, boasting promise was still fresh in his mind and rankled.

"He did. But he says he's busy."

Robert let the remark hang in the air; letting her reflect on how Gerald had let her down.

"Oh! I see. Busy! Gerald's busy." He was tempted to point out that Gerald had a job that required him to do very little. But he thought better of it, let Gerald's inadequacy speak for itself. "Oh, how … terribly unfortunate." He played with the deliberate pause to make the point.

"Yes, busy." She entirely missed the irony in his reply. Speaking in a matter-of-fact way, as if it was nothing, but clearly accepting Gerald's weak excuse at face value and not thinking that, perhaps, Robert might also be busy. As indeed he was. He was not pleased with either of them, especially Anna who was apparently refusing to see that Gerald was simply lazy.

Robert had been an articled clerk in a firm of Solicitors in the City specialising in the shipping business; he therefore knew the right person to approach was a shipbroker, someone whose business was the sale and purchase of vessels. His old firm had dealt with several shipbrokers, and Robert had been friendly with the clerks in one shipbroker's office. Anna was right, to discover the actual ship that the conspiracy had purchased would be a huge leap forward. Despite his reluctance to do Gerald's leg work for him, and his annoyance at the way Gerald had first tried to humiliate him by his foolish promise and had then shoved the task back to him, he could not deprive Anna of such a coup. It would not be fair. He therefore told her what he knew about shipbrokers.

"But look Anna. We must be careful not to alert the purchaser. The conspirators mustn't know that someone is interested in tracing their purchase."

"It needs a good plan?"

"Yes, and it is vital to be discreet. It needs a shipbroker who will respect your confidence."

"That sounds sensible. Robert, can you do it? You are the best person to do it."

He realised he had allowed himself to be led by the nose to the water and now had no honourable choice but drink it: he had promised to help her and could hardly refuse. He therefore agreed, wondering where it would lead him.

He approached an old friend, a clerk who worked for Henry Jones, shipbroker, provided all the relevant information and commissioned the firm to make the necessary search.

It did not take Henry Jones long to identify the transaction and he telephoned Robert within the week to report that he had found the probable deal, a purchase for £21,750 on 27th November 1908 in Liverpool. He sent Robert a report about the ship the conspirators had bought.

Steam Yacht Hermes.

The Steam Yacht *Hermes* was built on Clydeside in 1901. She has a steel hull and teak decking in good order. Mahogany main deck cabin structures, mahogany railing along the main deck, all in good order. Significant fire damage in galley and superficial damage to interior of the connected aft deck cabin. Requires refurbishing of all accommodation areas. Mahogany upper deck wheelhouse and connected sailing master's cabin. Ditto upper deck owner's cabin. She is 350 gross tonnage, 148 ft length, 23 ft beam. Needs at least an extensive engine overhaul. The engine is oil burning, not a modern steam turbine but an old, compressed reciprocating steam engine of about 250 hp, in serious need of major refit. However, if done should be capable of good reliable service. The engine refit, repair of fire damage and refurbishing probably explains the reasonable selling price. The vessel needs an extensive general refurbishment for the luxury trade for which she had been designed. She is probably able to cruise reliably at 10 - 12 knots. Max speed greater but needs testing. Owner's cabin and up to 8 passengers in sleeping cabins and 6 crew members. *Hermes* is well built and seaworthy and could be easily handled seamanship wise by a small crew, say master, engineer, two deck hands. Additional crew needed for long voyage, especially sailing master, engineer's assistant and third deck hand. Also running the galley, service to guests, accommodation, etc. would require appropriate staff. The word in the Port is that *Hermes* will be moved to a shipyard in Birkenhead for refit and other work.

There it was, after all their work, the discovery of a real steamship called '*Hermes*', a mythical figure whose winged sandals made him the messenger of the Gods. What mattered was that proof of the purchase brought the Sergio conspiracy dramatically to life. The Foreign Office had wanted 'facts', and here was an unmistakable fact, a real ship.

He telephoned the news to Anna. "Now you can tell the FO that Sergio's conspiracy is no illusion, there is an actual ship. This is surely the key fact they wanted to hear."

But some details in the report had interested him, what 'other work' were they intending to carry out and why? It could be important to know. The broker suggested that Robert should go to the shipyard where the refit would be carried out and see for himself. He passed the proposal to Anna.

"Robbie, could you do that for us?" she asked.

Regretting he had made the suggestion he felt he had to do as she asked. He contacted Henry Jones again, who agreed to commission Robert to visit the shipyard to discuss a contract for some marine work for one of his clients. It should be a good cover that enabled him to do a bit of snooping.

Arriving in Lime Street Liverpool, he booked into the Adelphi Hotel and unpacked his bag. Early the following day he took the ferry across the Mersey to Birkenhead and walked the side streets towards Taylor and Blanchard the shipyard where *Hermes* had recently been taken for refit. *Hermes* was indeed berthed there, and engineers were working on her engine. Stopping to admire the graceful lines of the vessel, Robert spoke to the foreman, who expected the engine overhaul would start soon and would take several weeks to complete.

"Will that improve her performance?" Robert inquired.

"Oh, she's not a modern engine, but she should be a good runner."

"What kind of cruising speed?"

"We'll do a sea trial, but I'd expect an easy 10 knots. Depends on the sea conditions and how much oil you want to burn."

"And something in reserve?" Robert asked, pushing his luck a bit.

"Oh yes, something in reserve. She was built to be able to do a pretty turn if needed."

"And on a cruise to Italy, for instance, what sort of crew would be needed to look after the engine?"

"She needs an engineer who understands the engine and can do any routine maintenance, and he would need a lad as an assistant for any long voyage like Italy."

Robert could see work in progress on the mahogany deck cabins, that were built fore and aft on the main deck. He was told that the interior of the large aft cabin, which had been the dining saloon, was to be refurbished because of the fire damage. Also, the aft portion of the upper deck, that was also a sun deck, was to be strengthened to support some heavy object. The two davits on the upper deck, used to lower the ship's boats, were also being 'improved' to increase the weight they were able to lift. The owner must, therefore, be planning to deal with some heavy cargo on their trip to the Mediterranean. Robert also picked up that metal shutters were to be fitted to the windows of the forward cabin on the main deck. Surprising as there were already blinds to screen the interior from the sun.

Robert noticed that another visitor had come to the Yard and was inspecting the work being done on *Hermes*. Robert inquired and was told the man was a marine engineer representing the new owners. Nothing unusual in that; the refit must be costing a lot of money. However, the man was then joined by a second visitor, who from his clothes seemed to be a man of business, a lawyer perhaps. He spoke to the first visitor and suggested adjourning for a private talk in one of the Yard's offices. As Robert heard them discussing security arrangements for a 'valuable cargo' his ears pricked up. He needed to find out more. What valuable cargo required special security arrangements? Gold, Guns?

The office to where the two men were directed for their discussion was in a single-story wooden building sub-divided into several rooms. Robert was using a desk in the accounts section in one of those rooms, separated from the room where the two men would be sitting only by a thin wooden partition. He should be able to overhear their conversation if he could get close to the partition. He moved quickly to be seated at his desk in the accounts section before the two men reached their office. There were only two clerks in the accounts section, and both were fully engaged in bookwork. But, when the two men began to talk, it was hard from Robert's desk to hear more than a murmur of conversation.

If he was to eavesdrop, he needed to be closer to the partition wall. He saw a filing cabinet alongside the partition wall on top of which was an assortment of reference materials, dictionaries, Bradshaw's General Railway and Steam Guide for Great Britain and Ireland, and so on. He pretended to consult the railway timetables in Bradshaw, as an excuse for standing at the filing cabinet with his ear close to the partition wall.

He could hear clearly what was being said as the first man, the marine engineer, spoke: "… the engine's a problem …I propose to replace it with a new steam turbine …"

"That's a major operation."

"Yes, but it would be sensible for what they want, and they can afford it."

"Very well. So do it."

"About the deck cabins, is the plan to strip all the fixed furniture? It will look odd. Do they need all that space for the cargo? Did you say rifles?"

"The cargo must not be mentioned. I agree, think we should leave the fixtures. It needs to look like a pleasure boat."

"You mentioned a place where a cargo of … coins will be safe."

"Of course. They will be in secure wooden boxes and need to be in a locked lower deck cabin; the door must be strong and fitted with a new lock."

The conversation continued and the first man mentioned work to strengthen the upper deck.

'Why do they want this?"

"… they need a stronger firing platform."

What? Robert asked himself. They intend to put a gun on the upper deck? Unless it was easily removable or could be disguised it would look completely out of place on a pleasure yacht. But maybe they were thinking of a heavy machine gun that could be carried up to the deck when needed and bolted into place only when required.

This conversation continued, but with alarm Robert saw that one of the account clerks was heading towards him. If he spoke to Robert while Robert was close to the partition, his words would be heard on the other side, and the two men would know that their conversation could have been overheard. Robert improvised quickly and grabbing the Bradshaw he virtually ran across the room, yanked the clerk by the arm and headed him out of the door.

"Do you ever use Bradshaw?" Robert asked him in a whisper. It must have sounded completely daft.

"Me? Bradshaw? Not much."

"Ah! That must be it! I've finished with it. Please return it to its place."

With which he handed the Bradshaw to the astounded clerk and walked off. It would be unwise to try his luck any further with another attempt to overhear them. Robert had learnt a lot and was sure that his visit had not been observed by the two men. The trip to Liverpool had been very worthwhile.

10

On the journey back to London Robert pondered the success of his trip. For one thing it was beyond doubt that, whoever was behind the conspiracy, had plenty of money to throw at it and was well organised. He wondered idly whether there was any way he and Anna could continue to track *Hermes'* progress. The ship would need a crew and he wondered if there might be a way to 'plant' someone in it who could report back. That seemed a useful idea, and thinking that Hugo would know how, he arranged to meet him in 'The Albert' in Victoria Street. He talked over his findings from the Liverpool trip and Hugo agreed that a cargo of gold did indicate a plan to bribe the Arab tribes around Tripoli to revolt against Turkish rule.

"I think," Hugo said, "that they want to strengthen the ship's davits to handle heavier loads. Probably unloading crates of rifles at sea into a small boat. Sounds as if they intend to store a cargo of rifles in the main deck cabin, which is why they are putting in metal shutters. I think from what you say that they plan to fix a mounting for a machine gun on the upper deck, probably for protection against the Arabs in case they get greedy when the gold is being dished out, and are tempted to rush the ship."

The Foreign Office had previously dismissed Sergio's plan for lack of supporting evidence. Now there was much more information and Hugo suggested that Robert prepare a written report for passing on to Blake. Hugo felt confident that Blake would have no choice but to 'take the bait', as he put it: there was clear evidence of a foreign inspired conspiracy based on Sergio's original plan.

Robert then asked Hugo about his idea to put someone who could be trusted to be their eyes and ears on board *Hermes*.

"You mean put a plant in the crew?" Hugo observed with a knowing grin. "What a splendid idea! Our own spy from the start, right on board. Just the ticket. I'll fix it."

Hugo said it would be easy to plant someone; the new owners of *Hermes* would appoint a British Master and then leave it to him to sign on the rest of the crew.

"Once we know they have a Master, we can get a 'suitable' friend installed in the crew. The position of ship's cook is probably our best bet. The Master will expect references and I can find someone who meets all the requirements."

"Will it take time?" Robert asked.

"No. I think I have the right man already. A fellow connected to my own RN Reserve unit, someone who has been at sea in a merchant ship. I can easily provide good references."

"But will they be references that stand scrutiny? The conspiracy are probably professional crooks!"

Hugo didn't like that, "We too are professionals. The references provided will be perfect. The chap I have in mind is Thomas Connolly. He is about 27, was born in Manchester, had a run-in with the Head Teacher and left school when he was 14. Well actually he set fire to the school gym. He was than apprenticed to a carpenter but didn't like it and went to work in an office. Went to night school and took a course in engineering. Didn't get on and left, then went to sea for a few years. Tramp ships and saw a lot of the world. Came home and has worked in the City as a warehouseman since. Referred to my RN unit by the City Police after he had a slight problem over an alleged break-in. We found him a job. And he has been useful to us."

Robert was staggered at the detail provided. Hugo had given him the chap's life history and had done it as if he had been prepared for this move. Surely, he must have anticipated Robert's suggestion. It left Robert thinking he had merely proposed something to Hugo that Hugo had already decided to do.

*

After receiving Robert's report Blake wrote to Robert inviting him and Anna to return to the Foreign Office. Robert passed the letter to Anna.

She phoned Robert. "Can you come with me to the meeting, Robbie?"

They agreed to meet, as before, outside Golders Green Station and take the Underground to Strand Station. She greeted Robert and smiled, "Robbie, you haven't said a lot about your interests these last few years."

This was the first time she had expressed any interest at all in his activities, a lack of interest that had considerably annoyed him. However, he was happy now to chat about trips to the family cottage in Norfolk, shooting 'for the pot' with a local farmer, about the old sailing dingy he kept in Brancaster Staithe on the north Norfolk coast, and how he enjoyed sailing her in the coastal estuaries and creeks. She was curious about sailing and hinted she might enjoy it.

Then, and as it turned out disastrously, he mentioned he had also enjoyed a recent trip to Paris with his friend Andrew, a trip which he blandly described as 'a visit to the Art Galleries'. She gave him a hard, mocking look that said she thought his explanation unlikely.

"You're telling me that two young men with money in their pockets go all the way to Paris just to visit Art galleries?" It was cutting and sarcastic.

Her reaction caught him unguarded, and he was not sure what to say.

"Robbie, you don't seem to be the gallery type. Or do you mention Art galleries just as a good excuse for enjoying … the other attractions of Paris?"

He saw at once what she meant; it hardly needed the meaningful pause to make the point. He could not believe what she was asking.

"What!" he protested.

"Are you using Art galleries as a good excuse to savour the other well publicised attractions of Paris?" There was a deliberate, nuanced provocation in her tone.

He could only think of being defensive. "Whatever do you mean?"

She clearly took his evasion to mean that her arrow had hit the mark. "Come on! You know exactly what I mean. Don't pretend! You were never any good at dissembling in the old days and you're no better today."

He should, if he was wise, have left it there and hoped for the best, trusting she had not picked up the gossip about his Paris trip. But he wasn't wise.

"Whatever do you mean by the 'other' attractions of Paris?" he demanded. "Particularly the lurid way you said it?"

If this was meant to embarrass her it wasn't going to work because he should have realised that she might have heard the talk and know he was being a hypocrite. He had indeed gone to Paris with his friend Andrew to have a good time. While they were not uninterested in the City's cultural attractions, including its fine Museums and Art Galleries, they had also arranged to meet two girls in a brassiere on the West

Bank and go dancing. They all went together to various clubs, and he greatly liked the new style of dancing, especially the syncopated rhythms of ragtime music. New dances, like the "Cakewalk" and the "Turkey Trot", were coming into vogue in slinky parts of Paris nightlife and they and their friends tried them all. Repeatedly. He took quickly and happily to the simple pattern of repeated steps and the freedom for expression. Their friends from the Brassiere then took them to a sleazy working-class district where they experienced bal-musette dancing – an even more relaxed style, simple, fast, and sensual steps holding very close. And afterwards there were indeed other physical pleasures, if not enjoyed in any of the gorgeous, lavish, and expensive pleasure establishments for which King Edward's visits to Paris were all too well known.

"Come on Robbie! You prevaricate. Don't young men who go to Paris usually want to enjoy everything it offers?" The way she said it could only mean one thing.

"What?" Her concern in what he had got up to in Paris shocked him. It was surely not proper for a 'nice well-brought-up girl' like Anna to take so much interest in what young men did on trips to Paris. He sensed however, he was in quicksand and his uncertainty about how to handle the situation forced him to pause. She read him; she always had been able to read him.

"Robbie are you really saying you didn't? And I hadn't heard you were that much interested in paintings."

Robert was taken aback by her boldness. Even if he saw it was delivered with a smile. No other girl he had ever known would have dreamed of interrogating him like that, which was surely more than just being modern and progressive, even for a suffragette. He saw her as a militant feminist ready to shove her advanced attitudes in his face. He knew of course before this conversation that she had changed.

She was not the same girl he had known so well when he was fourteen, but he was unprepared to cope in close quarters combat with this new Anna. He felt flummoxed, out of his depth and floundering.

"Anna! What are you asking?" It was an answer intended to put off the issue. He entirely grasped what she asked and, moreover, that she knew he had. Trying to avoid a straight answer was not a good way of handling Anna, who would not of course have approved of him making use of women for his pleasure. But at that moment he could think of no other reply.

"Robbie, I was asking for honesty!"

They had by then left the Underground station, had passed Trafalgar Square, walked through Admiralty Arch, and were on Horse Guards. The grand edifice of the Foreign Office was just five minutes' walk away and Robert strode out to make the pace.

"Anna, we must stop all this nonsense. We came here for a meeting, and we should go to it. Let's get on with it!" But he knew he had evaded the honest answer she asked for.

Arriving at the Foreign Office they were once again shown up the Grand Staircase, then along a long corridor into an impressive conference room. There was a large mahogany table in the centre, strewn with maps of the western and central Mediterranean, at which Hugo and Blake were gazing. Blake greeted Robert and Anna, and Robert got a knowing wink from Hugo. Blake invited them to take a seat at the table and they were then joined by another person, who entered and took a seat at the head of the table. Like Blake he was wearing morning dress and was introduced by Blake simply as Mr. Gandy, signifying a person of importance. He was tall, with grey hair swept back over a high forehead. Beneath which was a long nose and a closely clipped grey moustache. He had the patrician air and brooding presence of a superior person, one barely deigning to deal with those below him, clearly someone of substance, Robert supposed, close to those who advised the Foreign Secretary himself.

Gandy came directly to the point. "With the information now available, Sergio's plan is a real, well-planned, fully financed operation. It is indeed dangerous to our British national interests and should be frustrated."

He paused to look hard at Robert. "You already know that the Government cannot itself take any part in doing so. We would simply risk drawing public attention to it. Our best outcome is that Sergio's plan and everything about it, the money, the boat, any weapons purchased, all of it, lock stock and barrel, simply vanish without trace. As if they never existed."

He glanced around the table. "However, there is the possibility that Sergio might be persuaded to agree to withdraw or disown his plan, particularly if it was made plain to him that it is fully known to the British government and would be thwarted. He might accept that the best thing for Italy was for him to renounce his plan." He paused again, Anna and Robert exchanged glances. "However, I must stress that the British Government cannot in any circumstances be involved in any such dealing with Sergio himself."

Anna's meaningful glance gave Robert the message: it was what he was thinking himself.

Gandy is a miserable old fudger. He is blatantly fishing for us to volunteer to do what the Government itself ought to do. We did what we were asked. They promised to respond but they haven't. The Foreign Office just sits on its hands.

He guessed that Gandy's cautious words would alarm Anna and he wondered how she would react.

She did so quickly, speaking in a clear-cut voice. "I quite understand the difficulties that Sergio's plan presents to you. But I think I can help!" She emphasised the first-person pronoun, and the room froze in expectation. She played it like an experienced trouper; Robert was sure she had done amateur dramatics at college.

She held their full attention in complete silence for some telling seconds. "Yes. I'm sure I can help." Another pause for effect. "I will go to Tripoli myself and talk face to face to my cousin Sergio."

It was a grenade thrown into the room that stunned those present. No one including Robert had foreseen such an outrageous proposal.

She continued boldly, apparently unaware of the effect of her statement. "Yes. I will go to Tripoli and speak to my cousin Sergio. You see Sergio will not refuse to see me. I am family. He knows he is responsible for my mother's death. He will answer my questions. It is a matter of honour that any Italian would understand. I will tell him to his face he has my mother's blood on his hands and must cease his conspiracy."

There was a marked air of awkwardness in the room as her words sank in; everyone knew at once that her idea was a horse that wouldn't run. Or rather a horse that must not be allowed to run; Anna a young girl left to the mercies of wild North Africa. Hugo stared at her wide eyed. Blake and Gandy were frozen. Robert, momentarily lost at sea by her alarming announcement, was the first to recover.

"Anna!" he exclaimed. "What in heavens name are you saying?"

She gave him the hard stare that signalled that she had made up her mind. Yet the whole room knew she could not possibly be allowed to undertake such a mission.

Gandy was quick to declare the formal Foreign Office view. He spoke with a well-trained diplomatic voice. The condescending view he took of her outburst was all too clear. "My dear young lady, we naturally all respect your courage. But, such a venture by a young lady, to such a remote oriental Ottoman outpost as Tripoli would not pass unnoticed. It could easily create an unwelcome and embarrassing incident and place His Majesty's Government in a very difficult position. It could well jeopardise our present good relations with both the Kingdom of Italy and the Ottoman Sultanate in Constantinople. Your visit could well serve only to assist the dastardly conspiracy against this country that your cousin has planned."

Anna said nothing; she had not liked the tone or the content of his message. For their own reasons Blake and Hugo sat silent.

"Exactly!" Robert blurted out the word and seized the moment. He sensed that if he did not do something and at once the whole prospect of any sort of Government action would flounder and sink. He turned to Gandy. "With respect, Sir, you are right! Anna cannot possibly go." He paused, building the effect and addressed the room. "But it would be a different matter, entirely different, if it was I who made the journey to Tripoli!"

It was his turn to play the dramatic pause for all it was worth. "You see no-one would notice a visit to Tripoli by me. I can easily arrange it. I worked in a shipping practice until recently, I can find a client who will give me a good commercial reason to visit North Africa. I will go to Tripoli and deal with Sergio."

There was a stir in the room, followed by only a brief interlude before Hugo jumped in with both feet, or rather with both hands, for he vigorously thumped the table to express his support.

"Wonderful!" he declared loudly. "Splendid! That is a much better idea. A really good idea. It would work." He slapped the table again with his right hand in approval.

"Oh, would you Robbie!" Anna exclaimed. "That would be wonderful."

When he made his offer, Robert thought she might be annoyed at him taking control of her proposal. But, instead, she seemed pleased, and he did wonder if his offer had really been her object all along. She must have known that her own offer would be completely unacceptable to the Foreign Office.

Blake looked at Robert from across the table. "You make an interesting proposition young man. However, you must understand that the Foreign Office cannot ask you to take part in such a venture." He played on the work 'ask', meaning that the responsibility of such a trip would be Robert's alone. He was to be a volunteer, on his own. "Nor could the Foreign Office formally recognise such a visit. There must not be any involvement by the British Government."

In the hush that followed he looked at Gandy, who nodded. "Naturally any risk will be minimized if you make only a short trip to Tripoli."

A note of caution, but one that at least implied his consent in principle. It was sufficient endorsement for Hugo.

"I should say privately," Hugo said, "and off the record, that the trip's expenses, if you decide to do it, would be defrayed out of contingency funds I hold."

Robert was and looked astonished at this mention of contingency funds, surely yet another unexpected aspect of Hugo, a man who had apparent control of secret state funds.

"Yes. On condition that it remained confidential. Which would naturally also apply to the whole operation. No-one outside this room must ever know of it. We would ask for your written assurance of complete confidentiality."

Robert was taken aback at the alacrity with which his offer to visit Tripoli had been grabbed by the Foreign Office. He suspected, indeed, that his offer had in fact been carefully choreographed by Hugo, as if he was playing a careful hand at Bridge and had finessed Robert's Ace. Better perhaps, Hugo had simply gone fishing, waited patiently, and then allowed Robert time to catch the bait. But whatever his suspicions, what he had done he had done, what he had said he had said, and he was not someone to back out of a clear undertaking.

"You mentioned Turkish sensitivity," Robert asked, thinking he should explore Reggie Rands' analysis of Britain's relationship with a changing Turkish Empire. "Sergio's plan is aimed against Turkish rule in Libya. Is Turkey more sensitive since the change of government in Constantinople?"

Blake looked, for once, uncertain how to reply and glanced at Gandy.

Gandy replied in his dry, detached tone and in a matter-of-fact punctilious manner. "You mean I suppose that a group called the 'Committee for Union and Progress', or the CUP for short, has taken power from the Sultan's old regime. Well, the Foreign Office remains uncertain of their intentions."

"Ah!"

"We are advised by our Ambassador in Constantinople, on whose great experience we rely, that the new CUP government is no more than what the ambassador calls 'an oriental Jewish conspiracy' to seize control of the Ottoman Empire."

An oriental Jewish conspiracy? Robert thought it seemed a bit over the top, Turkey was indeed in the orient but was a Muslim state and the Sultan was also Caliph; surely a

Jewish take-over was most unlikely. Was the Foreign Office really being advised that? If so, was their ambassador out of his mind?

"Yes," Gandy continued, "our ambassador advises us that the CUP is a Jewish conspiracy, one allied to dangerous elements in central Europe that support Zionism and want to obtain a Jewish base in Palestine. In our view that presents a threat to British control of Egypt and the Suez Canal."

Robert had no idea about Zionism and wasn't sure what the reference to a base in Palestine meant, but Gandy was in full flow.

"The Government considers the CUP to be a dangerous clique of Jews and Freemasons, and fears it is bent on preaching a new aggressive pan-Islamism."

Robert felt clobbered by the onslaught of strange new concepts and thought that it didn't make sense that a 'clique of Jews and Freemasons' should be advocating the world-wide advance of Islam. He asked Gandy to explain.

"Pan-Islamism? It is a political creed that sees Islam as a world movement that crosses national borders. It is about the unity of all Muslims, Muslims everywhere, those living outside Ottoman rule as well as those within the Ottoman Empire. This naturally focuses attention on the very large number of Muslims living in the British, French and Russian Empires. But then it also stresses the role of the Sultan in Constantinople who is also the Caliph, the head and leader of Islam. In other words, Pan-Islamism advocates that the Caliph or Sultan must claim the right to lead Muslims everywhere in the World. Moreover, that he should in fact do so actively."

Robert could at once see the logic and the attraction of such a movement. A resurgent Turkey with such a political credo would be a new and powerful force on the world's stage.

Not good news for the old European Empires with their vast number of Muslim subjects.

"Given," Gandy continued, "the large number of Muslims who live in India, Pan-Islamism could pose a particular danger to the British Raj."

"Ah!"

"It will also stir up trouble in Egypt. The CUP government is therefore seen by us as intrinsically hostile to our interests."

Robert doubted the whole thing. He was no believer in the Imperial expansion philosophy, questioned the national resources that were being devoted to maintaining and expanding the Empire and was sure our future prosperity lay in enhancing our commercial relations with the industrialised world. A modernised Turkey sounded attractive rather than alarming, something we should support. At first Gandy had seemed merely typical of the limited, blinkered imagination he expected of the Foreign Office. Now, though, with all this talk of oriental conspiracies and world-wide extreme Islamist agitation he wondered if Gandy might be a bit deranged. Moreover, it was alarming that people like him were advising ministers and forming the whole direction of British foreign policy.

Gandy had said his piece and wanted to depart. "Thank you for your attendance. The government is grateful for your information. I will leave you with my colleagues to discuss more about your possible private visit to Tripoli." He nodded to Robert and Anna in dismissal and walked off.

Blake had a final message. "We would like you to think carefully about your proposal to visit Tripoli. And if having done so you remain sure you wish to make the journey, then please let us know."

11

Robert and Anna took the Underground to return to Golders Green. He asked her what she thought of the meeting.

"I suppose it was good that they have at last been persuaded to accept the facts about Sergio's plot." He gave her a calculated look: it sounded as if there was a caveat. There was.

"But Robbie, you see I'm really anxious about you going to Tripoli. It's all my fault you made the offer. I only said I would go because I thought it might persuade the government to do something. I didn't expect you to rush in. I really didn't like the way they just jumped in to say the visit to Tripoli is important, and then being so keen for you to go, but not being prepared to lift a finger themselves. I'm worried for you."

Her words echoed his own feelings about the meeting, feelings he didn't want to express aloud because it might look like cold feet. Nevertheless, he decided to be honest.

"I was feeling that myself. Look Anna, if they really think that the Sergio conspiracy is a danger to Britain, why doesn't the government find a way to deal with it? Is there any doubt that they have the means? We are constantly told that we are a great Empire, that we have far-reaching military power to defend our vital interests. Why then don't they act?"

"Then, Robbie, for goodness' sake you must tell them you're not going to Tripoli. I was watching them; they were over the moon when you volunteered. For them you are merely another pawn in their diplomatic game. And they will certainly disown you if anything goes wrong. They will abandon you without hesitation if it suits them. Did you notice how quick Hugo was to slap you on the back when you said you would go, but Gandy said that the government could not be involved in any way? That means they would not save you even if things turned out bad. What kind of people are they? They would leave you to rot in a Turkish prison."

He looked at her, for she had spoken his own thoughts. But then he had freely chosen to make the offer to go to Tripoli and did not like the idea of retracting what he had publicly proposed.

"Anna, I knew what I was doing."

"Did you Robbie?"

She was right, there was a question in his mind. Had he been the victim of clever operators, walked into a trap like a mug?

"Robbie, neither I nor my father want you to do anything dangerous. And Tripoli could be very dangerous. We never expected that these investigations into my mother's letters would lead to this. Please think about it carefully. I want you to tell the Foreign Office you've thought about it and decided against going!"

"It's too soon to do that, but since you ask, I will think carefully about it."

*

Feeling somewhat torn, he wanted to discuss the trip with his parents, who were still in the cottage in Norfolk. So, he took the train from Liverpool Street up to Hunstanton for the weekend. It would also be good to spend a few days in the quiet of the countryside, perhaps take his dinghy out for a sail. He could relax and review the Sergio affair calmly and objectively. He was pleased to discover that his father was in much better health and was, with his doctor's approval, intending to return to work within days. Robert respected his father's judgement and wanted his advice. His mother joined their discussion. Robert summarised the background, what had happened as a matter of fact and what he now surmised was the situation.

To his surprise his father was sympathetic, seeing the trip as an opportunity for adventure that might never come again. He said, "If you want an adventure, Robbie, now would be a good time. You're only just qualified, haven't any commitments and haven't yet bedded down in a steady job. It's an ideal time to take a break if that's what you want."

Robert was surprised at the interest his mother took in the trip to Tripoli. She was plainly in favour of him going. Not what he had expected.

"It will be a good experience for you to see another way of life." She told him. "The voyage will do you good and it will open your eyes to the world." She hesitated and looked at him. "You will see things here at home differently when you come back. You should go."

He was puzzled. "How would I see things at home differently? I am not going to be away that long. Two months at the outside."

"Yes. But going to Tripoli will separate you from what you're used to here. You will get a new perspective. And I'm sure, new and different friends when you come back home."

He saw at once what was in her mind. It was the way she said he would have 'new and different friends' when he came back. He suspected that there was one 'friend' she had in mind, and that must be Sybil. It puzzled him, for up to that very moment he had been sure that his mother liked the idea of his marriage to Sybil. Yet here she was telling him, in effect, that the trip would be the opportunity to finish with Sybil. What could account for such a violent change of opinion? He had always been on good terms with his parents and was sure that if his mother had changed her mind about Sybil, she would have a good reason. So, he asked her to be frank.

"Sybil is a nice girl and I know you like her." His mother began, the faint praise signalling her conclusion. "I did think that she would be the right girl for you. I can understand that you might well think you were in love with her." She paused. Robert knew the next sentence was going to be a bombshell and it was. "But before you think of asking her to marry her, you should be sure that she is likely to accept."

"I haven't proposed to her. But we have become quite close. I am sure that if I proposed she would accept!"

His mother looked at him without saying a word. She didn't need to. He could read the silence. And it was awful.

"You must mean she would refuse!" The idea that Sybil would do anything else but accept had never occurred to him.

"Yes Robert. I mean that. You may have misunderstood her real feelings for you."

"Whatever makes you think that?" He was shocked. "How can I have mistaken her feelings? They are unmistakable."

"Oh! You should realise what marriage is. A marriage would not just be about you and Sybil. It is that of course, but marriage would also be about our family and about her family, joining two families together. The families can't be ignored."

"Yes, but what of it? It is surely what she and I want."

"Robbie, she would not go against her family's wishes."

"Whatever makes you think her family would be against her marrying me?"

His mother was quiet for a long moment. As if hoping that she would not be pressed to answer such a question. Her hesitation forced Robert to insist on a reply.

"Mother, I do need to know why you think that."

"Yes, I think you do. And I know that you won't like it."

"Maybe but tell me all the same! You must."

"Very well. She has some aunts, one who I know slightly from my Monday Whist circle. She wrote to me last week to suggest a meeting in the Blue Boar Hotel in Cambridge. She did say it was most important and hinted it was to do with the family. I took the train from Hunstanton to Cambridge and a cab to the Blue Boar and we had lunch. She had come up from London specially. She said she was concerned about my father's difficulties in living in London. What difficulties? It was nonsense. He was a respected consultant in a big Hospital, had a good private practice, a nice house, servants and a family. Then she said that she admired my mother for her courage in bringing up children who were, as she put it, 'so different' to other children. Children 'who didn't always fit in.' Who might be looked at in the street. Might be commented on by neighbours."

"No! I don't believe it. How dare she."

"She did, and you know what she meant. She said that my mother must have been so brave, so strong. Not many women were strong enough to do it. Then she complemented me for how I had brought up my children. What cheek."

"Damned cheek!"

"Yes. It wasn't nice."

"So, she was in a devious way saying that a marriage with me would not do for Sybil. Because we would have children who looked different. Children who looked like me."

His mother replied, holding back her tears, "Yes exactly that."

"Are you sure? Might you be reading something into it that was not meant?"

"Yes, I am quite sure what she meant. There was no doubt. As she had spoken openly to me, I asked her directly if that was what she meant. She was really embarrassed that I put it so very bluntly, but I persisted, and she agreed that it was. It was not a nice conversation. I told her that I had managed very well with my children and saw no reason why my son's children should raise problems."

"Did she not accept that?" Robert asked.

"She said that I was an exceptional person. Sort of suggesting I am so thick skinned, blind or stupid that I don't notice the problems."

"No! How dare she talk to you like that." Robert was angry and banged his fist on the arm of his chair. "It is disgusting."

"That's how it was. It was quite tense and horrible."

"It must have been terrible for you." Robert was angry that his mother had had to listen to such insulting rubbish.

"I insisted her telling me if she was purely expressing her own opinion. She assured me that that Sybil's parents knew what she had just said to me and were of the same mind. Indeed, Sybil's mother had asked her to speak to me."

"Had she! But does Sybil think this way?" Robert asked. "If this is what she thinks why didn't she tell me? She could easily have. Is it perhaps just her relatives?"

"That is possible. But I am sure that she was speaking for Sybil. Whatever her own views may be, I know Sybil, and I don't think that she is strong enough to oppose her family, not the sort of person to defy her family. Sybil is a nice girl who in the end will do what her family wants. But I don't believe she wants to hurt you."

"How can I not be hurt! Horribly hurt. Good God Mother, I was about to propose. I trusted her and it's a stab in the back. I feel betrayed. And by someone to whom I thought I was so close. I had no idea. In fact, I imagined that she was expecting me to propose and would say yes. That's how wrong I was."

He felt utterly devastated by the news, shocked at the sheer nastiness of it. He had believed he knew her well and had never felt even a hint of any reservations on her part about their relationship. Learning just now, like a bolt from the blue, what she really felt about him, was so totally different to anything he had experienced in being with her that it came as a hammer blow. How could he have so completely failed to understand Sybil? So blind to the truth of her feeling for him? It was appalling.

"I've hated having to say this to you Robert. But I felt I had to."

"Mother, you were right to tell me. You can see I'm fairly shattered by the news. It's so unexpected. I am really upset by her attitude. It's awful to be told this but I'm pleased you told me. I could easily have made a fool of myself. A bigger fool than I already have."

*

He left the cottage and cycled up to Brancaster Staithe where he kept his old dinghy. The tide was coming in fast, and dragging it through the mud by the shore, he took the boat out to sea. He struggled to master the power of the sea; that was his way of fighting the crisis he felt had engulfed his life. He was uncertain at first whether to meet Sybil and confront her, or to simply never see her again. But to ignore her would be difficult as she was a cousin of his best friend, and it would be cowardly to say nothing. To slink away with his tail between his legs like a dog that had been given a good kicking was not his style. He decided he must meet her but wondered how on earth he was going to manage the meeting. Then the answer came to him in a flash.

He knew exactly how he would manage it. He would meet Sybil in some neutral place and tell her that unfortunately he had to go on a sudden, confidential, and perhaps risky, business trip to the Mediterranean. One that would take some time, months rather than weeks, indeed he was not sure when he would return. Given it was a trip that had some dangers, the future was so uncertain he might never see her again. Perhaps therefore it would be best if they parted company. If she agreed with her family's view of him, and their objection to marriage, she would simply say how sorry she was but of course understood he had to go. Implicitly that would be the end of the proposed engagement. That would be that. He would never see her again.

However, the devastating news about Sybil had cleared his mind of the confusion with which he had travelled up to Norfolk. Now he was perfectly sure what he would do about the Sergio business. The Sybil debacle had made up his mind for him. Going to Tripoli would end the relationship with Sybil without an unpleasant confrontation. Moreover, Tripoli would distract his mind from the appalling affair of Sybil, and he would return to England, as his mother said, with a new view of the world and could look for new friends. He would need to. Sybil had become a big part of his life and there would be a gulf to fill. So, he would go to Tripoli. It was the only decision to make. The rest was straightforward. He told his parents he was going to Tripoli and when back in London he would see the Gibson's and tell them the same.

12

So, a few days later Robert walked round to the Gibson's house. He would tell Anna about the cover story that he was proposing to write to Sergio, to explain his sudden decision to visit Tripoli. She greeted him nicely, accepted his decision to go and took him to the sitting room, where they sat on a sofa facing the garden. She listened quietly, pensively, as he talked, gazing at him with her big eyes. He knew the technique at once, she was softening him up for something. He said he would tell Sergio he was a lawyer dealing with the estate of the late Maria Gibson. His instructions were to visit Sergio in Tripoli to finalise a bequest to Sergio in a newly found codicil to Maria Gibson's Will, the gift to Sergio of a valuable property in Italy. It was the details of the bequest and Maria's personal wishes to Sergio regarding the use of the property, set out in confidential supplementary directions to Maria's Will, that he needed to discuss with Sergio personally.

"Yes, that sounds plausible."

There was a pause and it seemed to Robert that she was working out how to say something else, probably beginning with 'but'.

He was right and Anna came to the point, putting her hand on his knee as if to restrain him. "Robbie, it is very kind of you to volunteer for Tripoli. But I have been thinking about it."

So, there was indeed a reservation, something else on her mind "You see Robbie the whole thing about my mother's murder and Sergio is about our family, and we should deal with it. I mean that I should be the one to go to Tripoli and deal with Sergio."

"Anna! What are you saying? We have been over all this. It is settled that I am going to Tripoli."

"It is not settled!"

"Anna, you cannot be seriously thinking of going to Tripoli."

"I have decided. It is not a difficult journey. Times are different and women do this sort of thing now."

The harshness of her determination was tempered by the way she put her hand on his, a gentle gesture of affection, together with the slight smile on her lips as she looked at him face to face. Neither move was lost on him. She was stage-managing him, and he knew it.

"Anna! The idea of you travelling by yourself to a place like Tripoli is out of the question. You have no idea of the danger. How could I possibly let you put yourself at such risk. What you are suggesting is neither acceptable nor practical. On any condition."

Anna physically recoiled from the sharpness of his response. Not what she wanted. She looked upset and there were tears forming in her eyes. She moved to withdraw her hand from his. But he held it firmly, putting his other hand over it. She sat still and dried her eyes with the handkerchief he proffered.

"Very well, Robbie." She spoke calmly and carefully. "If you insist on making the trip, you must do so."

He breathed a sigh of relief; no explosion of rage and she had seen reason.

She put down the handkerchief. "But I shall come with you as the interpreter. You will need an interpreter, you have no Italian, and I am your best possible choice."

Robert's previous alarm at her impetuous idea of going alone to Tripoli was now replaced joined by annoyance at what he saw as her lack of common sense. "You cannot be suggesting that you come on a foreign trip with me. Anna, you are a young single woman. What you say is unthinkable! How can you imagine that you could possibly travel with me!"

She did not seem to be too surprised at his reaction. "Don't be so old fashioned, Robert. You are being bourgeois and conventional. You need an interpreter; I can do it easily and I am your best choice."

"Anna, you may have modern opinions about the role of women but what you propose goes too far. Even for a radical. It's well out of court. What do you suppose would happen to your reputation? What would it do to your father?"

"Can't you bear the thought of my company for so long?"

"Anna! You know that's not true. And no, it is not my reputation that concerns me. It is yours and you know it."

She refused to withdraw her plan to travel by herself to visit Sergio in Tripoli unless Robert agreed to take her as his interpreter. In the end he had to accept her terms, but only on condition that her father found her a chaperone. John Gibson suggested Maria's distant cousin Valeria. However, as he knew her to be a person of strongly held opinions, he also felt it wise for Anna and Robert to first talk to her and to decide if it would work.

*

Valeria lived in Camden Town and was the daughter of Maria's father's sister, Daniela. Now a widow, Valeria had come to London many years ago with her husband, who was then in the import business, and had two girls both now married with their own children and living in South London. She had been in regular contact with the Gibson family over the years and Anna was fond of her.

Anna arranged to visit her and asked Robert to accompany her – so that he could give Valeria the once-over as she put it rather indelicately.

Valeria took them to the sitting room and offered them a glass of wine. "Roberto! The last time we met you were about eight and now you're such a good-looking young man."

"Oh Aunty! It's still the same old Robbie! Only bigger."

"Only bigger! What do you mean? Have I not eyes in my head? Questo bel ragazzo!"

He guessed the gist of what she said and felt embarrassed.

Valeria was considerably less than medium height and judging by the family photographs on display had taken after her father, a plain rounded face with strong features, including prominent cheek bones, a large nose, generous lips, and big dark searching eyes. But when she wished to make a point there was a glint in her eyes that suggested powerful reserves of determination. She had rather frizzy and dark hair but the main thing one noticed about her face was her permanent contented expression, a smile playing around her cheeks, she seemed to be always smiling and it was infectious. Her hands were large and workmanlike with rather stubby fingers to match. She had, though, a good if full figure. With her hair style and as she was wearing a quite elaborate dress in sombre colours in an old-fashioned style, she looked much older than her actual age.

She explained to them that John Gibson had telephoned to tell her about the plan to visit Sergio in Tripoli.

"I must say," she said to Anna, "I was surprised that you insisted on going. Roberto has become a very capable young man. He is perfectly able to deal with Sergio."

"Yes of course Robert is capable. I'm not suggesting he is not. But dealing with that devil Sergio is personal to me. I must know why my mother was involved in this affair, find out what Sergio did or said to draw her into it, get her involved. It is personal for me."

"I can see that is worrying," Valeria replied.

Valeria turned to Robert. "Roberto, surely you can tell her this is stupid. Can't you persuade her?"

"I have tried, believe me I have tried. The idea of Anna coming to North Africa fills me with anxiety. There are so many possible dangers. She won't see reason. I'm sure you know how determined she can be."

"Indeed!" Valeria replied.

In the end it was settled. Valeria agreed to come as a chaperone.

"But if I'm coming, how do we describe ourselves? Something that makes sense as a travelling party and doesn't invite questions."

"How about me and Anna being cousins? And you can be our aunt?" Robert suggested.

"I like the aunt. But cousins? We are going into very foreign country, and I'm concerned about Anna's safety."

"You think there might be ..."

"I do! Cousins is not close enough. Too ambiguous. Turks and Orientals have a reputation you know!"

"Ah!"

"Yes. Brother and sister is better. No Turk would dare touch her if you were her brother."

"Don't be ridiculous!" Anna exclaimed.

"No Anna, Valeria is right. In the old days I always thought of you as a sister, it will be just like then." He was thinking that her beauty could well be a honey pot for the men of the orient.

"Then," Valeria stated firmly, "it's settled."

"Only," Robert added, "if I can call you aunty!"

"Delighted!"

Robert left the meeting being sure that he liked her, someone with a direct, even blunt approach that had no hidden edges, concealed nuances, prevarications, down to earth and no-nonsense, someone who said what she thought. Robert's sort of person. If there had to be a chaperone, he felt that Valeria would be fine. He could get along with her.

*

Much later that day Robert left the office to take some papers to the Midland Bank in Golders Green and by sheer chance encountered Gerald Morris. Gerald's father owned several premises in Golders Green and Gerald must have been there on business with a tenant. Gerald caught sight of Robert in the street and decided to intercept. Gerald looked agitated and moved in a menacing manner. His cheeks were flushed, his eyes blazed, and he was waving his arms wildly. He was indeed, thoroughly worked up. He came up to Robert like a maniac, shouting and yelling in an ill-mannered, uncouth fashion.

"You there! You creole! I want to speak to you!"

Robert made no reply but had to stop because Gerald physically blocked the pavement.

"You cad!" Gerald yelled. "You filthy cad!"

Robert remained calm. "Behave yourself Gerald and mind your tongue."

"You swine!"

"Control yourself Gerald."

"No! I'm telling you to forget this trip. I'm telling you. Forget it."

"Back off Gerald. You're making an idiot of yourself."

"Don't you dare speak to me like that. You dirty dog. What are you thinking? She won't tell me the details. I'm sure it's some nasty, sneaky, underhand plan. No doubt about it, a nasty, dirty trick to play on a girl. Drop it!"

"What Anna does is her business. What I do is mine. None of it is yours."

That infuriated Gerald still further. "Tell me it's off!"

"What I do is none of your business."

"You damn well will tell me. You dirty scum!"

"I told you, it's none of your business."

"I won't have it. You've tricked her. You miserable mongrel!"

"No-one's been tricked. And I won't let you call me ugly names. Back off!"

"I know what you are. And I will say it if I want to. You have some nasty foreign, mongrel way of tricking her. You despicable sambo!"

"What does that make you Gerald? Dirty white trash?" Gerald had got to him, and Robert was boiling with anger at his insulting words.

"How dare you speak to me like that. You filthy half-breed! What did you use? African witchcraft?"

"Gerald you are a fool. Your pathetic attempts at abuse are wasted on me. You are pitiful. You know nothing about Anna."

Robert confronted him face to face but did not raise his voice. "I know that Anna has a mind of her own. God, she must find you such a bore. Even your attempts at insults are pathetic."

With that Gerald's anger got the better of him and he went off the deep end. He jerked forward and prepared to lash out with his fists.

"You dirty black cur! How dare you! I'll not let you ruin her!" he screamed at Robert, lunging wildly with a swinging blow to the face, a hefty punch thrown with considerable body power, intended to floor Robert.

Gerald was not, though, a clever fighter and had too obviously signalled his intentions. Robert was not therefore caught by surprise by Gerald's move but didn't want to get involved in a street brawl. Robert knew he was both lighter and quicker on his feet than Gerald. So, as Gerald's fist approached, Robert simply avoided trouble with a quick backwards-leaning side-step, a dodging move he had learnt in docklands. Indeed, he helped instruct the boys in self-defence moves exactly like this. He had simply danced to one side and left Gerald punching thin air, which threw him off balance, leaving him floundering, and propelled by his own momentum he fell heavily onto the pavement.

Robert left him struggling to get up and walked away. "If you want to be a match for us sambos, learn how to fight smarter!"

13

Having debated various possible routes to Tripoli, the three travellers had eventually opted to take a steamer from Liverpool bound for India, disembark in Malta, and then pick up a local steamer to Tripoli via Tunis. Robert, Anna, and Valeria, therefore gathered in the splendid Passenger Hall at Euston Station and waited there to board the Liverpool express. Valeria swept in with the swagger of a seasoned voyager, followed by a porter with her travel-worn steamer trunk embellished with a magnificent array of brightly coloured railway, hotel, and steamship labels. By contrast Robert showed he was a mere novice in the travel game by displaying a brand-new leather trunk, just purchased for the trip at the Army and Navy Stores. Anna had no trunk but several large, handsome leather suitcases that had been her mother's luggage.

Advised by Special Branch about the activities of the Charlotte Street agents operating from Schwarz's Restaurant, Hugo had insisted that all their luggage be deposited clandestinely and securely at Euston station two days before they departed. Moreover, on Hugo's instructions they had all travelled together by underground only as far as Camden Town, where they had been picked up by a cab driven by one of his men for a roundabout final leg to Euston itself. Robert wasn't sure if Hugo, knowing the professional organisation and resources of their opponents, was taking no chances., or was simply showing off. Probably a bit of both, he concluded, thinking though that it was quite re-assuring.

But Valeria thought it all ridiculously over the top and said so loudly, that was her style. "Does this Hugo person really think we are being watched by agents of an international conspiracy? He is mad." Robert was obliged to tell her plainly that was, indeed, exactly the situation. The danger from the conspirators was real and not to be ignored.

"Hah!" she dismissed his caution.

*

Led by Valeria they made their way to their platform with porters trundling their luggage. Robert hung back because he had been advised by the ultra-cautious Hugo to be on the alert, just in case, despite his precautions, they were followed.

"We know," Hugo told him, "that the Charlotte Street people have been watching you carefully ever since the break-in at the Gibson's house. We don't want them to follow you to Liverpool. Watch out for anyone in the station who seems unusual or different."

Robert had a go at doing so, but picked out no-one of obvious unusual concern, although Hugo's advice was easier said than done in a busy cosmopolitan railway station like Euston. The place was positively crawling with people who looked 'unusual or different', whatever that meant.

Anna allowed herself to relax once the train had pulled out of Euston, and chatted to Valeria, who wanted to know the whole story of their dealings with the Foreign Office. Robert noticed Anna recounted the saga with accomplishment, her command of the language was attractive, and she had a good story-telling voice. He caught himself thinking she would be an excellent teacher, only to remember that the consequences of Maria's murder had destroyed any such prospect. He wondered how well he would cope if, like her, his whole future was to suddenly implode. However, while her conversation was an entertaining way of passing the long journey, he feared it just showed how bright and accomplished she was. She must surely find him boring and ignorant, his conversation exposing dreadful gaps in his education.

"But," he mused, "that is surely of no matter. I'm on this trip to forget about Sybil; be ready to see life through new eyes when I get back." The Sybil affair had hurt him. Although he wanted to forget her, it was all too brutally true that forgetting her and their manner of parting would not be easy. His main hope, as the train left Euston miles behind, was that the Tripoli expedition would drive the whole Sybil thing out of his mind. But that was a big expectation, for Sybil had been such an important part of his life this past year that her sudden disappearance left a gaping void. But a void, he had resolved, that he must not fill with another relationship built on sand.

The tedium of the long train journey was thankfully broken by two or three station stops, when it was possible to take a quick perambulation on the platform, and by two visits to the restaurant car on the train. They eventually pulled into Lime Street Station in Liverpool and took a cab to the steamer quay. They were dropped beside the vessel as many other passengers were milling around, and a large noisy group was busy trooping up the gangway into the ship. Robert and his party were travelling in two first class staterooms on a steamer bound for Bombay through the Suez Canal, though they were on board only as far as Malta. The ship, that would take three days or so to reach Malta, had been fully booked and it had taken all of Hugo's considerable influence to obtain their passages. Robert wondered which unfortunate Indian Civils had been bumped off the passenger list to make room for them.

On the quay they joined the crowd waiting to board, and then Valeria led them up the long gangway into the vessel. There, they were greeted and directed to their cabins on the promenade deck, where they were re-united with their luggage. Later, having changed out of their travel clothes, they met on deck to stand at the ship's rail and examined the hustle and bustle of the busy Port. The last passengers were by then hurrying to board and there were the usual last minute frantic efforts of stevedores and the ship's crew to complete the loading of stores for the voyage. Robert made a point of discreetly observing the last few straggling passengers to board. There were only one or two last-minute first-class passengers but several third class and even a couple of crew members. He still wondered if the Charlotte Street people might try to follow them. But there seemed to be nothing of concern.

Soon afterwards the pilot came on board and members of the crew carried hand bells along the decks, ringing loudly to signal and shout that those not sailing should disembark without delay. There was a flurry of activity on the ship as the crew rushed about hither and thither while passengers and their friends sorted themselves out, some having left disembarkation to the last moment. When eventually all was ready for sailing, orders were barked out from the bridge, the ship's warps were cast off, the tugs took up the strain and the ship's whistle shrilly blasted the news of their imminent departure. Then the vessel slipped away from her berth on the quayside, left the dock and entered the Mersey. Then they pulled away from the hubbub of small boats that had been attracted by their departure and their tugs cast off and dropped behind. Now alone, the steamer slowly gathered speed and gently steamed down the mouth of the

Mersey into the open water, gradually leaving the Liverpool skyline behind and standing out to the Irish Sea.

Robert had not been on a modern steamship of this size or sophistication, and he found it exciting, a proper beginning to the adventure. He went to the rail to take a last look at the famous Liverpool skyline and Anna joined him. Then they moved to the promenade deck and stood watching as the green slash that was the long Welsh coastline glided by. They could make out the distant purplish outline of the Snowdonia mountains, that approached and then fell gradually behind. There were many other passengers on deck to witness their sailing and they quickly gathered from many overheard snippets of conversation that most of them were in for the whole long voyage to India. That helped to create a camaraderie, perhaps that was why it was obviously customary to simply talk to everyone, whether you knew them or not. Similarly, after boarding, nearly everyone had changed into relatively informal clothes. It all made for a relaxed atmosphere that Robert found delightful and left him pleased they had decided to travel by sea.

For First Class passengers there was a single formal dinner sitting each evening. This was announced by a dressing bell at 6.30 in the evening, that caused everyone to saunter to their cabins to change for dinner. On their first evening at dinner Anna appeared in a close fitting, simple black silk dress that she had enlivened with an exquisite turquoise silk scarf, her mother's diamond and sapphire flower brooch, and a delicate white gold necklace lent by Valeria. Anna's ensemble was neither elaborate or expensive, indeed most other women present were wearing clothes and jewellery of far greater value and splendour. But Anna had a natural talent and sense for style and an innate ability to wear her clothes with panache. Indeed, she looked so elegant and amazing in her simple outfit that many heads turned. Robert observed her appearance with great pleasure, seeing her now so much calmer, relaxed and at ease than any other time since the murder. The tension was leaving her face and he was glad that Valeria was right, the sea voyage would do Anna good. Valeria herself had turned out smartly dressed in a cobalt blue dress and an impressive pearl choker, and by her manner was clearly enjoying the scene, studying the assembled company.

She entertained them with a string of none too sotto-voce comments about their fellow passengers. "Do you see that couple over there? The old dowager smothered with too much gold and huge diamonds. What frightful bling. Cosi ostentato."

She had more. "And look at that man over there with that frumpy woman. She must be his wife because he's clearly completely bored with her; you can see how he keeps eyeing the room for someone to pick up."

She carried on in Italian, enjoying the sport of picking apart selected victims in the room. Anna looked embarrassed and tried to restrain her, although it was unlikely that anyone near them understood Italian. Robert envied her fluency in Italian, his own Igbo did not go a lot further than simple words picked up from his mother for the family, like indeed 'nne', the Igbo for 'mother'.

During dinner there was a three-piece ensemble who played quietly for background amusement. After dinner there was a general movement to the Ballroom, which Robert's party joined. They found a table and Robert invited Anna to take the floor for the first dance, a traditional waltz. He realised it was the first time he had ever danced with her; dancing must have entered their social world only after he left school. He discovered that he liked the feel of holding her, and found that she was an excellent dancer, her movements were so lithe, supple, and graceful. He speculated whether there was anything at which she was not greatly accomplished. No sooner was the dance over and they were they seated again, than one of the several young men who had been eying her was in like a flash – as others were for the rest of the evening. He grasped that one of the consequences of the comradery on board was that everyone had quickly learnt that their little group was brother and sister and an aunt, going on after Malta to Naples for a family occasion and travelling by sea because their aunt needed a sea voyage for her health. Particularly, therefore, that as their fellow passengers took Robert and Anna to be siblings it was socially acceptable for a young man to approach Anna for a dance, with only a brief formal nod to Robert.

Robert noticed, though, that a couple of the single young men who had clearly taken account of Anna, and her beauty, did not make any move to ask her to dance. He knew at once why; because he and Anna were taken to be siblings, although Anna might appear to be European, because of Robert's appearance she was in fact more likely to be something other. Although he felt a personal hurt at their insulting attitude, he also wondered if she had realised the situation. From the way she behaved he guessed not.

Indeed, Anna's visible delight in throwing herself into the dancing presented a new face to Robert. Could this be the serious-minded girl who was quick off the mark for any political debate? Yet here she is, an enthusiastic party person enjoying every minute of it. And one, to boot, who conspicuously relished the company of attentive young men. He had got the wrong impression of the suffragettes, plainly they were not all the dull, blue stocking, killjoy crowd he had imagined. All of which he confessed merely demonstrated the limits of his imagination: because Anna clearly was capable both of supporting 'the Cause' and thoroughly enjoying herself.

Indeed, she was conspicuously having a wonderful time with a young, smartly turned out and good-looking cavalry officer. He was apparently returning from leave to re-join his regiment in India, and was an accomplished dancer, indeed their chic routine on the floor attracted much favourable comment in the room. By chance Robert caught snatches of their conversation.

"Don't you find India fascinating?"

"Inja? Well, I'm with the reg'ment most of the time. There's not much to see ..."

"Hunting ..."

"Oh yes! The huntin's great fun ..."

"And the Indians ...?"

"The natives? There's the reg'ment of course, mine's a native one so I see my men. Others? Not much except if I go to the bazaar and so ..."

"Isn't the culture enthralling ...?"

"Culture? ... I suppose .... I don't have much ..."

She was clearly having fun, enjoying the dancing with a charming partner. But he knew at once there could be nothing more to it, she would get bored stiff after five minutes. He wondered, perhaps hoped, if it was the same with Gerald Morris; what could she have in common with a man like that except their common religion, and surely that was not enough for a girl like Anna. Then he quickly feared that she might feel the same boredom about him but dismissed the thought when he recalled that their conversations had never been boring;

arguments, harangues, rows and raised emotions, never boring.

They sailed on leaving the choppy waters of Biscay and steamed past the rocky outcrops of Galicia down the coast of Portugal towards Lisbon. It was the day when the crew were put through the weekly boat drill. Of course, the drill was for the passengers too, they needed to know what to do if there was an emergency. It was a pleasant breezy morning to be on the boat deck. It was interesting and exciting to watch the crew manipulate the ship's davits, to practise swinging out the ship's boats and lowering them into the sea. The boat drill was good entertainment and a lot of fun to take part in it. It was a day at sea they all enjoyed, strolling the deck, reclining on steamer chairs, watching the distant shoreline, or other vessels ploughing their way to some distant Port. Chatting to the other passengers, who all seemed to Robert to be a thoroughly good lot, he thought of the steam yacht *Hermes* sometime soon working her way through the same waters. He wondered what the voyage would be like in a vessel so much smaller than this huge comfortable steamer. In a boat like *Hermes,* he imagined, one might get badly thrown around in any kind of rough sea.

Valeria's prescription of a sea voyage was certainly borne out, Anna's transformation in such a short time was amazing. It was good to see her so relaxed, so absorbed in her entertainment of the moment that she could forget for a while the sadness of her mother's death and her oppressive concerns with Sergio. The following couple of days on board were much the same. Valeria had said that the sea air would do them all good, but for Anna it was not just the sea air but a constant round of social engagements and the assiduous company of her new friends. She had no time or energy for distressing inward thoughts. The pallor and lines of strain left her face and she smiled and laughed often.

Robert left her to it, got a book and relaxed in a steamer chair on the promenade deck. Valeria joined him and in her shockingly direct manner asked him a pointed question, "Is there someone special in your life Robert?"

What she was asking was obvious. He welcomed the chance to unburden his concerns and decided to be frank.

"Funny you ask. I've known several girls, but it didn't work with any of them. Recently I was seeing a lot of a particular girl, Sybil. She's the cousin of an old school friend. We spent a lot of time together. I thought she was nice, and I liked her a lot. But..."

"Something was missing?"

"Yes, but I had no idea until very recently. In fact, I was about to propose."

"But?"

"I didn't because I learnt I had seriously mistaken what she thought of me." It was a crucial moment in the conversation. He was encouraged by Valeria's openness and direct approach to tell her the whole dreadful story of how and why Sybil had rejected him.

"Hah!"

There was an uncharacteristic silence. "Hah! In that case Robert, I will tell you bluntly that you are better off without her! Forget her! She is unworthy of you. If this girl has just gone along with her family's silly prejudices, you are better off without her. What use to you is a woman who has no mind of her own."

He agreed completely.

"And I will tell you it is also much, much better to know it now rather than later. A lot better. You may not like me saying so, but to be blunt you are lucky to be rid of her."

"You are kind, Aunty Val." It was the first time he had called her that and he liked the sound of it.

"No, not kind, honest. I say it as it is. I can see it upsets you Robert, but you should think of it as a fortunate escape."

Robert felt the talk had done him a lot of good. The Sybil affair had preyed on his mind. Valeria had reacted much as how he had, with difficulty, tried to convince himself he should see the affair. To hear it put so forcefully and instinctively by Valeria did wonders for his battered self-esteem. A self-esteem battered a bit more, he was beginning to realise, by observing Anna amusing herself so happily with her new-found admirers. For a gang of them was always on hand. They would play deck quoits, stroll the deck, try cards in the lounge, sing songs at the piano, and so it went on.

*

That evening, the last night of their short voyage to Malta, Anna was again beset after dinner with her admirers. Although up to now the band had followed a traditional repertoire of Waltz and Polka, they had been asked to finish the evening with a 'modern' touch. So, the band moved into their version of the new 'ragtime', which caused a bit of flutter in the room and was not to the taste of some of the older passengers. Robert grabbed Anna's hand and took her onto the dance floor, and once there pulled her into a tight body-hugging 'bal-musette' hold. A hold he had learnt on his Paris trip, his hand low down firmly around her waist, drawing her close into his body.

"Anna, I hope you like modern dance."

"I do!"

"Good! Because this is modern dance Paris style."

"So, this is Paris style." she whispered confidentially into his ear, smiling.

She was quick at picking up the simple steps and they moved easily and fluently, both relishing the freedom of expression and enjoying the looseness of the movement, so much in contrast to the stiffness and formality of conventional dance. Robert sensed her initial surprise as his hold brought them so intimately together, but she did not try to repel him. Indeed, the opposite, she must like it because her hand tightened on his shoulder. Robert realized he liked the close physical contact. It was then that he could no longer see her as a sister, a dear and old friend to protect and cherish. It was the first time he really saw her in another new light, as a beautiful woman who was not just capable of expressing strong emotional passion but one who enjoyed, and would reciprocate, physical experience. But it was much more than that, what he could feel was not just that she liked the dance, but that she liked him. The dance was for him a transformative experience, he regretted it had taken him so long to understand what he felt about her, and what he sensed she felt about him. How could he have missed it? What a fool he had been not to understand it. His childhood playmate had become the light of his life and he had been too blind to see it. The dance ended and they returned slowly to the table.

"That was wonderful Anna!"

He meant it and would have liked to continue to dance, but she was swept away by another young man.

*

The following morning, steaming between the north coast of Tunisia and Malta, Robert was at the ship's rail gazing idly at the strange effects of the changing light on the sea. He was fascinated by the rolling, slowly churning waves, ever in motion, mysterious, deep. Now that they were nearing their destination his mind dwelt on the unknown quantities that lay ahead for them. Anna came up silently behind him and gently touched her hand on his arm. He felt it and turned; she must have deliberately escaped her many admirers to see him, not what he expected.

"Anna! I was just contemplating the wonders of the ocean."

"Valeria said you had taken a stroll. What is this about the sea?"

"Oh nothing, just words. But the sea is so amazing, isn't it? I was thinking about what was in store for us on this trip. And about my own future. I discovered I don't know the answer. Perhaps even the question. It's disturbing to be confused about something so important."

"How come? Aren't you going to be your father's partner in the firm? We've always thought it was settled."

"Maybe I will. I haven't made up my mind."

"Your father surely expects that?"

"Yes, he does. I know that. But the question is whether I want to be a suburban solicitor?"

"Why not? It is a good living."

"Yes, but money's not everything. I worry that one day I would find that I am a typical suburban solicitor, with a typical suburban solicitor's wife."

He had spoken his thought aloud, thinking of Sybil, who not long ago had seemed likely to become his typical suburban wife. Indeed, he had wished it so, had wanted such a suburban life. The change of mind was worrying; a life he had wanted to embrace only weeks ago he was now seriously doubting. So, what did he want?

"You don't want a wife?"

"It's not that. I would like to marry and have a family. Although it would mean that I had to change some of my interests."

"Like Paris?" The question came like a flash and was intimately whispered into his ear. It was deliberately nuanced and naughty, so closely echoing their heated argument about his Paris trip. He might in other circumstances have been irritated that she chose to tease him like this. But after that dance his recent conversation with Valeria he recognized that Anna was playing with him. He knew from her voice, the way she gently held his arm as she spoke and the sly sideways glance that she was not playing with him like a cat with her victim. It was a tease, but one done with affection.

"If I had a wife, I would not even want to think of it." He looked into her laughing eyes as he whispered it with a broad smile on his face. He had meant "If you were my wife."

"But surely if Paris was so good, you would want to do it again?" She gave him an intense searching look. He knew what she was getting at.

"Things have changed. Changed completely. You see I learnt a lot in Paris, a lot about life .... and I learned a lot about women." He said the last words quietly with a half-smile. He wondered how she would she take it. She took it silently, did not respond.

"And Anna I can't imagine now that Paris would ever hold any ..."

"Robbie, I didn't mean to pry!"

"You're not prying Anna. I'm glad for someone to talk to. Meeting you again made me realise that I've been without anyone to talk to, I mean to really talk to. I remember in the old days we used to talk such a lot."

"We did."

He looked into her eyes. "That's why I'm so pleased we both came on this journey." He touched her gently on the arm which she answered with a little nudge on his.

"Actually, Robbie I'm also pleased we came!" She returned his gaze, looking at him straight in the eyes. There was a moment of intense intimacy in which he felt he was looking straight into her soul. He knew then at that moment that he loved her and was sure she felt the same.

There was another pause before he answered. "But not half as much as I am!"

Then he whispered into her ear. "Otherwise, I would not have got to know you again. And that is the best thing I have ever done!"

If it had not been a very public place, and if there had not been passengers around who believed they were brother and sister and might be scandalised, he would have taken her in his arms, embraced her closely and kissed her fully on the lips. He sensed that she knew that. He also sensed also that she had expected him to do so regardless of the circumstances and was disappointed at the non-event. She was bolder than he thought. But the moment passed; his own reticence had been overtaken by the arrival of other passengers and he kicked himself for his lack of resolve.

14

They reached Malta later that day and, together with only a handful of other passengers travelling on Colonial Office business, they disembarked onto a launch. For Robert and Valeria, it was just a matter of leaving the ship. But for Anna it was more complicated; there were scenes on deck of tearful farewell with the young men she had got to know since they sailed from Liverpool. Including an Indian prince who pressed her to visit his family.

Robert had already pre-booked rooms in a hotel near the Grand Harbour and enjoying splendid views over it. On arrival he checked the sailing times to Tripoli and found that they had two days in Malta before their boat sailed. He suggested that they take the chance to enjoy the sights of the Island. Valeria was an inexhaustible tourist and quickly organised guided visits to all the main sights.

"This City is fascinating," she announced back at the hotel after a lengthy afternoon tour. "And such an interesting history for one small island. Such a mixture of people and cultures. So many different influences. I really like it."

Robert agreed, he had noticed with interest the blending of people and traditions.

At reception he was given a telegram from Hugo at the Foreign Office in London. It was a harsh reminder of the real world, and particularly that they were in Malta for a purpose. Following the secret code he had agreed with Hugo in the Foreign Office, the telegram meant that 'Bird', a code for the Steam Yacht *Hermes,* had not yet sailed. Given so, Robert thought that the best thing was for them to proceed to Tripoli and get the Sergio business done as quickly as possible.

*

Unlike the modern, spacious, and well fitted vessel in which they had sailed from Liverpool, the coastal steamer to Tripoli was cramped, dirty, distinctly past its best days and uncomfortable. Moreover, their cabins were tiny, the public rooms poorly furnished and the standard of service decidedly patchy.

"This," Valeria commented bitterly, "is what we must expect from now on. We are leaving the civilised world. We may indeed have to experience a slight touch of Hell for a week or so when we're in Tripoli. But it will make home seem all the better when we return."

The journey to Tripoli took the best part of two days. The old steamer had a leisurely pace of its own and anyway had to call at Tunis. Soon after sailing from Valletta in Malta, Valeria made for a deck chair in a shaded part of the main deck and stayed there. Anna and Robert stood for a while at the ship's rail, gazing at the water, watching Malta fade into the horizon. They strolled the deck, fascinated by the diversity of their many fellow passengers. Europeans of all sorts: they could hear French and Italian in the various conversations but also other tongues they couldn't discern. There were Arabs, some in European dress and some in traditional dress. He had heard that there was a historic Jewish population in North Africa and identified, by their distinctive garb and headdress, a small group of Jewish passengers engrossed in discussion in a strange tongue.

On the second day at sea, with Tunis now left well behind them, the steamer was still hugging the uninteresting far-off coast of north Africa. Then Robert heard one of the passengers say in French that they were now sailing in the waters of the Turkish province of Tripolitania. This was the

Turkish province that ran eastwards from the border with Tunisia, then past Tripoli to the Gulf of Sidra. Beyond Tripolitania was the Turkish province of Cyrenaica, which bordered Egypt hundreds of miles to the east. To the south of Tripoli lay the Turkish province of Fezzan and the great Sahara Desert, vast lawless areas with a long history of insurgency and no effective government control since Roman times. The sheer size of Libya was hard to grasp. Robert felt a tingle in his blood that they were so close to their destination, a sense of apprehension that what up to then had been mere speculation was about to become reality. What indeed should he expect in Tripoli? He had no real idea. The Foreign Office had described Tripoli as an 'uninteresting and boring oasis, dirty, run down, devoid of any interesting architecture and surrounded by encroaching desert'. In other words, a hole. Another reason, then, why the visit should only be long enough to meet and talk to Sergio.

The steamer chugged slowly towards the city of Tripoli, staying parallel to the coast. Although it was not yet anywhere near high summer, in England only a pleasantly warm Spring, here the sun shone relentlessly bright. The air became disagreeably hot from a cloudless sky, forcing him to screw up his eyes, and blanching his view of the distant coast, the powerful heat making it hazy and throwing it out of focus. He recalled being forewarned by people in the Army and Navy Stores, where he had equipped himself for the trip, what to expect:

> "What you will find, Mr Strange, is an extremely hot semi-arid climate, where the summer months are always long, unbearably hot and very dry, while the winter months are slightly wet and warm."

Anna came out of the saloon, and he showed her the distant sight of the approaching land. As their course drew closer to the shore, he saw a long coastline that was largely a monotonous, repetitive stretch of variegated shades of yellowish-brown sand. This was broken here and there by the green and yellow-brown splashes of colour formed by the groups of palm trees that dotted the shoreline. But above all what stood out was the sea itself, that from where he stood on the ship was a deep, dark ultramarine, but closer to the shore became a fantastic blend of variegated greenish and bluish shades of translucent turquoise. Then as they got really close to Tripoli, they passed a long, drawn-out succession of rocky islets and jagged reefs, stretching out eleven miles from the harbour. It became clear that these formed an extensive rocky chain running out from the peninsula on which the city of Tripoli stood. They formed the outline of what had gradually become the much-silted harbour.

Even though the city was the centre of Turkish administration for the province of Libya, so far had the commercial condition of Tripoli fallen that the poor state of the harbour meant that any sizable ship had to anchor in the inner roads about a quarter of a mile from the City pier. So, well short of the pier Robert's party had to disembark from the steamer into small boats to be transferred to land. The scene there was all rather chaotic, but once on the pier he had his first close view of the City of Tripoli itself, a long white semi-circle of buildings looking out onto the harbour. The city seemed a haphazard network of largely single-story rectangular buildings, a sea of flat housetops broken by the upward thrust of many gleaming white, slender green-capped minarets, their gilded tops glinting in the sun. The walls of the buildings glowed in the powerful light of the Sun and the shadows it cast were black, hard, and strongly defined. But there were also occasional green gardens, and groups of palm trees, to break up the overpowering whiteness of the buildings. And beyond a palm fringe outside the city were the ever present reddish yellow dunes of drift sand blown in from the desert.

In the centre of the harbour front was the substantial reddish-brown structure of the fortress that the Spanish had built when Tripoli was briefly theirs in the sixteenth century. From the fortress flew the Sultan's huge red banner with the white crescent and star, the first time that Robert had seen it. It must mark the building that was the centre of the Turkish administration. A fringe of Palm trees disappeared to the east of the city. The whole scene was set behind the deep blues and turquoise of the sea. Tripoli hypnotised him with its brilliant display of light; the whiteness of its haphazard outgrowth of square, flat, rooftops and buildings seemed extreme, all bathed in dazzling, blinding sunlight.

Anna crept up to him. "Robbie, it's captivating! A whitewashed city oasis shimmering behind a transparent screen. It's fantastic. My first sight of the Orient. Unreal."

"Anna don't be fooled. It's just the heat that makes it look captivating," Valeria observed caustically. "From here it may well look captivating, but up close it will not be so attractive. Seeing it from this distance means you can't see the dirt or the flies. But the heat's real enough. What you call a transparent screen are the heat waves. We are fortunate to have arrived well before the real summer even begins. If it was July, you would really know all about the misery of the heat."

Robert agreed with Anna, it might be hot, but for him it was a wonderful sight: the Orient with all its mystery and history.

Anticipating their forthcoming encounter with Sergio he told Anna and Valeria he had gleaned some information from his guidebook about the 'Banco Di Roma' in Tripoli, where Sergio worked. The Bank was founded in Rome in 1880, soon opened branches throughout Italy and then opened foreign branches including Tripoli in 1907. The book said:

> *The policy was to create an increasing Italian presence that would eventually absorb Libya into Italy without the use of force.*

"There you have it," Robert said. "The aim is to achieve Italian colonisation by stealth and economic domination. But what does Turkey make of it?"

"More to the point, what they can do about it?" Anna replied. "Just look around you, they haven't the resources to resist."

What had at first seemed the quaint oriental charm of the place somewhat paled when, once on the pier, they were quickly pestered by huge swarms of flies against whom there were no real defences.

"Get used to it!" Valeria told Anna. "This is how it is."

However, they were pleased to be able to pass without ado through the dogama, or Turkish customs house. The customs officials appeared bored and indifferent, were not much interested in them or their luggage and asked no questions. They had each acquired Turkish 'Permis de Voyage' that would permit them to stay in Tripoli for a short time. But as their intended business could take longer, they would soon need to apply for official passport visas. Departing from the dogama, and pestered by myriad insects, they left the pier and passed the office of the Eastern Telegraph Company on the quay, part of the vast network of modern communications that made this oriental outpost only minutes away from London. From the quay they could now better see the old town of Tripoli, a rough pentagon enclosed by the mouldering, but still impressive sandstone city wall originally built by the Spaniards centuries before, still forty feet high in places. A host of decrepit looking Arab cafes lined the immediate quayside, but further down were the British and United States Consulates and the steamboat offices for Societa Nazionale, the German Lemit Line and the Compania de Navigation Mixte. Near the harbour was a Christian quarter, to its west the Jewish quarter, to the southeast quarter was the Muslim quarter and the main business streets, which, unlike the rest of the city, were paved and lit at night.

He looked forward to visiting what Baedeker described as the principal points of interest in the city. Baedeker said there were some. So, it was not true, as he had been told in London, that Tripoli was devoid of any interesting architecture. Baedeker spoke of the renowned Moorish baths and the fascinations of the true heart of Tripoli, the ancient walled Medina or Old City:

> *"... with its many covered ally ways, a captivating, exotic and bustling mix of narrow alleys, ornate doorways, elaborate mosques, various souks, or markets and intoxicating rich sugar and spice aromas."*

Then there was the reddish-brown structure that Baedeker described as the Serai, the fortress, an impressive building that had once been the Spanish citadel, that now housed a complex of barracks, Courts, prisons, and Turkish Government offices.

They made their way from the quay, with a string of porters following with their luggage, and set up residence in the Minerva Hotel, accommodation arranged for them at Hugo's request by Tom O'Brien, the British consul in Tripoli.

The Hotel was an interesting old building, with a Maltese owner who greeted them warmly and was delighted to find that two of his guests spoke Italian. The building was constructed in the Arab manner with an entirely plain exterior wall to the street, within which was found a spacious inner courtyard designed to capture as little heat but as much light as possible. This inner courtyard was surrounded by a balcony supported on stone pillars. Rooms led off from both the courtyard and the balcony. The courtyard was dotted with Palms and other plants growing in large terracotta and marble containers, interspersed with which were some tables and chairs. It all presented a pleasant, shaded, and relatively tranquil ambiance, much in contrast to the business of the city in the heat and dust outside. The proprietor provided them with two large adjoining rooms that led off the balcony on the first floor and looked out onto the inner courtyard. Robert noticed that their windows were shuttered and had fine lace curtains.

"That's to keep out the flies," Valeria explained. "In climates like this the flies are simply terrible. As you have already experienced, they are an awful pest, much worse, unbearable, when the heat really gets going in a month or two. Especially as you can see, the people just throw their rubbish into the street. And it just stays there and festers. It probably isn't too bad now because we're here well before summer. I'm told that the fly and rubbish menace is insufferable in high summer. You can imagine. The flies swarm everywhere in immense numbers and are both persistent and aggressive."

That evening, welcoming the dramatic drop in temperature and pleasant relative coolness of the air after the sun went down, all three of them left the Hotel and walked along the harbour front. They had of course to do battle with the swirling insects of the evening but also witnessed for the first time the astonishing spectacle of the Libyan sunset. The sky gradually transfusing into a bleeding blue, with the orange glow of the dying Sun seeping throughout the horizon, matching the orange and brown of the desert as it sank out of sight. It was a terrific, awesome, display of the power and beauty of nature.

The following day Robert and Anna visited Tom O'Brien, the British consul, a shipping agent whose office faced the harbour near the Hotel. Thomas Damian O'Brien had been a shipping agent in Tripoli for some years. An Irishman in his fifties originally from the southwest of Ireland, he had as a boy gone to sea in a Tramp steamer that happened to have called at Cork. He had never returned to Ireland, travelling widely but especially in the Mediterranean, where over time he had built a formidable range of shipping contacts and friendships. Eventually he had found his own special niche in the shipping agency business and a place in his present enterprise, which was now his alone. As they entered his office he rose from behind a large wooden desk and greeted Robert and Anna warmly, taking Robert's hand in a strong firm handshake, and Anna's hand in her turn in a rather more delicate hold.

"Welcome to Tripoli! Our oasis on the edge of the desert! I'm Tom O'Brien. Hugo Cavendish in London wired me to expect you."

He was sturdily built and wore an extremely crumpled and somewhat dirty linen suit, that might once have been pale beige. Underneath was a distinctly off-white shirt, it's top two buttons unfastened, and a loosened somewhat bedraggled bluish tie that hung loose well down his shirt. The most distinctive thing about him though was his happy, round, tanned face, discernibly flushed beneath what had become his permanently dark complexion. Then one saw his large hazel eyes, a small surprisingly neat nose, and ears that by contrast were at once noticeable because they were disproportionately large.

"You find the Hotel to your liking? The owner is a good friend so you should have no trouble. It should be all right for you but in fact there is little choice."

He went on to say that although he didn't know Sergio personally, he recollected him from various commercial transactions involving the Banco Di Roma and had seen Sergio at work in the Bank. Robert explained they had Permis de Voyage but would need to stay longer than a couple of days. O'Brien offered to contact the Turkish authorities and apply for passport visas for permission for a longer stay. He told Robert that they would certainly get a visit from a Turkish official.

"The Turkish authorities are not used to visits by British travellers. They will be curious, probably suspicious of your group. An Englishman and two women of Italian descent will be seen as very odd. Enough in itself to draw attention. Moreover, they know your trip concerns the Banco di Roma, a business that they certainly associate with the expansionist policy of the Italian Government."

"What are the Turks like to deal with?" Robert asked.

"The Turks? There's been a big change. They sent another man from Constantinople, one of the new lot there, the 'Young Turks' they're called. He's well educated, speaks good English and is sharp. Don't try and fool him, you won't succeed. I've found him fine provided that you're straight with him."

This was not the kind of Turkish official that the Foreign Office had led him to expect. Educated, speaks English and sharp.

"Not how the FO described the Turks."

"No? Well London is as usual well behind the times. They probably know next to nothing about the situation in Libya. But I'm sure you will find out the position for yourself."

*

As they had travelled all the way to Tripoli to talk to Sergio, Robert wanted to contact him without delay. So, with the help of one of O'Brien's clerks acting as their guide, he, Anna, and Valeria set out towards Sergio's house in a new development of Italian villas just outside the old walls. It was a walk that involved once again doing battle with the buzzing hordes of flies that beset the confusing maze of narrow streets and alleys of the old City. They passed a multitude of one and two-story Arab houses, built for the most part of sun-dried bricks and palm wood rafters, and covered in whitewash. Moreover, the narrowness of the alleys meant that they had no choice but to retreat into a nearby doorway from time to time to avoid an oncoming heavily burdened camel. But there were many unexpected delights, such as glimpsing through an open doorway the sight of an Arab weaving an intricate fabric on his loom. Anna pointed out the houses whose doorways were made of columns that had obviously come from a Roman ruin. Indeed, they noticed many bits and pieces of ancient buildings re-used for the modern city.

But their trip proved to be in vain. They discovered on eventually reaching Sergio's house that he was not at home. The door was answered by an Arab house servant who told them in Italian that Sergio was away. In response to Valeria's questions, he was unable to say to where his master had travelled, or for how long he proposed to be away.

They returned to O'Brien's office feeling despondent. O'Brien, though, would have none of it. "The Banca's staff," he said, "often take trips back to Italy. Your man will be back. Meanwhile, you must see the souks! The markets. They are like nothing you have ever seen before in Europe. But first I will myself show you a special place we call 'The Café'. You'll find it a good place to go."

They walked along the waterfront towards the ancient citadel built when Tripoli had been a Spanish possession. It was still an impressive, powerful edifice, the dark shadow of the old castle walls threw itself down and across the ground framing the reddish-brown walls bathed in bright sunlight.

"You can just imagine," O'Brien commented, "how those old castle walls hide so many stories of intrigue, romance and bloodshed, especially bloodshed. Remember that for centuries Tripoli was a pirate base. Ships used to sail from here to harass merchant shipping in the Med. They were chiefly interested in capturing slaves, especially European slaves. The slave trade used to be big business."

Just to the east, under the walls of the citadel itself, and bordering the sea lay the gardens of the Turkish 'Army and Navy Club.'

"This is what we call 'The Café'," O'Brien observed. "It is something of a social rendezvous for the foreign community here. A good place to meet people, talk over a Turkish coffee and hear the latest gossip. An ideal place to be when the shadow of the castle walls casts itself across the garden and then creeps away across that sandy space, which it where they hold the Tuesday market. I will introduce you so that you can return on your own while you are here in Tripoli. Let us go in and have something to drink. But remember this is a Muslim country and 'The Café' is connected to the Turkish authorities so you will not get alcohol."

They went in and sat down at a table in the shade and Tom ordered lime juice.

"How do you find living in Tripoli?" Anna inquired.

"For me it is good," Tom answered. "Once you get to know them and understand their ways of doing things, the Ottoman authorities are easy going."

*

The next morning, Anna awoke early and looked out of the Hotel to see the rose-flush of the approaching dawn. Then many hours before the Sun was at its zenith, the three of them, for Valeria had decided she would join them, went with O'Brien's clerk to tour the Souks, Tripoli's markets. In some streets business was carried out from what looked like nothing more than a hole in the wall of a house, outside which the proprietor sat cross-legged, fanning the pestilential flies, and hoping to be approached by a potential buyer. What was displayed by some shops to entice customers was fascinating. Brilliant displays of burnished brass and copper vessels, hanging lamps, ebony boxes, handsome leather cases and saddle bags, carefully worked leather goods of all kinds, silks, cottons and embroidered fabrics. So much colour and variety, all accompanied by the continual sound of the shuffling feet of the moving, swirling mass of people, and the insistent cries of the vendors. In another part of the Souk, they came across arcades under which were laid out a profusion of beautiful carpets and rugs, that O'Brien's clerk told them came from such exotic places as Persia, Afghanistan, or Samarkand.

In the produce quarter they saw, and above all smelt, the huge variety of spices heaped up in great mounds. The multitude of powerful aromas was intoxicating. They also saw the piles of grain, melons and tomatoes that created gorgeous splashes of colour under the dark violet shadow of the Souk. The displays of goods in the Souk were themselves exotic, but perhaps more so was the great variety of people who frequented it. Townspeople in coloured, striped gandouras, Arabs from the desert in their long, loose fitted djellabas, now they saw too Hausas from beyond the Sahara, wealthy Moors with richly embroidered kaftans, Algerians in hooded burnous. and indeed, the occasional European mixing with the local Arab population.

Robert had been promised that they would encounter a multitude of fascinating sights in the Souks, and indeed the promise was wonderfully fulfilled. But he had also been repeatedly warned that they would be appalled and disgusted at the amount of filth and rubbish that was simply allowed to gather and fester in the streets and public places, as if it didn't matter and was no-one's responsibility. Certainly, no-one seemed to care, far less take responsibility, for there was all too clearly a general attitude of indifference. It was all too obvious that the Turkish authorities were content to let it fester. But the quantities of uncleared rubbish clearly did matter, they were a major health hazard because the swarming flies and insects were simply left to multiply in vast numbers.

"What a filthy place!" Valeria declared. "I've seen some dirt in my time in Naples, but this as you say takes the cake."

The old City was indeed so disgustingly dirty, polluted by garbage and refuse to such an extent that it must be a dangerously unhealthy place to live. It reminded Anna of the stories of the great slum that was a large part of London in the time of Charles Dickens. The disgraceful, miserable warrens in which the poor lived that had so infuriated Albert, the Prince Consort. But in London those stories had prodded reform and a proper system of Public Health. Here, in Tripoli, well into the twentieth century there was no sign that the need to change was recognised in any way.

"The whole City could be wiped out by a disease like typhus," Anna told them.

"I'm sure you'll find that disease is a regular occurrence," Valeria replied bitterly.

Robert was disturbed not only to see the streets left so unkempt, abandoned to the stink and danger of such ubiquitous filth, but by the evident failure of the City authorities to do anything to clean it up. The abandonment of the streets to such garbage seemed to demonstrate what he had been told in London about the hopeless inadequacy of Ottoman administration. However, when he repeated his critical thoughts to O'Brien later, he got a stinging response.

"You're right," O'Brien said, "the streets here are filthy, and the Ottomans do just leave it like that. But be careful who you condemn. Is Lagos in Nigeria much better, or Calcutta, or the shanty towns around Jo'burg? Or most of the big cities in the British Empire? We all have a lot to learn about how we keep our cities!"

15

That evening they strolled along the harbour front to witness again the fantastic display of orange, red, purple, and yellow as the setting sun once again merged sky, city, and sea in an other-worldly experience. Now, as the clear dry air allowed the worst of the heat of the day to escape, they returned to the hotel to sit in the relative cool of its spacious courtyard, strewn in the Arab style with palms and flowering shrubs in big terracotta urns.

And it was in the hotel they received the expected visit from the Ottoman authorities about their visa applications. A squad of four Turkish soldiers and a corporal pushed their way roughly into the hotel courtyard. Robert thought it expedient to stand up to deal with them, but with a dismissive flick of his wrist the corporal motioned him brusquely to stay where he was. Robert obeyed; he had heard stories about the unpredictable behaviour of the Turkish military. He was struck by the poor condition of the soldiers' uniforms; dirty, unkempt, and clearly made of cheap shoddy material often held together with rough-and-ready patching. They offered a telling image of the reduced resources of the Turkish military, and probably the bankrupt state of this distant province of the once mighty Ottoman Empire, a State that according to the Foreign Office was now rotten to the core. Moreover, the soldiers then just slouched or sat by the side wall and lent their rifles casually against it. A poor impression indeed of the Ottoman army, although Robert did notice they were equipped with modern Mauser rifles. Robert wondered how such an apparently ramshackle, slovenly force would face a well-trained and disciplined European army. Then, however, the Turkish officer arrived, escorted by a somewhat cringing Maltese hotel proprietor, and the corporal straightened up and brought the squad to a ragged order, standing with grounded arms in a somewhat uneven line. However, a quick word of command from the officer brought them into line before he then ordered his corporal to stand them down.

The contrast between the soldiers and their young, good-looking officer could not have been stronger. Smartly turned out in a clean, tailored, white cotton-canvas short jacket with chest level buttoned pockets, his shoulder boards displayed a gold disk-shaped insignia and two stars designating his rank. His boots were highly polished and on his head was a kalpak, a khaki lamb-wool hat. On his leather belt, whose gilt buckle carried the Ottoman crescent, was a leather holster. Of medium height he had a pleasant open face, black hair, dark olive skin and a well-trimmed moustache. But it was the eyes that stood out, for although dark they were quite brilliant, alert and piercing. His manner from the first had conveyed not merely military authority but a sense of personal superiority, and he therefore surprised Robert by striding across the courtyard towards them and, with a smile, introduced himself in good fluent English.

"Allow me to introduce myself. I am Mustafa Ersoy, an officer in the service of the Sultan. I hold the rank of Yuzbashi, you would say Captain, in the Sultan's Army. I am presently attached to the Governor's staff."

Mustafa wasted little time on the actual reason for his visit, checking the formalities of Robert's brief visit to Sergio, asking various questions, and just listening with a blank face to Robert's explanation for the visit. Valeria, who was observing the conversation from not far away, afterwards told Robert that it was clear to her that Mustafa had not in fact believed a word about the supposed land transaction that was Robert's long-winded excuse for visiting Tripoli.

If Mustafa was a sample of a new self-assured, modern, Turkey, it was not hard to see that there could be trouble ahead with the old Imperial European powers. Yet glancing beyond Mustafa to his five soldiers, it was easy to see the dichotomy; Mustafa's men in their worn-out uniforms were now slouching untidily against the far wall, smoking cheap cigarettes, or squatting on the stone floor and rolling dice, figures of such evident proof of the realities of Turkish decadence. It was hard to see how a handful of people like Mustafa were going to be able to build their bright, new, enlightened, modern Turkish state. But if they did, the world would be in for a shock.

Tom O'Brien looked in on his way back to his office. "How did you find the Turkish Captain?" he asked.

"Pleasant and efficient," Robert said. "He talked a lot about how things have improved after the change of government in Constantinople."

"Ah the Committee for Union and Progress," Tom remarked. "Mustafa is one of the new people they have sent out from Constantinople to improve the way things are done. He has the ear of Constantinople, and the new Government. What did you make of him?"

"We were impressed," Anna replied. "Intelligent, good looking and very agreeable. Not what we had been led in London to expect from an Ottoman official."

"No, I'm sure! But understand that what they may have told you in London is probably accurate enough for almost every other Ottoman official. Mustafa is the exception. You are fortunate that he chose to handle your application. And was moved to concede it. The others might have refused outright and certainly expected a bribe. Despite all the ballyhoo from the new government in Constantimople, that is still the normal way of getting things from the Ottoman authorities."

*

Contrary to what they had been told in the Banco di Roma, only two days later O'Brien heard on his grape vine that Sergio had returned from Rome. O'Brien sent a message to Robert, who joined by Anna and Valeria, decided to waste no time in visiting Sergio's house. That was after all why they had made the long journey to Tripoli, although they did not expect the visit to be welcome.

With the help of a guide provided by the hotel they walked again through the Old City to Sergio's villa. It was a pretty, modern, residence in a distinctively Italian taste, that made no concessions to its Arab environment. Entering through a solid front door, they were shown through a small courtyard and then into a large rectangular reception room. Its whitewashed walls were hung with a selection of oil paintings. Some were typical Italian scenes, but the long wall facing the French windows that opened onto the covered terrace was dominated by large portraits of Giuseppe Mazzini and Giuseppe Garibaldi, two of the makers of modern Italy. On either side of the French windows and between them were various marble busts of Roman emperors. Nor, on one of the shorter end walls, could one miss the large gilt framed map of the old Roman Empire, embracing the whole of the Mediterranean and hung symbolically beneath an Italian tricolour. Around the walls were placed some substantial pieces of dark furniture, including an elaborate escritoire and an impressive mahogany armoire. The centre of the room was filled with sofas, small tables, and chairs. The terracotta tiled floor was scattered with fine Persian rugs.

"It's a nice room spoiled by its contents," Anna whispered. "All this Roman stuff, it's all about building a new Italian empire, trying to dig up the past. He's obsessed with the idea. It won't work and it's not the path that Italy should take. I'm afraid that it all will end in tears."

Sergio came to them in his own time. Although he greeted them politely, the look on his face indicated his disbelief that they had bothered to make the long journey from London. He was not a good-looking young man; too obviously overweight, with a head that was too big placed on a neck that was too thick. Robert guessed he was about 35, although he could easily pass for ten years older, of less than average height and build with long oiled black hair combed back from his forehead. His dark eyes shone out from behind a pair of steel spectacles. His skin was sallow, and he had a tightly trimmed moustache. He was wearing a pale linen suit, with a white shirt and bluish patterned tie. He had polished brown shoes. His whole appearance seemed to reflect a desire to look smart that didn't quite come off. Instead, he did rather fit Robert's pre-conceived image: Sergio the seedy villain, the disreputable conspirator, the deceitful cad.

"I had not expected this visit," Sergio said as he embraced Anna in a decidedly unenthusiastic, cold, welcome.

"Oh! Surely you have," Anna replied calmly, introducing Robert as her family's lawyer and Valeria as her mother's cousin acting as a chaperone. Sergio nodded without comment.

Robert reminded Sergio, through Anna, that he had sent both a letter and a telegram explaining the purpose of their visit. He also explained that Anna had agreed to act as his interpreter as he had no Italian.

"Ah, I received the letter and the telegram," Sergio said in Italian. "But I replied to say that a visit was unnecessary. We should deal with any problems about my cousin's estate by letter."

"My father and I insisted on a personal visit," Anna intervened.

"Really?" Sergio replied with an air of bored disinterest, "then indeed let us be seated." He signalled to an Arab servant to bring refreshments and indicated a sofa for Robert and Anna and an armchair for Valeria, while he took a throne-like chair facing them on the other side of the room. It was a formal and distanced setting: he clearly did not intend a cosy family chat.

"As you know from my letter," Robert said through Anna, "I have a question concerning Maria Gibson's Will. It concerns some family property in Italy."

Sergio nodded.

Anna leaned forward towards Sergio. "However, I should tell you that Robert has seen all the secret letters you wrote to my mother." She spoke first in English, deliberately and carefully emphasized the words 'all' and 'secret'.

Sergio flushed with indignation and began a barrage of words. His heated response in Italian and the agitated gestures that went with it showed his annoyance. Sergio was obviously startled that she had begun the meeting so much to the point, without any of the normal opening pleasantries. Robert hoped this had thrown Sergio off guard, so that he would talk more openly.

"They were private letters!" Sergio shouted, and Robert asked Valeria to give him a running commentary in English. "Private letters to my cousin. It is an outrage, for you a stranger, to read them. An insult to good manners."

"Don't be such a fool!" Anna continued. "He has read the letters and so have the Police and the British government. Your shameful underhand trickery is revealed."

Sergio stood up. "No!" he shouted, "You're wrong. Everything I did was done for Italy and is sacred. Absolutely sacred!"

"Sacred nothing! You blaspheme. Murdering my mother was the devil's work and you dare to call it holy. How dare you. You murdered my mother."

Sergio remained standing, staring angrily, moodily, sullen and hostile.

Valeria jolted him back into action by standing up herself. She denounced him loudly as if they were common fishwives in the marketplace. "You are nothing but a diseased cur! A disgrace to our family. A dirty stain on the reputation of our Italy. A shame that has no useful place in our lives." It went on like that for some minutes and although Robert could not understand a word of the Italian, it sounded magnificent and the gist of it was all too clear.

Anna took up the verbal assault on Sergio, who appeared to have been cowed by Valeria's attack.

"You lured my mother into your plan. And then you had her murdered. That is the truth isn't it." Valeria resumed the summary translation for Robert's benefit.

Sergio sat silent and glowering as Anna continued to yell at him. But then he just slumped back in his chair and there were tears in his eyes.

"It was not meant to happen. Your mother. But I had nothing to do with it. Look, on the cross I swear it. (He touched the small gold crucifix around his neck). I was angry when they told me what they had done to her. But I could do nothing. It was too late. I was angry with them, and I am sorry about your mother. I believe she was a good woman. And she did help me. And therefore, she helped Italy. I do grieve for her."

Robert was inclined to take Sergio's unexpected display of contrition at face value. But if it was true the implications were hugely significant: what went on in London and Sergio's plan for *Hermes* was no longer under his control.

"So," Anna asked quietly, "if my mother helped you why was she killed?"

"They told me she would help them no further."

"They? And who is 'they'? "Anna asked, "was there someone in London helping to organise your plan?"

"Yes of course! How can I run anything in London from here?"

"And before that did someone come to you here in Tripoli to discuss your plan?"

"Yes. People came to me here. They said they had heard rumours of my plan for Italy to invade Tripoli."

"People came here?"

"Yes, they travelled from Paris, although they weren't French. We talked in French. Since you ask, it was they who suggested the ship should be bought in England and I should ask a relative in London to help about the transfer of money."

"Why were they helping you?"

"They said they wanted to support Italy."

"You wrote to my mother about buying a ship?"

"You are interested in the ship? I thought something small like a fishing boat would do."

"That is ridiculous!" Anna yelled. "a stupid thing to say. My mother received a fortune in gold to buy the ship. And it wasn't to be a small fishing boat."

Sergio was looking more and more miserable. Robert was sure it was not an act. Sergio actually didn't know how his plan was being carried out by his 'friends' in London.

"Look Sergio!" Anna said, "we know everything about your plan. We know the ship that was bought, where it is now, how it is being refitted, when she will sail, about the gold that will be put on board, the weapons that will be purchased. We know everything." She paused to see the effect her words had achieved. "And everything we know the British government also knows. And they will stop your plan. It cannot succeed."

"Hah! So, you say. I don't believe you," Sergio snarled back at her; but the doubt was in his eyes.

"Then understand also that Rome has been fully informed about your plan. Rome does not support you. Rome does not want any part of your stupid scheme."

"So, you say!" The response was quick enough, but his hand was shaking, and he looked unsure of his ground.

"I do say so! The British government has spoken to Rome. Rome does not support your plan. Why else do you think we are here? Do you think we would come here without Rome's approval?" A glib lie but it had cut to the quick because it was influencing Sergio, who sat still now looking uncertain, anxiously fumbling with his fingers.

Valeria confronted Sergio face to face, screaming at him.

"Understand that if I inform the Turkish authorities about your plan, they will arrest you and throw you into one of their stinking goals. You know that means torture. They will make an example of you. No one will raise a finger to defend you. Rome will wash its hands of you. They will let you be thrown to the wolves. And you will deserve everything you get."

There was silence again, and Valeria asked, "are you afraid?"

She repeated the question louder. To his continuing silence she repeated, "You should be afraid."

Sergio tried to pull himself together. "You are all deluded!"

"No, it is you who is deluded. You should be afraid given the hornet's nest you are stirring for yourself."

There was a silence.

"How much have they told you, Sergio. Your friends in London? The name of the ship they bought?"

Sergio stared resentfully. "You are ridiculous, I don't need to know such details."

"Or what they paid for her?"

"Another useless detail."

"Sergio, they paid about twenty thousand pounds in gold. I know you didn't' have such money. Who did?"

"It was sent in my name."

"Not good enough. Sergio other people are running your plan for their own ends."

"No! They do it for me!"

"How can you say that when you hardly know them or anything they do?"

Continued silence from Sergio who was looking uncomfortable, unsure how to deal with his visitors. It was transparent that Sergio knew little of what was going on about *Hermes*. Someone had taken over the rough plan that Sergio had described in his letters to Maria Gibson. In which case there would no point in trying to persuade Sergio to denounce the plan. He was no longer in control of it. He looked rather a pathetic figure, an idealist nationalist dreamer whose plan for the conquest of Libya had been somehow stolen from him. But there were questions about her mother's murder that Anna was determined to resolve.

"You murdered my mother. The Turks will execute you for it!"

"Murder? I told you. I don't know about that. I was not involved."

"Sergio!" Anna shouted, "how dare you say you were not involved. We know about how the Carbonari were used. It is stupid to deny you are involved."

"I did not ask for her to be killed."

"No? Then who did?"

"I can't say! I did not ask them to kill your mother. She was just asked to handle the money, nothing more. I had nothing to do with killing her."

"Who then?"

"It was not me!"

"Sergio, you persuaded her to betray her own family. She would not do that freely. What hold did you have on her?"

"None."

"That is nonsense. I know my mother would not do what you wanted without some threat, blackmail. What was it that you used?"

"I used none."

"That is untrue! And I will not leave until you tell me."

"Your being here makes me afraid. You should leave."

"Good! You should be afraid. We will go when you answer our questions."

"You don't understand! Go! You will get us all killed."

"We will leave when you answer."

Robert could sense that Sergio was wavering. Sergio was looking like a cornered rat and Anna renewed the fray.

"My mother," she said, "would not freely engage in your secret, underhand dirty conspiracy. How did you persuade her? What threat did you use?"

There was silence.

"Understand this! I will denounce you to all our family. I will destroy your name. I will go to the Banco here in Tripoli and will denounce you at the top of my voice."

Silence.

"Sergio," Anna yelled at him, "I will not stop until you answer me!"

"When we've finished with you," Valeria screamed at him, "you will have no friends and no job. Your life will be destroyed. They will hate you here in Tripoli and they will despise you in Italy."

She used not just words but body language. Robert could see the effects on Sergio in his face. It did not take much more for him to crack. The shouting, strident nationalist advocate became a pathetic, cringing confessor of his sins, pleading for forgiveness from his accusers. He admitted he had by chance found details of how Maria's father had been convicted of petty theft at the age of 16 and sent to prison, although later released. He had told Maria that if he made the news public it would bring shame on her, her husband, and her family. He had insisted that she co-operate with him in return for his silence.

Valeria strode across the room and struck Sergio hard on the face with the flat of her hand. A powerful slap that reverberated around the room. She did it again.

"Bastardo!"

This one too made him reel. She then stood over him and screamed further unbridled torrid abuse at him in powerful street language. It took a while for the temperature to cool. When she had finished, he sat quietly and visibly shaken. Then he gathered himself together.

"You have gone too far!" he said quietly. "You must go home at once, leave Tripoli, forget about me and the letters. You risk all our lives. Mine and yours."

"You think we have finished with you?" Anna asked.

Sergio rose to his feet, "For our own good I tell you to leave Tripoli. Enough of your stupid interference into my private affairs. Your stupid meddling is dangerous for all of us. Leave Tripoli while you still can."

The warning was sharp but fell on deaf ears.

"I am not impressed by your threats!" Anna shouted. "But we will leave you only because we will be back." With which Anna turned her back on Sergio and headed for the door, followed by Robert. Valeria remained for a few minutes only to hurl further abuse at Sergio.

16

After the evening meal in the hotel the three of them decided to benefit from the cooler night air and take a short stroll along the harbour front. The evening offered, indeed, something of a relief from the heat and dust of the day. It was always a fantastic, magical experience to see how the dying sun bathed Tripoli in shades of pale gold and rose. Enjoying the relative freshness of the evening and chatting among themselves, they wandered further than intended.

However, their excursion had been noticed by Sergio's friends in the Italian community, for as they turned to walk back to the hotel their route was obstructed. An excited group of Italian speaking men were gathered in a noisy hubbub, milling around under the walls of the old citadel, blocking the road. That they were not gathered by chance became quickly apparent, the mob surged towards Robert and his companions as soon as they came close. The danger was unmistakable. The Italians were clearly worked up and agitated, shouting unambiguous profanities and insults. Waving their fists aggressively, their anger was well worked up and all too evident. It had progressed beyond being merely alarming to the stage where at any moment it would be a mob that could turn into a rampaging rabble bent on serious mischief. And their unmistakable target would be the three visitors from London.

Too late Robert regretted his failure to foresee the obvious danger and take precautions. He knew they had infuriated Sergio and that Sergio had many friends in the city. Indeed, word must have spread about their confrontation with

Sergio and his fury must have ignited his supporters in the nationalist community.

Anna sensed the seriousness of the situation, "it's bad Robert! They are shouting ugly things about killing us. And they sound as if they mean it!"

Valeria, though, was resolute. "Porco cane!" she yelled back at them. "They are pigs Anna! Don't give them the satisfaction of showing we care!"

One of the Italians came closer.

"Che palle!" Valeria yelled at him. Doubtless another telling insult.

"Careful!" Robert urged her. "We must keep calm! They mustn't think they can frighten us. We must keep together. Keep moving steadily and back towards the hotel. Do nothing to agitate them. While they merely shout at us, we are safe. If they stop yelling that is when they may attack."

"Cowardly pigs!" Valeria shouted at them. And got it back with interest.

"We must keep moving!" Robert urged. "Steadily! Slowly!"

"Hah! You are too careful Robert!" Valeria exclaimed. "These cretins don't bother me! Basta! Vaffanculo! Pezzo di merda!" She screamed at them, and a lot more. "They are lower than the scum of the backstreets of Napoli! And you can't get much lower than that!"

"Valeria!" Robert urged. "For God's sake! Keep your feelings to yourself! Say nothing that works them up! Please!" She agreed only with reluctance.

Robert had been walking with Anna on one arm and Valeria on the other. But if he was boxed in between Anna and Valeria, he was unable to react if they were attacked. He needed freedom of movement, needed therefore to quickly rearrange how they were walking. He whispered to Anna to be ready to take her arm away from his and take Valeria's arm instead. He advised Valeria in the same way.

"But", he insisted, "keep walking at the same pace in the same way!"

"Now!" he commanded, and they executed the re-arrangement smoothly. Robert slipped behind the others and was now one pace to the side of Anna. The Italians noticed but did nothing, continuing to shout and yell, wave their fists and arms and surge around them.

He had to exercise great restraint as one of the Italians darted up close, making obscene gestures and yelling taunts. They were looking for a fight and soon wouldn't just look.

However, if this kind of loud-mouthed taunting continued to keep the mob amused, they would remain safe, although it was frustrating not to be able to teach them a lesson. One of the men though, shouting obscenities, came too close to Valeria and she reacted. She hit him hard on the side of the face with her open palm at the same time giving him a verbal blast in Italian.

"Vaffanculo!" she yelled in his face. "Sfigato! Mi rompi I coglioni! Brutto cornuto!" Indeed, there was a lot more.

However, instead of enraging the mob, most of them seemed to enjoy the performance. Indeed, some of them appeared to agree with her. Just a bit of street theatre for them, an entertainment. Robert assumed she had questioned the chap's manhood and commiserated with any unfortunate woman to whom he tried to have intimate relations. Some of his friends seemed to find it funny.

"Keep it up!" Robert thought. "We can cope with this!"

Seriously slowed down by these charades, Robert and companions edged only at little more than a snail's pace back towards the hotel. A gradual movement to safety that could not last. The mob was liking the entertainment but, underneath, was still intent on blood. There would be a crisis when they reached the Hotel. Then the hotheads in the mob would choose the moment to attack.

Indeed, as they neared the Hotel entrance a group of three or four men detached themselves from the milling crowd and rushed at them. At the same time another small group ran round behind them to get between their victims and the Hotel entrance. They physically blocked any retreat into the Hotel. The others shouted angrily in Italian, intending to hustle Robert's group back along the street. The mob was screaming that they should have left Tripoli when they were told to. Now they would pay dearly for their refusal.

The situation had become acute and dangerous. Robert and his companions were forced to halt. Stationary, surrounded by the Italians and cut off from the hotel. Any moment the bolder spirits in the mob would rush them. They would be simply overrun by force of numbers and trampled into the ground.

Valeria bellowed at the mob, Anna joined in, together more than a verbal match for them. However, the mood of the mob quickly became menacing. Robert looked to see if any of the men carried weapons. He could see none, but the situation was dark and ominous. The mob boiled and would not hold back much longer. The leaders were pent up to launch themselves headlong onto the despicable intruders.

Robert knew that if there was a concerted rush his group would be quickly overwhelmed. It had therefore to be avoided and he had only one choice. That was risky, but attack was now their only form of defence. So, he would take the mob on, starting with the ones nearest to him. A chap of about his own age, leading a small gang of four. He looked a big agile young man with powerful arms, the most physically intimidating of the group. Two of whom were overweight and out of condition, while the fourth one was hanging back at the edge. Robert decided to take his target, the leader, by surprise. Disable him quickly and distract or hold off the others while Anna and Valeria made a run for the hotel.

He spoke to Anna quietly, "I'm going to smash the nearest one. When I do you must break through to the Hotel with Valeria the moment I've got the mob's attention."

She nodded. Robert sized up his target, gauging the right point of attack and the right moment. Timing would be everything. He would rely on what was, apart from surprise, his main advantage over the Italians. That was the benefit of an instructor in the East End who had learned the hard way on the quaysides of countless foreign Ports, who understood the unscrupulous wiles of street fighting and believed that in a tricky situation the only way was the dirty, no holds barred, school that anything goes that win.

Robert reckoned that a mean, surprise attack could throw his selected opponent before he knew what had hit him. Especially if the man had not anticipated serious opposition.

He picked his moment. Then he suddenly lurched forward; two fast running steps and he caught the man full and hard with a powerful kick in the groin. It felled him to the ground. He lay there, a crumpled moaning bundle, rolling miserably on the earth trying to escape his agony.

Robert immediately delivered a straight, left arm, sideways slice at the head of the second Italian. A blow that sent him reeling backwards with blood pouring from his nose. He tried to recover but a forward lunge and a powerful right arm punch in the stomach finished him off. The other two

Italians in the group were taken completely by surprise at the unexpected fury they had unleased and backed off.

However, one of them drew a knife, looking as if he intended to launch himself on Robert.

"Codardo!" Robert shouted at him. "Try your luck if you dare! But expect no quarter if you use a knife!"

The man hesitated. Maybe he expected Robert to quiver at the sight of the naked blade. When he didn't, the man dithered. He had just seen what Robert had done to his two friends. But he had drawn his knife, and honour committed him to use it. So, he growled abuse at Robert and his friends left him to do it. They hung back leaving him alone in front of Robert. There were yells of exhortation for him to attack and finish Robert off.

"Well! Are you a coward?" Robert taunted the man and moved in closer. He could tell from the man's stance and way he waved the knife about that he had no real experience of knife fighting.

"You want a fight! Come on!"

The man was slow on his feet and when he attacked his lunge with the knife was crud, an untargeted stab into space. Robert avoided the thrust without difficulty. He gauged the right side-step to trip him up as the man rushed forward. The man fell heavily to the ground, sprawling face down. Robert kicked him hard to dislodge the knife, which he dropped to the ground.

"Get up!" Robert yelled. "I've not finished with you yet!"

The man did manage to drag himself to his knees, yelling abuse in Italian. Again, launched himself at Robert, in a wild stumbling attack, thrusting his fist aimlessly forwards. Robert dodged it, grabbed his arm, and pulled it backwards in a painful arm lock. The man screamed in pain. Robert released the arm lock and getting his foot behind the man's back hurtled him forwards into the Italian mob.

"Want to try again?" Robert yelled.

He might, perhaps, have done so, or his friends might have tried their luck, but for sudden, loud, shouts of military command right behind them, followed by warning shots fired into the air. Turkish soldiers had arrived, unslung their rifles and their sergeant was ordering the Italians to pull back or they would open fire on the crowd. The mob heeded the order and withdrew, ill-humoured, resentful, muttering vile threats and taking their wounded companions with them.

It was over.

While Robert was relieved at the outcome, he was not pleased to see that Anna and Valeria had made no attempt to make a run for the hotel, as he had expressly told them. Instead, they had remained exactly where they were, facing down the mob. His annoyance was tempered, though, when he noticed that Valeria was holding a neat two barrelled Derringer. Indeed, the Italians had melted away in front of her, not doubting she would use the gun. And Anna had pulled out an evil looking short hunting knife from somewhere in the folds of her skirt. They had maintained a united front against the hooligans, and he could not but admire them. They could have run; indeed, they should have run as he had instructed, but had chosen to stand with him.

Mustafa then stepped forward through the Turkish ranks. He had come to the Hotel to tell them that word had been received that known criminals, one accused of murder in Sicily, were being brought in from Tunis by steamer. Mustafa thought that the purpose was to kill Robert and his friends.

"Your presence here has now become a serious matter. I can no longer indulge you. You have brought fighting onto the streets and a surge of trouble among the Italians here. Nor do I believe the story you gave me for your visit. I must warn you that lying to the Ottoman Authority to obtain a passport visa is a criminal offence. I now need to know the truth. I need to know why you are here in Tripoli. I have important business with the Vali, the Governor, that cannot wait, but I will return here tomorrow when I expect your full co-operation. I will also add that you must leave Tripoli. Whatever your business here, whether you think it is completed or not, you must leave. If anything happens to you it will reflect on both me and the government. It is to be avoided. I give you no choice. You must leave on the next boat."

The next morning Mustafa returned as promised. He brought dramatic news. Known criminals had gone to Sergio's house to kill him. But they had made a mess of it. Sergio had put up a fight and had fired at them, killing one of the assailants. Another had been wounded and arrested. Mustafa believed that more assailants would be back. He turned to Robert and spoke sharply.

"These are the criminals I mentioned to you. We know that they have arrived in Tripoli. We were informed that you were the target, now it seems that Sergio was also to be killed. They will probably try again. Now you must realize why you should leave Tripoli."

That morning, therefore, Robert booked for the next steamer sailing for Malta, which was in four days. He then called at Tom O'Brien's office and was handed a telegram just received from London.

"Bird delay two more weeks"

This meant that the Steam Yacht *Hermes* was probably still undergoing refit in Liverpool, and at any rate would not be at sea for at least two weeks.

17

As they could not leave Tripoli for a few days, Robert asked Tom O'Brien to organise a sailing expedition to explore the coast north of Tripoli. It would be an opportunity to also discover the merits of the distinctively oriental, triangular, lateen sail carried by the various Arab sailboats, which could be seen every day plying their trade, weaving delightfully in and out in the harbour area. The rig appeared in boats of all sizes. There were the big three masted cargo-carrying Xebecs, and large elegant Dhows, usually with their distinguishing long overhanging bowsprit and aft-set mizzen mast, also designed for carrying cargo, and often with three masts and a crew of twelve. But Robert was particularly interested in the small, fast, single-mast feluccas and xebecs that could often be seen zipping around in the harbour.

Robert was fascinated by their strange, ancient lateen rig and light construction; so different to his own much heavier-built dinghy on the north Norfolk coast. In the lateen set-up the sail was fixed to a long crossbar, the middle of which was mounted to the top of the mast. The large sail was angled to extend aft well above the height of the mast, and then forward to almost touch the deck.

He had early on mentioned to Tom O'Brien that it would be fun to spend a day sailing such a vessel, perhaps exploring the coastline, to experience the lateen rig first-hand. It would, he thought, be fun to handle such a lightly built craft at sea and compare its sailing ability to his own boat.

So, with their departure from Tripoli now imminent, O'Brien arranged with an Arab fisherman he knew for Robert to hire his xebec. The man's son, Ahmed, also a fisherman, would come with them as crew to show Robert the ropes. The idea was they would sail up the coast to the north of Tripoli, find a pleasant grove of Palm trees beside the beach and have a picnic in the shade. Ahmed would leave them there, to return some hours later to sail them back to Tripoli. It should be a lovely, quiet, and relaxing day.

A morning on the water did indeed sound an enjoyable prospect, and Robert was delighted to put the idea to Anna and Valeria. He was keen to introduce Anna to the pleasures of sailing and this presented a golden opportunity. Valeria had been quick, however, to say that small boats did not agree with her, and she was not a swimmer, so she would prefer to remain in the hotel. Anna, though, was keen to come and Robert knew from the old days in the Highgate Ponds that she was a strong swimmer. Robert asked the hotel to fix them up with a picnic lunch basket.

They boarded the xebec in the harbour and Robert signalled to Ahmed to take the boat out from the quayside. He didn't understand but Anna explained in Italian, of which Ahmed had a working knowledge, that Robert wanted to observe how he handled the lateen rig before giving it a go himself. Robert quickly saw that the lateen rig was not that different in principle to his own dinghy. The lateen rig, like his own boat was a fore and aft sail, quite different to the old square rig. The lightly built, indeed flimsy looking, xebec, though, was radically different in both appearance and design to his own dinghy, which was far more substantial, heavily built, and strong to withstand the buffeting of the North Sea and being roughly hauled over the coastal mud flats. It completely lacked the grace and lightness of a xebec.

But it was also clear that sailing a lateen rigged boat could be tricky; for instance there could be trouble if any sudden, powerful, squall caught the large, baggy sail unawares. Ahmed showed off his skills; he ran fast with the wind full behind, then changed course to tack against it, now racing, now almost idling in the water. It showed Robert how well the xebec could be sailed close to the wind. He also noticed how, on beginning a prolonged tack against the wind, the long crossbar or yard was difficult to operate and how Ahmed skilfully prevented the sail rubbing by allowing the yard to swivel round to the other side of the mast. It looked so easy to do but would take a great deal of learning the hard way to master such a tricky technique. Ahmed was not more than fifteen but plainly had that experience; in his hands the boat behaved perfectly.

Then Ahmed passed the helm to Robert who enjoyed the novel experience of handling the unusual rig, and immediately faced the challenge that it carried a far larger canvas than his own dinghy. He had heard that one of the advantages of a lightly built boat such as this, was its ease of handling. But that was not entirely true, in any serious wind or sea it would be hard going, although in skilled hands it did have an ability to take the wind. He found that the rig took some getting used to and that he needed Ahmed's help. Nevertheless, the boat behaved well, it was so agile it could, if well handled, just ski across the water.

They sailed north in a light wind through the shimmering azure waters on a course out of the harbour, and then round the string of small islands and rocky outcrops to the west. But as these were bare of trees and without any shade, they continued up the coast to the north of Tripoli, seeking a likely spot where they could beach the xebec, unload, and enjoy their lunch basket. A nice, long, picnic lunch with Anna on the beach under the shade of some handy palm grove could be idyllic.

Anna had come in a long skirt and a light, flowery silk blouse that billowed in the breeze. She had also tied her hair loosely, so it, too, flowed freely in the gentle wind, while a red silk scarf tied under her chin restrained her essential sunhat. She sat on a thwart midships and looked as if she was enjoying herself.

"This is wonderful Robbie! Is sailing like this in Norfolk?"

He had to admit that the cold waters of the Wash and North Sea were not quite as welcoming as these warm African seas. Although, as he tried to persuade her, in Norfolk one could dress warmly for the weather and the sharpness of the cold wind on the face was indeed refreshing.

"You see Anna, the sea air in Norfolk is so good for you! Bracing! Healthy!"

"Maybe you can persuade me to try it. But I should warn you it might be just the once if it's as cold as they say!"

"You will love it!"

After sailing north, they put into the shore and beached close to a Palm grove. Ahmed helped to unload the picnic and prepared to return to Tripoli, saying he would come back in five hours. Anna and Robert sat down beside a sand dune, well beneath the shady canopy of a lofty Palm, to examine and consume the contents of the well filled hamper. Pasta in the Italian style, Moroccan spiced pastries, a cold omelette with potatoes in the Spanish manner, Arabic baklava and kunafa, and much more. Fresh lemon juice to wash it down. Tripoli was such a melting pot of culinary cultures.

They decided on a short walk under the Palms before enjoying the picnic and then relaxed in the shade on the soft warm sand, beyond which were the turquoise waters, empty except for an occasional steamship far away on the horizon.

But it was in fact not much more than three hours before they were rudely disturbed by Ahmed's unexpected return. He tugged his boat out of the water and called to them excitedly in his version of Italian. Anna sat up and slowed him down so that she could follow what he was trying to say. She turned to Robert looking worried.

"It's not good Robbie! I think we've got trouble!"

"What's happened?"

"He says that when he got back to Tripoli, his father told him some Italian people had observed us sailing out of Tripoli. They saw the picnic stuff being loaded and saw him coming back alone."

"So?"

"There was a man with them, Ahmed's father thinks he was a German. Not Italian anyway. They were talking among themselves, a lot of shouting and arm waving. They talked about us. And then they hired another xebec to take the German up the coast. He left in his xebec about half an hour before Ahmed himself decided he had to sail to come here and warn us."

"A German! You think he was chasing us?"

"He must be!"

"Does that mean Berlin's on to us?"

"Ahmed thinks the German was certainly intending to find us!"

And why would he want to do that unless ... It didn't look good. It seemed that Berlin not only knew they were here in Tripoli but had sent someone after them. If the German had, indeed, a mission to kill them, if he caught them on the beach, they would be sitting ducks. The question was what to do. Robert had to think quickly.

"Ask Ahmed if there's a road from here back to Tripoli?"

Ahmed said there was, but it wasn't in good condition. Moreover, it would be a long hot walk. And any horses or carts would have to set off from Tripoli.

"Not a good prospect. Anyway, it's not viable Anna. If people in Tripoli are after us, they will think of the road and be waiting for us. You've seen the country, there is no-where to hide. We wouldn't have a chance."

But if so, what then?

Ahmed had another conversation with Anna.

"Robbie, he thinks the German must have come this way, but didn't spot us here and sailed past, further up the coast. I guess we must have been lying in the sand, out of sight. He thinks the German might have sailed quite a bit further looking for us. But then he will begin to retrace his route slowly, thoroughly combing the coast for us."

"That means if we sail back now for Tripoli, we probably have a reasonable start on him."

"Aren't we just as much at risk in the boat as on the road?"

"Anna, on the road we have no chance if they're waiting for us. On the boat for sure we take a chance but can use our wits."

"Then we sail Robbie!"

"You're right! But we must clear it with Ahmed, we're in his hands. He seemed to me to be pretty good as a sailor but it's his call. Ask him if he's up to it! That German has a gun and if he starts shooting, Ahmed's in the line of fire. He has to know that we'll need to take risks."

She turned to Ahmed and there was a sharp, to the point, exchange of words. Robert assumed she asked him if he was up to the challenge, and guessed that her words were, in the Italian way, probably graphic. Recalling their earlier confrontation with the Italian mob on the harbour front, he assumed it would be something like Valeria's down to earth street slang when she faced down the mob. He was concerned that Ahmed would take it badly and would want to back out. It was, after all, not his fight.

Alright, it's up to him. I won't blame him if he wants to quit. If I must sail the boat, I'll give it a go. I have no choice. But I'm nothing like as good a sailor as Ahmed. It may not go well!

But perhaps because the question came from an attractive girl, who had probably said it in a way that indicated she was perfectly sure of the answer, in fact Ahmed took it with a broad grin and concluded the conversation with a clear affirmative. Robert slapped him on the back. A lot would depend on Ahmed's seamanship, bravery, and readiness to take risks.

"Tell him that if we do meet this German boat, I hope he likes playing chicken!" Robert wondered how on earth one might say that in pigeon Italian, but Anna obviously got the message across because Ahmed doubled the grin and added a smile. He was on for it! They were in with a chance.

Anna lifted her long skirt, waded through the water lapping the side of the xebec, and clambered on board. Robert stood in the water to hold the boat steady for her. Then he helped Ahmed raise the big lateen sail and they pushed the boat off into the blue waters. Taking advantage of the strengthening breeze and in Ahmed's capable hands the boat handled well. Robert noticed that Anna touched the blouse that covered her neck and guessed that, in the Italian manner, she wore a small cross.

Very Catholic. Well, I hope whatever patron saint she was addressing is in the mood to listen!

But in fact, he envied her the comfort that the little gesture evidently gave her. He would have liked to pray for an uneventful sail back to Tripoli harbour and feel that there was some point to it. But he had never felt at home in a Church.

For some time, they skimmed merrily at a good lick through the water with the wind behind them. The lateen sail picking up the full force of the breeze. Robert thought hopefully that maybe they had worried about their safety for no good reason. It looked like plain sailing all the way home to the harbour. But just as they were completing a long loop into the roads outside the harbour approach, Ahmed attracted his attention.

"Attenzione!"

He was pointing to another lateen sailboat coming steadily south down the coast. And what was at once clear was that it suddenly and sharply changed course to head out to sea in a straight line towards them.

There was nothing unusual in seeing another boat, but this one was behaving with menace. They had seen other boats going hither and thither on their business, and none had taken any notice of them. This boat, however, was doing the opposite, deliberately changing course to head straight for them.

This makes no sense unless they intend to come alongside. And why would they want to do that if it is not the German's boat? And why would he do that unless he wished us harm!

Scanning it as best he could, Robert was concerned

It is clearly not out fishing, there is no sign of fishing tackle. And instead of the crew of three or four normal for a fishing vessel, it has an Arab crew of only two.

Then he spotted their passenger seated mid-sips wearing European dress and a large white pith helmet.

It is the German! There's no doubt of it!

Robert was alarmed for their safety. Berlin had murdered Maria in London, ransacked the Gibson's house and they had only just escaped from the Italian mob with their lives in Tripoli. They had just attempted to murder Sergio.

"Who dares wins!" He shouted at Anna. "Are you ready for it!" It was not a question, for that die had already been thrown when they decided to risk sailing back. But anyway, she raised her arm in support. The suffragette salute perhaps? If they got back in one piece, he must remember to ask her.

"Robbie!" Anna yelled; the other xebec was fast closing the distance.

It was indeed now drawing level, on their quarter only yards away. The German was trying to stand up and had pulled out a shotgun from a canvas bag. Ahmed saw the move coming and realised the danger. He yelled out a warning to Anna, signalling her to slither off the thwart and get below the level of the gunwale. Robert too saw the gun. Now they must take big risks and the bravest would survive.

"Anna we must go for broke!"

Despite the way his boat was swinging and swaying in the choppy water the German was nevertheless trying to level his gun at Robert.

"Ramm them!" Robert yelled at Ahmed, indicating with his fist what he wanted.

This was the crucial test, and Ahmed came through it with flying colours. He immediately steered straight for a collision, aiming to ram the attacker amidships. The manoeuvre also conveniently swung their own lateen sail to block the gunman's line of sight, making it even more difficult for him to aim.

The other crew, as hoped for, reacted quickly. Clearly desperate to avoid being rammed they spun their xebec violently away from a full-on side impact. The sudden lurching of the boat wrecked the gunman's aim and he fired both barrels harmlessly into the air. Worse, he tried to re-load and then overbalanced, falling heavily backwards into the boat. He was slow to move and probably hurt himself.

The outcome happened to leave the two boats sailing away from each other on opposite courses. Ahmed straight towards Tripoli, and the other boat out to sea. This did not last long as the other boat turned smartly towards Robert.

It was once again dangerous. Even though there was a natural difficulty trying to shoot, even with a shotgun, from a small boat bouncing up and down and from side to side in a choppy sea, there was always the chance of a lucky shot. Moreover, the German was obviously set on a killing.

'They're too cocky for comfort!" Robert shouted. "We need to make things more difficult for them! We must engage them!" He indicated with his arm what Ahmed should do.

Ahmed was up to the mark. He swung the tiller round, manoeuvred the lateen yard and the sail took the wind on a different quarter, fairly hurling them through the choppy water, sending a shower of spray into the air. The xebec was lightly built with a tall mast and expertly handled by Ahmed its sail caught the fullness of the wind. The boat properly skated across the water.

"Exciting stuff, Anna!" Robert yelled, enjoying the thrill of the high stakes, and hoping that Anna was liking the excitement. She was and had returned to her seat on the thwart.

"Keep down!" he shouted as they closed with the other boat.

Ahmed then changed course again, twisting the xebec round in a tight turn to charge headlong into the other boat. Robert could hear the German shouting orders to his Arab crew, but they had problems understanding the orders. The German made it worse by getting angry and screaming more orders in a louder voice that they didn't understand. Nevertheless, in a while they succeeded once more being on a course that might take them alongside Robert's boat.

Robert signalled to Ahmed to repeat their previous tactic. He did, closing in fast, but this time steering for a showdown, a direct frontal impact. He was banking on the sense of self-preservation that would cause the other crew to veer off at the last moment. They did. There was a resulting consternation on the boat. The crew had had enough, such a collision at sea would put everyone's life at risk. The German might have paid them well, but not well enough to repeatedly hazard their lives. Nor did they like the Italians in Tripoli who had insisted they hired themselves out to the German. They also knew Ahmed and his father well, fellow fishermen and skilled masters of their boats. They had given the German the clever stunts he had demanded and for which he had paid well, but that was enough for them.

However, their passenger furiously demanded another attack and yelled abuse at them. The German shouted to his crew to turn towards Robert, gesticulating wildly, but they would not do it and instead altered course for the harbour.

This in fact presented their flank to Ahmed, whose own course would cause him to ram them mid-ships. There was further chaos on the other xebec as the crew scrambled to take evasive action.

The German ordered them not to, presumably intending to use his shotgun as the vessels closed. He raised his shotgun ready to shoot. But he would be shooting just over the head of one of his own Arab crew and the steersman saw this and yelled to the gunman not to fire. The German took no notice.

His steersman shouted and let go his sail, so that it immediately flapped uselessly in the wind. The sudden unexpected movement caught the German unawares as he attempted to steady his shotgun and he fell overboard, where he could be seen floundering in the choppy sea.

For Robert it was an easy tactical decision to break off the action and make for the harbour. There was no point in turning back to engage the other xebec, he could see that she was still wallowing in the water, her sail flapping idly and the scene on board chaotic. The Arab crew were still leaning over the side of the boat apparently attempting to recover their passenger from the sea. He knew it was time to call it a day.

"Ahmed, home!" he called, waving his arm towards Tripoli harbour. Ahmed grinned broadly. He had obviously enjoyed the adventure.

"Are you all right Anna? It's all over! They won't catch us now!"

"I'm fine! Was he really trying to kill us?"

"Yes! Either with the gun or by capsizing our boat and drowning us!"

"So, this is the quiet sail you promised me Robbie"

He could see the smile on her face, she had enjoyed it. An escapade to remember. That was the old Anna all over.

"Next time I promise will be really quiet! Norfolk is known for being quiet!"

"Next time? Do you really expect me to trust you in a boat another time!"

"I do! Now that you've seen what sailing is like in these easy waters, I'll show you some real sailing in the North Sea."

He was sure, however, that she had relished the thrill of the dangerous game they had just played and won. She had always liked the adventures they used to play in the woods and fields when they were young. However, the incident worried him. He knew very well that they had been lucky. They had won but it had been a close-run thing. If the German had spotted them on the beach, they would have been certain goners, the German would have landed and finished them off. Doubtless they would have just disappeared without trace. And what the unexpected incident proved was that their enemies remained determined, persistent, and obviously planned to kill them. They would probably try again. The main puzzle was, though, who were these enemies? Who was that wanted them dead? Italian friends of Sergio in Tripoli? Nationalists from Italy? Or were they like the people who broke into the Gibson's house, German agents? If it was Berlin behind these attacks in Tripoli they were in deep trouble. WilhelmStraße did not mess about.

"Look! We'll sail back to the harbour. It's all over here!" Robert announced, checking again that the other boat was still dead in the water. When they got back to the city, he slapped Ahmed on the back, hugged him and gave him a huge tip, probably enough to set him up with his own boat. He deserved it. Anna said something obviously very nice to him in Italian and flattered him with one of best smiles. Ahmed just seemed happy with the whole affair.

Robert went to O'Brien and told him what had happened and, on his advice, sent a written report to Mustafa. They were already unpopular with the Turks and doubtless Mustafa would think today's incident showed they were nothing but trouble to the Ottoman authorities.

18

The next day soon after breakfast, they got a visit from Tom O'Brien.

"Things have moved quickly," he said, "Since the trouble in the street last night some of the Italians are really worked up. I think they feel humiliated."

"They got what they deserved!" Robert answered hotly.

"Maybe, but they are angry. They want the Governor to expel you."

"Hah! We're going anyway!"

"The big problem is that the Turks are annoyed with you. They may arrest you."

"Arrest us?" Robert asked, puzzled and concerned.

"It's about the Xebec incident."

"Why?"

"The man who fell overboard, he drowned. The Turks have recovered the body. He is a foreigner who arrived in Tripoli the day before. Some people, who were standing on the shore and claim to have seen the whole incident, are not sympathetic to you. They claim you deliberately rammed the other boat. They say you are a murderer."

"We didn't touch the other boat."

"The people on the shore say you are a murderer. And the man is dead."

"That's ridiculous! I did only what I had to do to save our lives. The German in the other boat had a gun and was plainly trying to kill us."

"I'm sure you're right! But the situation is tricky."

"It sounds it! What will happen?"

"Well, it's interesting. The Arab sailors told the police that the man on the boat paid them well to hire their boat. He was carrying a large canvas bag and told them to sail north down the coast. When they were well away from the harbour, he produced a gun from the bag. He ordered the Arabs to find your boat. They looked all along the coast but didn't spot you. Then they did spot you at sea heading back to Tripoli. Their man then loaded his shotgun and they realised he wanted to kill you. He threatened them. He fell over inside the boat when they swerved hard to avoid you. He recovered and demanded that they steer towards your boat. He stood up but when you came at them again, he fell overboard. He could not swim. They turned back to find him and pulled him from the water, but he was dead."

"Sounds a reasonably accurate account," Robert observed. "Did the Police discover who he was?"

"Yes, he had a French passport in the name of Claude Gissot."

"French?"

"Yes, French passport. But the Arab sailors said he was brought to their boat by two Italians and when he spoke to them it was not in French!"

"Wow! So, he might in fact be German?"

"Yes. Could be anything! Maybe just a killer for hire. But all that caused the Police to start to ask questions in the Italian community here."

"Sounds a busy time!"

"Yes! The sailors have been released so the Turks have quietened down the local Arabs. But the Italians are still on the rampage, especially about you. The Turks say you are causing too much trouble. They don't want an incident that draws in the British Government."

"So?"

"You can expect a visit from Mustafa. The other thing is that the Minerva is no longer safe for you. Even for a couple of nights. The Italian community are really worked up and angry."

"What should we do?"

"I suggest that you stay in my house. You will be safe there. But it is unwise to think of remaining in Tripoli or to think there is any possibility of visiting Sergio again."

As Robert, Anna and Valeria agreed that the Hotel was no longer safe they were grateful for his offer of accommodation. He gave them directions; it was not far off in the European quarter near the harbour. Robert went around accompanying some porters with all their luggage. O'Brien lived in a pleasant, squat white house at the edge of the city facing the sea. He had two Arab servants and a cook living in the house and had also, in anticipation of their short visit, arranged for the house to be watched by the police.

They spent a comfortable night at O'Brien's house, regaled by his stories of a wandering life round the Mediterranean. Not unexpected after O'Brien's warning that there were questions about the Xebec affair, the following morning they had a visit from Mustafa. He came, however, not about the xebec affair, but to tell them that the criminals had been back to Sergio's house and had another fight with him. His real and dramatic news, however, was that Sergio was dead, murdered by his attackers with multiple stab wounds. Not a nice way to die.

"He's reaped what he sowed!" Anna said bitterly. "After what he did to my mother, I can't honestly feel sorrow! None of it should have happened!"

"He is better dead!" Valeria exclaimed. "He has brought shame and dishonour on our family."

Mustafa told them that Sergio's house had been under Police observation and the police had caught the culprits in the street as they left the house. One of them had been persuaded to talk. Robert was sure this meant torture; maybe the new Ottoman way was not so different to the old.

"There's more," Mustafa told them. "He incriminated a Lebanese man in Tunis who had paid him to kill Sergio."

Robert asked if there was any link with Germany.

"The man is in fact a commercial agent for some German firms."

"German firms?"

"German merchant firms, shipping and so on."

"And the killers were German?"

"No, not German. We think they are a mixed lot, brought in for the job. We are still investigating."

Robert asked Mustafa if he and Anna might be allowed access to Sergio's house to examine his papers. "You see it is a family matter. Sergio discovered an old criminal offence by Maria Gibson's father when he was a child, and used it to blackmail her. Anna wants to find the documents and destroy them."

"Anything else?"

Robert said he wanted to find what connections Sergio had with Berlin. Mustafa gave him a hard look but agreed to them being permitted to examine Sergio's papers, on condition that Robert disclosed everything he discovered. With this permission, they set off for Sergio's house. They took Mario, one of O'Brien's Maltese clerks, just in case of trouble. One of Mustafa's junior officers, who spoke reasonable English, also came.

Arriving at Sergio's house they were taken to the room that Sergio had used as his study. It was a large room leading off the ground floor veranda. The walls were whitewashed with various portraits, including another one of Giuseppe Mazzini. A large wall map showed Libya as a province of the old Roman Empire. Two divans were piled high with embroidered cushions decorated with Moorish designs. Near the window there was an important mahogany roll top desk in a Spanish baroque style. Robert opened it and went through the papers. He asked Mario to glance at each of them in turn and tell him about the subject matter. There was nothing of any interest.

However, Anna found Sergio's diary in a drawer of the desk and began to read it. After a while she found an entry in Italian. She translated it for Robert:

"... decided will not ask R direct support plan. ..."

She supposed that 'R' could mean Rome and thought that it indicated that Sergio had not in fact involved the Italian Government. It was a conspiracy only of local nationalists like Sergio. Another entry said:

"... further meeting people from Hburg ... will do technical side for us ..."

Anna found later entries about similar meetings with 'Hburg' people and a reference to the money paid into her mother's account.

"... people from Hburg ... said banking in L was under control... had received funds via Vna for transit to Ma ... suggest I write Ma re purchase boat ..."

Later entries noted without specific dates that Sergio had been informed that further funds were sent to Maria in London.

"I think," Anna said, "that 'L' means London and 'Ma' is my mother, Maria. 'Burg' means city in German, maybe the name of a German city, therefore. The money is coming via 'Vna', where is that, sounds like a place but could be a person."

"We can check this later," Robert said, "but it does broadly tie in with what's in your mother's Bank Account."

"If there's a German connection in all this, 'Hbrg' could be Hamburg and 'Vna' could be Vienna."

"Brilliant Anna!"

"But why is the money coming through Austria?"

All this was interesting enough, but it fell far short of being the damning, incriminating evidence of a Berlin link to Sergio's conspiracy for which Robert had hoped. Also, the reference to Vienna in the transfer of money to Maria suggested a central European rather than Berlin link. They found nothing in Sergio's papers or his diary about Maria's death. Robert imagined that Anna had expected to find something revealing in the diary, but there was no diary entry at all relevant to Maria's death, not even the fact that she had died. Nothing about attempts to recover his letters to Maria or to break into the Gibson's house. The lack of any reference to Maria's death surprised Robert because there were other entries in the diary about Sergio's personal life, relatives, and affairs. Robert would have expected that he would mention Maria's death. Similarly, there's nothing about the purchase of *Hermes*, her refit, her sailing, her cargo, or her destination.

Since the diary had a lot of information about the conspiracy, these gaps were puzzling. Might all these details of such crucial ingredients of the plan be in some kind of operational document or documents that they had not discovered? But why?

"It is a bit disappointing!" Robert remarked to Anna. "I did think we would find more!"

"Specially about my mother!" She re-joined. "I found nothing about my grandfather's prison sentence. You think of all those letters he wrote to my mother and yet there is little, hardly a mention of her in his Diary."

"At least it seems likely that he was working with the Germans or Austrians!"

"Although he doesn't say why! What reason to ask for their help?"

"Well, they seem to supply the funds! Through Vienna! And what I remember from London is that he was using the Carbonari people in London. Maybe the conspiracy here in Tripoli left everything to be organised by their people in London!"

When they felt they had looked at as much as they could they decided to call it a day.

"You have done everything you could have done Anna!" Robert told her as they left Sergio's house.

*

Mustafa had asked Robert to come to his headquarters when they had finished at Sergio's house. He did so and Mustafa came directly to the point.

"Tell me what you were looking for, and what you found."

Robert wanted no trouble from the Ottoman authorities and did so as accurately as he could. Mustafa seemed to accept he had been honest and wished them a good trip home.

When he left the Turkish headquarters, Robert sent a telegram to Hugo via O'Brien.

S murdered. Attempt to kill us. Visa cancelled. Returning home.

Their departure from Tripoli was a public humiliation, staged by Mustafa for the benefit of the local population. They were paraded from the Hotel Minerva between a file of policemen, pursued by a jeering crowd of Italians blaming them for Sergio's death. When they reached the quay, their embarkation was supervised by a languid junior Turkish officer, who carried out a deliberately long-drawn-out examination of their luggage. Mustafa intended it to be apparent who was in control in Tripoli and that Robert's party were leaving at the Sultan's pleasure. Mustafa had, though, taken the precaution, in case of British questions, of insisting that Robert sign a statement, countersigned by Tom O'Brien as the British Consul, stating he was departing only because he had completed his business in Tripoli. Tom O'Brien was on the quay to see them off. He said he was sorry to see them go; their presence had brightened up the otherwise dull routine of his life. The feeling was mutual, he had made their short stay in Tripoli much easier and pleasanter than it might otherwise have been.

"Actually, I have a favour to ask," Tom said, as they turned towards the boats waiting to take them out to the steamer in the roads. "Arman Kocharyan is a good friend of mine in the local Armenian community. He has a nephew, Bedros, who is eighteen and from Damascus but staying here with Arman. You may have seen him the other evening in the International Café? Arman came across to speak to us."

"Yes," Robert answered, "I remember. A young man in a linen suit?"

"That's him! The thing is the boy's making his way to London to work for a distant cousin in an import business. My friend heard you were leaving for England and wondered if Bedros might travel with you? I'm sure that the boy would be fine by himself, but my friend feels responsible for him. What do you think? Would you mind? He shouldn't be any trouble."

Robert could see Bedros standing respectfully to one side, wearing a beige linen suit. He was a young man of medium height, with thick, straight, long black hair combed sideways from a centre parting. He had a typical Armenian oval, sallow skinned face set on a thick neck, with large dark eyes, a long prominent nose, and full lips. He noticed Robert's gaze and approached them, greeting Robert's party with Middle Eastern courtesy. Robert liked the look of him but was still pondering his reply when Valeria announced the group's decision for him.

"Of course, we agree!" she told Tom. "After all you've done for us how could we refuse." Then turning to Bedros, she said, "We will be delighted to have your company young man."

Bedros acknowledged her acceptance with a charming smile.

The four of them boarded the boat to row them to the steamer for Tunis and Malta that was moored in the roads. The steamer edged out of the roads and left Tripoli behind in its wake. Robert stood at the rail watching the white city fade slowly away in the dazzling heat haze. The visit to Tripoli was over; he could look forward to a pleasant voyage home and a new life with Anna. He could propose to her on the steamer from Malta, that would be perfect.

Arriving in Malta two days later he set about organising the trip home, but his plans were interrupted by an unexpected and unwanted telegram from Hugo.

Urgent. Bird now at large. Can't be caged. Bird must be D Jones. Confident you feel duty to assist.

This meant that *Hermes* had left England and was at sea. What's more it introduced a whole new kettle of fish about the Sergio affair. For Hugo was asking him to 'assist' to 'D Jones' *Hermes*. This meant that he was asking Robert to help to send *Hermes* to 'Davy Jones Locker', to the bottom of the sea. He was asking Robert to help to sink her.

He showed the message to Anna. "Hugo wants me to help to sink *Hermes*. But we're not at war. It would surely be piracy."

"Robbie, you can't do it! Sinking ships indeed. You must not do something stupid like offering to volunteer. You must refuse."

"Don't worry, I intend to."

He replied to Hugo to say so. Hugo replied quickly:

Essential national interest that Bird drowned. Bird is key link and must vanish. Tom needs your help. Essential you do. Implore you to have a go.

"Tom?" Anna asked.

"He's the seaman Hugo planted on *Hermes*."

"What! He put his own spy on board. Is there no end to his chicanery?"

Hugo's choice of words was disturbing. 'Have a go!' was so casual and nonchalant. Robert had last been urged to 'Have a go!' when he went to the hoopla stall with Sybil at the Fair on Hampstead Heath. But sinking *Hermes* was not remotely like playing hoopla. Hugo was planning a serious international crime.

"Doesn't Hugo understand what he's proposing?"

"You misjudge him. He understands perfectly well, and he doesn't care a jot." He felt she was right, and Hugo's casual attitude annoyed him.

"How dare he!" Robert thought. "I went willingly to Tripoli and put Anna and Valeria in great danger. We could all easily have been killed. And now he demands more."

He sent another message to Hugo to say he couldn't help. Hugo's response was quick, saying that *Hermes* was due in Malaga within 12 days and repeating the necessity for Robert's immediate agreement.

He had joined Anna sitting at a table on the Hotel's terrace and ordered drinks.

"Look at this Anna! It doesn't look right! What kind of British Foreign Office business is this, planning to sink ships?"

"If it's not the FO, what's happening?"

"It looks like Hugo is making the decisions himself."

"In that case Robbie, Hugo is not the junior FO clerk we thought he was."

"Alright, but what is he?"

"We surely must know the answer to that before we go any further. You must not engage in any new venture of his without knowing exactly what he is and who he is working for."

"Hugo says he wants me to go to Malaga and help Tom work out a plan to seize *Hermes*. That's not too demanding."

"Work out a plan? He could do that in London!"

"True."

"It doesn't make sense. What's the point of a plan unless there are people to carry it out? Tom can't do it alone. Hugo will get you into it by hook or by crook."

"You're going too far! It can't surely do any harm to help Tom make a plan."

"Are you mad!" Anna responded sharply, thinking him culpably naïve. "Do you honestly think it will go no further than making a plan?"

"Yes, I do. But I agree it needs to be clear that all I will do is help Tom make a plan."

"Robbie don't be so blindly reasonable! Hugo is not to be trusted."

"You're too suspicious. Just going to Malaga and drawing up a plan for Tom keeps Hugo happy. He has helped us in the past, and I feel obliged to give him the benefit of the doubt."

"Robbie! No!"

He ignored her forcefully expressed objections and despite her continued protests telegraphed Hugo.

Will go B and assist Tom make plan.

Anna was angry. More than that, furious that he so easily and totally disregarded her opinion. And was so blind and stupidly prepared to trust Hugo. They exchanged more than a few heated words, but he had made up his mind and believed he could handle Hugo. But he didn't want Anna or Valeria to risk anything, he would do it all himself.

"Look Anna, I feel I have no choice but to go to Malaga. But there is absolutely no need for you or Valeria to come. In fact, it's better if you don't. It's my decision and I will go to Malaga alone. Go with Valeria and Bedros and return to London."

"No Robert! We came out together and we must keep together. If you insist on going to Malaga, I will go as well."

She too had made up her mind. Therefore, Valeria would also go as her chaperone. Anna made Robert give her a promise, that once they reached Malaga, after he had examined the local situation, and after he had advised Tom about devising a plan to capture *Hermes*, that would be the absolute end of the Sergio affair. Given the choice, Bedros decided to continue with them to Malaga.

19

Valeria studied the steamer timetables, and the best route to Malaga from Malta was first to Tunis and then another steamer along the long Algerian coastline. On reaching Malaga, Robert settled them down in the Hotel Regina, a pleasant well-established hotel that lay on the north side of the stately Paseo de la Almeda, a fine, wide tree lined avenue in the centre of the City next to the Port. There they could hide as best they could from the summer heat while they awaited developments and the arrival of *Hermes*. It was in fact an ideal location to observe shipping movements.

Leaving the others to unpack he went to visit the nearby British Consul. There he found a message for him from Hugo. *Hermes* had put in at Lisbon, and Tom Connolly, the sailor Hugo had planted in *Hermes* crew, had contacted Hugo. A number of heavy wooden boxes had been transferred to *Hermes* from a German registered freighter in Lisbon and stored in a lower deck cabin that had a special security lock. Robert recognised this as the arrangement for a secure cargo of gold that he had discovered months ago in the Birkenhead Yard.

Tom also reported that the transfer in Lisbon was supervised by a man from the German Freighter who had remained on board *Hermes*. This 'German agent', as Tom called him, was now in charge of *Hermes* and giving sailing orders to the ship's master and crew. Moreover, he would remain on board *Hermes* for the rest of the voyage. Tom reported that *Hermes* would soon sail for Malaga and said there was word of a rendezvous in Malaga with a German freighter, *Ulm,* for more cargo. Probably rifles.

The main point of Hugo's message was to ask Robert to prepare a plan to capture *Hermes* in Malaga the moment its cargo of weapons was transferred from the freighter *Ulm*. Hugo informed Robert he had ordered Tom to 'dispose of' the German agent before *Hermes* reached Malaga. Moreover, if any German crew from the *Ulm* managed to board *Hermes* in Malaga they must also be killed. Robert should get hold of the ship, set sail, put out to sea, and then scuttle. Those on board could save themselves by using the ship's boats.

The prospect of having to assist Tom to commit not one but a series of murders was appalling. Bad enough in itself, but worse because it also brought Robert face to face with his own gullibility; at how he had allowed Hugo to dupe him, allowed himself to be fooled by Hugo's pretence of being a lowly Foreign Office clerk, been so naive in not seeing Hugo's involvement in murderous skulduggery. He put his growing concerns to Anna, mindful of his promise to her not to get further involved in Hugo's plans.

Anna was angry with him. "Robert, perhaps we were all fooled by Hugo. Can't you see that he must be part of some underhand outfit that does the government's dirty work abroad."

"Hugo has ordered his man Tom to kill the Germans. This means Tom must be a trained killer!"

"Robert you must see that you can't take any part in this!"

Robert agreed and feared the devilish mission into which he had been foolish enough to get enmeshed. Hugo had put murder on its agenda as easy as pie. But murder could not be justified, Britain was not at war with Germany. Who gave Hugo a licence to kill Germans? Moreover, Robert knew that if he assisted Tom in the planned killing, he himself would be criminally guilty as a participant in the murder.

"Hugo is just assuming," Anna observed drily, "that because you agreed to be part of the Sergio business, you are hooked into it for everything."

Robert agreed, it was shameless, and in a new telegram to Hugo he tried to exclude his involvement in any killing. Hugo rejected his hesitation.

National interest demands sink Bird and justifies whatever means necessary. Repeat whatever: You volunteered for Tripoli. Although scene different, aim is same. You must think very carefully about your own situation.

This might be worded like a caution, but without doubt it wrapped a naked threat. Robert would know as a lawyer that if he was part of a conspiracy to capture *Hermes,* he was liable for any deaths in the furtherance of that conspiracy, whether or not he himself took part in the actual killing itself. Moreover, the message continued:

Do not forget that your friend A is as much an accomplice in this as you.

Anna an accomplice; the idea was frightening. Hugo was threatening Robert that if he did not co-operate it was not only him but Anna too who would pay for it. And if the outcome was murder, Robert knew that an accomplice was just as guilty as the actual perpetrator. That could mean the death penalty.

"What will you do?" Anna asked him after he explained what Hugo had said.

"Do I have a choice?"

"Don't be stupid! He's a criminal! Of course, you have a choice. Of course, you must refuse. Tell him 'No' in terms that he cannot mistake, and we'll take the first train out. Hugo cannot be believed and certainly not trusted."

"There's more. Hugo's offering me an unlimited supply of cash. It's a bribe. Just imagine, he dares to lecture me about the path of duty, then offers me a bribe and blackmails me. What kind of a man is he?"

"Can you honestly you say you're surprised? Really Robert!" Anna observed ironically. "Have you quite lost your common sense."

"No! But Hugo has me over a barrel. I have to go with him."

"Rubbish! There is always a choice."

"But not a good one."

"Nevertheless, you must refuse. Cut the knot."

"It's easy to say that. But there would be consequences."

"All right! Take the consequences. Tell him to go to Hell."

"Anna that is too hasty. The consequences are real. Too real. I have thought about it. I had better do as he wishes. And hope for the best."

"Hoping for the best is not a good decision." Anna said. "Agreeing to do something stupid and hoping for the best is a very bad decision indeed."

Robert did not agree. If Tom murdered the Germans on *Hermes,* unless Robert captured *Hermes* there was more than a chance that the bodies would be found by the Spanish police. There would then be a police investigation and Robert would be implicated in the murders. Anna too. The British government would disown them, they would be thrown to the wolves in the national interest. God knows how they would fare, alone and without friends, in the Spanish criminal courts. On the other hand, if Robert's plan to seize *Hermes* worked, no-one would know about the murders. He was therefore sure the only sensible course was to co-operate with Hugo, actively assist Tom to capture the vessel, help him to sail out into the Mediterranean, scuttle the vessel and then quit. He decided that he would do it. Say 'yes' to Hugo. Whatever Anna thought.

He looked for a quiet place to work out how to capture *Hermes*. He wandered to a nearby café and sat with an iced lime juice in the cool shade of a tall Palm. A crude surprise attack on the ship wouldn't work, he hadn't the men to do it. Moreover, he must assume resistance; the ship's crew could all be hostile and armed. He needed a subtler approach. Working out how to scuttle the ship would also have to wait until after the ship was captured. He quickly concluded that the best way of seizing the ship was to employ trickery, and to wait to act for the ship to dock in Malaga, to complete refuelling and finish loading her cargo of arms. That would be the time to capture her. Thinking about it, he was satisfied that the little deception he had agreed with Hugo would do fine.

When Bedros joined him at his table in the café he decided to explain the idea. "Bedros, I agreed a little scheme with Hugo to get on board *Hermes*. Hugo applied to the Admiralty Court in Liverpool for a Warrant of Arrest for *Hermes*, on the grounds of a debt incurred by *Hermes* in England. He sent the Court documents to the British Consul in Malaga."

"A debt?"

"A fictitious debt."

"You say a warrant of arrest from a Court, but how do you arrest a ship?"

"By literally nailing the Warrant, that means Order of Arrest, onto the ship's mast. I have received the documents and I am arranging for the local Spanish court to endorse it with Spanish seals. It will look impressively official."

"Such cleverness!"

"Bedros, The only thing that matters is that it deceives them. I will arrange for a Spanish lawyer to arrive at the ship carrying the Warrant for Arrest. He will then go through the drama of nailing the Warrant of Arrest to the Ship's mast. It should look official and impressive. I and you will go on board with the lawyer, as his clerks. And we will stop anyone else including more Germans boarding."

"It's like a play."

"That's certainly the idea."

"And then what?"

"Then we sail off in the confusion."

It did sound all so easy, and he knew it could all go wrong. He didn't like to even think about the consequences.

Now, faced with the imminent arrival of *Hermes* and a probable spate of murders, what was all too clear to Robert was that Anna and Valeria would be at great risk in Malaga. The Germans had murdered Maria Gibson in London, had tried to kill them in Tripoli; if they believed that Robert and Anna were in Malaga to thwart the conspiracy they would not hesitate to strike. It was therefore obvious that Anna and Valeria must leave Malaga at once. He did not want to be hamstrung by having to think about Anna's safety. He had spoken to Bedros who wanted to help him carry out the plan. He had better tell Valeria and Anna they must return to London at once.

So, later that day, without any doubt that for her own safety Anna must leave for London without delay, he went to her room in the Hotel and put his concerns to her.

She brusquely dismissed his fears for her safety. "You are making too much of it! I know all this. You are exaggerating the danger. The Germans will not dare to touch us here. We are British and we are no longer in Tripoli. We are in Europe now. Spain."

She was defiant, her eyes determined. She knew about the danger, accepted the risk and wasn't going to back down.

"Look Anna ... "

"No! I won't be pushed away! Robert, you dragged me here. I told you to say 'No' to Hugo. I told you again and again. You insisted on coming. And you insisted on taking part in his silly plan. I didn't want it, but now I'm here I'm going to stay. I want to see what happens. Remember I came out here to settle matters about my mother's death. That's not yet done."

"Look Anna, you've done brilliantly, and we've learnt a lot. But with *Hermes* coming the game has changed. Our enemies are ruthless. They will stop at nothing. It's just too dangerous for you to remain."

She flared up, quite tense, on edge and gave him a steely stare. "No! You brought me here Robert. You were naive enough to be taken in by Hugo's lies. I'm here and I'm going to stay."

This seemed to Robert to be ridiculous and perverse, ignoring the facts that had become plain to him. It was obvious that Sergio's plan had been hijacked by the Germans, who would be pitiless in destroying anyone who stood in their way. He reiterated that Anna's safety was in jeopardy, and it would be too dangerous for her and Valeria to remain. Robert himself proposed to stay only because giving Hugo what he wanted was their best protection. But, he repeated, it was important that she and Valeria left Malaga as quickly as possible.

"Robert don't be ridiculous! You know by now I can look after myself. I am not afraid. I have made up my mind and you'd better accept it."

"Anna you will not be safe."

"Enough! Stop it, Robert!"

Nothing he could say about his concern for her safety had any effect. He was desperate to persuade her to leave and as words had failed to sway her, he took both her hands in his. She didn't like it and he had to tighten his grip, which she liked even less.

"Anna, I have known for some time that you are the most precious thing in my life! I love you! I want to spend my life with you. I cannot bear the thought of losing you. That is the only reason I am so concerned that you leave. I must know you are safe."

She stood there shaking her head vigorously.

"Anna, I love you! I want you to be my wife!"

She wrenched her hands free. "Don't! This is absurd! This is no time to talk of marriage."

"Anna, I love you and want to marry you!"

"Robert, you don't listen! This is not the time to talk about marriage."

"Surely you understand ..."

Her eyes flashed cold steel and she glared at him. "You're just using this as an opportunity to lure me into marriage! Then you would get what you wanted all along! What all men want."

"Anna!" Her meaning was clear, and Robert was scandalised.

"Isn't that what you want?"

"That is unfair Anna! I love you! Look this is how I feel!" With that he embraced her, wrapping his arms around her, holding her closely and pressing his lips on hers, kissing her fully on the lips. He sought to convince her of his argument with his passion. All he did was confirm her accusation.

"Stop it! How dare you!" She was repelled by the unwelcome physicality of what she took as his sudden display of raw desire. She pushed him violently away.

"Anna!" It was not what he had anticipated.

"Don't Anna me! Have you lost your reason?"

"Anna, please see sense. You must see the danger if you stay."

She was outraged at what she saw as the crudeness of his abrupt and inept advances. She shouted at him, clenched fists and beat them against his chest.

"You fool! I've told you I won't do it!" she screamed. "I can't even think about marriage. You're just trying to take cheap advantage of the situation and I won't have it."

He despaired of making her see sense, recognised that the situation was quickly slipping away from him. He grabbed her arms and pulled her close to him, and, too roughly, kissed her again furiously. She reacted strongly against what she saw as his false and aggressive behaviour, rejecting him, thrusting him forcibly away.

"Stop it!" she yelled. "Are you mad. How dare you treat me like this!"

"Anna ..."

"No! Do you think you are still in Paris? With one of your French tarts."

She stood back, angry, coiled as if she would spring at him like a cornered tiger if he came at her again. There were daggers in her eyes, if there was a weapon to hand, she would have used it. He realised much too late that he had made a complete mess of it. He had been moved only by concern for her safety, to protect the girl he loved. But she called him a contemptible fake. He was distraught at the violent response that his misguided advances had produced. It was not possible to mistake the harsh truth that she had hated the way he had behaved. He had not, however, immediately grasped her reference to his trip to Paris a year ago. Then it flooded back to him that she had once accused him of going to Paris to buy sex, which she thought despicable. It was a horrible moment. She glared at him as if she despised him. He stood there, his mind driven blank by the appalling emotion of the moment.

"What do you mean?" His question was stupid, he knew perfectly well what she meant, he had invited her contemptuous dismissal and he knew it.

"Don't pretend you don't know what I mean! Paris is where you learnt to treat women like this!"

"I'm trying to tell you that I love you!"

"Love! You treat me as some kind of object. Some plaything you can toy with. You may have treated your poor woman in Paris like that, but not me."

"Anna! I love you!"

"Enough! Go away, leave me."

Anna had intended to explain how terribly weary and worn out she was, and how unready she was for the conversation that Robert had suddenly sprung on her. She had wanted to say that she was in no state of mind to think about such a demanding life change as marriage. It was his fault though; he shouldn't have tried to force her hand like that. And then to have come on to her in such a rough, outrageous manner. Yes, she liked him a lot, but what did he think he was doing behaving like that? She knew that she had said too much. Of course, she hated the idea of men exploiting women for sex, and he shouldn't have gone to Paris for it, but she regretted having gone too far in condemning him. She was angry with him for creating the situation and with herself for how she had responded to it.

But the events had driven them both into silence. They could only stand facing each other, frozen for a moment in a battlefield stand-off, she glaring at him with fury in her eyes, he angry at her refusal to see reason.

"We have known each other for many years Anna. How could you even think such things about me?"

"Oh! Do you not want to use me like your Paris women."

"Anna! You must know that's not fair."

"Stop it! Paris shows you have no idea what 'fair' means!"

"Alright." He paused, knowing a brick wall when he was foolish enough to run into one full tilt, knowing too he was on the brink of disaster.

She was standing there saying nothing but fuming.

He had to make a decision. "I will just say this. Then I will go. What I set out to do on this mission I will finish. That is who I am. You surely know that. But it has become too dangerous for you to remain. That is a fact. You and Val must return home at once. And after what you have said this afternoon, you can't stay. Nor can I imagine after what you have said that you would want to stay with me."

"Don't think to order me around!"

"I am telling you how it is Anna. There is no choice. I will finish the task but you must go home."

"How dare you! I will decide if I want to go home."

"No Anna, there is no choice! I will in no circumstances let you anywhere near *Hermes*. You can't stay in Malaga."

She remained furious but accepted from the look on his face that he was adamant.

Valeria spoke to him later, before the evening meal, and said she had in the end persuaded Anna that they should leave Malaga the following day, a long journey via Madrid and Paris back to London. Valeria said they would take Bedros with them.

20

Several days after Anna, Valeria and Bedros had set off for Madrid by train, Robert was standing under the shady trees of the Parque. In the early morning the air was still fresh after the relative coolness of the night, although the sun rising now in a clear blue sky would soon see to that. He expected yet another stifling hot day when it would be too hot for comfort in the city. He was grateful to be missing the excessive heat of high summer, but by midday it would nevertheless again be roasting in the crowded, noisy, and dirty narrow streets of the old city behind him: too hot to think properly, even under shade of the plane trees. But at this time of the morning the sun was still young, and it remained pleasant, a good time to calmly contemplate the move that he must soon make, when *Hermes*, who had been expected for a week, docked.

He would give it a go, his best shot and see what he and Tom could manage to pull out of the hat. He was so completely distracted that he was not even vaguely aware that two figures were steadily bearing down on him from behind, moving through the dark shadows cast by the tall trees. He did not know anyone was there until they were almost on top of him.

"Anna!" Robert exclaimed, totally nonplussed to see her walking up as if nothing had happened. Yet so much had happened. Only a few days before he had stood on the platform at Malaga station and watched her train steaming out for Madrid. Only the day before that, they had had an almighty row and parted on execrable terms. He had certainly not expected to see her again until such time as he might return to London, at whatever distant point that might be. If indeed he lived to return.

"Anna!" His voice betrayed the alarm he felt. "Has something happened to the train? An accident on the line?"

Valeria answered his question. "What happened Robert, was that we changed our mind. We decided we had to return. We got to Madrid and came back."

"Don't get carried away Robert," Anna said sharply, "I have not forgiven you for your stupidity. But I have come back."

"I can see! What happened?"

"I have ..."

"I talked to her!" interrupted Valeria. "That's what happened! You were a fool, Robert. An idiot. But we are all in the same hole."

"Aunty..." Anna tried to say something.

Valeria interrupted again. "No Anna. You have both been idiots. You both need to see some sense. Now I shall leave you together and go for a cold drink in the Hotel. I need it!" She turned and walked off.

"Anna," Robert said, "she tore a strip off me for my stupidity in how I spoke to you. And I deserved it. I know I deserved it. I'm sorry. I have been a fool in so many ways. Please forgive me. I could not bear to think I'd lost you. It was awful. But she said she talked to you ..." He looked into her eyes.

"Yes, that does mean she talked to me about your frolic in Paris. You can't expect me to approve it. I don't. But I see I may have slightly misjudged you."

"That's something. I'm not asking for forgiveness for Paris ..."

"That's good because you're not getting it. I can't forgive you for what you did."

"Oh."

"I came back because I want to see this *Hermes* thing to the end. I can't expect you to understand, but it's about my mother. She was dragged into this business by Sergio, and they killed her for it. I can't rest until I know that the whole thing is over. It's nice of you to think of my safety Robert. It is. But I have a voice. And I want my voice to be heard. Of course, I know there are risks, and I am willing to run them. I have a right to make that decision, to decide to take the risk, and you should accept that right. However wrong you think it to be."

"Alright Anna. I accept it. But are you quite sure you know what you're saying?"

"Yes, I am! Quite sure!"

"Well ..."

"The thing is Robert, that if you are ready to take the risks, I want to be with you!"

"Anna!" He could hardly believe what she had said. "If only you knew how much I missed you." He kissed her again on the cheek, and she did not reject him.

"Robert!" Bedros had rushed up to them and was pointing out to sea. "*Hermes* is coming in tomorrow! I've just checked the Port register."

"Anna, tell Val. We've little time to get things ready."

Anna rushed off to tell Valeria and organise themselves. They had already booked into the Hotel.

Robert turned to Bedros. "It's good to see you again."

*

They spent a quiet night except for one thing. Anna announced that there was a change of plan, she too would board *Hermes.*

"There's no point you arguing," she told Robert. "I've had enough of being ignored. You shouldn't have listened to Hugo. We should never have come to this position. But now we have I'll see it through to the end."

Valeria said that in that case she and Bedros would come as well. Robert tried and failed over a prolonged argument to change their minds.

The following morning Robert walked again to the Parque and looked out to sea. Then, at last, far out in the Mediterranean, just beyond the harbour lighthouse, he saw that the long-awaited Steam Yacht *Hermes* was indeed coming into view. Her profile was unmistakable; it had been burnt into his memory during his visit to the shipyard in Birkenhead many months ago.

"She's here at last, surely a day of destiny!" he exclaimed and sent a message for Anna to join him.

"My God Robert! Is that her?" Anna was amazed.

The reason why they had come to Malaga and waited for long uncomfortable weeks, the steam yacht *Hermes* herself was steaming serenely into the Port of Malaga. The wisp of oily smoke rising high into the air from her stack even suggested an exclamation mark. A challenge perhaps? *Hermes* was still a striking beauty, although today something of an aging one. So not surprisingly heads were turned to follow her incongruous progress towards the quays. She still exuded an aura of wealth, luxury, and leisure in making her stately progress, contrasting sharply with the hustle and bustle of the somewhat chaotic working harbour. Her classic, calm, dignity, albeit dated, stood out against the hurly burly of assorted and often decrepit and invariably dirty tramps, ancient fishing vessels meandering about and bum boats hopefully searching for trade. She was no working boat like them, but a rare grandness, built not for trade but only for pleasure. She looked stunning. Her raked bow with her elaborate, gilded, and carved figurehead announced her presence; her burnished deck rails set off her sleek clean lines; the ivory whiteness of her hull showed off the dark teak of her decking and the teak cabins on her main and upper deck. Malaga did not often see such a graceful classic vessel as *Hermes*.

Robert took note of the Red Duster flying proudly at her stern, such a public demonstration of her as a British ship. But that of course was the point of the German plan: the whole dastardly beauty of the Berlin plot came dramatically clear to him. *Herme*s was intended to be seen by the world conspicuously flying the Red Ensign. Her Britishness would be noticed and be remembered. It would become part of a collection of facts that would later be joined together by Berlin like a jig-saw puzzle and promoted across the world to make a completely damning picture. A picture that would show how *Hermes* was a base, underhand British plot. There she was, a ship purchased in England, with English money, refitted in an English shipyard, and sailing under the Red Duster. She had already loaded a cargo of English gold sovereigns in Lisbon, then in Malaga she would pick up a cargo of British made rifles, cargos that she then unloaded in North Africa in Tripoli to instigate a revolt against the Ottoman Empire.

And when an international crisis erupted after fighting in Tripoli and across Libya, Berlin would unleash the story of Britain's disgraceful part in a devious and unlawful plot against the international order. One that would damn Britain as a hypocrite, ready to use piracy for her own ends.

Hermes would be used as part of a careful plan to incriminate Britain in a conspiracy to bring about a coup by Italian nationalist supporters in Tripoli. It would drive Turkey into the hands of the Kaiser, would threaten the security of the Suez Canal and the route to India. Moreover, in the event of a big European war, Turkey would close the Dardanelles and block the sea route into the Black Sea.

"So, this is the famous *Hermes*?" Bedros exclaimed. He had joined them.

"Indeed! She's a beauty isn't she! Just look at those lines. That grace. That charm. What elegance."

"You speak of her as a woman," Bedros observed dryly. "She does look a fine vessel. What a shame to sink her. Isn't there another way?"

"That's what Hugo wants."

"And what about you?" Bedros asked.

"A Good question! I wonder if I am expendable like *Hermes*. They want *Hermes* to disappear, they may wish I could disappear at sea with her."

"You don't trust your friends in London?"

"No! I fear it might be safer for them if I was left to sink with the boat!"

"Then we must make sure it doesn't happen."

As she approached the Port, *Hermes* signalled that she would proceed directly to the refuelling station, probably therefore intending to load the cargo, replenish fuel and galley supplies and make a rapid departure. Ideal from Robert's perspective, for provided they could capture the vessel they could sail away at once. Indeed, after refuelling, *Hermes* moved to the quayside and one of the crew went off to the market for supplies. Later a gang of local porters, accompanied by military guards from the City's garrison, arrived. They carried many wooden crates that they stacked on the quay. Robert assumed that this was the cargo of rifles to be loaded onto *Hermes*. A small crowd of onlookers gathered to view the steam yacht, and shortly afterwards two sailors with cap badges from the German freighter *Ulm* joined them. Robert assumed that their orders might be to board *Hermes* when they could.

He moved to the quay and stood at the back of the crowd. He had bundled up his black legal coat in a sack and given it to Bedros. Instead, he wore well-used porter's overalls and hoped he looked inconspicuous. A man who fitted Tom's description, short stature, and long black hair, appeared on the ship's gangway preventing the sailors from *Ulm* from boarding. They looked as if they might make an issue of it, which made Robert think they probably had orders to board as soon as they reached the ship. The situation looked tricky.

"This may look suspicious to the Germans," he whispered to Bedros.

"It is certainly confusing."

"Look! They will see there is no sign of the German Agent on deck. It will look strange."

He was right and Robert assumed that Tom must have 'disposed of' the chap. It meant that if they went ahead with the plan to capture *Hermes*, it had to succeed.

"And the sailors sent from *Ulm* are not being allowed to board *Hermes.*"

It seemed to Robert that things were going wrong. If the arms crates were not loaded at once the Germans might send more men from the *Ulm* to find out what was happening.

Robert whispered urgently to Bedros, "the sailors from *Ulm* must be allowed to load the arms crates onto *Hermes*."

It needed quick action and Robert pushed his way through the crowd, intending to yell instructions at Tom. However, as Robert got near *Hermes,* Bedros had somehow managed to get in front of him, to boldly push to the front. He was now there yelling loudly, and bizarrely holding aloft, high above his head two live and squawking chickens, which he clutched by their feet. He had in fact just that moment bought them from a trader working the quayside, seeing the chance of using them to get on board *Hermes*. Robert had no idea what Bedros was up to, but grabbed the opportunity to speak to him. Bedros went as close to *Hermes* as he could get, waved the chickens in the air, and bellowed at Tom.

"I bring you galley supplies from Hugo!" Bedros shouted in some strange language that Robert guessed might be Armenian, but the words 'from Hugo' in English came across loud and crystal clear.

That was why Tom allowed him to scramble on board. Bedros passed on Robert's message about the sailors, and Tom who was not a fool, did as requested. The chickens attracted some attention and amusement from the onlookers as Bedros carried them to the galley in a ridiculously outrageous, over-performed pantomime.

"He's a natural comic!" Robert thought, impressed by the gales of laughter from the spectators. Tom, meanwhile, having got Robert's message duly directed the *Ulm* sailors to pick up one of the crates from the quayside and supervised its transport onto *Hermes* and into the forward deck cabin. It was no great distance, and the loading was quickly done. They returned and lifted another crate on board. Other crates followed until all the crates were in place in the deck cabin. The arms cargo was loaded.

Robert had taken the opportunity of the hustle and bustle caused by the sailors coming up and down the gangplank, and had himself slipped on board, vaguely looking as if he was assisting Tom in the process. Once on board, Robert went below deck and told the engineer he should be ready with steam up in case the master decided to sail. The engineer was naturally surprised to see Robert but said that the master had already given orders to get up steam. This confirmed Robert's earlier impression that the plan was for *Hermes* to make only a short stop in Malaga.

So far so good, but Robert realised that he had to get Len, a new deckhand recruited by Bedros on Robert's instructions, together with Anna, Valeria, and Bedros on board, before they could sail. Then Robert saw that the German sailors standing on the quay, who had been loading crates onto *Hermes,* had been joined by another three sailors with *Ulm* cap badges. Together, moreover, with a person in a uniform who was probably another German agent from *Ulm.* All of them were looking as if they would make a move to board *Hermes* together in a concerted move.

Robert knew that this was a critical moment, one that could turn into a disaster. If all the Germans boarded and some were armed, his plan to capture the ship would be defeated. Luckily at that moment the attention of the crowd on the quay was attracted by the arrival of a noisy, colourful procession led by a small boy loudly banging a large drum. This was Pablo, recruited from their hotel kitchen, yelling for people to make way for 'Her Excellency' the 'Condesa Di Ligure.' He was repeatedly proclaiming: "Atención! ¡Atención! ¡Da paso a la Condesa! ¡Viene la Condesa!"

Behind him was Anna dressed to kill in an amazing flower decked hat, wearing a bright yellow dress topped with a bright magenta scarf, a vision of vibrancy against the greys and browns of the quayside. She held a vividly coloured parasol that she twirled from side to side as she moved through the crowd. Behind her was Valeria, elaborately dressed also carrying a colourful parasol, and as she walked, she exchanged greetings with the people around her. It was indeed the unexpected and grand procession of a young Italian Countess and her entourage, making a dramatic appearance. It was a proper stage entrance, for laughing and chattering loudly in Italian, Valeria shouting to make way, gesticulating wildly, and exchanging banter with the crowd. They did indeed fully engage the crowd, attracting everybody's attention as they arrived at the foot of the gangplank.

Pablo, enjoying himself, announced loudly to the crowd that Her Excellency the 'Condesa di Ligure' desired to examine the vessel, which she had seen in Naples two years ago. Taking her cue, Valeria declaimed loudly to the world in Italian the Countess's profound desire to board the vessel, recalling her fond memories of a party on board in the Bay of Naples. The Contessa and her entourage moved forward to board. Valeria and the personal maid started to follow her up the gangplank, but were halted by the Contessa, who commanded them to stay on the quay and wait for her. Which they did by standing at the foot of the gangway, effectively blocking it from the Germans. Anna continued to attract attention by promenading the main deck of *Hermes* demanding to be shown round the ship. Anna then went below decks into one of the cabins to change into the rough pants and blouse, the clothes of a deckhand, that Robert had managed to smuggle aboard. He joined her there and quickly helped her tie her hair in a long ponytail.

"Anna you were marvellous! What a performance!"

"I think you too are enjoying all these theatricals Robert. It reminds me of how we used to dress up as explorers in the old days."

"Absolutely! It was fantastic!"

In the confusion of Anna and her party boarding *Hermes,* Bedros had returned to the quay to take part in the next scene of Robert's playlet. It was fortunate he did for he saved the day again, managing to manifest himself at the foot of the gangplank, enabling Valeria to board *Hermes.* He pushed in front of the men from *Ulm* and prevented them from boarding. Bedros was now wearing Robert's formal, legal black coat, a ceremonial and impressive garment in a seventeenth century style, with a stiff black silk collar, puffed up cuffs, a line of fancy gold buttons down the front and a large, embroidered badge, the colourful embroidered arms of the Province of Andalucía, on his left breast. Best of all was his huge, fantastic, hat with feathers. With his back to the ship and facing the quay he occupied the gangplank. This would not have prevented a determined attempt to push him to one side, or leap onto *Hermes* over the ship's rail, but the *Ulm* group was clearly taken by surprise at the abrupt turn of events. Bedros's dramatic performance and impressive appearance had, as hoped, confused them.

Nor was it over, for he then shouted out loudly: "Esperar! Esperar! ¡El oficial viene! Esta barco es detenido!"

For the crowd on the quayside watching the comings and goings on *Hermes,* Bedros's latest entertainment added to their interest. The words 'es detenido', meaning is 'detained' or 'arrested', aroused more attention and there was some murmuring in the crowd. Many shouted out what Robert understood to be: "What's going on! What's all this!"

Well, what was in fact going on was the attempt to frustrate a German boarding party. A ruse that was so far working. The *Ulm* party were just standing around in a bemused huddle. They had probably had orders to board, even to use force, but what they saw was a situation they didn't understand. It obviously looked convincing, something they took to be official, and they would have no wish to get entangled with the Spanish authorities. It meant that for a critical moment, the Germans did nothing. Nevertheless, it was only a matter of time before they decided to use the weight of their numbers and rush the gangway. Robert knew he could wait no longer for the new sailor, Len. But then he saw a boat being rowed towards the side of the ship and at the oars was Len, the new crew member. Robert signalled to him to come alongside and get on board.

At that point the Spanish lawyer Robert had hired to take part in performing the 'arrest' of *Hermes* arrived on the quayside with two assistants. All were formally dressed in courtroom attire. The lawyer clutched a collection of large, sealed documents in his hand and was clearly preparing himself for a proclamation of some sort. Bedros was still there on the gang plank, so Robert went close to him and signalled to the lawyer to go ahead with his piece about arresting the ship, making sure they were blocking access to the gangplank. Meanwhile Robert got hold of Tom and told him to gather the crew, get boathooks and prepare both to pull in the gangway and repel boarders.

It worked. An ad hoc improvised scheme but it worked. The Spanish lawyer and his group stood on the quay, blocking access to the gangway, he read out in Spanish the long-winded terms of the order of arrest. It was a suitably flowery and lengthy document, and he was still reading it out, to the attention of the crowds, who were entirely puzzled, when Tom pulled in the gangway and let go the hawsers that tied the vessel to the quay. At the same time *Hermes* engine went into action, turning the screw, pushing the vessel away from the quay – with a little help from the boathooks wielded by Tom and the others. To cap it all Robert could see the *Ulm* group on the quay milling around in a state of consternation. Slow to react because of the confusion and surprise, too late they made a half-hearted rush towards *Hermes* rails. But the vessel was now too far off the quay for a jump. They yelled in frustration.

Robert rushed up to the wheelhouse and told the master to steer for the harbour mouth. The man was only a bit surprised; Tom must have given the order to start the engine and pull away from the quayside and had probably had a word with him about the likely change of command. Which the master obviously simply accepted.

21

As soon as they were clear of the assorted shipping that was milling around in Malaga harbour, and had steamed out of the harbour entrance, Robert ordered full speed ahead. He felt comforted by the gathering shudder under his feet as the engineer below decks let loose the full power of the engine. He looked way back over the stern to see the rippling wake showed how the screw was churning the water. He looked ahead to see how *Hermes* steeply raked bow was slicing through the choppy sea as they ran free into the Mediterranean. He felt an enormous sense of relief; the dangerous enterprise had gone so well, as good as he could have possibly hoped. Acutely aware of the risks they had run, the weight of responsibility on his shoulders for Anna and Valeria's safety lifted slightly. At least for the moment they were all safe, and for the moment he could think no further forward. But the need to do so, to face the future, would come and come soon. He knew that. He could hardly believe his luck that they had so easily tricked the Germans, got themselves on board, captured *Hermes* without a fight and cast off before the *Ulm* sailors realised what was happening. He needed to grip the handrail in front of him to reassure himself that he was in command of the vessel, that they were indeed unscathed and had really escaped into the open sea.

"So far so good!" he told the master.

"Aye! Tis that."

But Robert knew that when the Germans on the quayside woke up to the fact that *Hermes* and its cargo had been captured and was escaping their grasp, they were bound to pursue.

"What speed can she do?" he asked the master.

"She can easily cruise at 12 knots. Could put on a spurt if needed. Depends on the sea. We have just refuelled so that is not a problem."

A day or two before, Robert had wondered what vessel the Germans might use for a pursuit if something like this did happen. Thinking that most boats would be too slow, he had asked Bedros to make inquiries around the Port. He did.

"I was told of a vessel," Bedros reported back, "that is advertised for hire. It is described as a '*Narrow fronted, cutting bow, very fast, launch.*' I'd call it a 'speed boat' I've seen it in the water, and it looks as if it can really go!"

"So, it can go fast, but how many passengers can it take?"

"Only four."

"What sort of engine?"

"It has a heavy, gasoline powered, piston engine midships. It uses a lot of fuel and is probably noisy and smelly. But it has a top speed of at least twenty knots and probably more."

"How does she handle in the water?"

"The owner says she handles well in calm, still water. However, other people say that it is a lousy seagoing vessel and rolls heavily in any sea swell."

"So it's fast! But can carry only four and would be a poor firing platform unless the sea was flat calm."

Tom Connolly approached. "We've done it! But they'll try a pursuit. We must be well out to sea before they can get out of harbour."

"We'll know soon enough if they're after us."

"They will come."

"Then we will fight them on the water," Robert said it with confidence. He walked back along the upper deck to get a good view of Malaga harbour through the master's glasses. A soft sea breeze ruffled his hair, and he was aware of the hot early afternoon sun on his back. Bedros approached, having noticed him scanning the harbour mouth.

"Expecting company?"

"Yes. I expect the Germans will chase us in that speedboat."

"Ah! Then what?"

"They will close with us and try to take *Hermes* by storm. Try to board us. I expect they will open small arms fire. We need to be ready."

"We do."

"We need to rig up some cover against small arms fire. On both decks. Main deck and especially the upper deck."

"There is furniture in the deck cabins we could use."

"Yes, and mattresses from the lower deck cabins. Anything that gives cover. We need to protect the stern rails on both decks."

Robert was thinking that the upper deck offered a good firing platform to protect the stern, which would be the initial direction of approach by the 'enemy' – the word now seemed to be appropriate. The chips were down now, and if the Germans came after them it would not be with bunches of flowers. This was where the shooting would begin. And if *Hermes* engaged the Germans from the stern, they could open combined fire from both the lower and upper decks. An enemy attack on the bow would be more difficult to deal with, the hull had an upward inclining slope at the bow, a graceful line with the ornate bowsprit and gilded figurehead but one that also obstructed the field of fire. Moreover, the wheelhouse was vulnerable in a frontal attack.

For any kind of defence against the Germans, they would need guns. But that was easy; they would use the guns that the Germans had just loaded on board for their mission to arm the Arab tribes in Libya. He had, therefore, better find out exactly what weapons *Hermes* had on board. There was no time to lose to prepare, and he told Len, the new sailor, to go to the forward cabin where the crates containing the guns were stored.

"Break the crates open. Use a crowbar. We need to see what we've got."

Robert went himself some minutes later and examined the weapons. He had expected to see crates of rifles and ammunition, and he did. But had not expected several other long, wooden boxes. One had been opened by Len and contained carefully packed layers of a kind of projectile, each about two feet long labelled as "Hales Rockets". The box also contained what he assumed to be launching devices for the rockets.

"Rockets by God!" he told Len. Evidently also intended to arm the Arab tribes in Libya against their Turkish masters. But how do you use them? He had no idea.

"Maybe," he thought looking at the rockets, "they might come in useful some time."

He assembled the crew. Apart from himself there was Tom and Len, who had both served in the Royal Navy and could use a rifle. Bedros quickly volunteered and assured Robert that all Armenians knew how to handle a gun. Tom had spoken to the other sailor, Bill, who had been taken on in

Liverpool and he was prepared to 'give it a go' with a rifle. With Robert that made five men to use the rifles.

Robert had recognized the rifles as the British standard service rifle. He had belonged to a rifle club and had handled the SMLE, the 'Short Magazine Mark 3 Lee Enfield', which fired .303 calibre ammunition and was first introduced as the standard British army issue in 1907. It had a range of 2000 yards, was more accurate at 200 to 300 yards, but in combat would be used at 500 yards. Its magazine was loaded using a charge clip, an ammunition clip holding five rounds. The rifle's magazine could load all the cartridges of two charge clips. In combat a soldier would carry several loaded charge clips in ammunition pouches.

Valeria had observed Len unpacking the rifles. "Give me something useful to do!" she demanded.

"And me!" Anna added.

Robert asked both of them to start loading cartridges into the charge clips and to build up a quantity of loaded charge clips.

"Any tricks in loading?" Valeria asked.

"Yes. To avoid jamming, load the charge clip with alternate rims of each cartridge overlapping. And the charge clip needs a hard push downwards to load the ammunition into the magazine."

He explained that when the charge clip was loaded into the magazine the charge clip itself was then automatically ejected. Each spent cartridge case would be ejected after each shot was fired. In experienced hands the rifle could fairly rattle through its magazine.

Robert demonstrated how to load the charge clip, and then use the charge clip to load the rifle's magazine. They were quick to pick up the technique.

"You grasped that quickly!" Robert said.

"Robert, you are so condescending! You must learn that women are very capable." Anna said it in a sharp tone; he had walked straight into that one, as Valeria's amused side glance told him.

"I'll train Bedros and Bill." Valeria told him and started to instruct them. He noticed that Valeria was handling the rifle as if she was familiar with it. She saw him looking askance.

"Don't worry, I can use a gun!" she announced. "I was brought up on a farm with a gun in my hands. We had to be ready for anything. Wolves, thieves, bandits, you name it."

"Well, we might have to face thieves and bandits, but I hope not wolves!" Robert joked.

"Don't be too sure! I'll get on with it," Valeria said, grabbing Bill and Bedros and telling them how to take up a firing position.

"Now about firing. First, relax. Keep both eyes open to aim. Don't take too long. Control your breathing, take a deep breath when you're ready to shoot. Hold your breath and squeeze the trigger. Squeeze the trigger, don't jerk it. Hold the rifle stock firmly, apply a steady pressure. Just think of it as your first girl. Keep it firm but gentle ..." There were yells of ribald appreciation.

"Keep squeezing until the bullet is fired." An instruction that produced a fusillade of vulgar shouts. But it seemed to work, they were doing what she said. It was another side of Valeria.

Robert looked again towards the harbour mouth and could make out the tell-tale sign of a tiny white bow wave, indicating a fast boat coming out of Malaga. With the first shots fired at the speedboat, Robert realised again that 'enemy' was indeed the appropriate word. Now it was truly 'dog eat dog'.

Valeria got Bedros and Bill to tie mattresses taken from the cabin to the stern rails, to give cover against incoming gun fire. They brought up further mattresses from the lower deck passenger cabins to the upper deck, whose metal wire rails offered no cover. Some empty rifle crates helped to line the rear of the side rail as cover. When it was done the upper and main rear decks looked like a floating junk shop.

"There are only four men in the speedboat!" he told the master. "One steering, one is sitting next to him in the front of the boat and the other two are in the rear seats."

"So, only three men who can shoot!" the master observed drily. "And it's cramped. Not ideal."

"No! And we have five men who can shoot."

"What kind of weapons have they got?"

"I can't see any sign of a machine gun. That means they are armed only with revolvers and rifles." The conclusion was pleasing; they outgunned the Germans.

Robert looked back towards Malaga and saw that the German speedboat was coming away from the harbour at a good lick, throwing up a massive bow wave and an arc of spray as her powerful engine drove her sharp narrow bow to slice through the water. Robert decided to test the range of his rifle and lay flat on the upper deck, sheltered between two empty rifle crates, and opened fire. He couldn't see if any of his shots were on target, the sea had such a rolling swell that the speed boat was dancing up and down; correct aiming was difficult. Moreover, conditions for accurate shooting in the speedboat were far worse as the speedboat was being thrown and tossed around in the water as she launched herself headlong into the undulating sea.

Perhaps that was why the Germans seemed intent on closing with *Hermes* as quickly as possible. Probably try to board *Hermes*, a risky operation as both boats were moving, and the speedboat was a lot lower in the water than *Hermes*. The Germans would have to leap upwards from the speedboat, a chancy move, as *Hermes* would be shooting at them. Robert was therefore feeling confident he could deal with them.

He was just about to relax when he noticed the tiny white speck of a second bow wave. He realised with growing unease this meant a second boat coming out of Malaga harbour. Moreover, behind that was the white blob of a sail in what was clearly a larger vessel, a yacht perhaps. A support vessel for the speedboats, perhaps carrying a crew of sailors from the *Ulm*.

"My God another one!" he exclaimed.

He had not expected to be attacked by two speedboats. A situation that changed the odds. With two boats they could attack on both flanks simultaneously and divide *Hermes'* defensive firepower. Their chances of boarding *Hermes* had suddenly got a lot better. They were still too near Malaga to hope to outrun the speedboats, unless their engines developed a fault, or they ran out of fuel. He would have to rely on whatever rifle fire his hotch-pot of defenders on *Hermes* could manage, and *Hermes* ability to manoeuvre. He would have to re-act to the situation as it developed and play it by ear. He remembered sailing his dingy in the marshy inlets of north Norfolk, how he had to tack to outwit and defeat the wind and the fearsome currents of the racing tide. They could try the same tactics with *Hermes*, duck and weave to escape the Germans. He had seen enough already in their escape from Malaga harbour to know that *Hermes* had a turn of speed and was sleek and nimble.

"Does she handle well?" he asked the master.

"She's a bute! Like a leopard of the sea!"

"Good! She may need to be!"

They did not have to wait long. The first speedboat, still out of range and visibly dancing up and down in the sea swell, reduced speed to maintain distance from *Hermes.*

"They wait for their friends to catch up with them!" the master remarked, "and they want to save fuel!"

"They will try to get round to both port and starboard of us, and attack from both directions at the same time!" Robert said.

"What are your orders?"

"Keep this course until we see what they do. I think the main danger is boarding. They may close and use their guns, but any hit would be lucky. It's much the same for us of course. But we too have guns, no shortage of ammunition and a more stable firing platform. We wait for them to make a move."

Robert saw the second German speedboat catch up with the first. They hovered together for a minute or so. A menacing presence like a couple of tigers waiting to pounce. Then suddenly there was a rush and a roar of their powerful engines as both boats opened their throttles. Both boats quickly picked up speed, broke away from each other, separating to go wide of *Hermes,* one to her port side and one to starboard, hunting their prey.

"Right! They are attacking from both sides simultaneously!" Robert said, telling the master the obvious. "We are too few to engage both at the same time. But we can effectively engage one of them."

He thought only for a moment. "Quarter turn to port. Keep our stern presented to the German on the starboard."

Robert deployed his small fighting force. He would leave Tom to do his best to fend off the attacker on *Hermes* port side. The others took up position to deal with the attacker from the starboard, who he feared might try to close and board *Hermes* from the stern. From the port side of *Hermes* Tom opened fire on the other speedboat, which thanks to *Hermes* change of course was now wide and side on to *Hermes* bow. The master's orders were to continue to turn to match the speedboat's position. *Hermes* change of course meant that if the German original plan had been to launch a co-ordinated midships attack on *Hermes,* the Germans were probably now confused. They would need to adjust their plan, but had no way of communicating with each other.

"If they had any sense," Robert said, "they should just attack together on our stern. They have eight men and could hope to board."

While the port side attacker drove towards *Hermes'* bow, the starboard side attacker continued to surge aggressively near to *Hermes'* stern. There was some incoming fire but all of it seemed wild, very wide of hitting anything on *Hermes.* But Robert was suddenly aware of a fifth rifle engaging the starboard side attacker with rapid fire. From the sound the rifle was on the upper deck and looking upwards he could make out Valeria, lying prone on the deck and half hidden by a mattress. The firing was so continuous that someone must be servicing her. It could only be Anna. It concerned him that she was on the relatively exposed upper deck, but there was nothing he could do.

The speedboat attacking on the starboard side was now closer to *Hermes* stern. He could see that its glass windshield, designed only to protect the occupants from sea spray, was in fact shattered. *Hermes* guns must have scored.

Some comfort, but nevertheless the boat was alarmingly close to *Hermes* stern.

"Keep firing!" Robert yelled. The stern might be vulnerable to boarding but was also *Hermes* best defensive position as all their rifles from two decks could bear and would have a good target.

"Will they board?"

"They will try!"

"If they get under our stern they would be out of our line of fire. They will try to leap over the Taff rail to seize the ship."

"Might it work?"

"We will soon see!"

The speedboat was now rapidly closing with *Hermes* as if to ram her stern. But suddenly the speedboat cut her engine and as she neared *Hermes* stern, one of the Germans stood up unsteadily in the rocking boat waving a piece of white cloth.

"They're surrendering!" someone shouted. It had an immediate effect: rifle fire from *Hermes* stopped.

Tom yelled out that the Germans were not to be trusted. "Keep on shooting! It's a dirty German trick!"

"We can't. They're raising the white flag!" Anna cried.

Robert was in a dilemma, not sure what to do. If the Germans were indeed surrendering it would be against the rules of war and his sense of decency to continue shooting. However, like Tom, he instinctively suspected a trick. He also feared it would be foolhardy to allow the Germans to come on board *Hermes*. Especially as there was a second speedboat close by.

"I'll warn them off!" Robert shouted. Saying which he fired a warning shot, well over the top of the speedboat, which took no notice and edged closer.

"We have a wounded. Help!" One of the Germans in the speedboat shouted at the top of his voice in English.

"We throw guns into water," another German called out, ostentatiously chucking his own rifle overboard.

"Don't let them aboard!" Tom yelled. "It's a trick."

"Hold fire!" Robert yelled back. He dared not risk bringing them on board *Hermes,* yet he hesitated to shoot them down in cold blood. He thought of simply leaving them, they were after all afloat, and trust to them being picked up by the yacht that had come out of Malaga in support.

But at that moment of his indecision there was a loud explosion on the speedboat. A large blue-black cloud of smoke appeared on the sea where the speedboat had been, thrusting itself violently upwards into the air. From the smoke burst bits and pieces, fragments of what had been the speedboat. Robert felt the blast of hot air as he watched the smoke cloud, dark as thunder, spew upwards from where a moment before the speedboat had floated. The light wind only dissipated the smoke slowly, *Hermes* had moved on, and it took a while to see that nothing remained of the speedboat and her crew, except pieces of flotsam and wreckage floating on the water. There was no sign of human life. When the smoke cleared the boat and everything in it had simply disappeared.

"My God! They must have been carrying explosives." Robert exclaimed, collecting himself after the blast. "Perhaps on some kind of time fuse. One that went wrong. They must have intended to get alongside and blow a hole in *Hermes*. Or at least disable her. A desperate plan."

"Thank God it didn't work!" Valeria replied. "They nearly tricked us. A moment later and they would have had us at their mercy."

Hermes left the wreckage of what had only shortly before been the German speedboat, and pulled steadily away from what was now only an assorted debris of bits and pieces. The sense of relief on board was palpable.

"Thank God! We are rid of them. The dirty rats," said Len. "They were scum who would have done for us if they could." No-one dissented.

But it was not the end because there was a second speedboat. She was well ahead of *Hermes* and was moving rapidly to a position from where she could attempt to board *Hermes* port bow, a move that left her relatively protected from any rifle fire from *Hermes*.

Robert decided to bring the issue to a quick conclusion and ran up to the wheelhouse.

"Ram them!" he ordered, "sink the swine."

Just, therefore, as the speedboat moved close to their port bow, *Hermes* swung sharply to port to confront the oncoming speedboat head on. To avoid being run down by *Hermes* the speedboat banked hard, at top speed, veering wildly to change course at the last moment to escape the collision. But this sudden change of direction caused panic and consternation in the speedboat as its passengers were thrown violently to one side. The forced manoeuvre had also exposed them to fire from *Hermes*, Tom and Bedros had come to the fore deck with their rifles and were shooting. As the speedboat twisted away to save herself. *Hermes* was able to rake her with rifle fire, which was now rapid fire, so quickly had they learnt to handle the Lee Enfield rifle

The rifle fire must have found its mark because the speedboat's engine first began to stutter erratically and then spluttered and cut out altogether, leaving the boat wallowing helplessly in the sea. There were loud cries for help from the Germans, one or more of whom might have been wounded, but Robert was determined to ignore them. He would not take any of them on board *Hermes;* he would leave them to be picked up by the yacht.

"We sail on!" he ordered. "There might be more of them. We must get clear away from this spot."

Tom had the same idea for different reasons. "If anyone heard all that shooting," he said, "or heard that explosion, the Spanish may come and investigate. We need to get somewhere else. And fast!"

Luckily no-one had been hit by any of the shots fired by the Germans, although Valeria and Bill had sore hands from driving home the charge clips on her rifle.

22

They kept sailing on a coast-hugging course, reducing to normal cruising speed. The yacht Robert had spotted earlier did not attempt to pursue them and seemed to stop to pick up the survivors from the second speedboat. Later through the glasses he saw her turn back to Malaga. The pursuit was therefore over, they could relax, at least for the moment.

Robert kept a course parallel to the Spanish coast, wanting to find a quiet sheltered spot to moor for the night. By early evening, many hours later, they were off a pleasant looking fishing village east of Motril. It looked a good, safe place to anchor for the night, so they heaved too and dropped anchor just off one of the headlands that shielded the tiny harbour. They were in the lea of a rocky outcrop that protected the beach, where a number of small fishing boats were drawn up on the sand. Robert sent in a boat to buy fresh produce. There was general relief that they could all now relax. Everyone was exhausted and unless something came up to change matters, he suggested that the next day should be a day to rest and recover.

"We must also work out where we're going," he thought.

He organised a duty rota to keep watch during the night, which passed without disturbance, and most of them got a good sleep. Valeria and Anna used the owner's cabin on the upper deck, which had a door they could lock at night, although Robert noticed that Valeria also made a point of taking her rifle with her to the cabin. Robert and Bedros used sofas in the rear cabin on the main deck and the sailors and engineers used crew quarters on the lower deck. Next morning

Tom and Len rowed the launch to the village in search of more fresh food and milk. Robert had been eying the wonderfully clear and enticing water. He was a good swimmer and found it inviting. He called to Valeria and Anna, who were in the gally checking what supplies there were, to say that he as he was about to take a dive from the stern, they should look the other way. He stripped off and dived from the taffrail. The water was warm and a delightful feeling on his bare skin as he swam vigorously around the ship. As he rounded the vessel he saw that Anna, wearing a sailor's rough vest and short canvas trousers, had discovered a Jacob's ladder, hooked it to the taffrail and was about to join him in the water. She did, and called out how wonderful it was, how buoyant and fresh. They enjoyed playing in the water and then raced each together across the bay, after which they just floated contentedly in the sea beside the other headland. He realised that he wanted to kiss her and tell her she was fantastic; she laughed and returned the kiss. They kissed again. He felt wonderfully happy, just as he had before that awful argument in Malaga. He was at peace with himself. Then they saw Tom and Len as they were pushing their small launch off from the beach to row back to *Hermes*. They waved towards them and swam back to the ship.

Tom and Len had returned successful with fresh supplies and Valeria set about preparing a lunchtime meal. Later, Robert took the opportunity of them all being seated together for a meal to raise the question of what they did next.

"It's good! We have captured *Hermes* and escaped. But we must face facts; we are not safe on this boat. We need to get off it and soon. The Germans have come after us once and they may do again. And next time more powerfully."

"You're right!" Valeria agreed, and there were murmurs of support.

"My suggestion," Robert said, "is we take *Hermes* somewhere that has a ferry going to one of the big French or Italian Ports with rail connections and then abandon her."

"Abandon her?" Bedros queried. "She's a good sound vessel. Couldn't we sell her?"

"That would take time and attract attention. I think we should be rid of her as fast as we can."

"You're right!" Tom said loudly. "Before they catch up and kill us all!"

"In that case I suggest heading for Cagliari in Sardinia," Valeria said. "There's a ferry from there to Genoa in North Italy and another one to Sicily. It's off the main shipping lines, they won't have heard about any shooting near Malaga. Just the right place for us to quietly vanish."

It seemed a sensible idea and the others agreed. Robert suggested that as their present anchorage seemed secure, and as they all needed to recover from the speedboat attack, they should spend the rest of the day recuperating and set course for Sardinia the following day.

While everyone else was relaxing on the man deck, Robert decided to check the guest or passenger cabins on the lower deck. He found two of the cabins locked and noticed to his surprise that the cabin that had been fitted with a special lock was in fact unlocked, moreover with the key inside. Maybe someone had been examining the contents when they were disturbed. But as he expected when he opened the door, the gold cargo loaded in Lisbon was inside; twenty or more small wooden chests, each one firmly closed with a padlock. He had seen such chests before in London and calculated that each one contained rows of gold sovereigns, wrapped in cartridge paper tubes, of 50 or 100 coins. He guessed that the coins would be stacked several layers deep, perhaps 5,000 or more coins in each chest. That would make something like 100,000 gold sovereigns. It was a vast fortune in gold, dramatically confronting him with the reality of the huge scale of the Sergio conspiracy. Whoever was behind it had enormous resources; surely that showed it must be some hostile government, and who more likely than Germany. He tried to shift one of the boxes to test its weight, but gold was heavy, and the box must weigh perhaps a hundred pounds. Moving the gold would take much time and effort. That would be a problem.

He decided to keep the news about the gold to himself, which meant that he and Tom were the only people on the ship who knew the secret. However, the presence of gold introduced a further major issue into any question of abandoning the ship; the problems in moving it meant that it would be difficult if not impossible to take the gold with them. Simply abandoning *Hermes* would probably mean leaving almost all the gold on the ship. Hugo had said skuttle the ship, that would mean sending the gold to the floor of the ocean. Did he, Robert, really want to do that? Surely, he could think of a solution. Meanwhile he locked the cabin door, took the key, and made his way thoughtfully up to the main deck.

Meanwhile Bedros had inspected the upper part of the vessel. There were only a few bullet holes in the wooden structures of the cabins on both the main deck and the upper deck and one cabin window had been hit. However, this was only superficial and as far as he could tell there was no structural damage to the vessel.

They spent a quiet night at anchor, though Robert again organised a night watch rota in case of trouble. As they had decided to set sail soon after dawn on a course to Cagliari in Sardinia, Robert went up to the wheelhouse to discuss the charts with the master. The master had complained of acute stomach pain during the struggle with the speedboats and Robert was concerned about his condition.

"I'm not too good!" the master told him, and Robert could see he was not in a good state, with obvious renewed pain.

Soon after they set sail Len came up to the wheelhouse. He shouted a warning: "There's a vessel coming after us!"

"What!"

"Yes, whatever it is it's cracking on like the devil's on his tail!"

Robert left the wheelhouse and peered astern. He could see the distinct tell-tale sign of distant smoke and a dark smudge, hull down on the horizon. It did indeed signify another vessel and judging by the thick line of black smoke spiralling upwards from her smokestack she was coal burning. Moreover, Len was right, by the quantity of smoke she must be really shovelling the coal to put on maximum speed.

"Is she following us?" Robert wondered. "Or is she just by chance on the same course? I need to find out quickly if she's tracking us!"

He returned to the wheelhouse and spoke to the master, "there's a vessel behind us. We need to find out if she's stalking us. We'll change course due south and see if they do the same!"

They did so, and then repeated the move after a while. However, the vessel behind *Hermes* echoed their course alterations.

"They are definitely following us," he told the master.

Robert used the binoculars, but although it was not possible to make out the detail of their pursuer, it was plain that the vessel was substantial. This was no small speedboat.

He could just see through the glasses that there were the tiny figures of many men on deck. He gave orders for *Hermes* to increase speed and went down to the main deck where Tom was stowing a rope.

"We have another German rat after us!" he told Tom, who looked surprised but not astonished at the news. He used the glasses.

"You're right. No bloody doubt about it!" Tom replied. "They're not going to give up! It looks to me like an oceangoing tugboat. That's a big heavy boat, easily capable of ramming and sinking us. They'll have a large crew so they can board us. They probably mount a machine gun. It's a bad situation."

Robert already knew that. It was not a helpful opinion.

"But," the master said, "she's not built for speed, and we can outrun her."

"You think so?" Tom observed. "She's got some pace on her and seems to have plenty of coal to burn. They wouldn't have sent another ship after us unless it was capable of catching us."

"I'll talk to the engineer," Robert said.

The engineer was in fact sanguine. "We refuelled at Malaga. We should be well capable of outrunning them. In a big heavy sea, they would have the edge on us. But in this weather, it's different. I suggest we maintain the distance and keep a few knots in hand for a spurt in case we need it, for instance for some fancy tricks at night."

"Exactly what I was thinking," Robert replied, concerned at the significant danger that the tugboat presented. He had seen big sea-going tugboats in Liverpool, with high prows built to slice through the water, and capable of slicing through *Hermes* as well. Not to mention that as Tom said the vessel probably carried a larger than normal crew and some sort of heavy weapon. If they were able to close with *Hermes* it could be over very quickly, and all of them would die.

Back on the main deck he collected everyone except the master, who remained at the wheel, and the engineer. He broke the bad news that the fight was not over; news that had in fact already spread and caused a widespread sense of disquiet. He tried to be upbeat.

"We have to face it that it's a bigger, heavier ship than the speedboat, and that they have a lot of men on board. They can do us harm if they catch us. They could ram us or board us. So, we must keep ahead of them. But if it comes to a fight, and it may, we know how to defend ourselves. We have done it once and we can do it again. We have guns and we know how to use them."

"Do they have heavy guns?" Len asked. "Machine guns?"

"Bound to!" Tom said bitterly. "Look they've obviously come prepared to get us. They will have machine guns."

There was a murmur of agreement, the beginning of a mood of defeatism that Robert didn't appreciate.

"Why don't we ask them what they want and give it to them?" Len said. "Then they would leave us alone to go home."

"These people are killers! Pirates!" Robert insisted. "We couldn't trust anything they said. If they board us. We'll all die!" He assumed that the tugboat knew that *Hermes* carried a fortune in gold; there was no way they would be quietly allowed to go home.

There seemed to be a grudging acceptance of this by Len and Bill. Tom kept quiet.

"And don't assume they are well armed. We don't know what weapons they have," Robert said defiantly. "Whatever it is they have, we should be ready."

"Fight machine guns? Or worse?" Tom asked. "With rifles! Can't work. Stupid."

"No!" Robert shouted back. "That is not the attitude! We have beaten these German swine once and we will beat them again."

Tom was clearly about to object again but Valeria elbowed past him. "All you do is criticise," she challenged, "where's your plan?" Tom made no response.

"So! I take it you have none!" Tom didn't like it but did no more than mutter.

"Pity!" Robert said. "But I do have a plan!"

"Why can't we just ram on speed and outrun them?" Len suggested.

"We could of course try to outrun them. We do have the fuel. But for what purpose? I don't fancy getting to some port in Algeria or Italy being bottled up and picked off at will. We need a smarter plan."

No-one else offered a suggestion so Robert continued, "I propose that we continue this course until evening. We will keep our distance from them. Just before dark we will alter course south, mislead them that we are bolting for Algiers. Then once it is completely dark, we dose all lights and change course 90 degrees to steer north for the coast of Ibiza. We should reach it in four hours and anchor for the rest of the night. Hopefully, we've lost the tugboat during the night. Next morning there will be no sight of them."

"It's such an old trick! Won't they see through it?" Tom objected.

"Old tricks are sometimes the best tricks. We can only try!" Robert answered.

23

He followed the plan. In the late evening *Hermes* altered course south, as if heading for Algiers. The tugboat observed the change and followed suit. Once night had fallen *Hermes* increased speed, soon after altered course 90 degrees to head north for Ibiza. Robert organised a night rota to keep the engine going and maintain course. Valeria and Anna went to the upper deck cabin to sleep. When the sun came up at dawn Robert climbed to the upper deck to scan the sea. If the plan had worked, there would be no sign of the tugboat. Unfortunately, it was immediately all too obvious that the plan had not worked: the smoke of the tugboat was very much in evidence on the skyline.

The crew were unhappy and mutinous.

"You said you had a plan!" Len protested angrily. "Some bloody plan! Blasted useless!"

Comments from Tom were much ruder. "What an effing, bloody stupid waste of time! All that's done is to make them really annoyed. We'll be lucky if they want to talk to us now."

Len agreed. "We should have found out what they wanted."

Robert knew exactly what the tugboat wanted: get their hands on *Hermes* gold. And he was quite sure what would happen to those on *Hermes* the moment they got it. There would be no talking, only killing.

"Look!" he shouted back. "The plan was worth trying! I told you there was no promise it would work. We were simply unlucky."

"No! The plan was stupid," Len yelled.

"You're wrong! It was a good plan. The trouble is that their Captain is smart and worked out our ruse. He made the right guess about our little trick. We were unlucky that's all."

The sailors huddled in a complaining, conspiratorial group and continued to blame Robert. Valeria broke into their huddle, pushed Len aside and asserted herself to shut them up.

"None of you had anything else to offer. All you do is moan. It's pathetic!" She bellowed at them in Italian, Robert guessed it was vulgar and to the point.

She then turned to Robert. "You said the tugboat captain is clever."

"He is smart," Robert said, "he worked out what we would try. A night escape manoeuvre was an obvious option for us."

"Anyone could see that!" Tom spat. "I told you so."

"Look! It often works. He just made the right guess. No genius, just an intelligent, competent sailor who made a lucky guess." There was silence. It made sense.

"And what do you suggest now?" Valeria asked. Her assertive manner cowered the sailors, who were on the verge of mutiny.

"I propose that we do the same thing again," Robert replied. "He has to gamble on making the right guess about our trick. He was lucky once, but would he be lucky twice? The odds are reasonable for us. It is of course a gamble, but one where we have good racing odds."

There was silence on deck. No-one offered any other plan, but Len felt he had to make his presence known. He seemed to enjoy challenging Robert's authority to command. "I told you we should've talked! It had better work this time." The tone was aggressive; there was an implication of 'or else' that Tom endorsed by slapping him on the shoulder.

"Yes," Robert answered quietly, "it would be best if it did work. But we have fuel, and we could try it a third time if we need. There is no emergency."

"Absolutely!" Valeria cried. "We must keep our nerve."

"Our only other safe course," Robert said, "is to make a run for it, crack on at top speed and make a dash for somewhere far away. But Spain is not safe for us. In Algeria or Tunis, we risk being arrested by the French. Italy may be the same. You really want to hole up in Turkish territory. For myself I don't fancy my chances in a French, Italian or Turkish prison."

A comment which struck home with the sailors.

"I don't trust the Frogs!" Tom was derisive.

"Alright!" Robert announced. "You don't trust the French and there's no reason to trust the Germans. So, there is another possibility. If you're up for it."

"What's that?" Len demanded. "Another stupid plan that doesn't work!"

"No!" Robert shouted, "another plan that does work. We fight them!".

Tom was openly derisive: "Fight them. How? What with? How do we fight machine guns? It would be suicide. Better to heave to and see what they want."

Len thought Robert's idea was rubbish and said so. As Bill would go with the other sailors, Robert was about to lose control of his ship. He needed to take a strong positive stance.

"Right! You ask how we fight them? I'll tell you. We beat them with our secret weapons." A confident announcement that attracted everyone's attention. They had all assumed that they were absolutely no match for the Tugboat. And what were these 'secret' weapons?

"We can't fight them." Len dismissed the idea in a tone that reflected his incredulity.

"Listen and I'll tell you. I'll tell you how we fight them. We fight them by using our two crucial advantages. The first is surprise. They will not expect us to stand and fight. They think like Len that we know that their numbers give us no chance against them. They will expect us to give up. That brings in our second advantage. We have a secret weapon. A weapon they do not know about or expect. A weapon that will scare the life out of them. A weapon capable of destroying them in one engagement."

"Hah! What effing bilge!" Len, a natural doubter expressed what probably others also felt but hadn't had the courage to say.

"Secret effing weapon!" Tom scoffed. "What effing rubbish! You're talking bloody daft. Secret weapon. We don't 'av no secret weapon."

"Oh yes we do!" A bold, audacious assertion from Robert, spoken with a masterly outward air of complete confidence, a feeling that in fact inwardly he lacked. But if they were to survive, he would have to be a leader, assume the aura of command, dispel the defeatist sentiments he had heard from the crew and inspire them to fight. His words did indeed grab their attention and stymied an impending rebellion against his authority. In the circumstances he had no choice but put his blind faith in a weapon about which he knew almost nothing. A weapon that he had never seen in action and, moreover, one that he wasn't sure would even work. But the alternative was that Tom and Len would undermine his position as captain of the vessel and compel a disastrous negotiation with the thugs on the tugboat.

"We have the weapon, and you'll see it!" Robert asserted loudly. "It's fantastic! Like nothing you ever imagined. We will need to be bold. Daring. And be sure that with it we will win. Just watch."

With which he called to Albert, the engineer's assistant, who had been waiting outside the galley to come down to the stern. Albert was carrying a long metal tube over his shoulder, and a two-foot projectile in his right hand. There were gasps of surprise and doubt.

"My Gawd what's this?"

"What kind of thing is that!"

"Looks like Chinese bloody fireworks?"

"What's it do?"

"Bit of twisted metal! Wouldn't scare a crow!"

Tom pushed his way to the front to examine the rocket closely. "What the hell!"

Robert was delighted to explain. He had read the booklet he found when he first saw the Hales Rockets. Then, he was lucky. After the speedboat attacks he had gone down to the engine room and happened to have the Rocket booklet in his hand.

The engineer had noticed it. "Hales Rockets?", he inquired.

"Yes. We have boxes of them, loaded with the rifles." Robert explained that the rockets were part of the cargo that had been loaded in Malaga. "Do you know anything about them?" he asked.

"I do. I was in Durban in the South African war. The army used Hales Rockets there, although by then they were replaced by light field artillery. But they were still useful in certain conditions. You see the rockets and launchers are easily loaded on a mule, a battery of them needs only a small crew that is easily trained, and they can be used in places where it would be difficult to take artillery."

"Did you see the rockets fired?" Robert asked, hardly believing his luck that he had found someone who knew how the thing worked.

"Yes, I saw some practice firing. They're simple! You unscrew a safety cap at the base of the rocket. Then light the fuse underneath it. And bingo! It's quite dramatic! The body of the rocket is filled with propellant, a gunpowder mix. The design, by a chap called William Hales, is clever. It uses the power of the propellant to rotate the rocket, which keeps it on course. As the propellant burns, gases are expelled through an exhaust tube at the base of the rocket. This gives the projectile its thrust. But some gas also escapes through holes at the base. That makes the rocket spin around its longitudinal axis, giving it stability and enabling it to be aimed."

"You saw some fired, did they hit the target?"

"Yes. I saw them being fired. They were aiming at a target more than 1000 yards off and I was told they could get to 4000 yards. They were reasonably on target."

"And if it hits the target?"

" There's an explosive in the head of the rocket which goes off on impact. The whole thing is reasonably effective but doesn't pack the punch of proper artillery. Which is why it's been replaced in the army."

It was great news.

Robert told the engineer that *Hermes* had several ammunition boxes of the rockets and launchers. The engineer inspected the launch tubes and noticed there were two types. One was a long metal tube; into whose base a projectile would be placed. The tube would be supported at one end on a metal triangular framework, with a device to control the angle of launch. The other type of launcher was designed for fitting onto a vessel by clamping its framework, and its device for controlling the angle of launch, onto a ship's rail.

Robert was fascinated, the rocket might be old fashioned but could be useful to them. Then, with the tugboat launching its second attack, he had gone back to the engine room and asked Albert, the engineer's assistant, to come on deck and demonstrate how the launcher could be fixed to the rail. Now was the moment of truth, would it really work? The *Hermes* company gathered round expectantly, excitedly, attracted to the Rocket launcher like a new toy. Robert took one of the missiles and loaded the rocket into its launcher, unscrewed the safety cap at the base. So far so good, as he had practised this part with the engineer. The next part, though, would be a new experience.

"Stand well back! I'm going to light the fuse. I've set the angle of launch at 45 degrees. The thing will go up at a steep angle. Get back!"

There was a buzz of excitement and anticipation, and everyone took several paces backwards as Robert lit the fuse. He endured a prolonged moment of anxiety as the fuse seemed to burn too slowly. He wondered if the thing would just fizzle out, completely fail. Then there was a sudden roar I the rocket tube as the propellant caught fire, followed by an acrid, stinging, dense, cloud of smoke as the propellant ignited, followed by a dramatic flash of flame from the base of the rocket. Finally, the projectile was away, gushing through the metal tube, rushing high into the sky leaving a great trailing arc of smoke and sparks in the air as it soared upwards. All very theatrical and it certainly made more than 1000 yards before it plunged down and splashing into the sea. On deck there was a burst of spontaneous applause.

"Wow!"

'Crikey!"

"Look at that!"

"It's the work of the bloody devil!"

"If it hits a solid target it would explode!" Robert told them. "Imagine the effect that will have at close quarters. I fired at a distant target but think what it would do if we used it point blank against another vessel. One fired so close we couldn't miss. Firing into another vessel right next to us."

"Ah! The blasted tugboat."

"Yeah!"

"It would gut them!"

"Serve the bastards right!"

"Send 'em to Hell!"

They were impressed and Robert was keen to press home the effects of the demonstration.

"And not just one rocket, but a whole battery of rockets! All fired together, one big salvo."

"An effing inferno! The poor bastards!"

"Poor be damned! What do you think they would do to us if they get the chance!"

He was right in thinking that after witnessing the spectacular power of the Hales Rocket, if it came to it the crew would be up for a fight with the tugboat. But any such fight would be a risk. It would be a good deal safer to try to avoid the tugboat than fight her. So, Robert persuaded the crew to try a second night escape ruse, which would be a repeat of the same manoeuvre. So, when night fell, they once again changed course towards the coast of North Africa. But when it was completely dark *Hermes* would double back due north.

24

The night that followed was an anxious one. It seemed to start well; the tugboat duly echoed their first change of course. Then as full darkness fell, *Hermes* doused every chink of light and changed course again to double back north, then slowed the engine to conserve fuel. It was time to organise a night rota, ensuring someone at all times in the engine room and at the wheel. And as Robert was concerned by the crew's mutinous attitude about fighting the tugboat, and was worried what they might do if they knew about the cargo of gold, he altered the sleeping arrangements. He and Bedros would now join Valeria and Anna in the owner's cabin on the upper deck. So, Anna strung up a rudimentary arrangement of sheets suspended from ropes across the cabin to form a temporary partition separating the large bed from the rest of the cabin. They threw down a mattress for Robert and Bedros, any rest that they took would have to be fitted into their stints on the night duty rota.

When it came to his turn on the rota, Robert slipped out of the cabin, delighted to feel the soft night breeze on his face as he stood on the upper deck, feeling humbled by the vastness of the heavens above him. He stayed at the wheel until *Hermes* regained the Spanish coast, and with the master's help had found the bay he had previously picked out on the chart. With Bedros' help they anchored fore and aft. As he was by then worn out, he decided that, rather than disrupt the others, he would instead simply bed down in the main deck cabin. There, he stripped off his shirt and duck trousers and threw himself down on a mattress on the deck.

Perhaps helped by the substantial meal provided by Valeria, most people on board slept well. However, Anna woke long before dawn, her sleep disturbed by deep fears about what lay in front of them, believing that if the tugboat caught up with them, they would all die a horrible death. She anxiously walked the upper deck to stare out into the surrounding darkness. Gazing out to sea, the faint breeze brushed her cheeks and ruffled her long hair.

"Lord, hear my prayer!" she whispered. "Keep us safe this day!"

Her faith told her she must not abandon hope for their safety, but this did not stop her experiencing a powerful sense of blame for their perilous situation. If something awful happened to them all, as she feared it might, it would be her fault. It was she who had proposed the expedition to Tripoli. She was gripped by an acute awareness of her responsibility for the whole of the Tripoli enterprise. Dragging Robert into the Sergio letters, grabbing Reggie Rand's suggestion of a meeting with Hugo Cavendish, making her rash offer to go to Tripoli knowing it would be refused and that Robert would volunteer to go. She suddenly felt a keen sense of guilt for what she had led Robert into, knowing that if the tugboat attacked, he would not hesitate a moment to put his life in danger to protect her. That was how it had been in the old days, anytime they had ever got into a risky situation, and there had been some, he would always think of how to protect her before bothering for himself. Memories of the old days when they played together filled her mind. She felt desperately unhappy and returned to the sleeping cabin intending to share her thoughts with him, and above all seek his re-assurance that he would somehow, like the old days, find a way out of the mess. He had always been so confident that for any dangerous situation there was, somewhere, an answer if one only looked hard enough.

But entering the cabin and pulling aside the suspended sheet that partitioned it, she found that Robert was not there. She thought he must be doing his rota in the wheelhouse and went there to find him. But it was Bedros not Robert who was there, on watching duty only as they were now anchored. He told her that Robert had gone to the main deck cabin to sleep. She went down to the main deck and entered the cabin silently, closing the door behind her. Guided only by the flickers of moonlight through the cabin windows, she stood quite still and tried to pick out where he was in the gloom. Thinking she could see him, she moved slowly across the cabin and suddenly found that his slumbering body was right there in front of her feet. He was stretched out on a mattress on the floor, lying on his back. It was a jolt, she had not seen him naked since they were children, throwing off their clothes to swim in the Highgate Ponds. It was a shock to realise that just by her presence she was horribly in breach of the powerful social conventions that had once ruled her life.

But she didn't care. Nothing about this situation was anything like normal. The idea of normal surely belonged to a way of life of which she was no longer part. Anyway, was she not a thoroughly modern woman, no slave therefore to tired, old social conventions? And might not both of them shortly die when the tugboat caught them. Surely 'niceties' of social convention had no place in a situation like this. All that filled her mind was the thought that today fate would plunge them into an abyss for which she was responsible. At that instant all she cared about was the need to share her fears with him, and especially confess her guilt and hope for his understanding, if not forgiveness. So, she knelt beside the mattress and gently touched his bare shoulder.

His dark eyes sprang open in alarm as he felt the touch of her warm, soft, hand and he found himself looking up into her lovely face. Confused, he was at first sure he was dreaming, transported to some heavenly paradise. Yet the renewed touching of her hand gave a feel that was too real to be a dream. It was no fantasy.

"Anna!" he exclaimed, suddenly wide awake. But the unexpected sight of her made him think that she must bear bad news and had roused him in distress. He raised himself on his elbows and took her hand, drawing her towards him.

"What's happened?" he whispered, holding her close, now feeling through her thin nightdress her delicious softness on his bare chest.

She had dismissed conventional restraints and it did not even occur to her to feel embarrassed at being in such close contact. It just seemed entirely natural for their bodies and eyes to meet and when they did, a flicker of moonlight lit up his face and she had the feeling that she was looking through his eyes into his very essence.

"Robbie I've been on deck looking for the boat. There's no sign of it. There was nothing. I hope to God, we've done it!"

"Anna that would be marvellous. But it's far too early to be sure. We just must hope. Just believe we can do it."

"Of course, we can!"

He pulled himself up and folded his arms protectively around her. She felt his face close to hers and found his mouth with hers, instinctively gently kissing him full on the lips. He responded and his mouth covered hers. With his arms he tightened his embrace, drawing her closer, feeling a spontaneous ecstasy that he knew was entirely sincere for both of them. His lips returned to hers, intimate and loving. A touching that said to them both that everything was possible, indeed not just possible but implicitly desired. They found no need for words, she moved aside and pulled off her nightdress and he once more pulled her close. Their slowly developing tactile movements as their bodies came together were simply utter bliss. It lasted for not long but seemed an eternity. The softness of her lips was a delightful pressure on his own, and her warm body rubbed against him so that his blood boiled. He kissed her neck and wanted to kiss every part of her, this shoulder, that one, this breast, the other. They then kissed passionately, wildly, a mindless urgency overcame them both and when the tip of his tongue searched inside her mouth she responded, making the kiss full. He moved a hand to cup her breast and bent his head to take her nipple in his mouth.

They lay side by side on the mattress and mutually discovered the delightful experience of their newfound intimate physical contact. She held his hand and wanted to feel him explore her. His searching fingers found her and there were cries of pleasure. He moved to be above her, kissing her on the mouth, the neck, the breasts. He did not need to ask where they should go next, or she to ask for gentleness. Then finally, but not too soon, they were slowly moving together. Entwined and loving, a prolonged frenzy of pleasure began for both. Her slowly rippling moans of joy sang to him of her pleasure. Then finally in a crescendo of bliss she came with a loud sustained cry. He felt her grip on him and he wanted to shout. He waited for her to subside and kissed her again and again, keeping moving, a gentle continuing pulsating, now shallower now deeper, now faster now slower, a rhythm of delight that often renewed her cries of pleasure. It ended only when he could restrain himself no longer and finally exploded, giving himself to her in what was for both a wild, intense, and impassioned coupling that left both gasping for breath. He felt the last jerks as he emptied his body.

He had known women before. Sex was not anything new for him, but it had never before been remotely such a shattering experience. He had believed before this that he loved her, but now it was not just that his belief had been confirmed, he knew he had discovered the real meaning of love. He could not now image or want a life without her. They lay joyfully together. It had not lasted long but it seemed like years.

"Anna dearest! I love you! I think have always loved you! We were always made for each other. I want to be with you whatever happens. I love you!"

It was only then, so far after it was far too late for any meaningful regrets, that he was hit by the sheer enormity of what they had done. What he had allowed himself to do. He knew he had simply let himself be carried away by the raging tide of his impetuous love making. Without considering the consequences. Without thought. Yet he also knew that he wanted the consequences. All of them.

"Anna, I love you! Will you marry me? Will you be my wife?"

"Robbie! Of course, I will!"

An answer that quickly led to more passionate love making, but this time the passion that brought their bodies together moved more slowly, gently, and carefully. It was even better for both than the first time, another sublime ecstasy.

"Anna you're so fantastic!"

"Robbie!"

And so, it continued until at last, exhausted, they fell asleep in each other's arms and were only wakened by all too soon presence of reality, as the pale light of the slowly rising sun sent muted beams of pallid orange into the cabin. Finally disturbed by it, Robert woke with alarm and the sure knowledge that he needed to be up and about the day's business. He kissed her softly.

"Anna dearest! I want only to lie here with you for ever. And talk about our future together. But I must go on deck. You stay. There's no need for you to stir yet."

She awoke and returned the kiss. "Robbie, it was so marvellous! I had no idea! But have we done the right thing? I'm so confused, things seemed to happen so quickly!"

"Anna dearest! Yes! We have done the right thing! Don't be confused. We love each other and only did what we should have done weeks ago. It was so wonderful please don't think of regretting it."

"Oh, I don't regret it! How could I regret it? I'm just feeling overwhelmed by events. So much has happened so quickly. My life has suddenly taken such a leap. Where will it end?"

"Anna, we have made the same leap. Think of it as a fantastic start on our journey together into a wonderful future. Dearest, as soon as we can, we must talk about that future. Our future."

Saying which he kissed her again and got up, pulled on his cotton trousers, and grabbed his shirt. "But that will have to be later dearest! There are things that must be done to make sure we have a future."

He went out onto a still deserted and grey main deck. He could hardly grasp what had just happened to him, it would have seemed unreal if he could not still feel her hands on his back, clawing and insistent. As other sailors gradually appeared on deck he could see no sign, even distant, of the tugboat and there was general rejoicing at their apparent deliverance. One that meant he could relax and work out the details of a new life with Anna. But for the present he needed to get *Hermes* moving again so he organised raising the anchors, went up to the wheelhouse and rang the engine room telegraph for slow ahead. The master took the wheel. However, he was also cautious, it might be too early to celebrate an escape from the tugboat.

"It's too soon to be sure we have lost them," he told Valeria, who was preparing breakfast in the galley. "But if we have lost them, we need to discuss our destination. The master needs a doctor as soon as we can make it to a port."

25

The sense of relief and escape lasted only an hour and then vanished like a snuffed candle. For Tom, who had taken over at the wheel, poked his head out of the wheelhouse door to shout down to the main deck that he had just spotted a new smoke trail to the south and had examined it through the master's glasses.

"They're on to us!" he yelled, and indeed he was right, the tugboat had not been fooled by the second ruse and had found them again.

"Right!" Robert shouted. "Now we have no choice! We must fight! Let's get ready for it."

He told the master to increase speed to get further out to sea: they might need room to manoeuvre. He needed to decide what was the most effective way to deploy their surprise Hales Rockets. One factor in his mind was the need to protect the wheelhouse, which was relatively exposed and vulnerable to hostile gunfire. That suggested he should avoid a frontal engagement with the tugboat. He considered placing the rockets so they could be fired from the stern on both the main and upper decks. If so, he should allow the tugboat to come up astern of *Hermes*. Then, if the rockets were not effective, *Hermes* could make a dash to escape, using her superior speed. However, if they did that and engaged from the stern their target would be the relatively narrow profile of the tugboat's high steel prow. Moreover, if the tugboat had a quick-firing gun, it would probably be in the bow. An engagement from the stern of *Hermes* was not therefore the best idea. Eventually he concluded that they should engage the tugboat on her quarter, side to side, manoeuvring *Hermes* so that the tugboat came up to lie almost alongside, *Hermes* starboard quarter to the tugboat's quarter. The rocket batteries were therefore to be massed on *Hermes* starboard side to be engaged at close quarters at the last moment to maximise their impact. They would be fired as a single devastating co-ordinated salvo. It was, though, taking a serious risk, because if the tugboat had quick firing weapons and opened up before the Hales rockets were fired, *Hermes* could easily be raked. But he was sure that the enemy would want to capture *Hermes* intact, and would therefore avoid anything that might sink her, and the gold. The risk was worth taking.

"We have one chance, and we need to take it and hit her hard!" Robert told his crew. "There won't be a second throw of the dice in this game!"

He calculated that the captain of the tugboat would welcome the chance of coming to close quarters with *Hermes.* He would want that because it would make boarding her so much easier, and Robert was increasingly certain that the main purpose of the tugboat was to capture *Hermes* intact. That meant boarding. Nelson's old tactic: engage the enemy closely, board and capture. That made sense of the apparently large crew that the tugboat carried, doubtless criminal riffraff recruited hastily from the dockside. The sheer number of men cramming their deck was bad news if they were able to board, but a good sign that their main plan was indeed to board. For in that case, they would probably not devastate *Hermes* with any heavy weapon like a Maxim gun they might have.

He had worked out a plan and gave orders for the Hales rocket launchers to be fastened to the ship's rails on the main and upper decks. They were to be positioned to deliver the crucial powerful and decisive broadside blast at the tugboat, rather in the fashion Robert imagined that Nelson himself in his day might have chosen. The rockets themselves were to be placed in a firing position on the base of the metal launcher tubes before the tugboat closed with *Hermes*. All that would be required when *Hermes* was in the right position to open fire was to light their fuses. The firing tubes would, though, be conspicuous and to conceal their presence he looked in the deck lockers near the galley and discovered a quantity of colourful festival bunting, doubtless used in the past to dress the ship for a party or regatta. The bunting was liberally spread along *Hermes* port and starboard side rails on both decks, creating a strange sight for a ship in the middle of the Mediterranean. That didn't matter if it was a rudimentary but effective way of camouflaging the rockets. With luck the disguise would work, and the rocket launchers would not be noticed until it was too late.

As the fateful moment of actual engagement with the enemy drew nearer, Robert found Valeria and Anna surveying the distant smoke trail and told them that as soon as the tugboat came close, they must remove themselves to the relative protection from small arms gunfire of a lower cabin deck.

Valeria told him straight. "I'm not sitting in some pokey cabin below decks while the rest of you fight for my life. I can fire one of these rocket things. And I can fire a rifle. I intend to do both."

Anna supported her strongly. "No! Don't think of trying to box me away. If there's trouble, I'm going to be there with you."

Robert was unable to shift either of them, gave up and positioned them on the upper deck. The cabin there had opening windows on which rocket launchers could be fastened and which would give a good field of fire downwards onto the tugboat deck. Moreover, if they were standing inside the cabin rather than on the open deck, they would be some cover from any gunfire.

The big remaining and uncertain factor was whether the tugboat had a heavy weapon like a Maxim gun. The Maxim was an automatic, modern, machine gun that used the recoil of an expended shot to reload and fire. It was a deadly weapon and could fire an incredible rate of about 600 rounds a minute, the reason why it was credited with gaining easy victories in many British colonial wars. If the tugboat had a Maxim, knew how to use it, and had ammunition, *Hermes* was probably doomed: the tugboat could simply rake her with machine gun fire until she was disabled and surrendered. If the Tugboat had that kind of firepower it might be best to crank up whatever speed they could squeeze out of *Hermes* engine and make a run for it. He used the binoculars to investigate. Though still distant the tugboat was close enough for Robert to make out some details. On her prow was a huddle of men gathered around what was clearly some kind of machine. Then he took another careful look. What was on the tugboat was far too big and cumbersome to be a Maxim gun. His uncertainty was soon settled when the enemy gun opened fire, a short, uneven, even ragged, staccato burst that was not nearly as fast and even a rate of fire as a Maxim. It was fired from what was still some distance only as a warning, or perhaps a ranging shot, and the shots went nowhere near *Hermes*. But the damage it could inflict in a few minutes at closer quarters was nevertheless all too evident.

Tom, who had come up to the wheelhouse, had a good look at the tugboat and had recognised the distinctive pattern of firing.

"It's definitely a Gatling! They've got a Gatling gun fixed somehow on the prow!"

"Sure? A Gatling gun?"

"Absolutely!"

Not then a dreaded Maxim, but a Gatling gun. The Gatling was an old, outdated weapon long discontinued in any modern army. Moreover, this one looked too ungainly to be on a proper naval mounting. Rather it must be an old Gatling gun mounted impromptu on an army gun carriage, a gun carriage then hoisted aboard the tugboat and somehow roped ad hoc to the deck. Robert needed to think. Although this was an old piece, maybe not reliably secured to the deck, and although the Gatling was not as efficient a weapon as a Maxim, what they had on the tugboat was nevertheless potent. It could, if competently handled by its gun crew and if the ammunition was available, fire something like 300 rounds a minute. That was more than enough to wreak devastation on *Hermes*. However, he was not ready to abandon hope.

"Tom, what gun crew does a Gatling have?"

"About four to service it. And given how they've fixed the gun to the deck, the gun crew will all have to stand beside it. There is no cover for them. The gun crew is very exposed."

That was good news, an unprotected gun crew would be vulnerable to rifle fire, especially in this case because the Gatling was standing not directly on the deck itself but was raised off the deck on some kind of bespoke platform.

"You're saying the Gatling gun crew is exposed to our rifles," Robert observed. "And I think they are unlikely to be a trained gun crew. Just a scratch gang got together quickly. They are unlikely to get the best rate of fire. Or to know how to correct any technical problem in loading, or deal with any hitch if the ammunition feed jams."

"They also have to be careful how they fire the thing," Tom said. "They mustn't hole us; they don't want *Hermes* to sink."

"Good. I think the tugboat captain may just use the Gatling to fire high to terrorise us into surrender," Robert said, hoping he was right.

"We certainly have no answer if they use it for real. Maybe we should see if they will talk."

He did not like Tom's tone, again the mention of an impossible negotiation. But before he could reply, Valeria came to the wheelhouse. "I heard you say they have a big gun of some sort. Is it bad news?"

"Yes, they have a Gatling gun. And that means we need to take out the gun crew with our rifles the moment before we open fire with the rockets."

"Yes, but how?" Valeria asked.

"Having the Gatling they will be super confident. I expect they will fire a burst when they get close, but just to frighten the wits out of us. They will, I think, aim for a surrender. Probably open fire with the Gatling and then order us to heave to. They will be so confident of their superiority, and an easy victory, that they will not expect us to fight. So, we go ahead as planned. We will slow the engine as they will demand. We'll let them draw close. We will stand ready to fire the rockets. There will be four in their Gatling gun crew, all standing around it and we must pick them off with our rifles the moment we light the Hales Rocket fuses. Make sure that we also have rockets aimed at the Gatling. I and Bedros will deal with the Gatling gun crew."

"It's a good plan but you need to make one small alteration," Valeria pronounced, in a tone that gave no invitation to argue. "You are needed on the main deck Robert. I and Bedros will deal with the Gatling crew. I think we are the best shots. It's only a step back to the cabin where Anna is, so I will be able to help her fire the rockets in the cabin."

She was probably right, and Robert did not disagree.

When Robert was satisfied that they were as prepared on *Hermes* as they could be, he spoke to the master, who was hobbling in the wheelhouse but insisted that despite his stomach pain he was still capable of handling the ship. Robert told the master to slightly alter course and to signal the engine room to marginally reduce speed. It needed a delicate judgement by the master; it must not look as if *Hermes* was deliberately setting up a trap. The tugboat was approaching from aft on what she intended to be an intersecting course and the slight course adjustments made by *Hermes* would bring her closer to *Hermes* sooner. It must do so without making it apparent that this was *Hermes* intention.

Meanwhile Robert gave orders for the *Hermes* crew to take up their positions on the main and upper decks, and make sure that their rifles and a supply of loaded charge clips were close at hand. And needed they would be, for after the rockets had been fired, they should maintain a rapid rifle fire until *Hermes* had pulled away from the tugboat. Anna had been busy using the charge clips to load enough rifles for each shooter to have three or four rifles to hand. When it came to using them, *Hermes* should be able to let lose an impressive and continuous fusillade.

The tugboat slowly closed with them. As predicted, when still at some distance the Gatling let rip with two short bursts of fire. Aimed very high but an effective and menacing warning.

Eventually the tugboat drew close enough to *Hermes* quarter for Robert to use the speaking trumpet. The master's skilful handling ensured that although the tugboat slowly came up closer, it was not close enough for the tugboat crew to leap across and board. Many looked as if they were expecting to do so at any moment and there was a great deal of shouting and yelling from the motley crowd massed on the tugboat deck, brandishing their array of vicious looking weapons. Not just rifles and pistols but wicked looking cutlasses, pikes, and axes. Watching from the upper deck Anna shivered with apprehension and had little doubt that if that lot got onto *Hermes*, all on board would have their throats cut. And for her, before that she would be brutally and multiply raped. She resolved to throw herself into the sea if such a fate looked imminent.

"What do you want?" Robert shouted at the tugboat through the speaking trumpet.

"Heave too!" the tugboat captain yelled back.

To emphasise his words he ordered the Gatling to fire another short staccato burst over *Hermes,* enough to leave no doubt about the damage it could inflict. Robert could hear and almost feel the shots whining overhead, some seemed too close for comfort. The Gatling had to be stopped.

"If you fire again, I will open our stop cocks and *Hermes* will sink! I have a man standing by below to do exactly that. Tell your gun crew to lay off. At once! Stand them back!" Robert had thought of that threat on the spur of the moment. It could work, they would not want *Hermes* to sink.

"Alright! But you must heave to. That is an order. You have stolen the boat. I am coming aboard." The tugboat captain was standing on his aft deck surrounded by his crew of desperadoes, they were armed to the teeth and doubtless were the intended boarding party. Robert imagined that the captain had simply hired whatever disreputable rabble he could find at the last moment on the dockside. He must intend to board, why else would a tugboat have a crew of thirty men?

Robert watched and saw that the captain had indeed ordered the Gatling gun crew to stand down, they had stepped away from the gun.

"I have ordered the master to reduce speed to dead slow ahead," Robert yelled. "But you have made a mistake. *Hermes* is not stolen. This ship is lawfully seized by the Spanish High Court under a Court Order. It is the property of the Spanish government." He was taking up time to ensure the master could manoeuvre *Hermes* into exactly the right position to open fire.

"What?"

"This ship is arrested by Order of the Spanish High Court!"

"What?"

"This ship is the property of the Spanish state."

"What?"

Robert repeated it.

"That is not true!"

"It is true. I have the Court Order here. You will answer to the Spanish government if you ignore the order of the Court. The documents are here if you wish to inspect them."

The tugboat was now lying in almost exactly the position Robert wanted for his plan. Not close enough for her crew to leap across onto *Hermes* main deck, but well placed for firing his Hales Rocket battery. He could see that the tugboat crew were wildly brandishing their assorted collection of axes, cutlasses, billhooks, spears, pikes, rifles, pistols, even some muskets from a bygone era. Looking every inch the gang of desperate pirates they were, the crew were yelling themselves into a battle frenzy and ostentatiously flaunting their weapons at *Hermes* so that they glinted in the sunlight. The scene on the tugboat looked like a tableau from the middle ages. They were hoping for an easy prey.

"I will see your documents! I don't believe you. I will board." The tugboat captain stood on the deck rail ready to lead his men onto *Hermes.*

"Of course! You are welcome. But alone. And no weapons."

"I bring my mate!" the captain shouted back, and Robert judged the position of the two vessels was just about right for his plan.

"No! Alone! Comprende!" Robert gave his answer shouting the last word, which he repeated even louder: "Comprende!"

It was the pre-arranged signal to light the rocket fuses. All along the starboard side of *Hermes* the Hales Rockets were quickly and quietly lit one by one. On the upper deck Anna rushed to service the rockets positioned there.

"The mate must come," shouted the tugboat Captain. "Heave to!"

Any continuation of the discourse was frustrated by the sudden opening of rapid rifle fire from *Hermes* upper deck.

Two rifles, Valeria and Bedros, rained sustained fire down at the Gatling gun crew immediately below them. The gun crew was standing around the gun, unprotected and exposed to rifles only yards away. Sitting ducks.

At the same time the fuses on the array of Hales rockets on *Hermes* two decks were burning. The tugboat captain had clearly not anticipated that *Hermes* would open fire and was slow to react. He did shout to his Gatling crew to open fire, but the gun crew had been blown away by Valeria and Bedros.

And there was far too big a gap between the vessels for his assembled boarding party to leap across. So, most of the tugboat's assorted crew, who were massed amidships simply stood and shouted, idly brandishing their collection of weapons. One or two, though, managed to fire their rifles or pistols.

Robert was standing opposite the tugboat's after deck, where the bulk of the intending boarding party were massed, and as soon as he lit his rockets, he emptied a whole rifle magazine into the crowd.

Other sailors on *Hermes* did the same. The Gatling never opened fire again. Valeria and Bedros had picked off the entire gun crew one after the other.

Then the Hales fuses steadily burnt. One by one a battery of six Hales rockets from the upper deck and another eight rockets from the main deck were unleased at the tugboat. Each rocket streaked away with a brilliant flare of light as the propellant ignited, followed immediately by a loud whoosh and bang as the rocket screamed out of its firing tube into the air.

It was within seconds a scene out of Hades.

A sudden bright flare as each rocket was ignited. A fearful shrieking as the rockets screamed towards their target. A dense trail of billowing gritty acrid dark smoke followed each rocket as it sped through the air.

Loud repeated explosions as each rocket hit the steel structure of the tugboat and detonated on impact. Explosion after explosion added more dark smoke. Yells of pain and anger as the rockets did their work.

Dense smoke completely cloaked the tugboat's deck. Fiery sparks filled the air. As soon as their rockets were fired *Hermes* crew seized their rifles and opened rapid fire at the tugboat through the dense smoke.

No more than a handful of minutes and the battle was over.

Robert doubled up to the wheelhouse and at his shouted command *Hermes* engine ran at full speed ahead, pushing her steadily away from the terrible scene of destruction.

Through breaks in the clouds of black smoke he could see that the tugboat was badly hit. Its wheelhouse had taken a direct rocket hit and looked a shambles. The Gatling had been thrown off its carriage and its multiple barrels were pointed uselessly skywards.

The large crew, with which the tugboat captain had intended to board *Hermes*, had been mostly assembled near him on the aft deck of the tugboat and had disappeared. Perhaps wiped out as several rockets had been aimed at that part of the tugboat.

The surprise had been complete. The devastation far greater than Robert had expected. There was no return fire from the tugboat in response to either the rockets or the rifle fire from *Hermes*.

The tugboat was also clearly out of control, idly turning in a circle, her engine still adding billowing smoke to the inferno of the rockets. Robert nevertheless waited five minutes before shouting for rifle firing to cease. In no more than a few intense minutes their nemesis had been destroyed.

Hermes pulled steadily away from the cloud of billowing smoke, that was only gradually being dissipated by the light wind. The feeling on *Hermes* was relief mixed with triumph and palpable exultation. Some of the sailors did indeed raise a ragged impromptu cheer at their astonishing victory, but most on *Hermes* were simply grateful for a lucky escape.

Once keyed up for the battle, now that the exhilaration of action was over, Robert felt utterly physically and mentally drained. He knew he had taken an enormous gamble in taking on the tugboat, one that might well have ended badly for them all. Although they had been lucky and it had in fact gone well, he had no sense of personal elation; he was simply glad the thing was over. But he managed to raise the energy to yell out his thanks to the crew.

Then he made his way to where Anna and Valeria had taken station on the upper deck. He was desperate to know that Anna had not been injured. He found them both sitting on the deck, near the ships' boats, leaning against the starboard deck rail. He could see at once that there was something seriously amiss with Anna. She was half lying, propped up against a mattress, but quite inert, her neck drooping, her face ashen, completely drained of colour. She looked sick and unwell, miserable, shattered. Her clothes were torn, tangled, and dishevelled and her white blouse, face and arms were streaked black with soot from the rockets. If her appearance was awful, what was worse she was shivering, shaking all over and crying. Tears were running down her grime-streaked cheeks.

It was a moment of horror for Robert, and he rushed to her, throwing his arms around her as she just sobbed and sobbed. She was breathing heavily and sweating profusely, so he loosened the buttons of her blouse and tried to comfort her as best he could.

"My dearest love! Anna! It must have been a terrible experience for you. We are through it now. It's all over. You have been so brave!"

"It was so horrible. Horrible! I couldn't bear it!" She could do little more than croak the words.

"Anna Dearest! It must have been awful! It's my fault I should have insisted you went below deck. You are trembling. So bad." As he held her in his arms, he could feel that she was indeed shuddering, and he was worried. "You must lie down."

Valeria looked composed as always. "Well done, Robert! Anna, Robert is right you don't look at all good. You should lie down. Anyway, Robert has a lot to do, and we should help him by letting him get on with it. Come. Lie here on this bedding, we will rig up a sheet to keep the sun off you. The breeze will be good for you. I'll get you a drink of water."

In fact, it took both Robert and Valeria to lift her onto the makeshift bedding. She was reluctant to lie down but Robert insisted.

Valeria comforted her as best she could. "Robert," she said, "you have things to do around the ship. I'll stay with Anna. It's been a terrible shock to her. All those rockets and explosions. And on top of the speedboats. And everything else. She must rest. I'm sure she will get over it. She's strong."

"I had no idea that she would be so badly affected," Robert said. Too late he regretted he had not absolutely insisted that she went below deck before the fighting began. She would not have witnessed the awful scenes on the tugboat's deck as *Hermes* rifles and rockets did their deadly work. But Valeria was right, he had always known Anna as strong and robust, his first thought therefore was not to doubt that she would overcome whatever passing distress had been caused by the fight with the tugboat. This didn't stop him feeling shattered to be face to face with her distressing torment; it brought him close to tears.

Valeria tried to re-assure him. "I'm sure she'll be all right. It's just the shock of those rockets. It was a bad experience for her. But you couldn't have done anything else

Robert. You had no choice. They would have murdered us all if they got on board. Go and deal with the ship. I will call you if I need to."

"I don't like to leave her like this."

"You must. She will be safe with me. Go. When we can, we will move her to the main deck cabin."

26

He made a damage check of both decks and found that, surprisingly, there was nothing significant; probably the result of the complete surprise they had achieved. Nor had any of the crew been injured, although everyone was blackened with the smoke from the rockets. He spoke to the engineer who reported the engine was running well. After all this, it was almost an hour later that Robert went up to the wheelhouse to see how the master was faring. He found Tom at the wheel and the master in his adjacent cabin lying exhausted and in some considerable distress, clutching his stomach. Robert spoke to him and then went through to the wheelhouse.

"We will set a new course!" Robert told Tom. "Direct for Alicante. The master needs a doctor urgently."

"What!" Tom's face distorted in a scowl.

"We have to go to Alicante."

"Who says?"

"I do!"

"You say, do you!" Tom snarled, his face contorting with anger. He stepped back from the wheel, reached into a pocket, pulled out a Luger, a German automatic pistol, and pointed it at Robert's chest. He was so close he could not miss.

"No! I think not. You will carry out my orders instead."

"What!"

"You are no longer in command. I give the orders now. Take the wheel."

Robert did not move, and Tom jabbed the Lugar into him. "At once! Don't doubt I will use this."

"You dare to draw a gun on me. I am the captain on this vessel."

Tom dismissed his words with a sneer. "You fool!" He punched the gun into Robert's side to emphasise the point. "Understand me! Take the wheel. Do as I say, or I will kill you. Without hesitation."

"We must sail to Alicante."

"No! We stay on course. Take the wheel now or I will kill you without another thought."

Robert could not ignore his words. Tom would indeed kill him without compunction. He must have had orders from Hugo to shoot Robert. Robert moved towards the wheel intending to play for time.

"You intend to scuttle the ship?" he asked Tom.

Tom laughed right in Robert's face. "Scuttle! You are so funny. So stupidly funny. You think I am doing this to scuttle the ship?"

"Those are your orders, aren't they?"

"You are a fool!"

Robert suddenly grasped he had badly and completely misunderstood Tom's intentions. There would be no scuttle. "Ah! The gold!"

"What else!"

"You have orders to shoot me?"

"Clever aren't you!"

"Whose orders?"

"Mind your own business!"

"Don't you want to know why I want to sail to Alicante?"

"No! I'm not interested. Get on with it or I'll use the gun."

"I think you mean to kill me anyway?" Robert suspected that was Tom's intention from the moment he pulled out the gun.

Tom did not need to reply because an evil looking grin on his face spoke for him. It made sense if Hugo wanted the disappearance of everything connected to Sergio's plan, including him. Robert took Tom's threat seriously.

"Take the wheel or else!" Tom ordered. There wasn't a choice, so Robert did it. Tom edged to one side of him, holding the gun in his right hand close to Robert's left side. He could not miss if he fired.

"Now! Signal the engine room Slow Ahead."

Robert did so and *Hermes* gradually reduced way.

Robert's mind was in a whirl. Yes, it had been his suggestion to plant someone in the crew, but in fact he must have just played straight into Hugo's hands. All along Hugo must have planned to trick the Germans into loading *Hermes* with gold and then with Tom's help to steal it for himself.

"It's all about the gold isn't it!"

"Clever aren't you."

"So, you're not going to scuttle?"

"Oh maybe, when we've sorted the gold."

Tom said "we." He must have brought the other two sailors into his mutiny. That made the situation even more difficult; but before worrying about the other sailors, he had to deal with Tom.

"Was that why you killed the German agent? To get the gold. He is dead, isn't he?"

"Oh yes he's dead! But Kraut? No, he's no German." Tom spat out the last sentence.

"Not a German!" Robert had noticed the vehemence of the denial. "You told Hugo he was German."

"No! I didn't. Hugo knows he's not German."

"Not German?"

"You heard."

"He must be German!" Robert was stunned. The whole Tripoli story was based on the certainty that Sergio's plan was part of a conspiracy organised in Berlin.

"Hah! You are so gullible. You believe anything."

Robert had the horrible idea that Tom was right. He had believed far too much and too easily.

"Too clever by half." Tom was dismissive and contemptuous. Robert had been caught for a sucker.

"You think so?"

"I'm sure of it! And you're just another stupid mug."

Robert said nothing.

"You think yourself so intelligent. You and your clever girlfriend."

The reference to Anna alarmed Robert. Where was she? Was she safe? He feared not.

"Anna? What have you done to Anna! You had better not touch her!" Robert stirred as if to attack.

"Nothing." Tom jerked the Lugar into Robert's ribs. He could feel the steel muzzle. "She's safe. While you behave."

"She is not well! She's ill. What have you done with her?"

"She's safe. I told you."

"She had better be."

Tom scoffed at this feeble threat, "you're in no position to threaten me. Now, keep her steady, this course will do for ten minutes while we finish our little business."

Robert obeyed.

"Secure the wheel! Here's a rope."

Robert did so.

"You will now walk slowly out onto the deck," Tom ordered. "You will walk slowly in front of me. I will be directly behind you. I have the gun and I will use it if you do anything silly. We will proceed down the companion ladder to the main deck. Understand?"

"You must promise not to touch Anna."

"Must? You are in no position to say must! Understand? Now get moving."

Robert understood all too well. But why co-operate with Tom if he was doomed in any event. Maybe he could get Tom to make an unwise move.

"No!" he shouted suddenly. "You're going to kill me anyway. Why should I obey you? If you're going to shoot me, do it now." This reaction clearly surprised Tom, and Robert could see him thinking how to play it. Should he shoot Robert there and then? It might go beyond what he had said to the other sailors. It might alert Bedros, who might be still at liberty and could pose a threat. On the other hand, if he didn't shoot Robert, what should he do? He would have to do something.

Whatever that might have been was interrupted by the sick master. He had been lying in his adjoining cabin and had been disturbed by what was happening in the wheelhouse. He suddenly pushed open the door and staggered into the wheelhouse clinging to the doorframe to support himself.

"What's going on?" he cried out.

Tom was standing beside Robert with his back to the master and was taken by surprise. He instinctively spun round in response to the creaking of the opening door and pulled the trigger on the Lugar. He fired two shots in rapid succession at the master. The first hit him in the shoulder and he cried out in agony. The other, a moment later, hit him in the chest and he crumpled to the deck. Tom froze for a fatal moment.

"You stupid fool!" Tom exclaimed, "I needed you to run the ship."

So much for any remorse, the master was dead.

Robert seized the opportunity of Tom's momentary distraction. Tom was standing beside him, but had turned to face the master's intervention, and was holding his pistol in his right hand, a hand that was now close to Robert's right arm. Robert reacted quickly lifting his right arm and chopping it down hard onto Tom's right wrist, the one holding the gun. Another useful move from his dockland training. At the same time, he grabbed Tom's shirt collar with his left hand and jerked him violently backwards. Tom was thrown off balance and fell awkwardly and sideways onto the brass mounting of the engine room telegraph. He yelled with pain and dropped his pistol, which cluttered onto the deck.

The gun fell a few feet away from Robert. Instead of remembering his dockland training and finishing Tom off, Robert was unwisely tempted to bend down to snatch it. It was a bad move. Tom was a tough street kid, recovered quickly from his fall and saw the chance to spring back at Robert. Robert shoved him away but had not reached the gun.

Tom did not wait and came at Robert, fists flailing wildly. There was no time or space to avoid him, and Robert met him head on, bringing his fist round to hit him hard, then again, landing a punch to his stomach that winded him and left him breathing noisily. Then he launched one to Tom's jaw that left him staggering backwards. But he was not down, and he came at Robert again. Robert kneed him hard in the face, and Tom went flying backwards towards the wheel. His back hit the wheel and he yelped in pain. But he bounced back and got in a punch to Robert's face.

They wrestled and Tom managed to trip Robert and throw him to the deck. He then hurled himself on top of

Robert, going for his throat. Robert succeeded in pushing his arm away and was able to free himself to roll to one side. They grappled and struggled on the deck, rolling, wrestling, punching, pummelling, thrashing about, each one seeking to gain a crucial momentary advantage. Tom tried butting but Robert was ready for it and brought his fist up to jab him full in the face. Robert succeeded in getting in a hard blow to the chin so that Tom slumped to the deck.

Robert rose from his knees and looked around for the gun. But that once again that was a mistake that gave Tom the chance he wanted. He wriggled away and managed to get up, pulled out a knife and came up behind Robert, holding the knife to his throat.

"So! You traitor! You will die!" he bellowed. His face was seriously bloodied, but his eyes were bright, demented, and he grinned, excited at the prospect of a victim. Robert was sure Tom was set on finishing him off as he probably had killed the unfortunate German agent.

"On your knees knave!" Tom ordered. "On your knees or I'll slit your throat right now."

Robert made a quick decision to comply. Tom was probably no stranger to the use of the knife and unless Robert complied, he would be killed there and then. Tom took the opportunity of Robert kneeling to regain his pistol.

"A foolish move! Do not try and repeat it. I will kill you at once. Now we're going to go down to the main deck. Unless you want to die you will move exactly as I order you."

But for Bedros, if they had reached the main deck that would have been the end for Robert. However, Tom's earlier instruction to reduce engine speed, when Bedros knew Robert was in the wheelhouse, had taken Bedros by surprise. It was a warning that something was wrong. He knew that Tom was at the wheel and Robert was with him, so he had put two and two together. Whatever was wrong was connected to Tom, a man Bedros did not trust. Bedros collected his rifle and went up to the wheelhouse.

He heard Tom's two pistol shots as he ran stealthily up the companion ladder. He reached the upper deck and saw that the port side door into the wheelhouse was being slowly pushed open. He also heard Tom's snarling commands to Robert to obey and was sure that he was up to no good. He had just time to slip away to one side and creep round the rear upper deck cabin without being spotted by Tom. He then continued carefully round to enter the starboard side door into the wheelhouse. He passed the dead master and went straight through the wheelhouse, leaving it by the door that Tom and Robert had just used. He thus arrived silently behind Tom at the moment that Robert had reached the top of the companion ladder and was about to descend. Tom was standing with his back to Bedros, leaning forwards over Robert and did not either see Bedros or sense his presence. Bedros stood stock-still holding his breath.

"Start to descend!" Tom ordered Robert. "One step at a time. And don't try any tricks. Or I'll shoot. Go down feet first and put both hands on the rails as you descend. I'm right above you. And Len is at the foot of the ladder and will shoot if you try anything."

There was no choice. Robert started to shuffle towards the top step of the companion ladder. The ladder was vertical, and he turned round to feel where to place his feet. It was awkward and he was not going to hurry. Something might happen to his advantage; he hoped so without much faith that it would. But Tom repeated his order and Robert complied, putting one foot on the second step down and his hands on the rail each side.

"Get a move on!" Tom ordered, becoming impatient. "Keep it nice and steady and don't try anything."

Robert carefully moved his other foot to pass the second step down and felt for the next step. He would go as slowly as he could just in case an opportunity to reverse the situation might appear out of the blue. However, there was no sign of Bedros, Len was evidently one of Tom's men and Robert could hear movement below him that was probably Len. The other sailor, Bill, was probably controlling Anna and Valeria. Robert slowly moved another foot down to the following step, carefully and slowly. He was aware that Tom was standing above him, leaning forward and Robert could sense that his gun was pointing somewhere uncomfortably close to his head.

At that moment, however, Bedros crept silently up behind Tom and putting his rifle against Tom's head fired a single fatal shot. Tom, who had been leaning forwards, crumpled, and tumbled downwards over Robert, who realising what was happening, pressed his face close to the companion ladder and gripped the rails tightly with both hands. In this manner he was able to avoid being knocked off the ladder by the weight of Tom's body, which fell over him and tumbled down to the foot of the companion ladder..

Len had been standing at the foot of the companion ladder, holding a rifle. But had not aimed or fired it when Bedros moved behind Tom, presumably because Tom, above him at the top of the ladder would have been in the line of fire. But when Bedros fired and Tom's body cascaded down the ladder, Len just stood there frozen, immobilised for a moment by shock. He stepped back only just as the body reached him. Seeing Len with a rifle, below him at the foot of the companion ladder, Bedros did not hesitate to fire. His shot hit Len in the head, and he dropped dead.

Robert, who had hugged himself as close to the ladder as he could to avoid being dragged down by Tom's falling body, now recovered himself. He looked down with a shudder at the two crumpled bodies of Tom and Len at the foot of the ladder. Neither moved but he knew he had to get down quickly to the main deck and make sure they were both dead. It shocked him to think that it had come to this, the Master, Tom, and Len all killed in the space of five minutes. Of course, it could easily have been Robert, Anna, Valeria, and Bedros who had died instead. That had clearly been Tom's intention and Robert did not feel remorse at what had happened to Tom and his fellow conspirator.

"My God what a shambles!" he exclaimed as he managed to stumble around the two bodies. A quick look satisfied him that they were certainly both dead, both shot in the head. He looked up at Bedros standing at the top of the companion ladder.

"Bedros! Thank God you came. And are such a good shot."

"It was chance more than anything," Bedros answered. "I couldn't miss Tom he was so close and for Len I just fired blindly and hit him before he could take aim."

Bedros followed Robert down to the main deck.

"Robert, they got what they deserved!"

"You're right. But it's still an awful mess," Robert said quietly. "But I must find Anna. They must be held captive in the front cabin, and I hope to God they are alright."

Earlier, when Robert had said he was going up to the wheelhouse, Len and Bill had waited on Tom's orders until Robert was out of sight. They had then followed orders and were tying up Valeria and Anna with lengths of rope when Tom shot the master. Len heard the ensuing fight in the wheelhouse above them and broke off to see what was happening. He left Bill to guard Anna and Valeria. But Bill lost his concentration when Tom and Len were shot. That was when Valeria launched herself at Bill, using a rifle stock to batter him on the head, knocking him down with blood covering his face. She might have finished him off, but Bedros and Robert then arrived, grabbed Bill, and tied him up with a rope.

Robert found Anna lying distraught on one of the cabin settees, terribly shaken by the further awful turn of events. He hurried across and tried to console her, sitting beside her, and stroking her hand, whispering soft words into her ear. But she was still uncontrollably trembling and crying. He was himself badly shaken, certainly by the recent dramatic events but much more at seeing that Anna's condition was so much worse. But he knew he was responsible for the ship and all in her and that he had to pull himself together. It was time to get control of the situation.

Now only Robert, Anna, Valeria, Bedros, the engineer, Albert the engineer's assistant and Bill, the third sailor, remained. As Bill was needed to run the ship, Robert decided to ask him if he was ready to serve under the new command, warning him that any kind of disloyalty would be immediately punished. Bill, shaken at the death of his two accomplices, agreed at once and Robert untied him, having warned him again about his quick fate if he tried any tricks. Robert sent him up to take the wheel and went himself to the adjoining master's cabin to examine the charts. With the death of the master there was no experienced navigator; Robert would have to do his best, with his limited knowledge of seamanship and navigation, learnt in sailing a small dinghy off the Norfolk coast. Being in a much larger steamboat somewhere in the vast expanse of sea between Algeria and

Sardinia, he wasn't quite sure where, was, he appreciated, a very different business. But he had confidence; the principles and techniques of navigation were the same whatever the size of the vessel as were the means of fixing a position and using the maps. So, he used the old master's instruments to ascertain their current position, marked it on the map, checked their course for Cagliari and gave it to Bill.

It was also time for a council of war to assess the situation and most of all decide their future course of action. Leaving Bill at the wheel he called for everyone else on the ship to convene around the large table in the aft main deck cabin. Robert summarised what had occurred, much of which was news to the two from the engine room. Robert told them that he intended to take *Hermes* to Cagliari in Sardinia for supplies and fuel. There in Sardinia they would make a final decision about the fate of *Hermes*. No-one disagreed and Albert volunteered to join the wheelhouse rota.

27

After the engineer and Albert departed, and with Bill still at the wheel, Robert decided he must tell Valeria, Anna, and Bedros about the cargo of gold sovereigns. He said that the tugboat attack and then Tom's attempt to kill him had made it all too clear that the gold was a magnet for murderous thieves. While the gold was still on the ship, they were not safe.

"No wonder they tried so hard to recapture the ship!" Valeria said. "The gold is like a honeypot for them."

"That means," Robert answered, "the question is what to do with the gold. The gold and *Hermes* are literally a deadly combination for us."

"We must give the gold back!" Anna croaked. "It would be horrible to keep it!" She continued to cry. "It has blood on it, We cannot keep it!"

"You say give the gold back; but whose gold is it?" Bedros asked.

"A good question! " Robert said. "And there you have the problem. I assume it is the Kaiser's gold because it was loaded from a German ship in Lisbon."

"Yes, but *Hermes* is British registered," Bedros observed quietly. "Would the British government not claim the gold?"

"They might think of it, " Robert advised. "But they can't claim the gold without the whole story coming out. They won't want that; it would open a Pandora's box of diplomatic trouble. "

"Would Germany not demand the return of the gold?" Bedros asked.

"I think not," Robert said. "You see they could not claim the gold was theirs without admitting their conspiracy."

"You're saying," Bedros remarked, "that there is no-one who would claim the gold?"

"Yes! I am saying that."

There was a silence while people thought.

"Therefore, it's surely finders' keepers," Valeria asserted, "and we are the finders."

"You mean it's ours? Can we be sure?" Bedros wanted to know.

"No, we can't be sure," Robert said. "Flotsam or jetsam abandoned in the water is one thing. But what we have is a very valuable cargo of gold. What I remember about shipping law is that an abandoned cargo on British territory belongs to the Crown. And *Hermes* is a British ship. We're back to square one."

There was silence.

Anna, listening, was quietly crying, "The gold is covered in blood. We must get rid of it."

Another silence.

"Can I suggest something," Robert said. "We have the gold, but we know it is a magnet for thieves and that we must do something with it. We also know we must dispose of *Hermes*. Let's first decide what to do with *Hermes*."

There was agreement apart from a tearful Anna, "we should just throw the gold into the sea."

No-one else liked that idea.

"Simply throw away so much money!" Valeria objected. "Surely not. It is obscene when there is so much good that could be done with it. We must get rid of the ship, and then deal with the gold."

There seemed to be agreement.

*

Putting Albert at the wheel, Robert decided that they must bury Tom, Len, and the master, at sea without delay. The sea burial was of necessity a rough, improvised, event, Robert used Bill's experience and put him in charge of making the arrangements, finding some lengths of canvas and sewing materials. Robert himself conducted a brief service including a short prayer, in what he believed was the traditional manner. They used a plank covered with a "Red Duster" from the wheelhouse to slide the bodies over the side into the sea. For the master's death he had real regrets, for he had been an unlucky victim of Tom's treachery. For the other two he found it hard to feel any regret, for they would have killed him, and Anna too, if they had not been shot by Bedros. He knew he was lucky that the fortunes of war had been kind to him.

Since the sea fight with the tugboat, Anna had withdrawn into her own private, deeply troubled world. She looked wretched, and her continued weak condition worried Robert sick. It was made worse because he did not understand what had caused her symptoms. For such a strongminded person, someone so much in control of her emotions, someone who was so resilient, it seemed so out of character. Especially as no-one else had reacted in her way. He was confused and hated himself for being the author of her misfortune. He had no idea how to help her and felt helpless. Valeria repeatedly assure him that all Anna needed was a good rest, but Robert suspected that these were merely words designed to calm him. He feared the problem was far more complicated.

It was only after they had finished the grim business of the sea burial that Robert remembered that there was almost certainly another body on the ship. That of the German Agent who had boarded at Lisbon, the man Hugo had instructed Tom to 'dispose of'. Such casual words for murder, so typical of Hugo. As the man had not been seen after *Hermes* docked in Malaga, Tom have indeed carried out his orders. There had been no opportunity of disposing of the body in Malaga so it must still be on the ship.

The body of the German agent was indeed found inside his cabin, with a bullet in his head. A terrible sight that made Robert physically sick. The dead man's jacket was on a chair. In an inside pocket was a German passport in the name of Gunther Eisel, born 1872 in Hamburg, described as 'Engineer'. There was also a small oblong object propped up on the dressing table, wrapped in red velvet. He opened it and saw a small but beautiful Icon of the Virgin Mary, of the type sometimes found in Greek Churches.

Bedros had followed him down. "My God! This is disgusting! Another body."

Robert asked Bedros to have a last look round the cabin and bring the passport, Icon and any other personal object he found up to the table in the aft upper deck cabin. Robert himself returned to the wheelhouse to take over the wheel so that Bill could sew up the German Agent's body for another sea burial. When the burial was done, Robert went to the main deck aft cabin where Anna was still lying on a sofa. They were joined by Bedros, who placed on the big central table the collection of objects he had removed from the German agent's cabin.

"I found one or two interesting things in the cabin," Bedros said, holding out a large, heavy gold ring. "It has some interesting markings."

"What do you mean, markings?"

"Here," he said, holding out the ring and indicating a mark on the inside. "It was made in St Petersburg. It has the right assay mark and I have seen the maker's initials before. I have an uncle in the jewellery business. Look, the ring has two intertwined letters inscribed on the outside. You can make them out if you look closely."

"And what about it?"

"They are Cyrillic letters. The Russian alphabet. It must be a Russian ring. Strange thing to wear for someone who is not Russian? Must be something personal. What kind of story does that tell? The man had a woman in Russia, perhaps an old love affair in St Petersburg?"

"Where did he get it?" Robert wondered.

"He could have bought it at any Port," Bedros answered.

"Yes, but it is rather odd," Robert said. "How does having a ring like this fit someone engaged on the Kaiser's secret work?"

"And you should see the gun I found in the cabin," Bedros said, offering him a gun in its special leather case.

Robert took the gun out of its holster. He expected to see a Lugar, a German automatic pistol popular in the German officer class. This gun, however, wasn't a Lugar but a seven-shot revolver. Unusual. Examining the side of it he could see some lettering, also in clear Cyrillic letters.

"Look at these letters," Bedros said. "This is a Russian gun. The man has both a Russian ring and a Russian revolver. Can that be just a coincidence?"

Valeria came in and noticed the Icon in red velvet that Bedros had placed on the table. "This is a fine Icon. You say you found it in the German Agent's cabin. What is a German doing with a Russian Icon?"

Robert was taken aback. "A Russian Icon?"

"Yes. It's a good copy of a famous Russian Icon of the Virgin. It is very popular in Russia. This one is beautifully painted and quite old, the sort of Icon that might be a family treasure. It may be valuable."

"Are you sure it's Russian? Aren't there Icons like this in Greece?"

"They are not the same. The pose of the Virgin in Greek Icons is different and quite distinctive. The colours are different. There are many subtle ways that separate Icons from Greece and Russia. This one is definitely Russian."

"You're sure?"

"Yes! I knew it at once! It's a copy of a famous Russian Icon. The colours used by the painter are distinctively Russian, this is a pale green colour you will never see on a Greek Icon. The style of painting is not Greek. Look at the pose of the Virgin, it is uniquely Russian."

"What!" Robert was astonished. He had wrongly jumped to the conclusion that the icon was Greek.

"If it's a Russian Icon, that does make sense," he said thoughtfully. "A Russian ring, a Russian revolver and now a Russian Icon. It fits! And it makes a new situation. A Russian situation! My God it changes everything!"

"But why would a Russian Agent be on *Hermes*?"

They looked at each other for barely a moment, although it seemed an age. Valeria had a flash of understanding. "There would be a Russian agent on *Hermes* because, Robert, we got the conspiracy completely wrong. *Hermes* was never the German conspiracy we imagined. It is a Russian conspiracy."

"But that would mean the Tsar was conspiring against his allies?" Robert replied, searching for a denial of the logic that had suddenly turned everything upside down. "There is surely so much that implicates Berlin. The Germans who broke into the Gibson's house, were traced back to a German restaurant that was used by German agents in London. And what about the German ship?"

"A German ship?"

He paused and knew at once he had been a fool. He had too easily taken far too much at face value, relied on assumptions instead of reliable evidence.

"You're right! I am an idiot. Of course, a 'German' ship could simply mean that it was registered in Germany. But in fact, the ship might have been chartered by anyone."

"Including someone from St Petersburg."

"Absolutely! A Russian could charter it as easily as anyone else. And you know what, the largest shipping exchange is the Baltic Exchange in London. I wouldn't put it past the Russians to have chartered a German registered ship in London. What damned cheek!"

Anna had overheard the conversation. "What does that say about the gold, Robert?"

"It says that when I was told that gold had been loaded onto *Hermes* from a German vessel in Lisbon, I wrongly assumed it was German gold."

"When in fact it was gold paid for by Russia."

"Yes!" Robert said, "the whole idea of German control of Sergio's plan may after all be a clever hoax."

"They tricked you, Robert."

"Yes," Robert answered, "I blame myself. It was a mistake I shouldn't have made."

The full implications of what was emerging from the discovery of the Russian agent were hitting home.

"I remember now," Robert said, "that Tom told me just before he tried to kill me that the man we called the German Agent, was not a German. And Hugo told me that it was vital in the event of a major war in Europe that the Straits at Constantinople remained open for Russian shipping. Russia might therefore be looking for a ready cause to occupy Constantinople and the straits the moment a European war broke out."

"And," Bedros asked, "what situation would Russia need for that?"

"Russia would need Turkey to be Russia's enemy the moment war began. Then Constantinople could be immediately occupied."

"And that gives you the motive behind the *Hermes* conspiracy. Russia knew it was essential to capture Constantinople and the Straits."

"Looks like it!"

"Won't Russia want its gold back?"

"Perhaps not. Russia is an ally of Britain, and if the Tsar wants to keep the alliance, he cannot admit to being part of a *Hermes* conspiracy directed against Britain."

"You're saying," Bedros said, "Russia will not claim that the gold is theirs."

"Exactly. But we are still an easy target in this boat, We must get rid of *Hermes* as soon as we can. We seem to be back to sinking her?"

"Surely not!" Bedros said. "Sinking a sound ship is wicked. There are ways in which she can disappear. I suggested selling her for scrap. She would be cut up. Another way though would be to take her to a yard, like Athens, change her personality and appearance. Give her a new name, a new funnel, some changes to the upper deck, a new profile, and so on. She is a sound vessel, there is a market for her. We sell her for what we can get. She is a sound vessel and worth money."

"That sounds good," Robert agreed. "But we would need to think of a secure place for the gold."

"That's easy!" Valeria said. "The safest place for the gold is in a Bank."

"I like the idea of a bank," Robert said.

Valeria had a further suggestion. "We should bank the gold in Italy."

Bedros looked puzzled. "You mean in Cagliari?"

"No. In Genoa. It's Italy's major commercial City with reliable banks. It's not far from where my family comes. We have family contacts in the region. I speak the language, so does Anna. I know how to do business in Italy. That matters."

"Very well, you talk sense," Robert agreed. "If we combine Bedros' advice and yours, we should unload the gold in Sardinia, leave the ship, and arrange for *Hermes* to be sailed to Athens by another crew we hire for the job."

"But wait!" Valeria objected. "Someone has to be in Athens to make the business arrangements for a refit of *Hermes* and to sell her."

The long silence was filled by Valeria. "Would you do that Bedros? Would you sail *Hermes* to Athens?" Bedros looked doubtful; it would be a risky voyage if the Russians were after *Hermes*.

"I know it's asking a lot," Valeria said. "If the Russians are watching the ports, they will learn that *Hermes* was in Cagliari and know when she sailed. They may try another interception, like the tugboat. It could be dangerous. When we have reached Genoa and deposited the gold, we should of course find a way to transfer money to finish the refit. Don't you agree Robert!"

"Absolutely!" Robert exclaimed. "If it wasn't for you Bedros, we would all be dead. Tom would have killed us all. He nearly did. If we transfer the funds to you in Athens it should be plain sailing for you to make a good deal about *Hermes*."

Bedros still looked uncertain but allowed himself to be attracted by the proposal and then needed only a moment to endorse it but for one objection.

"I will take the boat to Athens," he said. "I will enjoy the challenge of transforming *Hermes* into another vessel. But I need to take only enough gold to pay off the crew. For the cost of refitting, I would prefer to wait for you to transfer money from Genoa once you have found a bank."

Bedros was saying that he completely trusted his companions. He was prepared for them to sail off to Genoa with all the gold. It was also the case that he was talking sense. To travel with any quantity of gold on board *Hermes* would be a risk.

"Fine," Robert said, "we will transfer funds to you in Athens as soon as we can. Give me an address there."

Bedros gave him the name of an Armenian merchant known to his father, to be used as contact point for Bedros in Athens. So, it was settled that Bedros would sail *Hermes* to Athens with a new crew hired in Cagliari. But agreeing to bank the gold in Genoa was only part of the story. What were they going to do with it?

"That's good!" Robert said, "we've agreed that no-one is going to claim to be the owner of the gold. Assuming we are right, the question is what do we physically do with the gold? We need to talk about who got what. In other words, shares. How do we divide up the gold?"

"You're asking how the gold should be shared?"

"Yes."

Anna who had been listening to their conversation with a scowl on her face and rather pointedly not taking part, now spoke angrily, "Don't try to pass any of the gold to me. I won't take it. Any of it."

"That's up to you Anna," Valeria replied calmly but firmly, "you can of course do what you wish with your share. If you want to throw it into the sea you can do so. Though it would be a wicked waste when there are so many good things you could do with the money. If that is how you think you honour your mother's memory, so be it."

Anna gave her a hard stare, "How dare you! It is not my share. I have no share. I refuse to take any share. I want nothing to do with it. I hate everything to do with *Hermes*." She went off in a tearful temper.

The final arrangement was easier than Robert expected, largely because Valeria made a proposal which Robert agreed.

"I think Bedros should get forty per cent. He has the risk of running the gauntlet taking *Hermes* to Athens. If the Russians assume the gold is still on board they may chase. That leaves sixty per cent between the rest of us. Anna's wrong to say the gold should be thrown away, but she's right to be worried that it has so much blood on it. If she has a share, I suggest it's used to support a charity in Genoa. And I want any share of mine to go to you Robert."

So, it was settled, Robert, Anna, and Valeria would take the next steamer from Cagliari to Genoa. The engineer and his assistant were told about the plan to sail to Athens with a new crew and were keen, in return for a handsome payment, to continue to Athens in *Hermes*. Bill was happy to be paid off in Cagliari with a ferry ticket to Marseilles. They kept some of the rifles for protection but the rest of the guns, ammunition and rockets were unceremoniously dumped overboard as soon as Sardinia was sighted.

28

Two days later they were approaching Cagliari on the southern coast of the island of Sardinia. Seeing the last of *Hermes* could not be soon enough for Robert, who was increasingly concerned about Anna's condition. Her disturbed state of mind had not improved, and she remained in evident distress, frequently tearful and shaking. The most devastating part of it for Robert was that she now shunned physical contact with him. She just repeated in a trance-like tone that she blamed him for everything bad that had happened to her on *Hermes*.

Valeria overheard her and was concerned. "Robert, you do realise that she's not herself. She was badly upset by what happened with that tugboat and needs a complete rest. You must get her away from *Hermes*. She identifies all her sickness with it. Now she starts to identify you with it."

"I know! As soon as we reach Cagliari, we'll get her off the boat into a hotel. That should help."

To avoid snoopers Robert anchored *Hermes* outside Cagliari harbour. He ordered Bill to take one of the ship's boats and cover the word '*Hermes*', painted in gold on the ship's stern, with white paint. A new name 'Athena' was inscribed in black letters. Modern telegraph and telephone systems meant the whole world was now inter-connected, and news of *Hermes* arrival could spread like wildfire round the Mediterranean. It could be too easy for the Russians, or whatever other gang was associated with the tugboat attack, to discover them and make another attempt to snatch the gold.

Then Robert rowed Valeria and Anna into the harbour to find a hotel, pondering how to organise the transfer of the gold from *Hermes* to the steamer to Genoa. The problem was that each of the twenty gold boxes was too heavy to be carried between decks in *Hermes and* was anyway far too obvious for what it was. Valeria proposed repacking the gold into small canvas bags, each one filled with about ten of the cartridge paper 'tubes' that contained the gold coins, and light enough to be easily carried up to the main deck. Valeria also proposed buying some strong wooden industrial crates in which to repack some of the gold, labelling the crates as her personal effects such as 'library books', or 'kitchen equipment'. The remainder of the gold would be distributed in their steamer trunks and personal luggage.

"Who would bother to steal books!" she said.

At her suggestion Robert telegraphed the Hotel Bristol in Genoa, which she knew from the old days, and reserved rooms. He also bought three steamer trunks to augment their luggage.

They had to wait in Cagliari only a few nervous days for the arrival of the steamer to Genoa. Just enough time to carry out the exhausting business of repacking the gold coins in their new canvas bags, shifting them to the main deck and then repacking them into the new wooden crates and steamer trunks. So, when the Genoa ferry approached, they were ready for it. *Hermes* upped anchor and Robert took her into the harbour; once tied up on the quay Bedros collected his new master and crew and organised them to unload the cargo and luggage from *Hermes* and carry it ready for the Genoa steamer.

Later with parting shouts of 'bon voyage' Robert and Valeria stood and watched as *Hermes* gave a piercing farewell blast on her steam whistle, cast off her ropes and with her engine gently purring slowly pulled away from the quay. They watched and waved until she had made her way out of the harbour and had disappeared from sight. As *Hermes* vanished from their lives, for Robert it was the end of a huge burden of responsibility, a moment to feel sheer relief that a terrible voyage was over.

He found Anna sitting by their luggage and was shocked to realise she was shivering. Looking into her face he saw also that there were tears in her eyes.

"Thank God she's gone," Anna whispered.

"Anna, you're right she has gone. Gone for good. It's all over," he said softly. "She's out of our lives. We're finished with her." He only hoped it was true. In the back of his mind, he feared that in fact the Russians might not be finished with *Hermes*; the repercussions of the Sergio affair could drag on.

"It's so easy to say she's gone," she answered, "you have no idea what it did to me."

Soon the Genoa steamer vented a powerful blast on her whistle and, as always, the passengers waved and cheered as the ship cast off. She edged slowly out of Cagliari's busy harbour to steam north along the coast of Sardinia, to then leave Corsica in her wake and veer east towards tiny Elba. Unfortunately, Anna was totally indifferent to the whole show, she just hunched down in a deck chair and refused to take any interest in the sights. Indeed, nothing dispelled her despondent, listless mood as the ship toiled on hour after hour. It was so utterly disappointing; both Valeria and Robert had been sure that witnessing *Hermes* departure from Cagliari, followed by the soothing experience of the sea air in a calm cruise to Genoa would break Anna's despair. By evening it was all too clear that her condition was much worse than Robert had feared. He retired to his tiny cabin for the night tormented by his inability to help her.

*

They docked in Genoa and Robert supervised the unloading of their luggage and cargo. Valeria rushed to disembark early and was a hive of activity in securing the services of a horse drawn wagon, and hiring porters to transfer all their possessions. She also found a nearby secure warehouse where they could deposit the crates and boxes that held their precious, concealed, gold cargo, now labelled as various parts of her personal household possessions, kitchen utensils, books, bedding and so forth. Satisfied that the property was secure they then made their way to the Hotel Bristol. Later Valeria took Anna and Robert shopping for some new, smart, fashionable clothes; if they were to turn up and deposit a huge sum of gold in a bank, they should look the part.

After that Valeria took Robert to the nearby Banca Commerciale Italiana to open an account and begin the deposit of the gold concealed in their steamer trunks and other luggage. Valeria took confident charge of the transaction in the Bank and doubtless made a point of her family's past commercial connections with the City. A barrowload of English sovereigns, an entirely acceptable international currency, spoke for itself.

Robert then went on to the British Consulate and asked them to send a coded telegram to Blake at the Foreign Office in London, summarising the whole story.

Blake replied, using Hugo's code, that he was not surprised at the news of *Hermes* being a Russian conspiracy. "We were more than annoyed at the goings on of Choristers Bridge. That is the address in St Petersburg of the Russian Ministry of Foreign Affairs, who operate a secret intelligence service, mainly concerned with pursuing the revolutionary cells that continually conspire against the Tsar. They use unscrupulous and violent methods in a pitiless pursuit of these groups. Especially in Paris, which seems to attract Russian exiles, but also in England. We strongly object to such behaviour and have told them so. But they do it all the same."

He went on with a crucial statement. "We have told Choristers Bridge that *Hermes* was attacked by pirates somewhere off the Algerian coast, that the pirates stole the gold and then sank the ship. The crew, though, luckily managed to escape in one of the ship's boats. We have made it plain to Choristers Bridge that the whole affair of *Hermes* is best forgotten by both Britain and Russia. There will be no questions asked about the gold."

The next day Robert and party set off from the Hotel Bristol to take the train to Santa Margherita Ligure and the hotel Valeria had recommended. The Grand Hotel Miramare was built on a small promontory that gave a magnificent view of the Bay of Rapello. The building was designed in the thoroughly up to date Art Nouveau style and did indeed exude all the qualities of the grandness, elegance and comfort Valeria had described. Anna perked up when they reached the hotel, entered the fine reception hall, and walked through to survey the terraces at the rear that commanded a superb view over the Bay.

"Ah!" she exclaimed. "What a view!"

"Aunty Val, the place is spectacular!" Robert said.

"Anna, it's wonderful isn't it." He tried to encourage her, and she did agree that the view was glorious. But there were still tears in her eyes and she avoided his touch.

The hotel stood in magnificent, lush gardens. The extensive area was filled with palms, pines, camellias, oleanders, pittosporum, and cedars. When they strolled through it the combined fragrance of the many flowers and bushes was delightful. The suite Anna shared with Valeria had a stunningly beautiful panorama; the rocky shore below them, the sapphire blue water in front of them dotted with small boats of various sizes, across the bay many lush terraces of trees and shrubs, colourful buildings sprawling down to the sea. A perfect place for Anna to relax and recuperate. He prayed that she would do so and recover her old self.

Much later, Robert was sitting on the terrace and was unexpectedly approached by a middle-aged man wearing a beige linen suit, a high old-fashioned collar, a bow tie, a well-trimmed goatee beard and steel rimmed pince-nez.

"You will perhaps forgive my impertinence in interrupting you?" He said, introducing himself as Dr Karl Steiger of the Klinik Otto Wagner in Vienna. He spoke good English with a distinctive Austrian accent. "I have not been able to help noticing that your attractive young friend, who is I gather from the staff is a Miss Gibson, is unwell. Unwell in the mind I mean. She was clearly distressed, and I observed her being sometimes almost hysterical if she felt stressed. I should explain that I am a doctor practising in Vienna. I am merely here on vacation. I specialise in the medical science of the mind, and I speak now only because I may perhaps be of some assistance to her."

"You will have noticed then," Robert observed, "that she is not quite herself."

"Indeed, it is unfortunately very clear that she is suffering serious problems. My interest was attracted because she displays symptoms that I recognise from my own patients as probably related to having undergone a serious traumatic experience. Is that the case?"

It was a straight question and Robert decided to accept that the stranger was who he said he was. He decided to be frank. "That is so. She had a bad experience."

"May I inquire the nature of the experience? I merely ask about the general nature of the experience. An unexpected death in the family? An accident on the railway?"

Robert decided it was safe to answer in general terms. "We were involved in having to save ourselves from some bad men who would probably have killed us."

"Ah! Were you in great danger?"

"Yes! They wanted us dead. Anna has been badly affected, in the way you have observed, but I am not affected and nor is her aunt who was also there. It seems strange that Anna reacts in this way, and we do not."

"Well, let me assure you that is not strange. It is the nature of the actual experience that a particular person undergoes that matters. People react differently to exactly the same event. The experience I have of an event is not the same experience you have of that same event. Perhaps I might ask you to describe the situation you experienced in slightly more detail? For instance, what was the nature of the danger to you, perhaps guns were fired at you? Were there many assailants? Was there a possibility of escape for you?"

Robert provided as much detail as he dared.

"May I ask you to describe the effect on her? I observed her sitting alone on the terrace crying to herself, I noticed in a conversation you had with her that at times she raised the pitch and level of her voice, sounded hysterical and her face shows all the signs of great underlying tension. Is there perhaps more, does she for instance become frozen? How often is she upset? How frequently? Are there episodes in which she is worse? How bad is each episode? How long does each last? How long to calm down each time?"

The Viennese doctor was thorough, and Robert answered as well as he could. He then advised Robert to be hopeful because in his opinion Anna's condition was one that could be helped by treatment of the right kind. She should with luck be able to make a full recovery in time. He finished by offering Robert his card and writing down the name of a medical colleague in Harley Street in London who might be able to help Anna. For Robert the unexpected conversation had introduced a wonderful and totally unexpected ray of light. He had indeed dared to hope that Anna's condition could be understood and that in time there might be a remedy, but it had up to then only sounded like wishful thinking. Now Dr Steiger had given him real grounds to hope.

29

But whatever prospects here might be for the future, for the present Anna continued to suffer. So much so that a week later Valeria suggested that as Anna's condition had not improved she should take Anna home to London. Anna herself was keen to go with Valeria, so Robert booked the train and hotel tickets for their journey. He himself would remain in Italy to complete the transfer of the gold to the bank.

As he and Anna left the dining room on their final evening in the hotel, Robert took this last opportunity for a few private words with her. Though really she just wanted to rest, she did not refuse.

"Anna, I'm really sorry you are going home with so much misunderstanding between us." Somehow his words totally understated his sense of total disbelief at the way ecstasy had turned so swiftly into despair.

"Misunderstanding?" she answered, giving him a cold look. "If you mean Paris, there is no misunderstanding."

"I had thought ..." he was thinking of that night of joy on *Hermes*. Surely, she could not have come to him that night and embraced him with so much warmth and desire if she still held 'Paris' against him. That would be unreasonable: his trip to Paris was well before fate had renewed his friendship with Anna.

"I'm sure you did! But it's not that simple."

"No?" It did seem all very simple to him.

"Really Robert! Don't be so dull-witted. I'm too tired to cope with your silliness. There's the whole thing about how you insisted on believing Hugo. And then dragged us all to Malaga."

He was astonished. "I dragged no-one to Malaga. That is not fair Anna!"

"Don't talk to me about being fair after the way you treated Sybil."

"Sybil?" He was non-plussed at the sudden change of attack.

"Yes Sybil! Did you tell Sybil about Paris? Did you dupe Sybil with your lies about Paris?"

"Lies? There were no lies."

"Sybil expected you to marry her. Yet you just threw her over when it suited you."

"I did not!"

"I know how you treated her. And what you did to her you could do to me."

"This is rubbish Anna. You have no idea what went on between Sybil and me."

"Oh! I do know. I know exactly."

"How can you?"

"Gerald told me!"

"Gerald!" He almost spat the word. "That oaf. What does he know?" He spoke harshly with a raised voice. "You listen to gutter gossip from fools like Gerald."

The look she gave him showed she found his tone aggressive and unpleasant. "Don't say such things! He was told the whole story by Sybil's family." She emphasised the last words, rubbing in the authenticity of her statement.

"Oh?"

"Yes. You told her that you were going away on a long sea voyage and were taking me so that I would have to marry you. Yet you were almost engaged to Sybil. She was expecting you to propose. It was disgraceful of you. Shameful. Can you be surprised that she rejected you?"

"Anna! That is not true."

"Oh! Did you not meet her just before the journey to Tripoli?"

"Yes."

"Did she throw you out?"

"Our relationship ended."

"Well then, it was exactly as I said."

"No, it is not exactly as you said"

"Oh!"

"Our ... relationship ended because her family didn't like me. It was nothing at all to do with the trip to Tripoli. Or for that matter with you."

"Please Robert! She had a lucky escape."

He was suspicious that Anna was inventing excuses to conceal her real motive. "Escape? If anyone had an escape it, was I, not Sybil."

"How dare you say that about Sybil."

"Anna are you suddenly bringing Sybil into it because you are really trying to tell me something you don't want to say openly? Well, if that's what you think, say it. Say it frankly so we know where we are."

For Robert had just had a sickening thought. Maybe he had been under a terrible misapprehension. Anna knew all about his family history, and he had been sure that she thought nothing of it: had always liked him for who he was. But both of them had changed, and now this sympathetic reference to Sybil made him wonder. Anna was making silly excuses for refusing him, but maybe her real reason was the same reason as Sybil had rejected him. But Sybil had done it because her family demanded it; Anna had no such excuse. Her parents would never entertain Sybil's objections to him. Anna must therefore be rejecting him of her own choice. And doing so despite what had passed between them the night before the tugboat attack: it was after all she who had come to him as he lay asleep. And how could she want to make love with such passion, as she certainly had, if her real opinion of him was as he now suspected? It just made absolutely no sense.

What was going through his mind was awful.

Being rejected by the girl I love is bad enough. But to discover that for years I've been so completely wrong about her true opinion of me is nothing less than a stab in the back. How could she have deceived me all these years.

It was a thought that smashed his trust in her into smithereens. But it made better sense as he recalled the time that her friend Gerald had come to their house, made fun of the family photographs, and called him a monkey. Gerald would certainly share Sybil's opinion of him. In anguish Robert grasped at what seemed to be the unpleasant truth that however much he had thought he knew Anna in the old days, since they parted as teenagers she had changed beyond recognition. In torment he looked at her again hoping to see some sign that told him he was wrong. But there was nothing.

Anna merely stared at him from a dazed, tear-soaked face. "I've said everything I want to say."

He simply had to be sure about his new assumption, force her to put it into unmistakable words.

"No! You have not told me the real reasons you turn me down. After everything we have been through together. Maybe you lacked the courage to say it to my face. Well, I want you to do it now. Tell me what you really think about me."

She glared at him without understanding.

"Alright. You say you know why Sybil rejected me. That means you know that she wouldn't have me because I am my mother's son. Is that right? Tell me that is correct, and we can be done with each other." It would break his heart, but if things were as he now guessed they were, there was no choice.

Anna indicated no apparent lack of comprehension at these words. But in fact she was exhausted, did not understand what was meant by him being 'his mother's son' and had no idea that Sybil had rejected him because of his African grandfather. Tired and distressed she simply wanted to end what had become an unpleasant conversation.

"Please Robert, I just want to rest."

"No Anna! If we are parting for good, we must be clear. Sybil made it plain she refused me because I am my mother's son. If you agree, that is indeed the end of it. Pity you didn't tell me earlier. Pity you didn't say it before we made love. You would have saved both of us a lot of heart ache."

His words, spoken sharply, were followed by a silence between them as they sat and stared at each other. Robert hoped for a response that changed things, but there was none. Anna was too miserable and unwell to think properly and grasp what Robert had told her about Sybil.

"Of course, I know that is why Sybil turned you down. She was simply saying how it is."

"So! I was wrong."

"Yes! Can you blame her!"

"And you have no comment?"

"No! Why should I?"

"In that case there is nothing more to say. I have been fooling myself about you for all these years." He left her to take the lift to her suite, and went himself into the bar for a stiff whiskey.

Upstairs, she lay on her bed, totally confused and miserable at the sharpness and sheer hostility of his behaviour, and a lot of words about his mother that she hadn't understood. Of course, he was his mother's son, but why did he make it into a riddle she didn't begin to grasp.

The following day Valeria and Anna set off from the Hotel for Genoa to catch the train to Turin and Paris. Robert went with them to Genoa Station and paid off the luggage porters. He felt sick and despondent but kept his emotions under control, wishing them a restrained and formal farewell. Then he kept himself busy transferring the remaining gold sovereigns to the Bank. The bank had received a message from Bedros in Athens, and Robert made a large bank transfer to him. To which Bedros replied saying he had formed a shipping business with Robert as his partner and work on transforming *Hermes* was well underway. As Anna had made it plain she did not wish to share in the *Hermes* fortune, Robert then arranged through the bank to establish a charitable Foundation, in Anna's mother's name, to support an orphanage in the City. A new dormitory block could now be built as well as a new Sister House nearby. It was, the Mother Superior said, the work of God. Robert thought "So much good will be done with the money, when Anna is once again able to see things clearly she will be pleased."

Maybe so, but for him, Robert thought, life was over: his world was shattered by Anna's departure , and he returned to the hotel feeling totally wretched.

"At least it can't get worse!" he thought.

He was wrong. It got worse a fortnight later when he received a letter from his mother in London. She had visited Anna and had insisted on telling her the whole unvarnished story about how Sybil's family had finished her relationship with Robert. The revelation left Anna appalled at Sybil's behaviour and feeling badly upset when she recalled what she had said to Robert. She had just kept repeating: "I had no idea! What must he think of me!"

His mother thought, however, that Anna remained quite poorly with her trauma problem and still insisted on keeping a distance from anything and anyone that reminded her of her bad experiences on *Hermes*. That unfortunately still included Robert.

Although glad that Anna now knew the truth about Sybil, he bitterly regretted that he had wilfully instigated such a disastrous and entirely avoidable misunderstanding between them in Genoa. He had totally failed to appreciate the continuing and devastating effects of the *Hermes* experience on Anna.

Moreover, two weeks later there was a letter from Valeria. Gerald had become a frequent caller at the Gibson house and Anna seemed to be under his influence. Valeria feared he was just waiting for the right moment to propose the engagement which he had planned from before the trip to Tripoli.

The letter blew Robert to pieces. In a state of jealous, angry fury he threw a shoe at the bedroom fireplace.

"I'll not let that swine Gerald have her! It'll never work for either of them. They'll both be miserable." He knew for sure that he must go back to London at once and save her: Gerald's intentions must somehow be thwarted.

30

After spending three long days in trains rattling across Europe, suffering a choppy Channel crossing and then a slow train to Victoria Station, he was eventually back in London. He had rashly expected that the long journey would enable him to sort out what he would actually do about Gerald when he arrived. It didn't. The problem was that even attempting to remove Gerald from the scene could easily make matters worse. If Anna really did have confidence in Gerald, a mistake in dealing with him might simply drive her faster into doing the very thing Robert wanted to stop. Gerald would grab her as a brilliant catch, a young, clever, attractive and of course Catholic, wife.

Moreover, if Robert wanted to make any move to win Anna away from Gerald, he would first need to be thoroughly dishonest. Conceal his true intentions from her. For he was sure that if she even imagined he had simply returned to London to propose to her once again, she would immediately cast him off, and this time for good.

Nor could he even speak to her without a credible explanation for his sudden return. He decided therefore to use the shipping business that Bedros had asked him to transact in the City, as the pressing reason why he needed to be in London. Then, to explain why he wanted to see Anna while he happened to be in London, he could say he had news about her health; the Viennese doctor's suggested treatment for her trauma that was available in London. In fact, he could give her the name of the doctor she could consult in London.

All very well but it left the bigger and basic problem, the quandary of how to deal with Anna's objections to him personally because she associated him with the cause of her trauma. Hopefully she now accepted she had been mistaken about Sybil. But unless things had changed, Anna would still reject anything he said out of hand because she continued to see him as the author of the hated *Hermes* trauma that was at the root of all her troubles.

He tried to think of a way of breaking the association she made in her mind between him and her bad experiences on *Hermes*. Bedros had just sent him a drawing of how the former *Hermes* would look after the work in progress was completed. The upper deck remodelled; the shape of the funnel changed, as was its position and colour; the hull repainted in a new livery, her name changed to 'Aphrodite' and with new luxury fittings inside. He could therefore honestly tell Anna that the old *Hermes* had gone for good. Maybe he could say that as *Hermes* herself had vanished, the connection with *Hermes* had also vanished. If so, could it be that the spell of *Hermes* had been broken?

While plausible, given what he knew about the intensity of her feelings of the *Hermes* experience it did sound like a distant hope. But even so, if it was the only game in town, he would have to give it a try. Would it work? Perhaps the *Hermes* experience had taught him about the iron law of unexpected consequences: anything could happen. He should forget all the forlorn arguments for doing nothing, he should simply trust to luck, visit her and try his plan.

So, he cycled round to the Gibson's house the following day and found Anna at home.

"Robert." It was a polite, formal, completely impersonal and coldly controlled welcome. He might as well have been the postman delivering a packet.

"I heard you were in London," she said. From the way she said it he understood her to mean: "Why are you bothering to be here?" He did his best to try his gambit, tell his prepared story. But she had absolutely no interest to hear how the ship was being re-modelled. When he mentioned the Viennese doctor's suggestion for a consultation in London, she waived it aside.

"Gerald's advising me about medical help."

Robert's whole ruse was an utter, miserable failure and he left her feeling wretched. He felt he had played all his cards and lost.

The rest of the week passed painfully slowly, and at the end of it he was sure he had totally failed. Returning to London had been a big mistake, and that was sounding like the story of his life. He spent Saturday doing nothing and sometime on Sunday morning his parents went next door for lunch, an invitation that had been kindly extended to him, but which he had declined as something he simply couldn't face. And as Mary their cook/general had the day off, he was therefore alone in the house. He had nothing to do and settled in front of a blazing fire in the lounge to catch up with the newspapers. He could not concentrate on any of the news because he kept reliving and regretting all the mistakes he had made with Anna. And that was a long list. But there was little to gain in continuing to idly hope that something would turn up and frustrate her likely marriage to Gerald.

He gazed idly through the French windows at the drab, lifeless, autumn garden, where the early morning drizzle had now worsened into a steady, dismal, drenching downpour. It looked thoroughly wet and desolate outside, and he was thankful for the coal fire burning brightly in the grate, making the room comfortably warm. Lost in his wandering, unhappy, thoughts he was startled by the loud ringing of the front doorbell.

There, standing in the porch, was Anna, to his horror in a terrible state. She was crying, the tears pouring down her cheeks, her long coat and skirt wet through, her hair dishevelled, her hat a sodden shapeless mess. She had obviously walked some distance through the rain. He looked at her aghast; the scene months ago last January, when she had come to this same porch in such a terrible state of despair to ask for his help, jumped into his head.

"Anna!" He knew that once again something bad had happened. Intuitively he stepped forward and held her close. "My darling Anna! What has happened?"

All she could do was whisper "Oh Robbie!" As soon as he held her, he realised instinctively, and immediately, that the *Hermes* spell, the jinx of her traumatic experience in the fight with the tugboat, her refusal to let him even touch him, had vanished. She was clinging to him tightly.

"Anna!" He hugged her as she collapsed into his arms, crumpled onto him, and cried miserably on his shoulder. He lifted her and carried her indoors into the lounge. He kissed her softly on the cheek then removed her sodden hat and her soaking wet overcoat. He laid her gently on the sofa in front of the fire and took off her wet shoes and stockings.

"Anna! You must tell me what's happened."

She could only almost cry, "I don't know what to do! It's James!" She sobbed, "I don't know what to do!"

He found a tartan rug in the Hall to cover her, a towel to dry her hair and telephoned next door to ask his mother to come home, Anna needed to be taken out of her soaking wet clothes.

Robert sat on the carpet beside her, holding her hand as she lay on the sofa, knowing that she had come to him for help, like last time sure she could rely on him. As always, she could.

She began to blurt out the story about her younger brother James. "It's awful! You see James has disappeared. He left the house three days ago. He hasn't been back since. He left a note saying he was going for good. He's only seventeen, what will become of him?"

"What! Gone? You don't know where?"

"We have no idea."

"Why should he want to go?"

"We have no idea. He had said nothing that even suggested he might run away."

"Did he have any money?"

"I think he took a little loose cash."

"That means he wouldn't get far. That's good Anna. He went on foot?"

"No, he took his bike."

"Ah! We could give a description of it. And look, he's probably only gone to a friend."

"No! You don't understand! We phoned everyone, we spent hours on the phone. Everyone he knows we could think of. But no-one knew anything."

"Oh!" It was not sounding good.

"Then the police called yesterday looking for him."

"The Police!" Robert tried to hide his mounting concern.

"Yes!" A Sergeant from the Hendon Station. He said he was calling in connection with a break-in at a Golders Green shop the day James went. He said they think James was part of a robbery at the shop. It's worse, the shopkeeper was beaten up to get the safe key."

"My God! But why do they think James is involved?"

"They have a witness who identified James."

"Maybe. But witnesses are often unreliable. Schoolboys look the same."

"They have a scarf found in the shop identified as belonging to James. It has his name on it. It must be a school scarf."

"Look that's something that could easily be planted! Let me think Anna. It may not be as bad as it looks." He said that to try and reassure her, but it did look bad. James was facing accusations of theft, if not robbery, and assault of a shopkeeper. James was a big strong lad for his age, physically capable of what was alleged.

"Is there anything else Anna? You must tell me!"

She cried miserably.

"Anna, you must tell me!"

"Yes, there is more! Yesterday afternoon Gerald came to the house. I was quite upset."

"Yes, naturally you would be upset because of James. Was Gerald there after the Police came?"

"Yes, we told Gerald that James was missing and about the Police looking for him to question him in connection with a break-in."

"Yes?"

"Gerald said James was a young fool! He would deserve what he'll get!"

"What!"

"He assumed at once that if the police were looking for James, the boy was guilty."

"No!"

"He said that must be why James ran off: he knew the police were on to him. But he said it won't work; James will have to face the music. It was awful"

"You're right!"

"I tried to say that the police were merely inquiring. He just laughed. I think he said 'Hah!' It was embarrassing."

"Anything else?"

"He said it was another terrible humiliation for the Gibson family. A stupid thing that mustn't in any circumstances involve him. Or his family."

"No!"

"Yes! What did he mean by another humiliation? He was plainly only thinking of himself. Gerald immediately thought James was guilty. Why else would the police come? He didn't care a fig that we were desperate because the boy had run off. That we had no idea where he was and were worried sick."

"The nasty swine!"

"Then he said the best thing for us is that James just disappears for good. At least that might avoid a conviction."

"My God! The bastard!"

"I was terribly shocked at his attitude. I had not expected it."

"No!"

"It got worse, I asked Gerald to help us find James. He was angry I had even asked and refused point blank. He said, 'Certainly not! I'll not get involved with this family's crimes.' I just cried and cried."

"The dirty dog!" Robert was angry. How dare that oaf Gerald treat her like that. Some friend he turned out to be.

"I pleaded with Gerald to help us."

"Let me guess!" Robert's blood was boiling.

"He was really cruel. He shouted: 'Don't be ridiculous! I can't afford to be connected with a criminal. My father is an important figure in the City and a Hendon magistrate."

"My God!"

"He said his family had a reputation to protect and couldn't afford to be involved with a fugitive criminal."

Robert exploded. "Gerald is despicable!"

"There is one other thing I must tell you. Just before he left Gerald insisted that any discussion of our engagement must wait until ...." She broke down again in tears.

"Until what?"

"Until the sordid business about James' conviction is settled! That's what he said."

"He said that! Sordid business about James' conviction. The dirty swine!"

"I asked him what he meant. He just shrugged his shoulders and said nothing."

"Talking to you like that! It's contemptible!"

"I lost it! I went wild! I hit him hard on the cheek. I was so angry with him!"

"Well done! You did the right thing Anna. Lucky for him I wasn't there."

Robert could easily imagine the scene. He had well remembered experiences from the old days of Anna on the warpath. Anna's eyes would have opened wide as she went berserk, venting her fury at Gerald. She said it had ended when she chased him out of the house with a kitchen broom.

"My God! That must have been something to watch. I'm sorry, I'm really sorry I missed it." He meant it and noticed that she had smiled. The first time for so long.

"I told him I didn't want to see him again! Ever!"

"Oh!"

'Yes, and then he just walked away. Quite abruptly."

"Forget him, Anna! James is the priority. We have to think what we can do about James."

"There's one other thing Robbie."

"Yes?"

"I had made up my mind anyway that I had to talk to Gerald about the marriage. He had proposed you know. I kept avoiding giving an answer. You see ... I knew I couldn't do it." She paused and looked at him hard through her tearful eyes. "But with everything else happening, there was no chance of saying anything. I felt so bad about it. He has been a good friend to my family." She burst into more tears.

Robert was not sure what to make of that. 'Couldn't do it' she had said. What did that mean? But this was not the time to delve into that, whatever it was. He tried to comfort her. "It's all over now Anna."

At that point Robert's mother rushed through the front door into the house. She went to Anna and hugged her tight.

"My poor dear Anna! What a terrible state you're in! You're wet through. You must change into dry clothes at once. Better, you should go to bed and get warm, there's a gas fire in the spare room. I will light it now and make up the bed." Anna protested that all this was unnecessary, but Grace Strange waived aside her protests.

"Don't be silly Anna. You will catch your death of cold. You must go to bed and get warm. I will put a nightdress out for you."

Robert carried her upstairs to the bedroom, and his mother hurried to get a thermometer and prepare her for bed.

"I think Anna's got a chill," she told Robert. "Her cheeks are quite flushed. If she's got a temperature she should stay in bed for a few days."

Leaving Anna sitting on the bed looking shattered, Robert left the room and started to go downstairs working out in his mind what he had to do to find James. It was only then that he fully realised the enormity of what had just happened. When Anna had come to the house and had flung herself into his arms, he had sensed at once that the old *Hermes* jinx was gone. She had allowed him to embrace and kiss her, allowed him to carry her and none of it with the slightest sense of reservation on her part. It must mean that the curse brought on by her experience in the fighting in *Hermes* had been broken. Gone! It meant that the spell of the whole appalling trauma that had separated her from him was banished. But it was only now that he realised what had happened was for him nothing less than a miracle.

The full force of the event hit him so hard he instinctively grasped the stair banister to steady himself.

It's not just that now I can touch her. And hold her. The thing is that she has dumped that bastard Gerald! Thank God for that! What a false friend he has turned out to be. And she knows it! Surely after what he said about James there can be no going back.

Yet if that meant that the two primary obstacles to marrying Anna had suddenly disappeared, as if by magic or like some divine intervention in a Greek play, this was surely not the right time for him to actually propose marriage. She was plainly physically and mentally exhausted, looking grey and unwell. Her mind must be a terrible whirl with so many things rushing into her life, and she must feel desperately worried about her brother. So, if fate had indeed opened the door that gave him the opportunity to propose marriage, it was a door that he must wait to enter. It would not be fair to do otherwise, to take advantage of her to bundle her into accepting him merely as a reaction to her despair about James' disappearance and Gerald's despicable conduct.

31

By the time he had walked down the stairs and reached the hall his mind was clear: to propose the marriage he so badly wanted he must first find James. But how? To rush blindly around the streets of London was pointless, he had no idea in which direction James had gone and it was now several days since he disappeared. The answer came to him quickly; the best hope would be Hugo. Indeed, the more he thought of it, his only hope was Hugo. Hugo had the contacts to launch a proper large-scale police search for James; which doubtless he would dress up as some kind of national intelligence operation. Robert knew from bitter experience that Hugo was good at getting what he wanted. He would therefore telephone Hugo Cavendish, ask for an immediate meeting and beg for help. But by the time he left the hall he had changed his mind about the begging.

No. Begging does not work with people like Hugo. I will have to crawl and buy his help. That is the only kind of transaction Hugo understands. But it's a price I've already paid by taking part in the Hermes affair. Hugo owes me. I will tell him what I want in exchange. He will think he's got a cheap deal.

So, he telephoned Hugo hinting he wanted a meeting to broker an important deal. Hugo invited him to a meeting in the Foreign Office immediately. Once there, Robert intended to waste no time in cutting to the chase, to ask for a speedy police operation to find James. He felt confident and began smoothly enough, but Hugo had other ideas and butted in.

"Hold your horses, man! Robert, you are the return of a conquering hero. You have given Blake a report about *Hermes,* but you were too modest. I had to put Blake right. You didn't give him the whole story by far."

He was right, but how did Hugo know that?

"You underestimate our information. To start with I got a full report from our consul in Tripoli. Then from Spain. The Spanish coastguard in Malaga put out when they heard guns firing at sea off the harbour. They picked up the chaps from the two speed boats and the yacht. The men talked to the Spanish police. Whoever was employing them dropped them like leppers, disowned them. The Spanish got the whole story. The men had been paid to storm the vessel and kill the lot of you. But they had not been told *Hermes* had a cargo of gold. Our consul in Malaga picked up the whole saga from the police and passed it on."

"Well, I'm glad that there were survivors."

"And then the tugboat. It must have been one hell of a show, one of our destroyers out of Gibraltar bound for Malta saw a rocket you fired, must have gone high, and heard the sound of distant explosions. They rammed on top speed and found the tugboat in a rather blackened, knocked-about state. She was French registered, flying no colours and full of weapons. There were dead and wounded crew armed to the teeth all over the place. Clearly a big battle had taken place and the tugboat lost. The destroyer towed the tugboat to Oran in Algeria. The French interrogated the crew and got the full picture. Some of them said they had been attacked by a British gunboat packed with soldiers and armed with a fantastic new rocket weapon with banks of machine guns, but the French didn't believe them and decided they were pirates. What a story! Pity we can't give it to the press. But if you go into the Army and Navy Club in Pall Mall – I've taken the liberty of proposing you for membership by the way - you will find the tale is well known and that quite a few of the chaps want to buy you a drink or two. For the public, though. it has to be kept under wraps, and we must all keep our mouths shut."

Robert thought that as so many people were apparently in the know, keeping it under wraps might be tricky. However, telling the tale of *Hermes* around town had apparently pleased Hugo, and Robert decided to exploit the opportunity to raise the question of James' disappearance.

"I assume," Hugo said, " that you and Anna Gibson are back together. You would hardly be so bothered about her brother were it not so, I think."

Robert nodded. And told Hugo what had happened including James' involvement in the alleged robbery.

"And?" Hugo inquired.

"I need a big police dragnet to find James before he gets into more trouble. Anna is desperate with worry."

"Then have you not asked the police? Are they not in fact looking for the boy because of the robbery?"

Robert felt blindsided. Hugo must have understood what Robert was asking. An ordinary police search for James was unlikely to deliver the goods. At best James was a petty thief, small fry not nearly enough to justify a full-scale police dragnet. What was needed was the all-out national priority that only Hugo, with so many fingers in so many pies, could supply. But he wasn't offering and must be forced. Robert decided to play his trump card.

"The police won't do the kind of search I need. But I believe that you could get it done." He paused and gave Hugo a hard look. But there was no reaction, so he had to put his demand in plain terms. "It's simple Hugo. I did what you asked about *Hermes*. I went to Malaga and captured the boat. I destroyed the conspiracy; there was no Arab uprising in Libya; Britain's reputation was unsullied. You got want you wanted."

Hugo just laughed. "After your little trip to the desert you come back talking like an oriental camel trader! Your trip to Arabia has muddled your head. You think to bargain with me like a trader in the bazar. Or do you perhaps see what you did on *Hermes* as an investment that you can cash in? You're wrong. I am neither a camel dealer nor a banker. There is no question of payback. What you did about *Hermes* you did because you chose to. There is no reciprocation for the *Hermes* affair, if that is what you mean. You did what you decided to do and did it well. We are grateful for it. The country is grateful for it. But understand that we owe you no favours. Don't come here and imagine I feel any kind of obligation towards you. I don't."

It was a slap in his face. A stinging, brutal rebuke. He had thought Hugo would negotiate, instead he was slamming the door shut. He sat still and considered playing another card, a dangerous card, the threat to go public about the *Hermes* affair. To take the story to the newspapers. He knew he wouldn't do it because it would damage the country's reputation, but maybe just a hint of the threat might finesse what he needed from Hugo.

Hugo must have read his mind. "*Hermes* is over Robert. That book is closed. And you would be unwise to even think of opening it, any of it, ever again. Our national interest is at stake; we could not permit you to damage it."

Robert could only sit and stare. He knew Hugo was right and meant what he said about 'could not permit you to damage it'. No newspaper would be allowed to print the story. In that case Robert had only one recourse, only one line of approach, and he would have to take it if he was to have any real chance of getting Hugo's co-operation in the search for James.

"Very well. I see I must accept reality". He sat back and turned his face to the window, an uninteresting autumn scene. Then he turned back to face Hugo again, beginning an entirely different conversation.

"But there is another matter." He went on to say he had considered Hugo's earlier suggestion about joining the Royal Navy Reserve. Having thought it over he would like to apply.

Hugo's flexible face adopted a new smiling mask, expressing pleasure and surprised delight at Robert's news. As if he had not deliberately played the scene with the intention of eliciting exactly that application.

"Wonderful! Knew you would see the point! Overjoyed! Glad to have you on board! Consider it done. You'll get a letter from the Admiralty of course, but it's only a formality. Acting lieutenant. Initially."

They shook hands. Robert noticed that this time Hugo's handshake was perfectly normal, unlike the first time when he had tried, and failed, a crippling wrestler's grip. Robert was pleased he had correctly anticipated that Hugo would not repeat the first performance. It meant that Hugo had got his measure and felt no need to test him again. It also meant that Hugo was sure that Robert had fully grasped the unstated conventions of the situation and knew not to disappoint.

"But," Hugo continued, "I believe there was something else?"

"Yes. A personal matter." Robert explained again about James's disappearance, making no mention of the fact that he had already done exactly that. This was to be an entirely different transaction to the one he had unsuccessfully first raised.

As expected, Hugo immediately recognised the nature of the new transaction; it was indeed exactly his kind of arrangement. He might deny being a camel trader, but this kind of dealing was his bread and butter. He held both hands open towards Robert, not in prayer but to say that he was open for business and wanted to proceed to clinch the unspoken bargain. It did look exactly like the bargaining gestures used by the merchants in the Tripoli Souk.

Hugo then quickly established the detailed facts about James' sudden disappearance, the police intervention, and promised to do whatever he could to find the boy. Robert knew without doubt that he would carry out his side of the business. That was the secret of Hugo's success, reciprocity was the key, Hugo always delivered his side of the deal. But equally Hugo would demand his price: whatever it was that he would ask from Robert - and there would be something - he expected to be performed.

Hugo than returned to the *Hermes* issue. "I hope that Blake has told you that I knew nothing about Russia's part in *Hermes* until you were already in Tripoli."

"He did, yes." Robert decided to force the pace, sure that Hugo had not been entirely straight with them. "But that leaves questions …" He left the rest of the sentence in the air.

"Yes?" Hugo was evidently not going to roll over.

"What did you know about the *Hermes* conspiracy before we arrived in Tripoli?" The question was designed to require a straight answer.

Robert waited, recalling that when they first met Hugo in the Foreign Office Hugo had evaded answering their questions.

"Well, you shall have a direct reply. Blake will have told you that I am only nominally a Foreign Office clerk. And that I am involved in what you might call ad hoc intelligence work. It is all a bit informal and haphazard at the moment, but we will reorganise our national security services and that will change. Anyway, as to your question. Blake has good contacts in Rome and a while ago we heard whispers that a nationalist working in Tripoli was looking for funds for a scheme to cause unrest in Libya. I was chasing it up, but I knew no more until you blundered into the Foreign Office with Sergio's letters. There, suddenly, was the whole plan given to me on a plate. It was a fantastic breakthrough. And when it was obvious to us that Sergio had in fact got hold of the money he needed, I assumed, because of the rumours in Rome, that it was Italian money. But then all our Italian contacts denied this, and it looked like a German plot – as St Petersburg had always intended it to look. I only discovered Russia's involvement by chance a lot later."

"And decided to stop it?"

"Exactly! It had without question to be stopped, and at any price, or our crucial alliance with Russia was in jeopardy. But all I had was Tom Connolly, the chap I planted in the *Hermes* crew. There was not enough time to get another man out there. Once *Hermes* sailed from Malaga it would be too late. My only hope was you. To somehow persuade you to go to Malaga and work out some scheme with Tom. But I never thought that Anna would go to Malaga with you. Why in God's name did you allow it!"

"I had no choice. She insisted. And because of what happened she's still in a bad way because of it."

"I know and I'm sorry. I am truly sorry! I can only hope that her problem is transitory. I know I should have guessed she was the kind of girl not to stop halfway. From what I hear she did a damned good job on *Hermes*! You should be proud of her. But I should have made sure she stayed in Malta with her aunt."

"But you didn't."

"No. And I do genuinely regret it. You have my word on that!"

Robert was inclined, despite the history, to give him the benefit of the doubt. And anyway, as Hugo implied, he really should have stopped Anna from joining him in Malaga.

"Well of course I accept that." What else could he say.

"I gather Blake has told you that St Petersburg accepts the story that *Hermes* was taken by pirates?"

"Yes. He said that they will make no claim on the gold."

"Look! It's politics. Forget about Russia. It's been a bad experience for them, and they want to forget it."

"That means ..."

"That means you must decide what to do with the gold. But for God's sake be careful. There will be questions if it's splashed around like confetti."

"No splashing. A lot of the money has gone to an orphanage in Genoa. A lot will go to Athens. Our Armenian friend took the ship there for ... transformation, and the gold will finance that and a shipping business."

"Excellent news. You have your Armenian friend Bedros in the shipping business in Athens? Splendid. I suggest you back him. I wonder if in your contacts with Athens you have picked up any gossip about Greeks going to war again." A question which signalled to Robert that Hugo probably knew about his and Bedros' commercial affairs in Athens.

"Not a great deal. Bedros told me just before I left Genoa that the word on the street is that the Greeks are gung-ho for a war. He mentioned it because he is expecting some good business if there is a war. We are buying another two coasters for the shipping line, and he's keen that I finish that deal while I'm in London. I could ask him for more information. I need anyway to write or perhaps telephone about another transaction I must complete at the Baltic Exchange, a long-term time charter for an oil tanker."

"Excellent! My information is that the Greeks will go to war at the first opportunity of a successful strike at Constantinople. We are told that they believe they can gain more territory in the north. If they go to war though they will need a logistics plan to move the army and its equipment. It would be helpful to know if they have chartered any forward shipping space for munitions and troops."

Hugo then leant forward. "There's another matter while we're talking."

"Oh."

"This is confidential. The Government will sometime soon, I don't know when exactly, establish a British secret intelligence service. I expect to be part of it. Officially. But I will keep my position in the Navy Reserve because I need to present to foreign powers and will need to deal with foreign military, so the uniform and Naval rank is helpful."

All of which, Robert thought, made sense.

"So, I'll come to the point. I have a job for you in Athens. We are sure a Balkan War is on the way. The problem for us is that several of the interested parties each have their greedy eyes on Constantinople as a war prize. That includes Greece, Bulgaria and of course Russia. Reaching the warm waters of the Mediterranean has always been an aim of the Tsars. It is a tricky situation for us, and we need to be well informed on what is going on in all the players. We want amongst other things, therefore, to have someone close to the Greek Government and Greek military."

"You mean a spy to find out what's going on." Robert interjected.

"Exactly! We need to know about planned Greek troop movements, logistics etc. All the plans that they must have to back up any serious advance on Constantinople."

"And my role?"

"Get to know the Greek intentions and military supplies. Any big military movement will require shipping. From what you say, as you have shipping interests in Piraeus you are brilliantly placed to know about that. And a naval rank will give you the status to talk to the Greek Navy. After what you did on *Hermes*, I'm sure you're the right man for the job."

Robert was astounded. Not long ago he had thought Hugo was trying to kill him and even now he had doubts about trusting the man. Yet here was Hugo offering him a sensitive and important mission close to crucial British foreign and defence policy.

"I appreciate your confidence in me."

Hugo did not react, he wanted more than an appreciation.

"Naturally I accept." Robert knew he had to if he wanted Hugo's help in finding James. He noted wryly that already it was far more than simply joining the Navy Reserve. He had no doubt that Hugo would not stop there.

"Glad to have you on board! The Ottoman Empire is going through major changes so are the Balkans and we need to understand them. The eastern Mediterranean is an area of great political and strategic importance to us. You will be a great asset for us. Naturally I will speak to the Admiralty at once, you will need to have a temporary acting rank more than lieutenant if you are representing us in Athens."

Robert had barely been in the room for ten minutes and already had been promoted to a naval rank that would take the ordinary volunteer a lifetime of hard grind to attain. He realised of course that he would be expected to earn it and did not doubt that Hugo had every intention of getting his money's worth from his new 'national asset'. Had he now become only another cog in the wheel? Hugo's wheel. Or was he rather merely another asset that could be easily expended at will in the name of some spurious 'national' interest? Time alone would tell. And time was marching on as the War clouds gathered again over the Balkans. Would it stop there?

32

Robert returned home. Anna was still in bed and still running a temperature, sweating, her breathing laboured and feeling tired. Robert went up and sat beside her on the bed to tell her about his visit to Hugo. He told her that Hugo had agreed to use his contacts to ensure an effective search for James. She seemed overpowered by the news.

"Anna, Hugo will help us to find James. That's what matters. Together we will find him. I'm sure we will." Her eyes filled with tears and Robert put his arm around her.

"That is good news Robbie. But I'm so worried about being tied up with Hugo again. Do you have to?"

"Hugo is the only person I know who has the influence to get a proper search for James going. So, the answer is 'yes', we do have to."

"It worries me, Robbie."

"Anna, we have to find James. And Hugo has the means, the access. It may not be easy, but we will do it whatever it takes. James must be somewhere. He can't have gone that far. At any rate let's hope not! He hasn't the money to easily travel far. My father will deal with the local police. We will get to the bottom of this accusation. It will be alright Anna. Have faith!"

"Poor James!"

"Whatever it is we will deal with it. Trust me, Anna!"

She held his hand. "What did you have to give Hugo in return for his help? I need to know. He wouldn't have agreed without getting something from you. I must know. What was it, Robbie?"

Robert had no choice and explained that he had made a bargain. At some time in the future Hugo would ask him to undertake a visit to Athens to brief Hugo on the Greek government's plans to charter shipping space in the event of a Balkan war. He kept it general and as a future possibility rather than as a certainty in the next six months. He downplayed the risks in the whole thing as he didn't want to alarm her, but it wasn't the full story and he felt a bit deceptive, even if it was for good reasons.

"Was there no other way?" Anna cried. "Another mission for Hugo. I don't want to think of you in danger out in the Balkans. And all because of me. Anything can happen there. It seems such a wild, lawless place."

"I'm afraid there wasn't an alternative. And don't worry about me. Hugo wants me to go to Athens, not to Bulgaria or Albania where there has been actual fighting. And Athens is quite safe, I'll have Bedros there. I'll not be alone."

His words didn't console her. If it was a mission for Hugo, experience told her it was bound to be risky. But Robert managed to persuade her it would be safe. Reassured that she seemed ready to reluctantly accept the need for his visit to Athens, he moved on to bring up the suggestion of the Viennese doctor for a consultation in London.

"It's good you are getting over the worst of the *Hermes* experience, Anna. But we need to be sure of it and see you back as you were, your old self. I think a consultation with the specialist would help." He was taking a risk, the last time he had mentioned such a consultation, only a matter of weeks before, she had virtually refused, and he feared a repeat. But instead, she merely sighed.

"If you think so, then let's do it." A response which gave him confidence that the Gerald business was indeed over;

previously she had told him only that she would do whatever Gerald advised.

*

The next few weeks passed uneventfully. Anna felt much better, and the colour returned to her face. Then Robert took her to an appointment with the psychiatrist, Dr Green, in Harley Street, as recommended by the Viennese doctor. He listened carefully to her account of the shock of James' disappearance and its effect on her traumatic symptoms from *Hermes*. Dr Green thought that while her traumatic condition was not yet fully understood medically, her reaction to learning about her brother's disappearance was indeed a plausible explanation for the release of her symptoms. There was, he considered every prospect of the release being permanent, but he nevertheless advised her to avoid contact with events that might remind her of her experiences in *Hermes*. He recommended no further treatment beyond rest, a quiet life, and another consultation in six months to review her condition. Robert drew great comfort from the meeting and from the fact that Anna was obviously relieved to hear Dr Green's opinion that her *Hermes* trauma was as good as over.

*

But then, within days, he was summoned to meet Hugo. "I'll come to the crux at once." Hugo told him. "Things are stirring in the Balkans. Our man in Sofia tells us that the Bulgarians are getting ready for another war. So far only the paperwork but they clearly prepare for an all-out assault on Constantinople and its capture."

"And when the Greeks hear about it ..."

"They will sharpen their spears, sound their trumpets, launch their triremes and generally prepare for war."

"Ah!"

"Yes, it means trouble. All the usual suspects will want to get in on the act – Russia, Serbia, Albania, Bulgaria, Austria as well as the Greeks. That's why I need you to be in Athens before May. We have to bring the plan forward."

It was bad news, but it could have been worse because Hugo still gave him till the end of April before he had to travel to Athens, leaving him some clear months in London.

"So, will you marry her before you go?" Hugo asked, having assumed that was Robert's intention. "The thing is you can never tell how long these Balkan tea parties last, how many come to the party or how messy the party becomes. Could drag on for years, or on the other hand be over like a passing cloud in a summer sky. If you want my opinion, get the wedding done and over with while you have time in hand."

He had put into spoken words the very thoughts that had flashed across Robert's mind. But somehow Hugo's reference to time made him think of counting the months that remained open before he would have to depart. And connected with what Anna had said about not being able to accept Gerald's proposal of marriage. Time must be the essence of it, especially the number of weeks. That must be the link between her words that she 'couldn't marry' Gerald, and what had happened that night on *Hermes* when they made such passionate love. Of course! It must be more than twelve weeks. He had been stupidly blind. Twelve weeks that now seemed an eternity so much had taken place. A magical twelve weeks that could be the reason why she couldn't marry Gerald. Why hadn't he seen it before? Worked it out? Wasn't it obvious? But then if it was true, why hadn't she told him she was pregnant? Why wouldn't she tell him? Yes, if she knew she was carrying Robert's child, her conscience would not allow her to accept Gerald's proposal. But surely once she was released from the *Hermes* trauma, there was no reason why she could not tell Robert she was pregnant. It would have been easy enough. And what else could she do but tell him? She would not even think of an abortion and surely, she would not want to be an unmarried mother. Then the thought struck him that perhaps she had indeed told him, and he had been too deaf to hear it and too dim-witted to understand what she was telling him. But if that was right, he had to do something. Above all he had to know the truth of it.

And when I am sure of the truth, I must marry her without delay. Time is already running out.

But marriage was nevertheless a big question and he hesitated.

Look! She is not yet fully recovered, is still tired and James is still to be found. Would it be fair to force her into a decision to marry me?

Maybe not, but the alternative was bad. If they did not get the marriage done within weeks, who knew when he would be back from Athens. The wedding might have to wait for six months or even a year. Balkan wars were unpredictable. What would it do for their child, or for Anna, if the marriage was delayed too long? He knew he had to act. And at once.

*

She was in bed resting when he got home. However, she had in fact been up and about in the house until she complained of feeling tired, when his mother sent her back to bed. He went upstairs to her and kissed her gently on the cheek, breaking the bad news from Hugo that he would have to be in Athens sooner than planned. He sat on the bed and held her hand.

"Anna dearest, do you remember a night about three months ago on *Hermes* when I asked you to marry me?"

He had decided to risk the reference to *Hermes* and the tugboat affair. He felt her reaction in her hand as he mentioned the ship and the battle with the tugboat, she tightened her hold on his hand. He sensed that she knew what he was about to say. He had been right to speak.

"I do remember. How could I forget."

It was a wonderful answer. "Dearest, I'm hoping that your answer is the same now as it was then!" He bent down to kiss her again. "Anna dearest, I love you, will you marry me?"

"My answer is the same, Robbie! Yes!"

They embraced.

"Well, If I have to be away in Athens later on, lets marry before I go!"

He had hoped for an enthusiastic positive reply and was disappointed when in fact she said nothing, although continuing to hold his hand tightly.

"Dearest Anna, it does seem best ... There is no reason to wait if we both want it." He continued, but she interrupted him.

"Robbie there is something I must tell you."

He looked into her eyes knowing what her next words would be. He was right, Dr Dunlop the family's GP had been called to see her about her high temperature. He had examined her as a matter of routine and had then confirmed the pregnancy. Robert had made the right guess.

"Dearest Anna! That is such fantastic news! Such marvellous news! It's just wonderful!"

"Robbie! I'm so pleased you're glad!"

"Glad! Of course, I'm glad! But the joy I feel is more than feeling glad! It's the very best possible news you could give me!" They embraced fondly and he knew she felt he same.

In the circumstances it needed to be a quick wedding: they were open with their parents about the pregnancy. Robert said that as he had no deep religious convictions he was ready to be married in a Catholic Church, her Church, provided that she understood that for him religion was a coat to be worn lightly. He was concerned how she would react to what he feared she might see as insincerity, a somewhat nonchalant attitude to the Church, whose practices were important to her. Moreover, he couldn't help feeling bothered by the thought that at the back of her mind she would compare him to Gerald Morris, whose proposal she had come so close to accepting not so long ago. But if she was disappointed at his attitude, she said nothing, maybe she appreciated his honesty. Maybe, as the Priest had hinted when they discussed the Church's conditions for the marriage, she was sure that he would in time come to embrace her faith.

When Valeria was told the news of the marriage, she suggested having the wedding in St Peters, in the Clerkenwell Road, near Gray's Inn Road in Holborn. It was a Church much at the centre of the Italian community in London. That was a great idea as it would turn the event into a proper celebration, which it certainly would be if James was also discovered in time. Robert felt confident about that happening, Hugo would not let them down. He would not let them down because he had the means at his disposal to find James, more than that, he would want to tie Robert to him with a debt of gratitude. It was nevertheless a relief when Hugo telephoned to say that his men had tracked James down to a dingy hotel in Dover. Apparently, he was intending to take the ferry for Calais but had not already done so for lack of cash. Hugo came by car to deliver James in person to the Strange house, typically saying little, letting the deed speak for itself and then driving off.

"Here he is. He's all yours. I've sorted out the break-in stuff. They've caught the real culprit. You'll hear no more about it." He was saying that he had performed his part of the bargain, now it was for Robert to carry out his part.

Robert's mother had opened the front door to Hugo and lost no time in making clear to James that this was now his home. "Your sister is staying here until she's feeling better. Your father has a housekeeper but he is not up to looking after you. It is far more sensible for you to be here for the moment. You had better go up and see Anna, she has been quite anxious about you. And has some news for you." James looked embarrassed when she hugged and kissed him but did what he was told and went upstairs.

He was down in a rush some ten minutes later and grabbed Robert. "Anna's told me the news Robbie! It's so good! If I'd only known that you two ..." He tailed off, lost for words.

*

For Robert, still reeling at how the wheel of fate had turned full circle, the following days passed in a whirl of activity organising the wedding. But, he thought, if so much had transformed his life in so short a time, how much more was simply waiting to happen in the wings. Perhaps there were events just biding their time to embrace him, things that could prove as momentous, as equally life-changing, as the *Hermes* experience. Yet if he was a religious sceptic, neither was he a believer in the pseudo-magical properties of some mysterious force of fate beyond human control. Surely our future was ours to make. Even if this philosophy did not seem to entirely explain the extraordinary turn of events that had begun that day in September when he happened to meet Anna at the Golders Green Underground station. A chain of events that was now about to give him the love of his life as his wife, and then sometime launch him into another unpredictable adventure in the Mediterranean. Could he honestly claim that he had much had much real control over the tumultuous course of the *Hermes* affair?

For Robert the wedding ceremony, that a few weeks ago had seemed so unlikely to ever occur, passed in a blur. Having anticipated the claustrophobia of facing a high altar in the overpowering baroque style he associated with Catholic Churches, St Peter's was a pleasant surprise. It was, unusually, a Church designed with the spaciousness and sense of light and air of a Roman basilica. Standing on the rich, red carpet in front of the sanctuary, taking in the lines of marbled pillars on each side of him, the colour of the images around the altar, gazing up at the bright blue ceiling of the apse, the huge semi-circle above him, there was a feeling of light and vibrancy in the building that lifted his spirits.

Valeria's story, and that of how Robert and Anna had redeemed the honour of the London Italian community, had done its rounds and had been well received. Indeed, the priest who was to celebrate the wedding had made a point of welcoming Robert as a 'true son' of the Italian community. Robert's mother had instructed him to relax and enjoy the occasion, and he quickly found that despite at first feeling uncomfortable in the strange environment he could in fact do so. He had wondered if he might have an eleventh hour fit of nerves, or that Anna would change her mind at the last moment. Nothing of the sort happened, she entered on her father's arm, radiant and beautiful, right-on cue. When she finally stood beside him, he touched her hand and felt he was in heaven. Although he had quite forgotten the quick guide to the marriage service given to him by the Priest, he simply went with the flow of events, virtually oblivious of the unfamiliar language and alien ritual of the Mass. It even somehow gave a seal of unity to the extraordinary journey that had begun outside Golders Green station only a bit more than a year ago.

After the service, everyone departed for the wedding breakfast and reception, boarding hired buses and a fleet of taxis for the short distance to an Italian restaurant in Soho. The affair was perfect except that after the speeches and the eating was over, when the band struck up and dancing was well under way, an uninvited guest entered surreptitiously. Who else but Hugo. He approached Robert, who was talking to his parents, and took his arm.

"Robert, I have important news for you!" he announced, thrusting a letter into Robert's hand. "The plan's been brought forward. All that political trouble in Morocco has heated up conspiracies in Sofia; we think the Bulgarians are up to something. It means that matters are developing fast all over the Balkans and I've brought you urgent Orders from the Admiralty."

Robert starred at the embossed envelope in disbelief. Marching orders delivered by hand on his wedding night: it was extraordinary. He tore the letter open and read it. "What! You say there is trouble with the Bulgarians. But I know nothing about Sofia and the Balkans."

Robert's father took the letter from his hand and read it carefully. "It says only that you're instructed to proceed immediately to Athens. There is nothing about Sofia. But what's so suddenly urgent about some business far away in Bulgaria to interrupt a wedding? Everyone knows that the

Balkans have been rumbling for months. Anyway, Britain is not directly involved."

Hugo ignored the comment. "Robert, you are to leave for Athens at once and pick up further orders there. You see it clearly written, at once, without delay!" He looked around at the roomful of wedding guests. "Whatever your plans might have been, you have overriding obligations to me. And I want you on the boat train for Calais and the connection to Italy by tomorrow lunchtime at the very latest."

With which blatant exercise of power, Hugo turned abruptly and left the room. Somehow, he had forgotten to congratulate the happy couple, or even notice that they were in the middle of their wedding celebration.

"He comes and goes like a thief in the night!" Valeria said, having overheard Hugo's words and noticed the paper in Robert's hand. "May I see?"

He gave it to her. "Robert, Hugo told you these are Admiralty Orders. But the letter has a Foreign Office not a Board of Admiralty heading. And if you look at the signature, he signed it himself. Robert, he is taking you for a ride!"

"Maybe, but they are still orders. I have to go. I gave my word. I made a promise." Did they not understand what that meant? That he had made an agreement with Hugo to find James and was committed in honour to carry out his part of it.

Valeria would have none of it. "Are you mad! You talk about giving your word. You say you made a promise. What about the solemn word you have just given in Church, the promise you made to Anna? Does marriage mean nothing to you? You cannot do this to her! Again!" Her eyes blazed. "Yes, I do mean again! I said nothing to stop you being tricked by Hugo, ignoring Anna and going to Malaga those months ago. I will not be silent now!"

"This is different."

"It certainly is! Robert, you are married and have a child on the way. Anna's not fully recovered from the business in *Hermes*; you know that. Don't you understand that she has to face childbirth. Don't you understand what terrors that gives her."

"You don't see my problem."

"Your problem? What about Anna? Actually I see your problem all too well. That man Hugo is playing you like a puppet on a string. Time to cut loose!"

Robert's father was still there. "Robert, even if you have some agreement with this man Hugo, it is surely reasonable to discuss it and especially the timing. This is certainly no time for you to leave Anna. And how can it be necessary for you to rush off in the middle of the night?"

Valeria delivered the most bitter blow. "Robert, do you really want her to believe she married the wrong man? Would Gerald even think of walking out on her so near to the child being born just because some jumped up busybody told him to take a silly trip?"

Robert was stung by the rebuke and ashamed by the comparison. He suspected Valeria was right, in his situation Gerald, who had little respect for civil servants, would certainly have told Hugo to 'Buzz off'. But then Gerald had not given his word to Hugo. Would that have made a difference?

"Look, none of you grasp that I had to make a bargain with Hugo. I thought I was doing the right thing for James. I thought it was the only thing I could do. It's too easy now to think I was too hasty. The fact is that I knew what I was doing. I made a clear promise."

"What's all this about making a clear promise?" Anna had walked across, attracted by the raised voices. " And what is this decision you have to make Robert." She took the letter from Valeria's hand and read it carefully.

Her tight-lipped expression and hard eyes reminded Robert of that time about a year ago in the Foreign Office when she had boldly confronted Blake and finessed the British Government's promise to think again about Sergio's letters to Maria.

She returned the letter to Robert. "I see. Well Robert, you say that you made a promise, and must make a decision. So, do tell us what you've decided!"

Historical Postscript.

Italy fulfilled the old nationalist agenda by invading Libya in a war against the Ottoman Empire that began in September 1911 and ended in October 1912. Italy used the secret agreement of France and Britain, given before 1900, to cover its seizure of Libya. The actual trigger for the war was the 'Agadir' incident in Morocco, lasting from April to August 1911. France had used the excuse of a rebellion against the Sultan of Morocco to persuade him to ask for French military help. But Germany saw this as a move against the Franco-German agreement not to alter the independent status of Morocco. Germany sent first a gunboat then a cruiser to Agadir as a gesture of discontent with France. Britain then pronounced strongly for France and sent battleships to Morocco, prompting a German compromise accepting a French Protectorate in Morocco in return for territorial concessions in Africa. But Italy had taken the Moroccan affair as an opportunity to invade Libya without the need to consult Germany and Austria, its formal allies in the Triple Alliance.

The Italian navy bombarded Tripoli on 3rd October 1911 and troops were landed on the coast. Turkey was unprepared for the attack, having sent troops from Libya to deal with a revolt in Yemen, and its small navy was no match for Italy. Some Turkish officers, including Kemal Ataturk and Enver Pasha, who later became the leaders of modern Turkey, made their way secretly to Libya to lead largely local and irregular Arab forces against the invaders. But without avail, and the Peace Treaty in 1912 gave Libya to Italy.

After the Great War began in 1914, there was a Russian inspired meeting with British and French Foreign Ministers in St Petersburg. Russia wanted British and French agreement to a carve-up of the Ottoman Empire, including a permanent Russian occupation of Constantinople and Russian expansion through Caucasia. France and Britain lodged their own claims to Ottoman territory. Britain wanted Iraq, Jordon, Palestine and continued de facto control of Egypt. France wanted Syria. At the end of the war Britain and France got what they had claimed and Libya was left with Italy. But after the second world war, under the terms of the Peace treaty with the allies, Italy renounced all claims to Libya, which became an independent kingdom in 1951.